The Hartwaker ᴜ
written by Daniel J. Barnes.

DJB

HÄRTWÄKER

The End of Kings

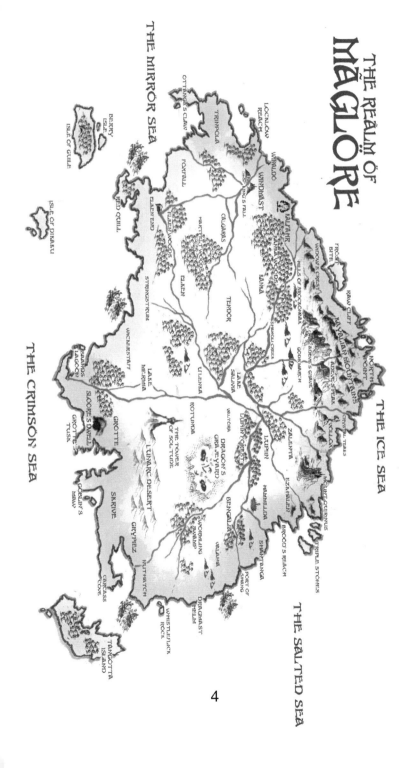

4

CHÃPTÉR 1
THÉ WÃR ÖF GÖDS ÃND SÉRPÉNTS

 thousand years ago (or more), the realm of Maglore was conceived. The wise scholars of the past wrote of Gods moulding the realm from fragments of hir own infinite imagination. Three Gods were responsible for everything that grew and gave breath within this vast new world that had been created. Gargantuan beings whose domed heads brushed the stars that burned high above. Adeve was the first God, flesh pale, body strong with enchanted white eyes that danced with visions of what could be. Adeve would show nothing but love for all things that were created and cradled the realm in hir arms, protecting it the way a mother would a child. Adeve would quiver with excitement with every unique creature or flora that was created, everything that evolved from the God's touch was made with the truest love.

The second sibling Merru, shimmered in a tone the colour of a prehnite gemstone. Merru's physique was slender and sleek, a crescent moon horn grew from hir forehead and a long tail like that of a carp formed from hir waist in dazzling scale. Merru was given control over the four seas and left the other two siblings as soon as the seas were formed.

The last God, Sloore, slightly smaller with a gentle tint of crimson that caressed hir flesh and two short horns that protruded from hir cranium. Sloore had black eyes that shimmered with mischief and serrated teeth that constantly drew dark blood as ze would bite down on hir forked tongue, to conceal words of jealously and bile towards Adeve's creations.

Adeve shaped an orb of cold pale light so ze would not have to work in darkness. But on seeing this Sloore looked to gain Adeve's admiration and formed an orb of hir own making, constructed by fire and heat. Adeve was not amused by Sloore's vulgar creation and so was forbidden from assisting in the inception of Maglore. Sloore wallowed in a deep pool of hir own bitterness and watched on as Adeve created a haven, a world draped with beautiful periwinkle skies, still and motionless, which were accompanied by scattered clouds that would flounce through on a calm warm breeze, gently bumping into each other.

Still, Sloore remained silent immersed in hir own jealousy.

Adeve formed exquisite dew soaked valleys that stretched for days, smothered by a million shards of emerald, almost as sharp as ice in appearance, but as soft as the clouds above.

Sloore grumbled, but allowed hir teeth to slice away at hir fleshy tongue and allowing words of conceit to be muted by hir own thick gore.

Adeve grew from strength to strength in a glorious frenzy of creativity and made all manner of flora and large trees, that contorted together in a forbidden erotic dance. Frozen in time as they reach to the skies above, clinging onto their various leaves and mysterious fruits, stubborn and greedy, unwilling to share. The riotous display of colour created by the flowers that rose above the entangled foliage, standing tall and proud, with an aura of arrogance, soaking up the admiration of any onlookers that are halted in their tracks by such beauty. Adeve made rivers that rolled into vast lakes of reflection that were silent, tranquil and unapproachable.

Sloore remained silent and petulant, but Adeve did not notice hir sibling's ugly jealous gaze and continued with hir masterpiece, hir Maglore. The pale hands of Adeve burrowed down into the earth of the realm and with much exertion retrieved gigantic shards of rock. The God heaved with all hir might and majestic peaks rose from the earth, slicing through the defenceless clouds with its snow capped blades. With such an arduous task now complete, Adeve collapsed with exhaustion into a throne shape etched into the mountains and slept.

While Adeve dreamt of the delights ze would create for the realm, the mischievous Sloore used hir deceitful tongue to caress hir sibling's conscience. Manipulating hir kin into allowing hir to help shape the world below and when Adeve finally arose ze welcomed Sloore to hir bosom.

Together ze created all manner of creatures and beings. Those called Furs were shrouded in a cloak of hair, with razor sharp claws and teeth, ravenous and primal. Cloud Skimmers were created with the gift of flight, intricately pinned with feathers of all different colours and detail.

Serpents were dark, mysterious creatures, limbless, sleek and moist in design, moving like no other, their bodies armoured with more scales than one could count.

Aquatic life of all sorts, bred and evolved quickly, but languished in rivers and lakes refusing to leave.

Then came the Skin Wearers, moving on two legs, and unlike any other creature before them. The beings were intelligent and evolved at an exceptional rate, showing tremendous survival instincts. These beings called Elf were the first, Adeve moulded them and gave them the power of rational thought and a heart to love and care. But with every being ze created, Sloore would have the last laugh by instilling the poison of jealousy and hatred that dwelled in hir own heart to each Elf that set foot on Maglore. Next came the Dwarves instilled with knowledge of construction and a hardworking mentality, which was diluted by Sloore's gift to them which was paranoia and bad tempers. Giants came with strength and a self loathing of others, Fairies with beautiful wings and blessed with handsome features, but bitter tongues. Then came Man, which had all the strengths and traits of what had come before, but Sloore's kiss of death gave them all the inadequacies ze had bestowed on Adeve's other creations, it would take a very long time for Man to become dominant with all these unwanted deficiencies.

Adeve looked on in horror as the beings ze had created started to wage war against each other for something as crude as power and wealth. After many decades of watching hir spawn do

8

battle, Adeve grew tired with the world ze had created and the life that dwelled there. Sloore would whisper discouraging words of extinction and starting again, but Adeve would not hear of it. In hir boredom they created hybrids of hir creatures, Skin Wearers and Serpents, The Furs and the Cloud Skimmers. But the biggest mistake the Gods made was forging together a beast of unimaginable power, that was seemingly indestructible. Adeve thrust hir hands into the orb of fire and utilising all that ze had learnt from every creature ze had created, from the beast like features of the intimidating Furs, the sleekness of the Serpents armoured appearance, the ability to dwell with the Aquatic life and the ability to fly like the Cloud Skimmers, but with the most important element being the intelligence of the Skin Wearers. In Adeve's cupped hands ze held a golden serpent that opened its eyes meekly and cried at its creator, its wings spread out and caressed the air. Adeve then did the same with the orb of pale life and withdrew an identical creature but with scales of shimmering silver. Sloore was not impressed by Adeve's latest conception that ze had dubbed Dragon, until Adeve reached up and snatched a star from the sky and broke it in half. The power that circulated inside the star was immense and as ze cradled each newborn serpent in hirs caring grasp, he fed them with the liquid contents of the star. They drank glutinously and it is said that their eyes blazed with flame before they burst into the sky flying at such fantastic speeds, until they halted and unleashed fire from their very bowels.

Sloore cowered behind Adeve for ze was scared of the shear power that ze saw before hir.

Adeve announced that the golden Dragon that was forged in the orb of fire's heat would be called Selym and the orb would become known as The Sun of Selym. The silver Dragon was female and ze dubbed her Tenaj and the orb of her birth would be known from here on out as The Moon of Tenaj. They grew immensely and at speed, they gleamed with magnificent silver and gold plates and would amuse Adeve with their frolicking, but Sloore did not trust them and ze feared them and unfortunately Sloore was right to do so.

Selym and Tenaj had superior intelligence and learnt very quickly and they soon believed that they should be the ones to rule Maglore.

They continued to evolve and had the ability to conceive their own young. Tenaj's innards had evolved giving her the capability to incubate her young in shell.

Sloore discovered a cluster of eggs in their nest deep in the bowels of a large volcano called Vollox. Thirteen large eggs of varying colours stared back at Sloore and ze held one in hirs hands, feeling the eggs delicate vulnerability between hirs fingers ze could not resist and ze crushed it, leaving nothing but visceral discharge and the underdeveloped fetus that was covered in lavender scales. Selym and Tenaj caught Sloore before ze could destroy any more of their offspring and sent hir fleeing. The Dragons were furious and spat flame, immediately taking to the sky and giving chase over the Kayalian Mountain range in pursuit of the fleeing Sloore , who headed for the safety of Adeve's bosom. Adeve pushed Sloore aside, ashamed of hirs actions, ze turned hirs back on Sloore allowing Selym and Tenaj to attack.

Sloore felt the flames lick at hirs flesh and ze fled to Maglore where ze burrowed deep down into the earth, creating hirs own bitter dwelling place known as the Shrouded Realm, a place of bitterness and darkness where ze would remain in fear of the Dragon's wrath forevermore.

But Tenaj and Selym's fury was not only directed at Sloore but at Adeve too. To the Dragons the Gods were all the same and to protect their unborn they attacked their creator, engulfing Adeve in silver and golden flame. They say that Adeve's cries shook the realm with groundquakes and skystorms that lasted for three days and three nights. The God fell onto the mountain range which was destroyed under the colossal impact, creating a canyon in the centre of the mountains. The fire had taken its toll on Adeve and ze was dying, but ze rose in one last attempt to fight. The God could not allow these beasts to rule hirs realm. He grabbed Selym squeezing with all hir might that his bones inside shattered and Selym fell to the earth dead, his massive remains falling on a cluster of various trees known as the Lover's Woods, which was engulfed in flames, burning every tree to black ash. Tenaj shrieked with pain and fury to see her beloved fall to his death and fled to Vollox to retrieve her eggs, but as she tried to leave Adeve swatted her out of the sky with hirs massive hand and sent the eggs hurtling towards Maglore, all of them falling in various places within the realm. Tenaj attacked with fire, teeth and claw tearing away at Adeve's

11

flesh who finally fell to the realm ze had created all those centuries ago. Tenaj hung in the air, tears of pure silver falling from her eyes as Adeve's prone body lay on the earth of Maglore. Adeve closed hirs eyes and hirs chest began to vibrate, a red glow lit up hirs pale flesh and as Adeve gave hirs last breath a ball of flame burst forth and hurtled towards Tenaj. The red flame took shape and for a moment was every creature and being that the God had ever conceived, until it sprouted a slender beak and claws of its own, surrounded by feathers of ferocious fire. Adeve's heart had become the most powerful being in existence, Sirod, The Phoenix.

Sirod penetrated the unsuspecting Tenaj and her once impregnable armour shattered and she fell to the earth and joined Selym on his deathbed of fire and ash.

Sirod rose into the air and spread its glorious wings of flame before turning flamboyantly in the sky and then hurtling with reckless abandon back where it came, ploughing through Adeve's open chest and disappearing forever. The blood of the God seeped into the broken world, unleashing all its secrets and sharing them with the earth and water. Magic was unleashed on the world, and there it stayed dormant, waiting to be discovered...

There was a sigh that seemed to echo around the high stone walls of the room. Pooka looked up from his mass of parchment that had been bound together with leather and twine. His oversized eyes looked like two orbs as they shone in the torch light. He glanced around the hall of young children who sat at wooden desks before him, each one with quills in hand eager to hear more of Maglore's history. His eyes found the culprit and narrowed, as he focused on a boy who's elbows leant on the desk to support the two hands that cupped his handsome but uninterested looking face. His hair was a mass of golden curls, as purest gold as the scales of Selym they said.

"Master Jasson!" Pooka snapped, his strange voice was a croaking and shrill and it echoed around the hall and woke the boy from his musing.

"Sorry, Pooka." Jasson replied, blowing a golden curl that dangled in front his face out of the way.

"Thank you for disrupting my lesson!" Pooka announced and his tiny frame sat back in his chair. "Is there something you wished to say to the class?"

"Keep it closed, Brother." Came a whisper from the girl sitting next to him, she resembled him but her skin was dark, like the purest bronze. Jasson turned to her and grinned, as mischievous as Sloore hirself. Their emerald eyes sparkled at each other, she wore the scowl of someone wanting to get on with her work and he wore the raised brow of foolery.

"Yes, Pooka there is!" He announced and stood, the wooden chair scraped across the tiled floor obnoxiously, causing Pooka to wince with discomfort.

"Oh, here we go again." His sister Xen exclaimed and her head fell to the pile of parchment on her desk.

"I echo your sisters sentiments Jasson, but go on." He sighed.

"We have heard this tale many times. The tale of Gods and Dragons, none of these things interest me for none of them exist."

"Really?" Pooka grinned, his broken teeth protruding for a moment before disappearing back into his maw and being replaced with a stern look.

"Forgive my brother Pooka, but it would seem he was born without the manners bestowed upon the rest of us."

"Kindly shut thy hole, Sister!" Jasson barked and stuck his tongue out at her.

"Now, now, there is no need for that is there?" Pooka said as the two siblings shared scowls, two pairs of matching emerald eyes burning into each other.

"And thank you Xen, but you do not have to make excuses for your brother. Now Jasson, what seems to be the trouble?"

"All I want is to hear some new tales." He looked around at the rest of the children sitting at their desks. "I know I cannot be the only one here that is fed up with hearing these ancient myths!" There is a muttering throughout the children and some acknowledge Jasson's proclamation with nods and mumbles of agreement.

"Ha!" He cried in triumph. "You see! I am right."

"Very well, Jasson." Pooka announced and gestures for Jasson to take his seat again. He then closed the large parchment that stood on a plinth before him. The noise was deafening and an ancient plume of dust escaped from between the crumpled and torn pages.

"Oh great, Brother! Thank you for that! I have not yet finished my notes." Xen seethed.

"So!" Pooka said as he made his way down the custom made steps that led to his Man sized chair, his tiny frame skipping nimbly down to the children and walked up and down the line of desks with his hairy hands clasped in the small of his back.

"What tales would you like to hear? What adventures through the history of Maglore could I tantalise your young minds with?" Pooka asked, his large eyes looking up at each child as they looked down at him as he passed. He span on the spot and walked back to the front of the class.

"Go on, don't be shy." He smiled as he struggled to climb up on an empty desk for them all to see him.

"Dragons!" Xen squealed, "I want to hear more about Dragons!"

"That's all you ever want to hear about Sister!" Groaned Jasson. "You're as bad as Pooka with all this repetition!"
Jasson realised what he said and stared at Pooka.

"No offence meant Pooka."
There was a pause and the hall was silent, the children sure that Pooka would unleash a tirade on Jasson, but instead Pooka smiled.

"No offence taken," he chuckled, "I teach only what is acquired for you children to know, and yes, I am well aware that you have heard these tales many times. So in light of that, please give me some suggestions and I will gladly be your bard."

Pooka's words had lit a fire under his students and ideas came in abundance.

"The War on the Lake!"

"The Battle of Black Moon!"

"The Age of Scales!"

"Oh yes!" Pooka exclaimed. "What great tales to tell."

"Can we not hear of the Twelve Dragons of Maglore?" Pleaded Xen.

"Maybe next time, Xen. But I believe that The Age of Scales is a perfect..."
Jasson interrupted Pooka with a grumbling, petulant sigh, and he slouched into his chair with his arms crossed.

"Why doesn't anyone ever ask me what I want to hear? Nobody ever listens to me! I am of royal blood you know!" Complained Jasson.

"Jasson, I wish I could take these peculiar long ears of mine and tie them up in a bow on my head, just so I don't have to hear your complaining." Pooka mocked.
The children laughed and Jasson sunk lower into his chair.

"Tell us Master Jasson, what tale should I bestow on you and your friends."
Jasson smiled and slowly rose from his seat again, standing proud he said without a stutter the words that caused the rest of the class to gasp.

"The Dark Reign!"

"You do know that knowledge of The Dark Reign is forbidden to fall on such young ears?"

"I do." Jasson replied, that mischievous grin caressing his lips again.

"I don't think you are ready for such a tale young Sir."

"Well, I disagree!" Announced Jasson.

"Pooka said no, Brother. Now sit down!" Xen hissed.

"Why should I?" Jasson cried, "Pooka wants to tell us the history of the realm, that is why we are here, right?"

Heads nod in agreement.

"Then we should now everything that came before us and not be spared of such ghost stories if they are part of our history."

"You are correct, Jasson." Pooka nodded.

"I am?" Gasped Jasson.

"He is?" Echoed Xen at the same time.

"Of course!" Pooka smiled. "I believe that you should all know the truth of Maglore's past and the tales should not be allowed to be watered down because you are children. But I warn you, these myths and ghost stories that you speak of," he shook his head, "this tale is truth!"

"But how can we know for sure? How do we separate myth from truth?" Xen asked.

"I can place my hand on my heart and pledge an oath to you all that this is truth that I speak."

"He's just setting the scene to scare us." Jasson scoffed, but in his eyes he looked unsettled.

"Oh I know it is truth, for I lived it!" Pooka said and there was a hush the fell over the class, a shroud of anticipation

17

had smothered them. Pooka jumped off the table and walked over to Jasson's and stared up at him.

"I was there Jasson," he whispered, "I saw it all!"
Jasson's widening eyes looked down into Pooka's dark bulging eyes and in them he saw the truth, there were no lies on the chapped lips of the tiny scholar. He sat back in his chair once again and for the first time that day was quiet. Pooka returned to his seat on the desk and clapped his hands together and smiled.

"The Dark Reign...where to start..." He pondered for a moment, his eyes flitted around the ceiling of the hall and noticed the busts of the Kings of Maglore that had ruled in the past and stopped at one specific bust and smiled.

"Of course!" He exclaimed excitedly as he looked out over the faces of anticipation, excitement and fear.

"It all started with a dream...NO! A vision!"

CHÃPTÉR 2
Ã DÃRK VÏSÏÖÑ

o some he was known as 'The Reluctant King', to others, 'Sebastian the Worthy'. If you were to ask Sebastian Hartwaker, he would truthfully tell you that he should never have been King. The fourth born son of 'The Bloody King' Cecil Hartwaker, who successfully reigned as King of Maglore for almost thirty years. A name that was legendary in the scrolls of history. He was most famous for thwarting 'The Goblin King' Grotte in his final charge against Man, bloody battles with Goblins that earned him the monikers 'Red Cecil' and 'The Goblin Slayer'.

Sebastian had three brothers that stood between him and the crown. The eldest Harold III was unfortunately born with a sickness of the mind that effected his limbs and ability to think and speak for himself. It was known very early that he was unfit to rule or conceive an heir and would never take the crown. So the second born, Roxon was groomed for the role from birth, he was truly meant to be King. And at the tender age of eleven years he was, claiming the throne when his farda, King Cecil passed peacefully at a good age of fifty. Roxon was ready and took to the role with vigour and enthusiasm, but unfortunately in some circles was dubbed 'Roxon the Unfortunate' when his Queen Annette, of House Bloodgaard died during childbirth. Their son Brode was born with illness and only gave breath for a few hours before passing. It was all too much for Roxon who was haunted by the ordeal and after refusing any help to build the funeral pyre, he placed the babe Brode in his marda's arms and wept as he watched their remains turn to ash. He spoke to no-one and returned to his chambers in the highest tower of Windmast Castle where he removed his crown and without second thought stepped out of the window, hurtling silently to his death.

With the death of Roxon Hartwaker, sister Florence was the next sibling in the bloodline, but the laws stated that only a Man could sit on the throne and rule the realm. A law which many thought old fashioned but dared not say such words, for these laws were made only by the tongues of Kings and Gods. She was unfazed that she had been passed by as she knew the laws and went on to wed Lord Lucas of House Forrestor and have two beautiful children Eemma and Tomas. Like Sebastian, brother Viktor had not planned to ever take the crown and so had paid more attention to the three loves of his life, slaying foes on the battlefield, drinking ale and debauching women. Viktor's conquests in battle, taverns and brothels may have been legendary but as a King he was unworthy. An arrogant drunk with a thirst for blood was not a good combination and the good people of Maglore knew this bestowing several undesirable monikers on their unwanted monarch, such as 'The

Drunken King', 'Viktor the Despised' or more simply and effectively, 'Viktor the Pig'.

Reluctantly Sebastian was compelled to step in and assume the role of leader, forced to carry-out the daily burdens that were bestowed on to a King, burdens that King Viktor neglected. For the majority of his reign Viktor remained in his royal chambers, consumed by wine and ale, not to mention the companionship of several local whores, who no doubt robbed him blind while he slept off each sordid adventure. It still remains a mystery to this very day who took highly toxic Reaper-shrooms and mixed them with King Viktor's ale, poisoning him. Who was responsible? Who can tell? For the list of suspects was as long as the tail of a Dragon. Viktor was unmarried and had no children, his brother Sebastian was his only mourner at the pyre, maybe more out of family loyalty than out of love.

So Sebastian became King, married his sweetheart the beautiful Marie Ann of House Vespa and reigned well and in relative peace. Sebastian 'The Obliging' was a great warrior, brave on the battlefield, but was also a peaceful Man that longed for the realm of Maglore to be at peace from the attacks from The Shrouded Realm and the constant bickering between the Houses and races. King Sebastian gave all the races their own right to rule their own kind, which was a decision respected by all the Giants, Dwarves and Fairies. He said it was improper for him to rule great races that he did not understand. He also left the great Houses of the realm to conduct their own laws upon their own lands and people, which was seen as very admirable for the young King as many rulers of the past would have manipulated these Houses for their own gain.

King Sebastian was loved by all and in his twelfth year of his reign, Queen Marie Ann gave him the gift of a child, a sweet green eyed girl with curls of spun gold. Maglore had lived in peace since King Sebastian had acquired the throne, but his dreams were less than peaceful, dark visions invaded his subconscious and poisoned his fragile mind with death and destruction. For several cycles of Tenaj's moon, he was haunted by these disturbing fantasies. Sebastian would delude himself by accusing the overindulging of various cheeses which were known to be the bearer of bizarre reverie.

"A King does gorge himself on such luxuries. Tis my only vice!" He had said to himself on many occasion but never really believed the words he spoke. Deep down within his soul he knew that he had always possessed a strange third eye within his mind, seeing events before they had taken place. He remembered the passing of his farda, and the death of his brother Viktor, a hand pouring poison into the last drink he ever consumed. He also saw the death of Queen Annette, Prince Brode and his brother King Roxon, but the images were so quick and so full of death that his mind dismissed it as soon as he had woken from his slumber. But this was different, the violence hurt his mind physically, fire rained down upon the Higher Houses of Maglore with reckless abandonment, nobody that he cared for was left alive, he saw all their terrified faces consumed in thick magenta flame. No matter what happened in these ghastly images the end was always the same, darkness, as

22

though a shroud of the thickest linen had been draped over the realm. He told no one of these premonitions, not even his own beloved Marie Ann even when most nights he would bolt upright and breathe heavily, consumed by a bleak sweat that felt both hot and cold, as though he had been taken by fever. But the eeriest occurrence of all was when he woke and looked out into the darkness of the chamber, he heard the unmistakable whisper of a serpents tongue. He would rise from the bed throwing back sodden sheets and fur and creep to the side of his sleeping babe Vai-Ra, always convinced that the sound came from the crib, but there was only ever his daughter. The Princess sleeping as sound as innocent babes always did.

CHÃPTÉR 3

THÉ BÏRTH ÖF THÉ SHÃDÖW BÉÃRÉR

lenka had been the birthplace of the horned colts known for centuries as Unicorn. A solitary Unicorn that was called Hartax, is said to have risen from the remains of the great God Adeve, to act as the realms Light Bearer.

The Unicorn became a symbol of light, goodness and hope to all that dwelled in Maglore. These wondrous creatures have walked the realm with a lifespan of one hundred years, entrusted with the heavy task of bearing light and preserving the sacred bond between her and The Sun of Selym.

The glowing orb of sky fire had become hypnotised by her beauty and followed her on her daily journey throughout the realm. The sun sleeps when she sleeps and makes way for The Moon of Tenaj, who will in turn guide nocturnal travellers through the darkness. It is this darkness that becomes the source of evil doers power, one in particular has been waiting patiently for his chance to unleash this dark world upon Maglore. This mysterious, hateful creature believes that by destroying the Unicorn, The Sun of Selym will cease to exist.

That fear will wrap its icy coils around the people of Maglore and darkness will rule unopposed.

The year is 257 AE, the Season of Floret is in full bloom which indicated the lifespan of another Unicorn had come to an end. The beautiful mare known as Unico lolloped towards her final resting place atop a peculiar shaped chunk of stone that protruded from the earth, in the place known as Ulenka. Her majestic golden alicorn that protruded from her forehead glistened proudly and all seemed right with the realm until she saw the stone reaching to her like a caring hand. She came to an abrupt stop and her hooves jolted nervously on the spot, disturbing the soil beneath. She gazed upon what would become both a bed for birthing and her final resting place. Her long eyelashes flickered as if to stop tears from falling from her bright blue eyes. She had always reflected hope and love, but now in those eyes there was a flicker of fear, fear of the end, fear of death. She cantered on the spot shaking her head from side to side, her luscious mane and tail of auburn fire flicked at the air anxiously and finally she looked to the sun. The Sun of Selym hung in the transparent vanilla sky and it beamed back at her lovingly. She could feel the warm rays caressing her pale skin, calming her and she knew it was her time. Something inside whispered to her, soothing her and reminding her that her time had come and another will take on the burden of light. For when one Unicorn lay to die, it would always spawn another to take its place. Unico's time walking the realm was over, it was time for another to walk with The Sun of Selym.

Unico collapsed onto the stone that felt cold on her warm flesh, causing her muscles to convulse, fear seemed to clench her again but the sun comforted her once more with its warm kiss. Her eyelids felt heavy and she let them close, shrouding her sparkling blue jewels. She felt movement from inside her swelling paunch and for the first time in her one hundred years she felt pain, as if the searing heat of Selym's rays had penetrated her flesh to boil her innards. Suddenly Unico felt cold, but it was not death, not yet, her nostrils twitched as she smelt the rotting aroma of evil. She opened her eyes to be greeted by darkness, she was alone and seemingly without the love of Selym, who had become shrouded by a black veil of darkness. As she lay there vulnerable, she felt icy daggers prick her flesh and a mist the colour of wild orchids circulated around her.

Panic-stricken she cried for help, she was frozen, held down by invisible cold clamps. The points of daggers tiptoed up her spine and then she realised they were fingernails, long blackened fingernails that belonged to bitter pale hands. Through the orchid mist a figure concealed in torn black rags rose into the air, hovering over her like some hideous harbinger of death. The dark apparition cackled grotesquely and swooped down caressing her slender muzzle as it whispered to her through the venomous flickering of its tongue.

"Your time is up dear Unico." It wheezed. "You will birth a foal, but it shall be of my seed!"

The words seemed to linger in the air and the apparition disappeared from Unico's view, had this spectre finally left her to birth and die in peace? Was this a Shadow Scythe that Man so rightfully feared? Or was this just death. Unico tried to move, her shaking limbs forcing themselves upright, hooves scraping on the stone as they looked to find traction to help her rise from the bleak grave. There was a sound of burrowing from the earth and she froze in fear again as small, spindly creatures emerged from the ground, blackened by the ashes of hellfire, their moist yellow eyes, beady and dancing with mischief. It was time for the Children of the Shrouded Realm to frolic. The Black Imps cared not for Man nor beast but to inflict heartache and sorrow wherever they appeared. They scuttled towards her and she was forced back to the stone, clammy hands seized her, clamping her fetlocks and making it impossible for her to move. The apparition was back again, she could feel its presence behind her, smell its foul breath on her face. It caressed her hide with one cold hand and with the other playfully ran its tapered talons through her luscious mane.

"The realm has been bathed by the sun for too long." Hissed the apparition. "It is time for darkness to reign and for the Children of the Shrouded Realm to play."

Those horrendous claws gripped her mane and hide simultaneously, those sharp fingernails piercing her flesh causing her to cry out in pain. But she was helpless, bound by the shackles of devilry, she succumb to the defiler who became one with the mist and entered the poor creature. Unico's head slouched and she gave up the fight, there was no way she could win such a one sided battle. When the mist withdrew and the deed was done, a single tear fell from her eye, its journey was a short one filled with false hope as it trickled down her muzzle, fell and burnt into the head of a salivating Black Imp, who in turn rubbed at its head with its scrawny digits and hissed at her.

Unico's eyes closed again and she lay still as the mist moved around her in some elaborate dance, before forming into that menacing figure once again.

"And so..." It hissed, "...let it be!"

The bulging stomach of Unico swelled hideously, pulsating in various areas as if something was fighting to get out.

"Yes!" The apparition cackled.

Unico's rear erupted with visceral discharge, its heat was immense and seemed to burn the stone beneath. A dark snout appeared from the confines of Unico's corrupted womb and she appeared.

"Come forth my child, come forth!"

A moist layer of fluid dripped from the skeletal appearance of this dark Unicorn, and it slipped and faltered for a few moments as she tried to gauge the mobility of her legs. Then she shook herself free of any remaining residue left from the placenta. Its mane and tail were crimson red and the sight of it swaying in the breeze pleased its maker.

"My child, you shall be known as Gri'ul!"

The reaper stroked the rotting dark flesh of the Unicorn's muzzle and caressed the newborn foals dark alicorn, that glistened like pure obsidian and grasped it in an icy grip and whispered sacred words.

"My Gri'ul, you will not totter and shake like some petrified foal. You will grow strong and quickly."
And with those words the Unicorn grew rapidly to adulthood, its awesome eyes burned like the fires of Sloore's sanctum. Gri'ul pounded the ground proudly with her thick hooves that were feathered with crimson hairs.

"Take your rightful place as The Shadow Bearer and swaddle this realm in darkness." Declared the apparition and Gri'ul bowed her head in respect before cantering away into the darkness. The apparition cackled loudly as The Black Imps scuttled away and tunnelled back to the dark bowels of The Shrouded Realm. The mist blended with the apparition and dissolved into nothingness.

There was darkness and the besmirched carcass of Unico lay broken on the stone, the faint chattering sound of the defiler's laughter could still be heard as a whisper on the wind. Unico's eye opened, the dazzling blue jewel flickered with life and her mangled stomach began to convulse again, and with all her might she pushed and out slithered a tiny white Unicorn on a tide of internal fluid. It lay motionless, covered in blood and all manner of internal seepage as Unico's eyes died, she joined them.

Unico's bravery left Maglore with a fighting chance, a sign of hope and a light that would continue to burn through the darkness, that of the little foal of white called Ulla.

Ulla twitched and kicked her hooves to free her from her tenacious confines and stood, teetering from side to side, small in stature even for a foal, mane and tail as white as the snow that tipped the Kayalian Mountains. She licked at the corpse of her marda as she started to dissolve into the earth and stone, feeding the realm as Adeve did all those centuries ago. The Son of Seylm appeared, burning away the dark curtain created by the apparition and Ulla looked to the burning orb for some kind of direction. She closed her eyes and she felt the warming touch of her guide and all was right, her eyelids fluttered and two silver eyes shone in the light. She neighed and reared up onto her hind legs before galloping away to the West. Somewhere the apparition shrieked with frustration as its plan had been thwarted.

If there is still light, then there is still hope.

CHÃPTÉR 4
Ã KÏ𝖭G ÖR Ã FÖÖL

ing Sebastian held the golden chalice in his hand, his full attention focused on the thick dark Elf berry wine that swirled in its deep cup. The chalice had some weight to its body, it was solid gold and forged from the crown of the first King of Maglore, 'The Elf King' Argo Calgaras. The Elves were an arrogant, despicable and greedy race, Calgaras was no different and amazingly his reign had lasted for 363 years, many believing that Elves were immortal and would indeed live forever. But Elves found out the hard way that they were not invincible when impaled by Man's steel. During the war that had become known as 'The Rage of Man', the first Hartwaker, King Grayfall led Man's uprising, wiping out the entire race of Elves and claiming the realm and the throne in one foul and bloody swoop. It was Grayfall who melted down Calgaras' crown into the chalice that would be drunk from by every king thereafter. Even 'The Dwarf King' Haggart Hammillaxe drank from it, but twas the blood of his predecessor that filled the chalice in a flagrant mark of disrespect. He had taken the throne for his short tenure as king for just 11 years in a tie that became known as 'The War of Two Kings'. Haggart Hammillaxe had outmanoeuvred the beloved

King Brode Hartwaker and slaughtered 'The Dragon Slayer' on the battlefield.

The same chalice was used by his successor 'The Dwarf Slayer', 'The Saviour of Man' King Grayfall Hartwaker II, who paid the same disgusting tribute by tasting the blood of 'The Dwarf King' before spitting it onto the floor declaring that it was as bitter as Haggart's heart. It was also the same chalice that delivered the poisoned wine to the lips of King Viktor.

Sebastian held history in his hands but was looking to the future with his musing, ironically he was ignoring the present until he heard an almighty cheer from his congregation, the sound of drunken triumphant calls exploded up to the rafters of the high ceilings of the great hall. Sebastian saw that a large boar was being carried out by two stewards on a silver plater, a succulent red apple stuffed in its tusk filled maw. His musing had ceased and he was back in the room, his great hall, on his throne surrounded by his people. He heard the twanging of several lutes as talented musicians worked the strings in time with the drunken voices of Windmast Castle. A smirk appeared behind his chestnut beard as he scanned the room taking in all the merriment of the affair. The heads of all the Higher Houses were there for this very special celebration, the first name day of his daughter, the beautiful Princess Vai-Ra. His eyes found the heads of the Houses with ease, each was clad in their House colours. The burgundy tunic caught his eye as he made eye contact with the Head of House Forrestor, Lord Lucas, his brother in marriage by wedding his sister Florence. Sebastian

32

lifted his chalice to acknowledge the Lord Lucas who reciprocated the gesture of his King.

Sebastian's eyes passed to Lord Trent of House Lacey, another smile and a lifted chalice. The acknowledgements went on as he scoured the room, Lord Bartholomew of House Bloodgaard, stood out like a sore thumb, his wild fiery red hair shook as he guffawed loudly over a large tankard of ale. Lord Grayhorn of House Tudor stood playfully lifting up his daughter Acala in his arms. She had had four name days, her hair was dark and thick, her laughter was contagious and her dark skin shone under the hundreds of candles that lit the great hall as if she had been from moulded from bronze.

The realms best Knights also celebrated heartily, Free Knights and House Knights brought together singing famous songs that only these brave protectors of the realm know. No armour weighed down their movements tonight, the Free Knights wore fine tunics emblazoned with their very own sigils, the House Knights the sigil of the House they had sworn to protect. Their swords hung at their sides, sheathed in scabbards, taking a well earned rest from slicing flesh and tasting blood. The King smiled at them all arm in arm and swaying from side to side, a part of him envied them and their adventures, a King was allowed to fight battles but never have adventures. Famous Knights such as 'The Golden Rose' Lady Jennifer Salt of House Seaclau, Sir Reginald Plume of House Smythe and even Gareth 'The Glum' of House Vespa seemed to have let his hair down this evening. Famous Free Knights of wars past were treated like royalty and rightfully so, for their loyalty and bravery. Such infamous names as 'The War Boar' Sir Daan Vilguaard, 'The Fish Hook' Sir John Shore and 'Gods Will' Sir Terrence Thomas.

Sebastian felt very peculiar, he felt like a stranger at his own festivities, as though he were an uninvited guest or a fly on the wall. He knew that he was not giving off an aura of approachability as he sat solemnly surveying the contents of his chalice. The huge wooden doors to the hall burst open and yet more food and beverage was brought in by stewards and maids, who arranged the platters on the long wooden tables that seemed to stretch the entire length of the hall. As they left and the doors were closed behind them a warm breeze swirled around the huge hall, it flicked at Sebastian's shoulder length hair that hung beneath the rim of his crown. It made him take in the hall and found himself staring at the thick stone that had been constructed centuries ago by unknown Elf hands and hoped in his heart that Windmast Castle was indeed as impregnable as the wagging tongues announced. Windmast had been built upon a waterfall originally known as 'God's Falls' before being renamed by King Calgaras as 'The King's Falls'. The castle was a chore for invited guests to even reach the drawbridge let alone marauders who wished to take the throne for themselves. The castle was safe enough, he knew that but he also knew there were ways in and out of Windmast through underground caverns, that many believed were barricaded after 'The War of Two Kings' knowing that was how the Dwarves took control all those years ago. Sebastian wondered whether there were other entrances that were missed, paranoia swept across him, perspiration appearing from beneath his crown. His mind wondered again as the breeze caressed the gigantic banner of House Hartwaker, vivid red and trimmed in gold twine, an extravagant golden Phoenix rising from flames emblazoned on it, the sigil of the House of Kings, House Hartwaker.

Beneath it the triangular banners trimmed in gold of all the Higher Houses that supported his rule hung proudly, a spectrum of luscious colour slapped at the stone wall in that warm Floret breeze. Colours danced in front of the King's detached stare, the forest green and vaulting elk of House Tudor, the burnt orange and fox of House Smythe, the saffron and hornet of House Vespa, the ivory and rearing colt of House Bythe. It soothed his heart and mind to see these sigils and know that they stood by his words. The carp on marine cloth of House Seaclau appeared to be swimming due to the breeze. The blue and charging ram of House Lacey, the burgundy and wild boar of House Bloodgaard and the lilac cloth of House Forrestor with a flaunting black crane. It comforted him to know that his people and family had the support of other strong Houses, they would need such strength in the coming months, if his dark visions were indeed true. Just the whisper of the darkness seemed to send his imagination into a frenzy as he gazed up at the banners and they all burst into magenta flame. He was lost in the vision and could feel the icy fingers of death caressing the hairs of his nape.

"My King!" Came a drunken cry severing the disturbing tie to his dark fantasy.

"You're drunk Sir." King Sebastian smiled.

"My apologies!" Chuckled Sir Winstone Vespa as he fell into the Queen's throne, wine spilling from his goblet and staining his crimson tunic.

"The Head Knight of the King!" Sebastian sighed shaking his head in mockery.

"That's me!" He giggled mopping up the spilt wine with his coarse hands, the hands of a man that had spent many a year gripping the hilt of a sword.

"And they call you Winstone 'The Wise'?"

"Apparently so!"

The pair laughed and embraced.

"My King your chalice appears to be quite shallow." Sir Winstone mocked starring into the King's chalice and swaying from side to side. "Here let me fill it for you." He added revealing a flagon and attempted to pour.

"No more for me my friend."

"My King! My friend!" Sir Winstone said taken aback.

"My head needs to be clear for what I am about to say."

"But Sire this is the finest Elf berry wine from House Plume, the famous vintners of Valania, they say the berries are picked from the Berry Isle off the coast of Guile."

Sir Winstone looked around to see if anyone were eavesdropping and leant in closely to his King's ear. Sebastian winced, overwhelmed by the aroma of stale wine spewing from his Head Knight's mouth.

"They say…" His voice now but a whisper, "…that the virgins of Guile crush the berries between their ripe thighs!"

They laughed again together and King Sebastian allowed him to decant the remaining contents of the flagon into his chalice.

Sir Winstone eyed a young maid that was pouring wine for a guest from a hefty looking flagon.

"Girl!" He cried and when he had caught her attention waved her towards them. She smiled and made her way across the room, her face blushing preparing herself to serve the King, her breasts heaving over the low cut of her flimsy cotton dress, her waist pulled in tightly by her laced corset seemed to accentuate her bosom which Sir Winstone 'The Wise' ogled perversely as she approached.

"Maybe this fine maiden is a berry squeezer." He murmured.

"I highly doubt it Winstone." Sebastian laughed.

She arrived and Sir Winstone dropped his empty flagon to the floor and took her in his arms and sat her on his lap. She squealed and laughed as Sir Winstone buried his weathered face into her cleavage.

"Forgive Sir Winstone, for he has already had too much wine, me thinks." King Sebastian said shaking his head in disproval at his friend's conduct.

"Oh, it's okay Your Highness I'm used to it." She giggled. "Ere, your chin hair is tickling me!"

Sir Winstone removed himself from the dark crevice of her breasts with a surprised look on his face.

"You mean you are not one of the legendary virgin berry crushers of Guile?"

"Me Sir?" And she laughed loudly, stepping away from him and his reaching hands. "Oh no I'm just Neeta from Nuthatch."

"You are not chaste?" He exclaimed in, his face full of farce.

"Oh, I've been chased alright and caught many a time." Sir Winstone took the flagon and shook his head, before smacking her round backside and sending her on her way.

"Then be gone you hussy! Only virginal berry crushers are welcomed." He bellowed. "But leave the wine."

They all laughed as the maid left, Sir Winstone could not help but examine the motion of her plump behind.

"I think I shall marry her." Sir Winstone said and then burst out into a fit of laughter that his king did not join.

"My King, something troubles you?" He asked, his tone suddenly sounding serious as if he had sobered that very instant.

"Yes, my friend, there is a lot that troubles me."

"Surely you are not still contemplating this foolhardy journey?"

"Foolhardy?" King Sebastian laughed. "Foolhardy it may be, but as King of Maglore I must be the one to take action. Only I can bring the races together to fight this... whatever evil it is that looms upon us."

"But these are but visions...dreams! There can be no truth in such fantasies!" Sir Winstone scoffed.

"Say what you will my friend, but these fantasies do not

materialise in front of your eyes, but mine! When they do, you will have the right to an opinion on matters."

"I'm sorry if I have offended you, my King." Sir Winstone bowed his head in apology.

King Sebastian wrapped an arm around the shoulders of his Knight and smiles.

"There is no apology needed my friend. I appreciate your foresight, but I have made up my mind."

"Then I shall support your decision."

They grip each others hands tightly.

"You are a good friend Winstone 'The Wise'."

"I only ask one thing from you my King."

"Ask my friend and hopefully I can grant you your wish."

"Let me accompany you on your quest. I beg of you to let me be your shield."

"My friend I must do this alone..."

"But your quest is a treacherous one. For the King to travel alone is unheard of."

The two had become drawn closer in conversation and neither had noticed that from across the great hall, Queen Marie Ann observed them suspiciously as she cradled the young Princess in her arms. "If I arrive at each of the mighty Houses with a Knight in toe then they will take my actions as being hostile and I can ill afford war with any of them."

"But they owe their independence to you. You alone made the declaration that they may rule their own kind. They should fall on bended knee for you and anything you ask of them should be obeyed!"

"My friend you are a great Knight, but you have a lot to learn about politics."

"Politics! Bah!" Taking a hearty swig from the flagon.

"This is a delicate situation that I have to handle myself."

"They will think you're mad, my King."

"Maybe so..." He pondered, "Maybe I am..."

"What?" Came the velvety tones of his wife and queen, who had quietly crept towards them with Princess Vai-Ra flailing playfully in her arms.

"Marie Ann, my love! You startled me." Sebastian cried and stood up to allow his queen his throne, she bowed her head slightly, long strawberry blonde platted hair coiling itself around her body like a serpent. She took the throne with the Princess still in her arms, Sir Winstone knew it wrong to remain seated next to his Queen and departed from the throne with a bow of his head.

"So what are you two Imps discussing?" She asked and Sebastian knew that he could not hide such matters from his dearest.

"I was informing Sir Winstone of my journey that I must take."
Her eyes widened in despair.

"But Sebastian, you cannot, you must not."

"You know I must my Queen." He knelt and clasped her hand lovingly. "I have told you of the horrors that I have seen, the evil that hovers over the realm like a plague ready to seize us."

"Can you not talk him out of this madness, Sir Winstone?" Queen Marie Ann cried, the Princess stirred in her arms.

"I wish I could my Queen, but words fall on the deafest of ears and the stubbornest of minds."

"But what of us, what of the babe?" Queen Marie Ann whispered, her long eyelashes holding her tears prisoner.

"My Queen, I leave you in the protection of the loyalest friend and greatest Knight."

Sir Winstone bowed to her, he had suddenly sobered knowing that the discussion had turned serious.

"You will be quite safe, you have my word."

King Sebastian bowed before her, kissing her hand that held their only child as tightly as a Dragon clutches her eggs.

"But what of your safety, Sebastian?"

"I shall be fine. I promise."

"Do not make such promises." Her words were accompanied by a single tear that cascaded down her slender face and fell on the forehead of Vai-Ra, causing the child to babble and reach out to her farda, kicking her legs vigorously.

"She wriggles like a little snake." Sebastian smiled, allowing her to grasp his finger in her podgy mitt.

Sir Winstone leaned in towards his king.

"My King!" He whispered in his ear. Neither of them had realised that the music and merriment had stopped and the congregation now watched the peculiar scene that was taking place at the top of the dais on the thrones.

"You must address them, my King."

41

Sebastian nodded, but leant forward and kissed his Queen on her moist lips, tasting the saltness of her tears as he did so and gently caressed his daughter's plump face with the rough flesh of his finger tip. The child's eyes widened and chuckled at him, grabbing for the finger and holding it tightly. Sebastian smiled.

"You will both be fine, no matter what happens. I shall see to that."

King Sebastian stood and turned to address his audience, his fur lined cape cutting the air and wrapping itself around him. He gazed out at the faces that stared back at him in confusion. Faces of those he knew well, who he loved and called family. Faces of kith and kin, all of those eyes depended on him, he knew that. Some might say that what he was about to do was foolish, some might say it brave. He would say it was a sacrifice for the people he loved.

"My friends!" He called from high atop the dais that homed the thrones.

"I must leave you for a while..."

Mumbles throughout the crowd ascend to the rafters.

"It is my duty to tell you that I have learnt of an evil that approaches. An evil that looks to plunge the realm into darkness."

"What is this evil, Sire?" Came a voice from the crowd, that was immediately joined by several other anxious pleas.

"I cannot say for sure."

"Then what is there to fear?" Someone called which was accompanied by harmonising jeers.

King Sebastian turned to his Queen and his friend, their eyes both said to not tell them where he received such information or they would truly he think him mad.

But he could not and would not lie to the people who depended on him.

"My friends I have never lied to you. You all know this, I do not have it in me lie to my people. I have seen visions…"

There was a silence from the crowd that gathered around the foot of the throne. House Lords looked at each other with eyebrows raised.

"Apparitions have cursed my dreams, growing stronger each night. I see the end, I see the darkness, I see Maglore engulfed by magenta fires."

There is still silence as King Sebastian looks around at his flock, curious stares meeting his gaze.

"My King!" Came the thunderous voice of Lord Bartholomew of House Bloodgaard. "It may be that you have partaken in too much of the Elf wine this evening?"

There was laughter throughout, an anxious laughter that tried to lift the mood. Sebastian smiled back at Lord Bartholomew and started to descend the steps of the throne and join his people.

"Lord Bartholomew, my friend, although the Elf berry wine is of the highest standards I admit that hardly a chalice full has passed my lips tonight. These words that leave my tongue are the words of a sober and rational Man."

He walks into the crowd, they part and allow their King to wander into the centre of the hall.

"I do not lie to you. These words I speak are the truth, by the great God Adeve they are true and if they are not then let hir strike me down where I stand."

There were gasps from the crowd at the mention of such a threat for many still feared the wrath of Gods, that some even waited with nauseous anticipation that he might burst into flames there and then.

"I would be a truly terrible King if I ignored this would I not? To dismiss it and leave us to our deaths?"

Some heads nodded in the crowd.

"You may start calling me Sebastian 'The Deranged' instead of the titles you have bestowed on me like Sebastian 'The Worthy' or 'The Obliging'! But know this, I believe the words I speak and I believe in you all and I will not stand by and leave you to this fate!"

There were some cheers that rang out from the crowd, it soothed his heart to know that he had some supporters, but he knew that some would still need convincing.

"On the morn I will leave on my journey…"

Queen Marie Ann clasped a hand over her mouth to suppress her dismay.

"…I will visit the heads of each race in turn, a journey that will take me to the Giants of Kanka, Valtora the Fairy Kingdom and Hammillda to parley with 'The Dwarf King', Dagyan 'The Defiant'."

"All hail Sebastian 'The Deranged'!" Someone called from the crowd and Sebastian laughed along with the others.

"Aye, I shall join you there."

There was raucous laughter as they knew that the Dwarf King was a bad tempered old Dwarf and negotiations with him would be very difficult.

"I will even call on the Grand One, Pagmai and consult his Mystic Circle. And I will travel alone."

There was a sudden gasp from the crowd and then there were a number of Knights declaring that they will accompany him and protect him. The mammoth of a man known as 'The War Boar' Sir Daan Vilguaard pushed through the crowd and stood in front of his King, towering over him, his bald head glistening in the candlelight, with his long red beard drenched in ale.

"I shall go with you, my King." Sir Daan boomed, releasing his sword known as Tusk from its scabbard and lay it at his king's feet as he knelt before him. Others followed suit and before too long every Knight in the realm was knelt before him, their arms laid at his leather boots.

"You humble me, my brave Knights. But please rise. I mean no disrespect, but I will be venturing out on my journey alone."

"I hope you do not think me speaking out of turn my King, but why?" Asked Sir Grey Snowfell as he stood and slipped his sword known as Ice Talon back into its sheath.

"If I am right about this darkness then Maglore will need the might of all its brave Knights. I could not bear it if any of you were to fall protecting me on my journey. Your place is with the people."

Many in the crowd patted the Knights on their backs as they rose and he could see that he had won the people over, not all of them perhaps, but that he knew was politics and in the world of politics no man is truly loved by all, there will always be neigh sayers what ever decisions are made.

"I understand that the Lords and Ladies of other Houses may wish to return to their own domains and make the necessary arrangements to protect their own people. But I want you all to know that you are welcome to stay under the protection of the royal guard. You will all be safe here at Windmast, as you know the walls of this castle are impregnable! And I leave you all safely in the hands of the army, lead by Sir Winstone 'The Wise'. You need not worry for I will unite the races and we will stand together against any plague of darkness that threatens Maglore!"

There is a roar from the congregation as King Sebastian made his way back up the steps of his dais to be united with his Queen and daughter.

"My King!"

A trembling voice broke through the cheers and silence fell. The crowd turned to see the small daughter of House Tudor, Acala standing nervously at the foot of the steps, dainty hands toying with a long golden belt that was encrusted with green emeralds that matched the colour of her dress. Her farda ran to try and stop her from addressing the King but as Sebastian turned halfway up the steps he waved him away.

"Yes, child?"

"What if you die on your journey?"

Eyes flitted around the room at each other as if that had been the same question that had danced on their tongues, but daren't be released.

"I will be fine little one." He smiled.

"But if you die, we shall have no King?"

The silence was nauseating, no one spoke, it seemed that everyone was holding their breath, waiting for an answer. They knew that King Sebastian had no male heir to take the throne and that he had no other brothers to take the crown if he should fall. Sebastian slowly descended and bent down to Acala's level, he whispered something in her ear and she smiled broadly before Sebastian turned and mounted the steps again.

There were calls for answers from his people and he gained his composure with each step closer to his Queen and then when he reached the top he embraced her and relieved her of the burden of the child she had been cradling in her arms all evening. He looked into Vai-Ra's eyes, glistening green that matched his perfectly.

"I have given much thought to this question and I have come to a decision that may not be to everyone's taste. But I am the King, am I not? I have always made decisions according to the laws of Man, but for the first time in my tenure as King I am changing one of those laws."

He turned on the spot cradling his daughter in his arms with tears in his eyes.

"I King Sebastian Hartwaker hereby declare that when my last breath leaves my body and my bones burn on the royal pyre. My crown, chalice, sword and throne will be bestowed upon my daughter, Vai-Ra!"

There were gasps from the crowd and open mouths greeted him, it was a sight that brought a smile to his face. His eyes met his Queen's, they were filled with tears of pride. He removed the band of gold that rested open his head, encrusted with rubies and expertly engraved with the same Phoenix in flames as the House sigil. He placed the crown in her delicate little hands, she immediately nuzzled on it, her gums that would soon break enjoyed the coolness of the cold and it soothed her.

"Maglore will have Queens. And Vai-Ra will be your Queen! Queen Hartwaker the first!" He cried holding her aloft for all to see.

There was silence, the people of the court were in shock but before it could become an issue Sir Winstone unleashed his sword and held it aloft in the air.

"When the time comes!" Sir Winstone cried. "Vai-Ra will have my Shard!" And he knelt on the stair and lay his sword down on the steps.

"Vai-Ra will have my Tusk." Bellowed Sir Daan Vilguaard who knelt and he to lay his sword down for the princess.

"You have my Quill, Princess!" Came Sir Joseph Deerheart.

"You have my Starchild." Said Lady Saara Lexon.

"And my Sovereign!" Said Lady Elizabett Wylde.

More Knights knelt and more names of swords were announced as blades caressed stone. Legendary names of swords echoed through the great hall, Gravestone, Thorn, Whisper, Confessor as the entire congregation joined the Knights on their knees.

King Sebastian kissed his daughter on the forehead and handed her to his Queen before unsheathing his own sword, the sword that had been wielded by every Hartwaker King before him. He held it aloft, the hilt sculpted into the neck of a phoenix, the pommel showing the head and curved beak, the cross guard two wings of golden flame. He knelt before his Queen and daughter and lay his own sword down before them.

"My Princess I give you Reignmaker. For it is rightfully yours."

Cheers of 'All hail Princess Vai-Ra, The future Queen!' Rang out in the hall and the music and merriment started once more with a famous song of the realm caressing everyone's lips... A Song for Maglore.

A SONG FOR MAGLORE

In times of peace and in times of war,
We sing the words for our realm, Maglore.
Let the words reach the stars above,
And let the mighty Gods believe our love.

If there is light, there is hope,
Sing out loud for the realm.
If there is light, there is hope,
Sing out loud, sing out loud.

Sing out loud for our protector,
Our Hartwaker King.
To keep us safe from harm,
And deliver us from sin.

If there is light, there is hope,
Sing out loud for the realm.
If there is light, there is hope,
Sing out loud, sing out loud.

In trying times of dark and ruin,
Our hope will see us through.
Our brave King will bring us hope,
And love to see that light be true.

If there is light, there is hope,
Sing out loud for the realm.
If there is light, there is hope,
Sing out loud, sing out loud.

Light, light, light,
Hope, hope, hope,
Sing, sing, sing for the King.

Sing for the king, for the king, let us sing,
A song for the realm of Man,
A song for our kin,
A song for Maglore,
so sing, sing, sing.

CHÃPTÉR 5

Ã KÏNG'S QÛÉST

It was a fresh Floret morning as the Sun of Selym peered over the jagged peaks of the Kayalian Mountains, its golden eye flickering sleepily as it began to slowly rise. King Sebastian stood in the courtyard of Windmast Castle, the constant flowing of the waterfall beneath the castle was soothing, it was a sound that the people of Windmast had become used to, many said it comforted them and helped them to sleep. He had beaten the cock's crow and eagerly readied his steed, Dayboy. A huge palomino colt of brawn and speed, Dayboy was the fastest colt in the kingdom and the King's personal mount. It busily chomped on an apple, a gift from his master as an apology for such an early rise, Dayboy's devotion to his King was never in doubt, but the stallion could become grumpy so the sweet ripeness of a apple from the royal orchard acted as a distraction for the early rise. Sebastian had finished tacking up Dayboy for what appeared to be a long journey. There was no armour on himself or Dayboy, he thought it illogical to wear armour when going on such a long journey, there was no sense in overloading his steed for it would surely double the time his quest would take. However

Sebastian had taken a tunic of chainmail as a precaution, something that his Queen and Head Knight had insisted on, he humoured them and packed the garment, but his desire was that he would not to have to use it. Dayboy was draped in a beautiful red barding trimmed in gold displayed the sigil of the flamed Phoenix. The Phoenix had been the symbol of House Hartwaker since it was adopted by the third Hartwaker King to be crowned, King Willem I. A creature that Willem had sworn he had seen light his way during The Battle of Black Moon when all had seemed lost. According to the scrolls of history Sirod the Phoenix has only ever been seen once when the great God Adeve fell to hirs death.

Sebastian smiled as he watched his steed devour the apple and then he nudged his face with his huge damp muzzle.

"Ha! Same old Dayboy, only happy when your stomach is full." Sebastian chuckled as he affectionately stroked the dark forelock that hung between his amber eyes and then scratched at his long slender forehead, a sentiment that was a personal favourite of the enormous colt and Dayboy nudged at the King for more of the same.

"You are a soft one Dayboy, are you not?"
Dayboy neighed and nudged the King's face again.

"I'm sorry my friend but I have no more apples for you."
Dayboy neighed loudly and shook its head from side to side in disagreement before reaching around and gnawing at a sack tide to the colt's saddle, which homed food supplies including fresh apples. Sebastian laughed loudly.

"I can get nothing past you my steed."

Sebastian surrendered and retrieved another apple for his steed which Dayboy munched through greedily.

"Surely you would not leave us without saying goodbye!" Came the bellowing cry of Sir Winstone Vespa from across the courtyard.

King Sebastian turned to see his Head Knight and best friend making is way towards him across the cobbled stones, joined by his cousin the Queen who cradled Princess Vai-Ra in her arms, as well as a plethora of other royal stewards and council.

"Of course not." Sebastian lied unconvincingly, he wanted to get away without any fuss. "I was just readying Dayboy for the trek."

Queen Marie Ann kissed him on the cheek and whispered into his ear. "You are an awful liar, my lover."

"Maybe that is why he is such a good King?" Sir Winstone laughed and he clapped King Sebastian on the back.

"Agreed, cousin." Queen Marie Ann said. "The people would not be so loyal to a liar."

"Your Queen speaks the truth, my King. You have the support of the people on your quest."

"That is good to know." King Sebastian smiled as he adjusted his scabbard and made sure his dagger and his sword Reignmaker were in place. Before holding the saddle and attempting to mount his colt, when the hand of Sir Winstone fell on his shoulder.

"I plead with you one final time, my King. Let me

accompany you on this quest. Let me take some of this burden I beg of you."

There were visible tears in the Knight's eyes, he did not wish to allow his friend to take on the trials and tribulations of Maglore alone. He knew that the King was naive to affairs outside the walls of castles. He believed his King knew nothing of the horrors that awaited him.

"I have told you my friend that you are needed here." Sebastian sighed as if he grew tired with the attempts to change his mind about the quest. "If I do not go and inform the leaders of these Houses, then who will?"

"Let me go in your place!" Sir Winstone said as he collapsed onto his knee, head bowed. "I am known by all the Houses they will know the words I speak true and that they come from you."

"No, Sir Winstone!" Sebastian replied sharply. "It must be me if they are to believe such a bizarre tale. You say I am no liar and they know this also. It needs to come from my lips to their ears for it to believed I fear. I am sorry but that is the way of it."

"There is nothing I can do." Sir Winstone sighed.
Sebastian knelt and looked his friend in moist eyes and smiled.

"Protect the people, protect the castle, protect my Queen and my daughter. That is what I ask of you my friend."
They rose and Sir Winstone nodded, standing proudly he agreed. "If that is your decree, then I will protect them with my life. I will be their shield."

"You are a good man, Winstone." Sebastian clasped his forearm and then pulled him in for a tight clinch. "And a good friend."

Winstone fought back tears and pushed his King away and turned to the entourage and dismissed them.

"Come now!" He bellowed. "Leave the King to say goodbye to his Queen."

The council members and stewards bowed and returned to the keep, Sir Winstone followed, he turned and smiled at his friend.

"I will keep them safe my King, you have my word."

"Your word is stronger than any sword my friend."

"Good Journey." Bowed Sir Winstone and he disappeared into the keep.

"He loves you my King." Queen Marie Ann said brushing her smooth hand across his rough bearded face. Sebastian closed his eyes and could not believe that he would not feel that touch again for the turn of many moons.

"I know, and I him. But he does not understand the rigours of being a King."

"No, he does not." She sighed and turned her attentions to swooning over her beautiful child. "Sometimes neither do I."

"I know you do not wish me to take on this burden, but I must."

"What if you are wrong?"

"Then I am ready to be ridiculed for the rest of my life for being Sebastian 'The Deranged'."

She embraced him, and he her, the child wedged between them started to grumble.

"Am I going to hear of your concerns now little one?" Sebastian laughed as he kissed her on her head and those green emeralds reflected the rising sun and gleamed, making it very difficult for Sebastian to leave at all. But he turned away and passionately kissed his Queen before effortlessly mounting the huge steed.

Queen Marie Ann choked back her emotions as her eyes met her King's and the two felt a cold uncomfortable caress harass their spines, their skin prickling with gooseflesh. It was an uncomfortable feeling but neither of them spoke of what it could mean.

Queen Marie Ann took his hand and caressed his wedding band that fit snugly around this rough finger, the thick gold band that held a red ruby within, a gift for him from her on their wedding day. She kissed the ruby and smiled up at him.

"Come back to me." Queen Marie Ann wept.

"Like the great Phoenix Sirod, I shall return my love."

"You promise?"

"You said it yourself my Queen, I do not lie."

His words lingered on her ears before coming lost under the hammering sound of Dayboy's hefty hooves as they galloped away.

CHÃPTÉR 6
THÉ SÉRPÉNT ÏN THÉ STÃRS

 hooded figure shuffled across the harsh terrain at the foot of the Kayalian Mountains. His slender feet were stained with the rigours of a long journey through hot desert sands. His pale toes were tipped with misshapen claws that hung over the sole of a pair of tired sandals made from the leather of a Juug. The figure came to a halt at the harrowing entrance to the Caves of Zalenta, which led to a labyrinth of ancient tunnels that ran through the belly of the mountains. These large tunnels had been caused by the burrowing of a Dragon! A Dragon known as Vlaag, a gigantic wormlike creature that is like no other Dragon, completely blind with no limbs but stumps to help push its way through the caverns. It has no need for wings on its moist, scaleless body, it is said to have discarded them centuries ago. Whether or not the fabled Vlaag still dwells in the caverns remains a mystery, but the visitor remained cautious. He took a deep breath and the sound of his nervous swallowing reverberated around the moist walls and returned to his ears causing him to shiver, having tasted his own fear riding the echo. He moved slowly and cautiously into the gloom, his nostrils flinched as he fought the urge to vomit, as the morose aroma of Vlaag's stale oral secretion hung from the walls. The retched aroma did not mix well with the other scents that attacked his delicate senses, like the decaying bones of Man and Goblin, fresh loose Troll dung and the bleak flavour of burnt animal flesh and hair that drifted out from the cave on a warm sickly breeze. While the nerves was still with him, he waddled into the cavern, his small frame was hunched and he struggled to hold the mass of scrolls and worn parchment that he cradled in his arms. He wandered around the tunnels aimlessly for what felt like hours, fatigued from the long journey from the Lunarc Desert and burdened by the weight of his cargo he felt like just relieving himself of the scrolls and leaving. But he knew that could not happen, for fear kept him bound to his duty, not the fear of the wormlike Dragon, Vlaag that may or may not still reside in the mountain tunnels. Fear not evoked by the Man eating Trolls, poisonous ten legged Decapods or long necked Bat-Fiends, but something much worse. The fear of disappointing his Master, one that does not take kindly to failure, he was not quite sure whether the information he had gathered would even please him. There was the sound of a distant cackle that drifted from a nearby tunnel, he turned and moved as quickly as his fatigued legs would allow and finally he saw a light flickering in the dark, illuminating his destination. He hurried on, scrolls slipping and sliding from his grip, somehow he managed not to drop them, until he heard the voice, that voice of fear, the serpents hiss of his Master.

"Astronomer!" The sound pricked at his skin which rose like the dimpled flesh of poultry, immediately the scrolls and parchment fell from his quivering hands, long nailed fingers that now nervously interlocked.

"You have been away too long." The words were shrill to his ears, like the flicking of a serpents fork.

"I am sorry my Master!" Came the stuttering reply as he scrambled to pick up what he had lost.

"Come forward, I grow impatient." Growled his Master. The Astronomer swallowed hard and moved forward into the light that danced on the cavern wall, bathing it in all manner of colours. He stepped into the clearing his murky eyeballs seemed to double in size as he witnessed all manner of animal carcasses engulfed in flame on a small pyre, the flames licking at the ceiling in a riot of colours. Two hooded figures stood over the pyre, gazing into the spectrum of flames as if watching something unfold before them. The Astronomer shuffled towards them but could see nothing in the fire except the eyes of burning creatures, their fear of sudden death captured and frozen in time as hot flame licked at their fur and flesh. The larger of the two hooded figures turned to face the visitor, his face hidden by shadow but the hiss of his voice was enough to show The Astronomer that his Master was displeased.

"It has taken you many moons to return G'nora." The smaller hooded figure cackled mischievous as skeletal hands broke the spine of a fat rat that struggled in his grip.

"Forgive me Master, but it has taken me many days travel. To read the stars the sky must be clear and..."

"I tire of excuses!" The Dark Master snapped and turned back to the fire.

"Yes, Master!" G'nora replied bowing his head, his eyes flitting back to the dark corners of the cave that appeared to move as if alive, dozens of yellow eyes gleamed in the glow of the fire, watching him. G'nora could not make out just how many eyes watched him from these walls that moved, flowing like water, surrounding him. The tunnel fell into darkness where it was not touched by the burning flames, making the task of counting these curious beings impossible.

"For too long now I have waited in the shadows. My time to rule is now, I can feel it!" The Dark Master groaned.

"I hear news from the East that darkness has already fallen upon it. The idiots that dwell there believe that The Season of Gloam has come early and a month of eclipse awaits them." G'nora said trying to sound positive knowing that his Dark Master failed in bringing his black shroud over the entire realm.

"It is not enough!" He spat and the flames rose higher as if mirroring his rage, spitting out flecks of cinder into the frightened old face of G'nora. His face illuminated for the first time, the long white beard that hung from his chin jittered under the wrath of his master and he fell to his knees, parchment and scrolls falling at the bandaged feet of his Dark Master.

"Forgive my insolent tongue Master."

"Stop your blubbering and show me what you have found Astronomer."

61

"Yes, Master, of course!" He sputtered as he rummaged around in his fallen findings and retrieved a scroll that he open to show all the stars in the Maglore sky. With his hand shaking a finger quivered out from underneath his huge sleeve to show where the stars seemed to have joined.

"Look Master, the stars aligned in the shape of a..."

"A Serpent!" The Master wailed in triumph and he snatched the scroll away from him to examine it in the light of the flames.

"Well, possibly..." G'nora attempted to intervene, but his words fell on deaf ears.

"You see Kelda my dearest, the stars show that a Serpent will save Maglore."

The smaller hooded figure was hunched over wicker cages that detained the sacrificial rodents. She cackled maniacally. "It was never in doubt, oh, Dark Master." Kelda added in a cracked tone that sounded like a heavy boot treading on gravel.

"But, my Master..." Said G'nora, again trying to interrupt, but to no avail, the Dark Master ignored him as he circled the fire staring at the scroll.

"Yes, the prophecy is written in the stars and cannot be undone. A Serpent shall rise and take Maglore. That Serpent is me!" His voice bellowed through the caverns and the walls with the watching eyes moved in a flurry of excitement. The euphoric cry caused something large to stir in the darkness, whatever it was sent a chill down G'nora's spine and its presence even caused those glowing yellow eyes to withdraw.

"No Master!" G'nora finally shouted as he stood holding another piece of parchment in his hands.

"Who dares say no to the Dark Master!" Cackled Kelda and suddenly she was at G'nora's rear, hands wrapped around his throat, squeezing with all her might, her jagged talons sinking into his flesh and drawing blood.

"Kelda! Release him!" The Dark Master announced.

"As you wish." She spat and as quick as she had pounced, the old hag was back where she had once stood another rat in hand. She snapped the poor rodent in half and drank its blood in one gulp. Crimson dripped down her pointed chin and settled on one of many hairy moles protruding from her horrendous face. She smiled a witches' smile and licked at the rodent's juice with her rough tongue. G'nora shuddered and clasped his hands over his throat, dabbing at the puncture wounds with his fingertips. G'nora turned to see the Dark Master looking down at him, his face still concealed by the shroud of his hood, but G'nora could still sense the malice. A stale sickly odour escaping with each heavy breath as he waited for G'nora to speak.

"Forgive my interruption Master!" G'nora quivered, holding out a second piece of parchment. "But this reading shows the prophecy in more detail and it could mean another."

"Another!" The Master screeched, the sound ricocheted against the cavern walls, sending those dark creatures into retreat, scuttling across the craggy surface for the safety of a darker corner. Whatever colossal beast sat in the far end of the tunnel stirred seeming not to appreciate The Dark Master's wailing.

The Dark Master snatched the parchment from G'nora's trembling hands and gazed at the stars that were joined together by lines of ink to form what resembled a long winding snake.

"Y-You see my Master that with the stars joined then the prophecy looks more like snake than Serpent and does not resemble a Dragon."

The Dark Master was silent for a while as he studied both pieces of parchment, as Kelda relished snapping rodents and hurling them into the fire.

"Snake!" The Dark Master scoffed. "A snake is a Serpent, a Dragon is a Serpent. I feel it is you that is misinterpreting the prophecy Astronomer, not I!"

"Of course my Master." G'nora bowed his head again.

A tinted black claw that protruded from a pale finger traced the line that formed the snake in the stars.

"You cannot take prophecies too literally my old friend. It clearly shows a Serpent and if you were to add the surrounding stars then do they not show wings?"

G'nora examined the parchments closely his Master bringing his attention to the neighbouring stars that had not been joined by the Astronomer's ink.

"It is possible..." G'nora murmured, but did not sound convincing in his belief. He flinched when he smelt the vile stench of rodent blood and turned to see at his side, the long wet entrails of Kelda's latest sacrifice hanging from her craggy maw. G'nora felt like vomiting, but knew if he did he would end up broken in half and heaved on the pyre. Her evil eyes looked glazed over like those of a blind Man, her nose was pointed and peppered with moles of all sizes, she was hideous but it was the smile that terrified G'nora the most, that sadistic enjoyment that she got from the torment of others was plain for all to see.

"I...I..." He stuttered.

Kelda sucked up the dangling entrails which splattered her chin with blood as she chewed it slowly, never taking her eyes of the Astronomer. G'nora vomited in his throat, it was hot and burnt away at the back of his gullet, reluctantly he swallowed it down and immediately felt the urge to retrieve it once more, but he fought it.

"I see it now my Master, a Dragon! The prophecy shows that the most powerful Serpent of them all will rule Maglore. The Dragon!"

"Yes!" The Dark Master hissed and discarded the unwanted piece of parchment into the flames. G'nora's old shoulders dropped in dejection as his work was eaten up by multicoloured fires, something that had taken many moons gone in an instant.

"Now that I see it is written in the stars that the prophecy is true that it will be the Dragon that will rule the realm, I am ready to show my hand."

"But still the stars have been known to be wrong from time to time. There could be another..."

"No!" The Master raged, the flames rose up and licked the ceiling and again something stirred in the tunnel. "There is no one else that can lay claim to such a prophecy for I am 'The Dragon Master', I am the one to speak in its tongue. Who else could the prophecy imply but me?"

G'nora knew that he should say no more and did not but nodded in agreement with The Dark Master.

"I sense that you are not so sure Astronomer?"

G'nora said nothing but stared wide eyed at his master.

"But I have not put all of my hopes in the stars and astronomy. I also believe in magic! Kelda has ways and means to look into the future."

Kelda spat the blood from the rat's innards into the fire and the flames burned magenta and white, a vision of Man's castles engulfed in fire as Goblins slit their throats, the sky turned black as a festering looking black Unicorn strode into view and the pale hand of the Dark Master holding in his icy grip the King's crown. A gigantic black Dragon rose majestically into the sky and engulfed the sacred tree, The Willow of Kalfahr into flame, the vision faded away and the hooded figures turned to stare at the frightened face of G'nora.

"I suckled at the dark teat of Sloore, ze gave me life when I was forgotten, ze told me this day would come. I will no longer hide for I am the prophecy! The Dragon Master! The one who will bring balance to this realm, those who choose to disobey me will burn in the fire pits of The Shrouded Realm!" The Dark Master declared triumphantly.

"But Master..." G'nora stuttered, "You have no Dragon!"

The Dark Master laughed and Kelda joined in with her high pitched cackling, together creating a deafening cacophony of evil. The large creature that had been stirring in the tunnel moved forward and was touched by the light of the flames. Shock attacked G'nora's face and he fell to the floor of the cave on his knees and a single tear fell from his weary eye, for he knew that he was wrong, there was no other. The vision he had seen was truth as the flames licked at the gigantic head of the legendary black Dragon, Demios.

"Finally the Serpents will rise and take their rightful place as the Gods they were born to be." The Dark Master hissed. "And with my guidance will rule Maglore in a shroud of darkness, as it was meant to be."

House under the care of current Lord Nathaniel Vespa, but he wanted to move on quickly with this quest and he would feel obligated to stay longer taking part in banquets and ceremonies and he could ill afford the time. Something pricked at his mind like an icy talon of restlessness warning him that there was little time to waste.

"That looks as good a place as any for us to bed down for the night." Sebastian said having spotted a small tavern at the end of the street. "What say you Dayboy?"

His tired steed grunted and trudged on in the direction of the tavern. Torches burnt brightly outside the tavern which had been erected adequately, although a little lopsided, it had been built strong with various types of stone. Light came through the slender windows and to Sebastian looked so inviting. The tavern's sign depicted an old tree that had been attacked by a severe winter, the name etched below it read *The Withering Tree*. Its hinges croaked loudly on the evening breeze like poorly played music, but it did little to deter the King who's hungry gut was far louder and more important. He dismounted the huge colt who breathed a sigh of relief having ridding himself of the heavy burden. Sebastian led Dayboy by his reins to a trough that was filled to the brim with water.

"Drink my boy, you have earned it."

Dayboy drank like a glutton and Sebastian rewarded the steed with caring caresses and pats.

"Steady on Dayboy! You drink more like a boar than a colt!" He laughed.

Dayboy replied with a snort that caused the water to bubble and froth in a flurry of resentment.

"I am not one to speak of such matters as I too shall be filling my belly very soon. And hopefully with a pitcher of fine wine to accompany it."

"You'll be lucky!" Came a small voice that seemed to mock him.

The King turned to see a small plump boy that could not have had more than 6 name days, sitting nonchalantly on a barrel picking at a piece of wood with a small knife, as if trying to carve something that resembled a feline.

"You startled me little one."

"Yeah, I get that a lot, Sir."

The boy hardly made eye contact with the King and carried on carving layers of shavings from the wood in his dumpy hands.

"What did you say just then?" Sebastian asked.

"You want wine?" He shook his head, a mop of greasy brown hair covered his focused eyes. "You won't find no wine ere."

"I see."

"They only got ale. My farda says that it's the best ale in Tendor."

"Oh really?" Sebastian smiled. "Well, at least that sounds promising."

"Nah!" The boy scoffed. "It tastes like piss. My farda has to say that, it's his pub isn't it."

Sebastian smiled, he liked the boy, this raw kind of honesty that you don't find very often when you are of royal stock and surrounded by yes Men.

"What is your name lad?"

"Ernest. Ernest Copperpot. Well, that's the name I was give, but everyone 'round ere calls me Ern."

"Well, Ern. If this is your farda's establishment would I be correct in presuming that you are the stable boy?"

"I guess I can be." He shrugged. "For a price of course." Ern glanced at Sebastian from under the greasy veil of hair and then quickly back at his wooden block that was starting to take shape now, with hind legs and a tail.

"And how much do you charge for such a task?" Sebastian chuckled.

"Have to be worth my while you know, I'm very busy."

"I can see that. What is it a bear, no, wait a liger?"

"Nah!" He held it up to Sebastian who examined it. "It's a Binturong. But my farda said they don't exist anymore, says they're a-stink."

"Extinct."

"That's the one!" He said jumping down and laying his carving and knife on top of the barrel. "Farda said that the Ferals from Tangotta were responsible."

"Very true. The Ferals are cruel beasts, many creatures have become extinct due to their lust for flesh."

"So if you want me to stable your colt, I'll need..." He stopped and looked Sebastian up and down, "You a noble?"

"You could say that." Sebastian laughed again.

"Gonna have to be three dollins." Ern announced, folding his arms as if that was his final word in the negotiations. "Not little nuggets either mind!"

"Three!" Sebastian whistled sarcastically. He opened his purse that hung from his belt. "Would you except coinage?"

"If it's gold I'll have it." Ern nodded as Sebastian poured three perfectly pressed dollins into the boys filthy hands. Ern whistled as he examined the coins, turning them over and over again with his stubby digits, watching as the gold caught the torchlight and flickered in his wide eyes.

It was more money than he had ever possessed, he was ready to haggle over the price as most nobles did and usually he would walk away with maybe one single dollin if he were lucky and more often than not it would be a small nugget. And to see the authentic Maglore currency stamped with the King's face astonished him. Ern stopped for a moment and stared at one of the coins, then looked up at Sebastian, staring at the bearded face from under the shroud of his hood. The sun had now disappeared almost completely and their was an amber glow across the sky that seemed to add an aura to this tall noble Man that stood before him.

"It's you!" Ern gasped, "You're the Ki..."

Sebastian shushed him and bent down to a knee to meet the young lad face to face.

"If you keep this information to yourself young Ernest, then there may well be another couple of dollins in it for you."

Ern nodded vigorously, eyes wide and mouth gapping.

"Now take Dayboy to the stables, feed him well and bed him down." Sebastian said. "Then come and find me and I will make sure to pay my debt."

"Yes, yes of course!" Ern danced excitedly on the spot.

"Good lad!" Sebastian said ruffling his hair. "Now be off with you!"

Sebastian chuckled as he watched the young lad take the gigantic steed by his reins and lead him away towards the stables.

"I can't believe that was the King! Bloody hell what a shock! But it'll be our little secret Dayboy and I will take good care of you."

Sebastian decided to keep his hood up as he strode into The Withering Tree, he still did not wish to acquire any unwanted attention that would slow down his quest. He was immediately welcomed by a warm greeting from the fireplace, as the heat comforted him, even more comforting was the smell of some homely cooking, it smelt like coney pie. Sebastian inhaled the aroma, it tantalised his tastebuds and made his mouth water. It had been so long since he had tasted coney. He was used to such richness as boar and elk, tender peagle or duck or on special occasion some fresh carp. This was informal and raw, this was proper cooking, home cooking and Sebastian could not wait to fill his belly with it. As he approached the bar, several eyes watched his arrival, eyes that said. 'You are familiar noble Sir. But I cannot place you.'

A group of rowdy Free Knights occupied a tabled, several faces that he had seen before as allies in battle or had had the pleasure of witnessing them compete in The Deerheart Games. One Knight in particular was standing with tankard in hand and his foot up on a chair speaking in a loud and obnoxious tone as he told tale of his gallantry under seemingly impossible odds. Sebastian knew the Knight and knew him well, his name Sir Maximillous Mondt, who referred to himself arrogantly as 'The One'. He claimed to have been knighted by Adeve hirself, the God and creator of the realm, which of course was preposterous, but it did not stop him wearing a depiction of the God as his sigil. Mondt was an exceptional tournament Knight and there was not many games that he did not excel in, almost always ending the tournament in victory. But as a Knight of battle and war he was mediocre, the majority of his time was spent shying away from battle. He had a huge personality and an even bigger mouth, and loved to tell stories, very, very tall stories.

Sebastian made sure that he kept his back to the group of Knights as to not draw attention to himself and waited at the counter for someone to serve him, he could hear grumbling and the rattling of pots and pans bleeding out from behind a tattered curtain that separated the tavern from the kitchen. As Sebastian waited he took in his surroundings, the uneven stones of many shapes and sizes would have made the establishment gloomy and uninviting, but the torches that were protruding from the wall somehow disguised its craggy interior, the glowing amber flames flickered to conceal the harsh walls, making them look almost alive. The gigantic fireplace was the focal point of the tavern and for some reason several colt shoes made of brass were hung on the chimney breast, the shoes caught the light of the torches and glistened. Sebastian tried to block out Mondt's booming voice who had now moved onto the time he had tangled with a gigantic Cyclops high in the Kayalian Mountains on The Bridge of Quildor. Sebastian rolled his eyes and turned his attentions to the other customers slumped in chairs, half asleep from a rigorous days work, others shared stories over large tankards with frothy ale spilling over the rims. Four old Men surrounded a wooden checkerboard, engaged in a traditional contest of battalion chess. One ravenous Man tucked into a huge piece of Coney pie, his fork digging through gravy soaked pastry to find the tender meat within, Sebastian could feel his mouth watering again and turned to bang an impatient fist on the wooden counter. He heard a loud grumble from behind the curtain and the barkeep appeared looking very flustered.

"Who's bloody making all the noise?" The barkeep grumbled. A round man waddled out from behind the flea-bitten curtain, a thick black moustache turned into a grimace as he wiped a hand through his receding hairline.

"Just a hungry traveller, Sir." Sebastian smiled, trying to look as friendly as possible to extinguish any hostility.

"Well, there's no need to come in ere banging about now, is there?" The barkeep mellowed slightly, but his flesh was burning with strain.

"My apologies, Sir." Sebastian bowed his head.

"Well, no harm, no foul." Sighed the barkeep. "What can I get you?"

"If coney pie is still on the menu, I will take a hefty helping of that."

"Agatha!" The barkeep shouted loudly and there was a clanging of pots and another round figure appeared from behind the curtain, a large woman her hair in two tight bunches either side of her head, her complexion as red as the barkeep's, obviously running a tavern was an exasperating job.

"What is it now Arthur?" She cried. "I'm trying to mash these spuds. We need an extra pair of hands back there."

"Oh shut up woman!" He groaned. "Do we have any coney pie left?"

"Aye." She said.

"Good!" Arthur nodded. "A bowl for this gentle Sir."

"Do you want mashed spuds with it Sir?" She asked looking curiously at Sebastian's shrouded face.

"That would be delightful M'lady."

"Oh M'lady!" She blushed and disappeared back into the kitchen.

"M'lady my arse!" Arthur scoffed. "Can I get you a drink?"

"Yes, I have heard that your establishment serves the best Ale in Tendor?"

"Ha!" Arthur chuckled grabbing a tankard and giving it a courtesy wipe with his cloth. "I see you ave met our Ernest."

"I have indeed." Sebastian chuckled. "He's bedding down my steed. Would you have a room available for an evenings rest?"

Arthur poured the bubbling ale into the robust tankard and slid it over the damp counter.

"All I can offer you is the attic room and it's a bit drafty, but in this weather it could be quite refreshing."

"That will be fine."

"All these bloody Knights have taken all the best rooms. They're on their way to the tournament in Wickerstaff. Is that where you are headed?"

"No, my journey lies East."

"Ugh, Dwarf country. Good luck with that!"

Arthur held out his podgy hand awaiting payment. Sebastian slipped six shiny coins from his purse and dropped them into his palm, Arthur's eyes doubled at such a sight.

"This is too much kind Sir."

"Not at all my good Man." He smiled and taking his tankard he worked his way around the maze of chairs and tables to fade into a shadowy corner near the fire.

As he sat he watched the Knights roar with laughter as they mocked Mondt's words.

"Believe me not brothers and sisters, but I swear to you on Adeve's grave that I took God's Hand." He unsheathed his sword and held it aloft, torchlight licking at the blade making it appear as if were made of flame. "And drove it into the Cyclops eye, right up to its hilt!" He gestured the actions with the great

78

sword. "And I watched as his gargantuan carcass fell to its death into the icy waters of Crystal Tears."

There was silence from the surrounding Knights as Mondt sheathed his sword back into its scabbard. Sebastian watched their faces as they took in what Mondt had just declared. He knew these Knights, Sir Dustin Droggon, Sir Manfred Moxley, Sir Theodore Lunde, Sir Thomas Tolos, 'The Tall' and Lady Maye Kessler.

"What a load of shit, Mondt!" Declared Droggon and the party burst into hysterics.

Mondt collapsed back into his chair sulking like a petulant child, his long blonde hair falling over his face.

"What know you of true bravery!" He grumbled.

Sebastian smirked and sipped his ale, Ernest was right it did taste like piss, but it was cold and wet and it quenched his thirst. The Knight's conversation had turned away from Mondt's heroics and onto the upcoming tournament, as Mondt was no longer the centre of attention he turned away and looked curiously at Sebastian as if he were trying to place him. The King noticed this and immediately manoeuvred his gaze away from the Knight and towards the kitchen doorway, his stomach rumbled and he had started to yearn for his supper. The curtain was suddenly drawn back and Agatha came shuffling out with a big wooden bowl a big wide smile squashed between two plump rosey cheeks. She beamed as she drew nearer to him, he made the assumption that Arthur had informed her about the extra coinage he had contributed and by the look of his bowl that swelled with coney pie and topped with two thick portions of bread she was very grateful.

"Here you go Sir." She said enthusiastically as she laid his supper out in front of him.

"Thank you M'lady."

"Ohh M'lady." She tittered and then leant over to whisper in his ear, her huge bosom almost suffocating him. "Thank you for your generosity. I have made sure to give you a double helping."

"Yes," He chuckled staring at her cleavage, "I can see that."

She left and Sebastian looked around to make sure Mondt's eyes were elsewhere, luckily they were, he was up again telling tales of how he had slain 32 Goblins at the Battle of Grotte's Tusk, Sebastian sniggered to himself knowing that this specific battle was well before Mondt's lifetime. With no eyes on him and believing he had enough shadow to shroud him, he removed his hood, he could wait no longer and dove into his meal, tearing at the bread with fingers and teeth. The coney was juicy and tender, the texture of the pastry crumbly and the gravy thick and rich. The ale may taste like the piss from a dehydrated boar, but the pie was some of the best he had ever tasted and he was a King that had sat at every noble table in the land and ate all manner of meticulously prepared food, but Agatha Copperpots' coney pie at The Withering Tree was sublime.

"I shall hire Agatha to be my new head cook." He mumbled under mouthfuls of pie as he devoured his meal.

80

Another obnoxious claim from Mondt's lips travelled in the air, one that he had beaten Sir Winstone Vespa in hand to hand combat. There was a grown from the other Knights.

"I grow tired of your self righteous juug-shit, Maximillious." Groaned Lady Male Kessler, she pushed her chair out from under herself and staggering drunkenly away. "I'm turning in."

"You go!" Mondt seethed. "What do women know of battle anyhow."

"Fuck off!" Came the reply as she disappeared upstairs.

"You didn't beat Sir Winstone, Mondt." Said Thomas 'The Tall'. "There is no way you would have bested him, with sword or by hand."

The others cheered with agreement.

"I tell you the truth. I would wager none of you have even seen Sir Winstone fight." Mondt added.

There was no answer to this as many of these Knights were younger and had only heard about Sir Winstone's reputation.

"Ha! You see!" Mondt snapped. "You have no right to tell me my adventures are folly! He fell to his knees and begged me not to tell the King that I had bested him or he would lose his position. Being a noble man I allowed him to rise and said nothing of his embarrassment to King Sebastian."

"No, but you'll tell it to a room full of drunken Knights." Laughed a very drunk Sir Theodore Lunde.

Sebastian scoffed loudly at Mondt's words, unfortunately the Knight heard and turned around quickly to face him.

"Do you have something to say Sir?" Mondt asked arrogantly.

Sebastian said nothing, but continued to finish his meal.

"Sir!" Mondt called loudly. "I am addressing you."

The tavern fell silent as all eyes were on the Knight and the stranger in the shadows. When there was still no reply, Mondt moved closer.

"You do me a great dishonour by ignoring my words, Sir!"

Arthur and Agatha hurried out from behind the curtain.

"Hey now!" Arthur cried. "I'll ave no roughin in ere."

"No roughing barkeep!" Mondt said edging ever closer to Sebastian. "I only await an apology."

"You will wait for a long time Knight. You will get no apology from me." Sebastian said as he chewed on the coney meat.

"How dare you! I am a Knight of the realm and should be respected!"

"For a Knight to be respected they must earn it on the battlefield my friend."

Mondt's face glowed red with anger as he strode towards Sebastian with reckless abandon.

"Who are you to disrespect me?"

"I'm no-one." Sebastian answered shovelling mashed spuds into his maw. "Just a tired journeyman wanting to finish his supper in peace without the name of a dear friend being dragged through the mud with your lies."

"Lies!" Mondt bellowed, his hand wrapped around the hilt of his sword. But Mondt was joined by Sir Manfred Moxley and his intervention stopped Mondt from making a terrible mistake.

"Forgive my friend Sir." Moxley said trying to lead Mondt away. "He has partaken in too much ale I fear and his tongue is getting away from him."

"It is not a problem." Sebastian replied as Mondt was led back towards their table, but Mondt pushed Moxley away and turned to face Sebastian again.

"You say you know Sir Winstone?"

"I do, Sir."

"Then prove it!" Mondt spat.

Sebastian was about to rise and take matters to the next phase with Mondt, but Moxley stepped in again to act as peacekeeper.

"That's enough now Mondt." And he pulled him back to their table.

"I have seen this Man before, he must be some false Knight that I have beaten somewhere or another that still holds a grudge. That must be it!" Mondt declared as he sat back down and downed his tankard, but continued to show Sebastian eyes of anger.

Ernest came hurrying in, almost bounding with excitement and headed straight towards Sebastian who was just finishing his meal and trying to ignore Mondt who was still burning a hole through him.

"Sire, I have bedded down your steed!" Ernest whispered.

"Good lad," Sebastian declared. "I too am off to bed down now."

"Oh!" Ernest said, all the enthusiasm seeping from his young face, he was hoping to sit and hear tales of the King's life, his conquests and his adventures.

"Maybe in the morn I can talk to you more. You will have Dayboy readied as The Sun of Selym rises, yes?"

"Of course!"

"Good, good!" Sebastian stood and pulled his hood back over his head. "Here is what I promised you young Ern." And with that dropped more coinage into his hand and turned to leave.

"Oh thank you, my King!" Ernest bellowed and then clapped a podgy hand over his mouth as everyone turned to face the rising stranger.

"King?" Mondt questioned.

"The King!" Arthur and Agatha waddled out from behind the counter towards Sebastian who reluctantly removed the hood again.

"Imagine The King of Maglore in our tavern, eating my coney pie!" Agatha swooned and bowed down before him.

"And drinking my ale!" Arthur declared kneeling down before him.

"Please rise." Sebastian said. "You owe me nothing. Your courtesy and hospitality has been more than enough, I should be kneeling before you."

Realisation that they were in the presence of the King of Maglore and quickly patrons and Knights in the tavern collapsed to their knees. Mondt was in a state of shock and slowly slid down from his chair like an embarrassed snake, bowing his head, so that his long golden locks concealed his reddening face.

"Please!" Sebastian announced. "There is no need to stand on ceremony, please go back about your evening. I wish to retire and I will be on my way at the break of dawn."

The patrons rose and returned to their seats, but the Knights remained on bent knees. Sir Dustin Droggon rose and approached King Sebastian before kneeling again in front of him.

"My King!" Droggon said.

"Sir Dustin, please rise." Sebastian replied nodding his head in respect of the Knight.

"I apologise on behalf of us all for not paying you the respect that you deserve."

"There is no apology needed, Sir Dustin. You were not to know that it was me. I travel under a shroud to quicken my journey."

Droggon stood and the other Knights followed suit, Mondt rose slowly and remained behind them, no longer loud and obnoxious as he hid his shame.

"I would be most pleased if you took my cot for your own, Sire." Droggon said.

"No, I cannot."

"It would do me great honour, my King. I have been unable to join you in battle because of my young years. But my farda served your farda in The Battle of Grotte's Tusk."

King Sebastian tried to intervene, but Droggon was welling up with emotion and continued.

"He and my brother also served by you and your brothers at The Raid of Raw Cliff and at The War of Crows. Where they lost their lives. Please let me give you this small offering." Droggon choked.

"My farda spoke most highly of your farda, Sir Laymon. He was a brave and loyal Knight, as was your elder, Sir Gant. It was an honour to fight alongside them. I will take your offering, Sir Dustin." He smiled, placing a hand on the Knight's shoulder. "But only if you will take my quarters in return?"

"Of course Sire. It will be an honour."

"Good! Arthur here tells me its best room in the inn."
There was laughter as they all knew that it was drafty and prone to leakage.
Sir Theodore Lunde came forward bowing his large head, he cleared his throat as his voice seemed always full of gravel.

"My King!" He said, "I am…"

"Sir Theodore Lunde, I know of your ability in battle and on the games field with lance and mace. They call you 'The Bear' and I can see why, brutish strength and a hunter's mind."

"You honour me with your words, Sire." Lunde bowed.

"I shall honour you all with my words."
He acknowledged them all by name and each nodded their heads, beaming with pride being mentioned on the tongue of a king.

"Sir Manfed Moxley, 'Tall' Tom Tolos and even you Maximillious Mondt. Your words may be stretched to the realm of fantasy on occasion, but there is no debate that you are a wonder with a sword and master of the joust. You are all exceptional Knights and although the lands have been at peace now for the majority of my reign, I may well have need of your services one day and I hope you will all rise to the call."

The Knight's swiftly drew their swords and lay them on the ground towards their King.

"Our swords are yours, my King." Declared Moxley.

The other Knights agreed with shouts of 'Aye!'.

"You honour me." Sebastian said. "It is pleasing to know that the realm has such loyalty to the crown."

"Please join us for a tankard of ale, so we may celebrate this prestigious occasion." Tolos said with a smile as broad as he was tall.

"Aye!" Moxley agreed. "It is not everyday one gets to have counsel with the King."

"Aye!" Shouted Arthur. "The ale shall be on the house!"

There was a cheer and Lunde slapped Arthur on the back almost knocking the rotund barkeep over.

Sebastian raised his hands and a hush fell over the room.

"If you will excuse me. I must retire early if I am to make good time in the morn."

There was a nodding of disappointment and the band of Knights parted to allow their king through towards the wooden staircase near the corner of the room.

"Sire?" The voice of Mondt halted King Sebastian on his way to the stairs, he knew what would be asked, words that he was hoping he could avoid.

"What is this journey you speak of?" Mondt asked and Sebastian sighed a heavy sigh for he knew he could not lie to his people, it was something that he had learnt from his farda King Cecil Hartwaker, his words were engraved in his mind... *Let truth be the way, give people the truth and they will love and respect you. With love and respect you will have their loyalty.*

"It is a solitary quest, Sir Maximillious. It is something that I must do alone."

"But the road is a treacherous one to be travelling on alone, my King." Said Mondt. "Let me make amends for my behaviour and my corrupt words and accept me as your travelling companion to defend you."

"Aye!" Lunde cheered. "Let us all join you and see you safely to your journey's end."

The Knights became rowdy with cheers again, but Sebastian had to silence them and strode around the room as he told them about his visions and about the darkness that he believed would sweep over the land. He looked on as their faces contoured with disbelief, the way one would look upon a madman, the enthusiasm seeped out of their pours and Sebastian understood why. Why would they follow a Man on a fool's quest? They should not and would not for he knew that a fool must journey alone if he is to see clearly again.

When Sebastian had finished his declaration there was silence for the longest time as they tried to come to terms with what had been said.

It was Sebastian himself that disrupted the silence.

"I do not expect any of you to believe these bizarre words I speak. I too have trouble believing them myself. But that is the truth of it and I must go alone. But know this, if what I have seen is true, then your oaths sworn to the crown may well be called upon."

Sebastian readied himself to leave when Ernest appeared, he had been sitting on a nearby table taking in the whole affair. His eyes were full of wonderment and he stopped the King in his tracks by holding his hand. Agatha gasped at her son touching the royal hand and thought it an offence but Sebastian smiled down at the boy.

"Yes, Ern?"

"I believe you Sire, I will always believe your words." Ernest said beaming.

"That means everything Ern." Sebastian said before ruffling his hair and attempting to climb the stairs.

"ALL HAIL THE KING!" Mondt cried and knelt again. Sebastian turned and nodded at Mondt, he was the only one of the Knights to pay tribute.

"What's with all the fucking the noise?" Cried Lady Maye Kessler stumbling down the stairs in a drunken state.

"Excuse me M'lady." Sebastian said as he passed her on the stairs.

As he disappeared, she stumbled in shock and slid down the stairs landing in a heap.

"Fuck me, it's the King." She belched.

The tavern exploded in a ruckus of laugher and Knights and patrons went about their business as if nothing had happened.

"I would wager that the King has lost his mind!" Droggon said to the table of Knights, now all seated with tankards clenched in their large mitts.

"I would say it is you that has lost your mind, Dustin." Chuckled Lunde.

"And why, pray tell? I am not the Man declaring some evil darkness will sweep the land and destroy us all!"

"No, but you gave him your room." Chuckled Lunde. "Who is more the fool?"

The table burst into laughter again, all apart from Maximillious Mondt who sat in silence.

CHÃPTÉR 8
THÉ KÏNGDÖM ÜNDÉR THÉ FLÖWÉRS

ing Sebastian had made sure that he had risen early after his interesting evening spent at The Withering Tree. He had looked to avoid anyone and everyone and leave Tendor as soon as possible, the visions still poisoned his dreams and he knew now that time was against him. Sat high upon Dayboy they lolloped slowly along the banks of Lake Salivia being sure not to get to close, for Sebastian had heard the legend of a Dragon that dwelled in its dark depths. Salinka was said to be of deep blue scales on a slender body, it had no need for wings, but is said to be able to swim faster than any carp. But Dragon sightings in Maglore had become so scarce over the last couple of decades that Sebastian believed the species obsolete or as Ern would say, 'a-stink'.

Sebastian smiled and delved into his saddle bag and retrieved the skillfully carved depiction of a Binturong. Ernest had risen early too when Sebastian was due to leave Tendor, either that or the boy could not sleep due to the sheer excitement of that evenings events. The King had crept downstairs, careful not to rouse any of the sleeping Knights, but had found Dayboy awake and saddled ready for departure. He would never forget the smile of pride on Ern's face knowing that he had helped his King with his quest, Sebastian made sure to tip him handsomely with coinage but as he mounted the large colt, Ern presented the carving as a gift to him. He had ridden away with a tear in his eye hoping that he would one day see that young lad again.

"His skills with a knife to carve with such precision is as good as any experienced sculptor I have met. Hopefully young Ern will follow this calling into the fine arts as an occupation and not get stranded pouring ale at The Withering Tree for all time."

Dayboy grumbled and scoffed as they travelled through The Woods of Salivia, his rotund stomach already calling to be fed again.

"You and your belly, Dayboy." Laughed Sebastian. "Do you think of nothing else but food?"

Dayboy snorted and shook his massive head from side to side, his blonde mane sweeping across Sebastian's face.

"Okay my friend, we are almost there. I believe that the outskirts to Valtora lies through these trees."

King Sebastian was correct of course, although he did not travel as much these days he still knew his realm well from his days as Head Knight and the right hand to his brother's, King Roxon and then King Viktor during their reigns. It was his job to travel to other Houses and deal with any quarrels that had arisen, he fought in battles all over the realm and had good relationships with the Lords and Ladies of both the Higher and Lesser

Houses. These were all things that made him a good King for he never forgot the realm or the relationships he had forged.

As they emerged from the woods a glorious view awaited them, acres upon acres of elegant flowers as if a blanket of colour had been spread across the land. It was a beautiful sight to behold, and there appeared to be an aura given off by the petals of the flowers, glowing slightly as if protected by some enchanted shield. Sebastian dismounted Dayboy who trotted off to eat some shrooms that grew at the foot of a tree.

"Steer clear of the crimson ones Dayboy or else your head will be lost in haze."

Sebastian looked out at the vast field of flowers and knew that they were indeed enchanted and the aura acted as an early warning system to those that lived below the tulips, daises, lilies and dills. If any trespassers were to cross that threshold then they would be in for some hostility.

Sebastian crouched down and took in the various scents that arose from the petals and cleansed his nostrils, the delicate colours fluttered in the light breeze and above was a soft cornflower blue sky that had been abandoned by cloud, it was as if The Sun of Selym only had eyes for Valtora and gave it all of its warming attention.

"A beautiful scene for the senses, but will the welcome be as warm in the kingdom that lies beneath those quivering petals, I wonder?"

He thought not, for below the mass of flowers stood the kingdom of the Fairies. An astonishing species that was proof that Adeve's touch was indeed filled with magic. A race that was

93

originally created by Adeve to watch over the plants and flora of the realm, ze had called them hirs Greenskeepers and instilled attributes and magic in them that ze did not give to any other. The main gift bestowed upon them was the ability to fly with magnificent wings of transparency and colour, the flying of a Fairy was truly a sight to behold. A species that could stand in the palm of a Man's hand and instilled with such hypnotic beauty that to gaze upon one for too long can make one fall in love with them and would gladly do their bidding if asked, a trait that Fairies have used to manipulate other species and races and keep themselves safe through the centuries. Any aggressor against the Fairy Kingdom of Valtora were usually entranced and forget why they were even there in the first place and overlook the Fairy species altogether. This is why many do not even believe in the existence of Fairies to this day. But with all their powers they are vulnerable and knowing this has left them paranoid of any visitors, it had made them ignorant to the world outside their kingdom and why they have never taken part in the battles and wars of those that walk above them.

"Dayboy?" Sebastian called and his head looked up from his nuzzling of shrooms.

"Remember to steer clear of the crimson ones please, you are a weight that I could not carry if you become intoxicated by vis-shrooms. Stick to the pink and yellow ones Dayboy."
Dayboy snorted as if to dismiss his master's words, he was not a careless or naive colt, he knew which fungi was toxic and which was not.

Sebastian readied himself and stepped into the bed of flowers, he could feel vibrations as he walked towards the centre of the field, he knew the Fairies had been alerted to his presence and it would not take long for them to besiege him.

"HALT!" Came a voice from below, Sebastian did as he was asked.

"I wish to parley with your Queen." Sebastian answered, his eyes flitting around his feet for the voice but he saw no one.

"You are trespassing!" Came the voice and Sebastian followed the sound of the aggressive tone and focused on a large fawn coloured coney that capered out from behind the cover of foliage. The creature was saddled by a noble looking male Fairy, clad in teal shaded silks that were trimmed in gold, a golden circlet wrapped around a head of black hair indicated that he was of royal blood.

"All I wish is for an audience with your Queen and then I shall be on my way." Sebastian answered and had noticed that silently he had become surrounded by Fairies clad in fine armour, with beautiful different coloured wings sprouting from their backs and two long antennae that protruded out from the tops of their heads like the ears of a coney. They stood at his feet, on the back of quails or appeared from the confines of petals. All the Fairies held sharp spears that looked like mere needles to the King, but he assumed it would not feel pleasant to be pricked by one. He knelt down to address the royal Fairy that steadied his attentive coney, spears were gripped even tighter as he descended and several Fairies appeared hovering around him.

"I am King Sebastian Hartwaker, King of the realm and sworn protector of Maglore. I wish to speak with your Queen."

"You are no King of our realm!" The royal Fairy spat. "And when have you ever shown the people of Valtora any attention or indeed protection?"

"You do well keeping intruders at bay yourself I hear, through hypnotism and manipulation."

"A despicable lie if ever there was one! For such a slanderous remark I should cut your tongue from you head, Hartwaker!" He said pulling a sword from his scabbard, his face contorting grotesquely with anger.

"It would take a much larger blade I fear." Sebastian smirked and although it was not his intention to provoke he was not going to stand by and be insulted with no just cause.

"How dare you!" He leapt from his Coney and flew to face Sebastian, sword raised and wings flapping at ridiculous speed, they even changed colour to reflect his mood and changed from turquoise to red within an instance.

"I am Prince Valian Sitruc, the son of Queen Oleander and heir to the Fairy Kingdom. You should lose your life for such disrespectful words."

"I mean no disrespect by my words Prince Valian, but you place me in a corner with your hostility."
Prince Valian said nothing for a few moments but Sebastian could tell by his wings that he was calming.

"I do not trust Man." He announced sliding his sword back into his sheath.

"That is your right young Prince. But I have come to your kingdom under a banner of peace. I am accompanied by no army or Knights. All I bring with me is a message that your Queen must hear and then whatever the outcome, I shall be on my way."

Prince Valian turned away from Sebastian and signalled to his army that had gathered, they lowered their spears and he flew back down to his saddle atop of the coney.

"I shall take you to see my marda." He announced turning the coney around, with a swift tug on the reins. "Ellon, prepare him." He called to a nearby Fairy as he hopped away through the foliage.

The majority of the soldiers disappeared into the cover of the flowers and the quail riders scampered away after the Prince.

A pretty Fairy who had been riding one of the quails approached him, launching herself effortlessly into the sky, swirling around, blurs of greens and purples flashed in front of him. She came to an abrupt stop in front of his face and smiled pleasantly, their was a hint of flirtation in her twinkling eyes.

"My Lord, my name is Ellon." She bowed in the air as her wings fluttered behind her.

"It is a pleasure to make your acquaintance young Ellon." Ellon giggled sheepishly, her wings turned pink for a second and the crowns of her antennae glowed vibrantly.

"Have I offended you?" Sebastian asked.

"Oh no Your Majesty! You pay me a great honour."

"How so?"

"I am 227 years old, my young days are well behind me I fear."

"Well, you do not look a day over 108." Sebastian smiled.

"You are too kind."

Ellon's eyes twinkled and Sebastian could understand now how Man have fallen for these beautiful creatures, it would be easily to fall under Ellon's amorous charms. Sebastian drew his eyes away from her glance for a moment to clear his head.

"My Lord, I must ask you to close your eyes." She said in a whisper that felt like a summer breeze at his ear.

"But why?" Sebastian asked cautiously.

"You will see. But no harm will come to you, you have my word."

She was hovering so close to his face now, he could feel the gust of her vigorous wings caressing his nose and he closed his eyes. Fairy dust formed in Ellon's hands, it sparkled all colours of the spectrum and she blew it into his face, he felt it tickle his eyelids, nostrils and lips, it tasted so very sweet. He felt as if he were falling and was as light as a feather, he hoped this sensation would last forever, unfortunately it did not.

"You can open your eyes now, Your Majesty."

He did as he was asked, his eyelashes beating away excess Fairy dust that had settled on his lids and when he gazed back at Ellon he was the same size as her. He was taken aback at first, but then when he looked around and saw the Kingdom under the Flowers he was astonished and wore his wonderment plainly for all to see. The cornflower blue sky was still there above him but it looked as though it would take a Fairy's lifetime to reach it, even the flower heads that swayed above were as big as the towers of Windmast Castle.

"You awe me with your kingdom, Ellon, for it is truly beautiful."

"Thank you, Your Majesty." She smiled coyly, her whole aura a radiant glow, she was truly intoxicating.

Ellon led the way through the kingdom, he was closely followed by two armoured guards clutching spears.

Sebastian saw houses built into the stems of the flowers and trees, Fairies came and went at rapid pace, a plethora of colours flashed in front of his face from their vibrant wings. He received many a strange look from the inhabitants of Valtora, obviously wary of this outsider, it was a look that mirrored the ones he received while entering the small town in Tendor. He realised then that there was still a fair amount of fear in the realm of Maglore, he believed that his knowledge of the realm had become a little disjointed, for he had lived safely behind the impregnable walls of Windmast Castle for so long. He knew not of the hardships and the people, to see the fear in the eyes of Man and Fairy distressed him immensely, what did they fear? Was it just a feeling that they shared? Did they too wake up wrapped in sweat soaked bedsheets from terrifying visions of fire and death?

Sebastian was in a world of his own, dazzled by the beauty that surrounded him and disheartened that the people of the realm would feel like this. So hypnotised by beauty and guilt was he that he did not hear his guide Ellon mentioning points of interest to him. They stopped abruptly which brought an end to his reverie.

"There it is." Ellon announced proudly.

Sebastian was agog as he gazed upon the glorious splendour of Castle Sitruc. It had been constructed entirely out of glass, several shades of colourful shards were used to create a sight like nothing Sebastian had ever laid eyes upon. A tall and slender structure built inside the stem of a magnificent pink dahlia in full bloom, swaying gently across the canvas of soft blue. Several sky blue banners flickered subtly in the breeze, displaying the sigil of the House of Sitruc, which was emblazoned with elegant Fairy wings, finished with many precious stones sewn which made the design come alive as they caught the light.

"You are favoured King Hartwaker." Ellon announced. "There are but a handful of your race that have had the privilege to gaze at Castle Sitruc and the Kingdom under the Flowers."

"I am unworthy of gazing upon such exquisiteness." Sebastian announced as he craned his neck up towards sharp steeples that pierced the sky. All around him his senses were besieged by colours of all manner of flowers that hung in the air and the sweet scents of various nectar tantalised his tastebuds. There was a sudden clanging of bells and Sebastian looked up to see a smartly dressed Fairy striking a row of bleeding heart flowers that drooped from a glass tower. The doors to Castle Sitruc opened and Queen Oleander exited surrounded by a huge congregation of Fairy nobles and armoured soldiers.

"Welcome!" The Queen declared her face beaming, eyes twinkling like two black diamonds, her dark hair wrapped up upon her head like a bee hive which was embellished with small flowers. Her long slender antennae glistened above the shine of a golden tiara. Her son, Prince Valian was at her side still wearing that same look of sternness, it was a look that could curdle milk.

"Your Majesty!" Sebastian bowed as she approached. Queen Oleander glided effortlessly across the soft blanket of grass beneath her bare feet, choosing not to use her abilities of flight, but her followers used theirs to hover towards Sebastian, he thought maybe it was an act of arrogance to flaunt their powers.

"You honour us with your visit, King Hartwaker of Man." She smiled arrogantly, Sebastian knew she had addressed him as King of Man to notify him that he was not her king and his crown had no influence or relevance in the Fairy Kingdom.

"I have heard tales of your beauty Queen Oleander, but they do not do you justice." Said Sebastian as he lowered himself to acknowledge her outstretched hand and caressed his lips across her pale flesh. He felt her magic on his lips, they tingled briefly as if they were crazed by some irritating itch. She giggled at the sensation of his beard bristles tickling her hand.

"You flatter me King Sebastian. I had no idea you were such a handsome Man." Her eyes burned with lust and Sebastian fought hard to divert his gaze, he did not wish to fall under her spell and remain in Valtora as her slave... or did he?

"What a beautiful place Valtora is. Who would have thought that there was such beauty to rival the flowers themselves."

"Yes, The Kingdom under the Flowers is a magical place. If I may be so bold, I would wager there is nowhere in the realm that looks as splendid as Valtora."

"I have ventured to ever corner of Maglore Queen Oleander, but I am yet to see anything like this."

"Indeed!" She smiled.

There was a silence between them for a few moments, she realised that he was indeed a Man of honour and could never be tempted away by her powers of seduction, she was a little upset by that, as she did desire him.

"We could stand here all day and speak pleasantries King Hartwaker, but tell me what brings you here."

"He is a trespasser and should be killed!" Snapped Prince Valian.

Queen Oleander was swift with her punishment and flicked the back of her hand around her son's face.

"How dare you!" She scalded. "This Man is a King. Show him some respect."

"Yes, Marda! My apologies, King Hartwaker." Consumed by embarrassment, Prince Valian sank away into the crowd holding his reddened cheek.

"King Hartwaker, I have never met you but I hear you are a Man of honour and trust. It was my farda, King Algamoth that ventured to your kingdom many years ago on your invite. He told us all of how you gave all the races the right to rule over their own and I respect you for that. I had heard many tales that Man were nothing but a race compelled by waring with each other and greedy for treasure and control. You have made me second guess myself and my congregation will tell you that, that is a very rare occurrence."

Her congregation agreed with a flourish of laugher.

"But to receive you here in my kingdom alone worries me. Why are you here King of Man?"

"You may call me Sebastian, my Queen."

She nodded.

"And you may refer to me as Oleander. Now what troubles you?"

"How did you know that something was troubling me Oleander?"

"You would not be here. There is a reason you are here and I can see in your eyes that something troubles you."

"You have a keen eye." Sebastian chuckled.

"Call it Fairy's intuition." She smiled playfully and that intoxicating allure seeped from her once again, if she wanted him he felt now that he would be impotent with his resistance to her charms.

"The words I speak are true..."

King Sebastian recited his tale leaving no stone unturned, bearing his soul and fears with the good people of the Fairy Kingdom. He glanced at the faces of The Fairies, confusion was all that looked back. Prince Valian was almost smug as if every word that spilt from Sebastian's mouth was preposterous. Only Queen Oleander and Ellon's gaze were different, showing traits

103

of pity. He did not know whether they thought him deranged, but their sparkling melancholy eyes forced him to end his narrative. As his words ended no one spoke, only the fluttering of wings met his ears, that was a judging sound in itself.

"Sebastian," Queen Oleander finally announced, taking his arm. "Please walk with me."
Her followers looked to follow her but she raised a hand and they bowed low before stepping back into place.

"I hear your words and I believe them to be true Sebastian."

"You do? Oh that is most pleasing." Sebastian smiled.

"You are a Man of truth and honour I know this, I can see it in your eyes. I see the love that you have for your wife and child, that is the only reason I would not take you as my own, even though it would be within my power to do so."
He nodded, he believed that if she wished it, he would be hers.

"And although I believe these words of a darkness that will shroud Maglore, it is not to persuade my people to go to war. As you know we have never felt the need to get involved in the battles of those above our kingdom, I mean no disrespect but this forthcoming, war does not effect us."

"How can you say that!" He cried, pulling away from her grasp and clasping her forcefully by her arms. Her army led by Prince Valian looked to move forward with weapons gripped but she told them to halt.

"This effects us all, don't you see that?" Sebastian pleaded.

"It effects us not. I will not send my people to their deaths for you and your kind. We will be well protected by our magic here. Fire and brimstone cannot penetrate Fairy magic."
He released her and stepped away.

"You are arrogant to believe that this does not effect you and your people."

"Maybe so, but I will not have my Fairies spill their blood for a cause that is not ours."

"Your magic will not protect you, Oleander, not this time. This is different, it is not Man or Dwarf, or Giant or Goblin. It is death itself."
She caressed his face and stared into his passionate eyes.

"I know that you feel what you are saying is true, but we do not involve ourselves in your wars, we never have and never will."

"If that is your final answer then I will take my leave."
Sebastian said turning and walking away.

"You could always stay with me Sebastian, be my King and be protected by the magic of Valtora. I would see that you come to no harm."

"And leave my wife and child to die? My people to burn under this dark plague?"

"Yes."

"I'm sorry to have wasted your time Your Highness!"
Sebastian snapped and left abruptly.
Ellon joined Queen Oleander as they watched him leave the kingdom and slowly start to regain his true height, growing like a Giant above the tops of the flowers.

105

"Is what he said true Your Majesty?" Ellon asked.

"I believe his words were pure and true, Ellon."

"Then what shall we do?"

"We shall do nothing. Just like we always do, we shall do nothing." A tear fell from the corner of her eye and it sparkled, she could not help Sebastian, her people would not allow it. It is all she had ever known.

King Sebastian emerged from the flowers, rapidly returning to his original size, his hefty leather boots stomped through the plants that surrounded the Fairy Kingdom, his frustrations being taken out on their feeble stems. He swivelled in the dirt and gripped his hips defiantly, his bearded face brushed with a shade of aggravation.

"What arrogance!" He growled in his irritation, he felt like he had again been treated like a fool, even though Queen Oleander declared that she did indeed believe him that she could do nothing, for her people would never spill their blood for those that lived above the Kingdom under the Flowers. The King's complaining brought Dayboy trotting out from the cover of the woods where he had wandered off in search of more wild shrooms. At first he thought his King may have been in distress but on returning saw that he was just sulking and he continued to nuzzle through dried leaves in search of fallen nuts or berries.

"How can such a powerful species be so blinded by their own ignorance?" Sebastian asked himself as he looked back over the field of flowers.

"If it's any consolation, I believe you." A voice rose up from the flowers.

Sebastian looked around for the speaker, but saw nothing or no one.

"Who goes there?" Sebastian asked. "Show yourself!" He was in no mood for games.

"There is no need for hostilities, Sire." Came the voice again.

Sebastian followed the sound of the voice and saw a leg dangling from confines of tulip, the barefoot swaying back and forth in a casual manner, mimicking the gentle movement of the flower as it was caressed by that subtle Floret breeze.

"Who are you?" Sebastian asked kneeling down to peer between the petals.

"It is I, King of Rum!" He announced his voice wavering with intoxication as he appeared from behind the curtain of tulip petals, like a thespian taking to the stage. His hair was in disarray, his long antennae drooped and he wore clothes that were ragged and heavily stained by rum and pollen. He smiled a crooked smile, his eyes almost shutting with the effort as he swayed back and forth unleashing an oafish burp that caused the petals of the tulip to quiver.

"See how the King of Man kneels before me!" He laughed and snorted. "Oh the irony."

"A drunken Fairy!" Sebastian scoffed. "That is all I need."

"I would wager my words would be of more benefit than from the fools in Valtora." The Fairy's demeanour changed and he appeared angry at the mere mention of the kingdoms name.

A Man's thimble appeared clutched in his hands and rum spilled over its lip, he took a hefty swig, the rum ran down his chin, he cared not.

"How can I believe any words that spill from a drunken Fairy's lips?"

"Ah, what words are truer than a drunk's?"

"All that I hear is rum talking." Sebastian scoffed and stood, readying himself to turn and leave.

"You are correct in your observation of the Fairy race, Sire." The Fairy hiccuped. "They are a species born out of arrogance. Over the centuries they have managed to isolate themselves from the rest of Maglore and perfect the fine art of being complete arseholes." The drunken Fairy burped again loudly and enjoyed another swift swig from his thimble.

Sebastian turned to face him again, confusion causing his brow to crease.

"Who are you?"

The Fairy stood up and staggered from side to side, his limp wings drooped lifelessly behind him.

"I am the first born, unwanted, drunken outcast of House Sitruc." He said proudly before falling backwards into the stamen causing pollen to erupt and consume him.

"You are the first son of Queen Oleander?" Sebastian gasped.

"Indeed!" He stood again, holding his thimble tightly, amazingly not a drip was spilt. He wiped away the excess pollen. "Prince Ekim at your service." He bowed before him and smiled.

"You look like no Prince I have ever seen."

"One of a kind, me!"

Ekim sat on the petal of the leaf and nonchalantly swung his legs back and forth like a child.

"What happened to you?" Sebastian asked, returning his knee to listen to this eccentric waif's tale.

"Ah a sad tale to say the least. Let's just say I outgrew the Kingdom under the Flowers. My voice no longer became of any value to my marda, my brother Valian had her ear and he poisoned her against me."

"That is a shame." Sebastian said sympathetically. "It can be so hard growing up in strong families, it can become a war in itself when siblings are battling for a prize of power. I myself was never born to be King. It was through the death of my brothers that I have found myself on the throne."

Ekim nodded and sighed, taking a small sip of his rum, before holding it out for Sebastian to partake, Sebastian smiled and shook his head.

"Aye, families, you cannot choose them."

The pair sat in silence, Sebastian remembered his brothers fondly. Harold III born with disabilities of the mind and body and seen unfit to rule. Roxon who took his own life after the death of his wife and child, he even thought of Viktor who was a boar and a lout but still his brother, still of his blood and he loved him.

"Aye!" Ekim announced calling the king from his woolgathering. "The constant drinking and debauching of women had nothing to do with it."

Sebastian frowned crossly having been taken for a fool by the Fairy Prince.

"You make a mockery of your family name." Sebastian snapped.

"Mockery?" Ekim laughed. "It is they that are the mockery, they are so ignorant to the world around them! I said that I believe you and those were words of truth, I have seen what evil lies in store for Man."

"What evil have you seen?" Sebastian asks.

"There has always been evil Sire. Man have just been blind to see it, but it is everywhere, concealed in shadows, hidden in crevices of cave and soil. The dark beings of Sloore will rise again." He took another swig of rum, his eyes span in his head. "I give no blessing to this rise of darkness, I merely choose to make myself scarce and stay out of its way."

"You say that you are different from the other Fairies?" Sebastian announced. "But you are one and the same. You flee from your problems just like the others who bury their heads and pretend that this darkness does not affect them."

"Very true, I am a coward by nature. But my reason for staying away from this evil is to stay alive, it is not born out of ignorance."

Sebastian whistled and he was joined by Dayboy who snorted at the drunken Fairy.

"Their ignorance will be their end." Sebastian announced as he mounted his huge colt.

"Truer words have never been spoken King of Man. They will all perish! They will all burn!"

Sebastian stared at him for the words rung true, he had seen the visions, he had seen the flames.

"And what of you Prince Ekim? Will you not suffer the same fate as the people of Valtora?"

"Not me," Ekim scoffed leaning back on the petal and making himself comfortable as if he had no troubles. "I'll be drunk in some brothel in Strigstrum no doubt, lost in the hefty cleavage of some whore."

King Sebastian had had better days, he scowled as he looked at the drunken Fairy who knew all and cared not.

"I ask one thing of you Prince."

"Name it."

"Prey that I am wrong."

Sebastian kicked his heels into the torso of his steed and with an uncomfortable bray Dayboy took off for their next stop.

CHÃPTÉR 9
ÚNDÉR WÃTCHFÚL ÉYÉS

he King had been travelling for several days across the harsh terrains of Maglore. He trudged through The Marshes of Hoss, with a firm grip on Dayboy's reins he heaved him through the shallow swamp, eased him over rocky terrain and steep hills, cleansed his weary hooves through the rivers that ran down from the Kayalian Mountains. The steed's tenacity was tested through the hardships as was the King's sanity as they lost several days in the thick mists on the desolate Moors of Geral.

"The King draws nearer Master." Kelda wheezed with animosity.

Those yellow eyes continued to watch from the darkness as two hooded figures clutched a large cauldron, they were watching intently too. A vision of a focussed Sebastian Hartwaker atop a fatigued Dayboy trudged towards the entrance to a forest, a blanket of night looming over them. The vision quivered, becoming distorted as ripples of bubbling liquid swept across the deep cauldron. The withered hand of Kelda touched the surface of the liquid and manipulated the vision, stretching the image for a more intimate view of the thirteenth King of Man.

"His shoulders slump and his eyes are heavy, as he carries the burden of the realm." She squawked.

"How pleasing!" Cackled the Dark Master.

"Do not be deceived by this observation." Kelda snapped. The two hooded figures stood over the vision that swayed in front of them, framed by the black circular rim of the cauldron. Kelda continued to caress the broth with her clawed fingers, chipped shards of fingernails sliced through Sebastian's journey through the woods.

"There is determination in those tired eyes. His heart is fire and it burns with courage." She turned to her master, eyes like murky pearls. "He will not stop until that fire is extinguished."

"Do you speak the truth, Kelda?" The Dark Master asked as he left the cauldron and wondered over to the dark cave wall that shone with dampness.

"I always speak the truth to my Master. My tongue may be coarse and bitter, but the words that are meant for my Dark Master are always sincere."

"Forgive me." He sighed, his pale slender hand stretched out from the confines of his dark sleeve and began to massage the damp walls of the cave. The cave wall moved and light from the flames that licked at the base of the cauldron shimmered on black scale, unveiling Demios 'The Black'. The Dark Master touched the Dragon lovingly, could it be the only thing in this realm that he loved?

"You owe me no forgiveness, but heed my words for they bring with them a warning." Kelda returned to her cauldron, those vacant eyes burning into the king, scrutinising his every move.

"It surprises me that a mere Man could have such courage against the horrors that lie in the coming darkness?" He asked, Demios' gigantic nose nuzzled at him as though he were an affectionate pet.

"He is not like other Man, Master." Kelda hissed. "He has the blood of his ancestors running through his veins. King's blood! Pure and blue, like the kings of those who reigned before him. Grayfall, Willem, Brode, Cecil... Names of brave Kings that formed who he is. He will not stop."

"Then we must stop him ourselves!" The Dark Master snapped impatiently, tired of hearing about heroes from House Hartwaker that had been triumphant during their reigns. Demios snorted lilac vapour from its nostrils, it's eye the size of a boulder gleamed like a magenta stone in enthusiastic anticipation.

"No Demios!" The Dark Master cackled. "My, my you are an eager one. But not yet, it is too soon."
Demios grunted and trudged away into the corners of the cave like a sulking infant.

"What do you suggest, oh Dark Master?" Kelda licked her lips, salivating, longing to finally sink her dirty talons into something wretched. The Dark Master returned to the cauldron and watched Sebastian's progress through the dark woods.

"Where is he now?" He asked.

"The Lupiin Forest." She hissed. "Shall I unleash a fatal spell? A poisonous mist to constrict around his throat and choke him to his death?" Strands of salvia dangled from her cracked lips with foul anticipation and bloodlust.

"No!" He replied and the magic that formed in her glassy eyes died like her hopes of sudden death and extinction of life.

"As you wish, my Master."

"There must be no magic involved in his demise or questions would be asked and a dead King would bring forward armies of Man. To maintain our advantage we must remain shrouded by shadow and conduct our plan subtly until the time is right. They must not know it is their end until it is too late."

"Then what do you suggest?" Kelda asked.

"We must call upon others to do the deed."

"Others? But we must not show our hand yet and apart from the Children of the Shrouded Realm we have very few allies."

"Man has many enemies. If some were to learn that he were alone and vulnerable, there would be some that would take advantage of that and if they succeed then Man's retaliation would be fall at their feet."

"But who?"

"The Cult of Crypor would prosper from such a deed. Their hate for all those that follow the laws of Adeve would be enough to spur them on to commit such an act, claiming it to be a sacrifice for their Crow God, Crypor."

The Dark Master conjured a glowing sphere of amethyst in his palm and allowed it to fall into the cauldron, it caused the broth to ripple and the vision of Sebastian Hartwaker disappeared replaced by a glowing mist.

"Your power grows , oh Dark Master." Kelda salivated as something began to form in the cauldron, a bird of some kind.

"I am not yet at full strength, I am only capable of these parlour tricks." He waved his hand above the bubbling liquid and a large black crow rose from it, feathers matted by the mystical placenta. "Only when I have The Orb of Quirinus in my grasp will I be all powerful."

The crow hovered in the air, an aura surrounding it as it outstretched its wings and screeched loudly. It took flight and drifted around the cave, Demios' humongous head swung out from the shadows and took an unsuccessful lurch towards it, but it manoeuvred past its barbed maw. It screeched again in mockery of the gigantic beast and settled on the outstretched arm of its creator.

"Seek out those known as The Cult of Crypor and lead them to the Man King. They will do the rest."

The crow squawked and gave flight leaving the dark caverns of the Kayalian Mountains far behind.

CHÃPTÉR 10

TÖÛCHÉD BY GÖD'S HÃND

ebastian yawned as he trudged through the Lupiin Forest, a pile of kindling grasped in his arms. Night had taken the sky, but as Sebastian looked up through the trees something felt odd to him. It was a different kind of darkness that seemed thick, tar-like and he thought it strange that there were no stars to be seen. He thought no more of his peculiar observation as he entered a clearing lit by a small fire he had constructed by discarded branches and dried leaves. Dayboy was unsaddled and had already settled himself down by the warmth of the fire.

"I see you have made yourself quite comfortable." Sebastian mocked as he knelt by the fire and added his findings to it, immediately increasing its size and heat. Dayboy grunted in reply, but his eyes remained closed.

"You rest well my friend, you have earned it." Sebastian said settling down himself on a makeshift pillow of items taken from his saddlebag, the Hartwaker family sword, Reignmaker was at his side and he lay back staring at that starless sky, waiting for his eyelids to catch up with the rest of his body and relax. The warmth from the fire soothed him and his mind felt

117

clear for the first time in a long time, he would have no visions or nightmares tonight he could sense it. Maybe it was because of the fresh air and the peace and quiet or maybe it was because he was exhausted, several days travel had taken its toll and he had not eaten a proper meal since the coney pie at The Wintering Tree. Living off the land on a diet of fruit, nuts and shrooms was no diet for a King. The closest he had been to indulging in wine was chewing on some harsh berries, such as the sharpness of the sun berry or the sour prickle of the old berry that did little to tantalise his tastebuds. His tongue worked its way around the inside of his mouth, it was dry and barren of taste, his stomach joined in and pleaded.

"I should eat." He sighed opening his eyes and rising slowly to his feet, his stomach churned again and he realised that hunting in the dark was an ill advised concept, he could hear all manner of critters moving around in the foliage, communicating to each other in blips and whistles that only their own kind would understand. He heard the warbling of peagles, the cooing of passenger doves and the hooting of a lonely owlex.

"I can hear you, but finding you is a different matter altogether." Sebastian whispered as he looked around the forest, outlines of black tree trunks played games with his vision, he appeared to be surrounded by misshapen beasts but it was but a shadows jest. The snuffling of a verbbit which was a distant cousin of the coney, known to be slower and dim-witted. Scratching came from above, tiny claws on bark, teeth freeing nuts from their outer shells, a cacophony of gnawing and splintering could mean a feakal or perhaps a skerkal. Then Sebastian heard the distant sound of running water, he realised that the Crystal Tears River rolled down from the Kayalian Mountains into Lake Salivia and thought that some fresh caught carp would go down a treat.

"Creatures of the Lupiin Forest your lives are safe tonight." He jested as he grabbed his dagger and a length of rope from his saddle bag and draped it over his shoulder. He retrieved a hefty branch that was burning nicely in the fire and held it aloft to act as torchlight to guide his way. He did not say goodbye to Dayboy for he was fast asleep and did not wish to disturb the sleeping stallion, so he made his way towards the sound of the stream.

The torchlight illuminated the forest, causing all manner of wildlife to scamper away seeking refuge from this hungry Man with fire and blade. The shadows that teased him now danced for him like the jesters at court, but he did not laugh, he was too hungry for such merriment.

At the bank of the stream Sebastian lodged the torch into moist earth, its flames exposed an abundance of speckled carp swimming along nonchalantly, unaware that a hungry King waited above the surface of the water.

Sebastian retrieved his dagger and his length of rope, he gazed at them, and he reminisced of when he was but a small child and he accompanied his farda, King Cecil, on a hunting trip within the Hartfelt Woods. It was there that he was shown how to attach the rope to the daggers handle, using a specific knot and the right amount of rope. He used these memories to recreate with what he had learnt with his own knife and clambered up onto a nearby cluster of boulders, where he crouched and waited. The carp swam at an alarming speed, masses of them passed him by, speckled scales shimmering provocatively in the torchlight, inviting the King to try his luck. He positioned the dagger in one hand and the rope in the other and tried to focus on a particular carp, he readied himself and then eagerly launched the dagger into the stream, he was too eager and he missed, the blade hitting nothing but rock in the shallow waters. The blade floated in the depths, inquisitive carp approached it to see if it was edible. Sebastian gave a yank on the rope and the dagger came back out into his hand, the ruckus caused the carp to swim around in disarray for a few moments before they returned to their familiar swimming pattern.

He tried again and again and again but was unsuccessful.

He needed to focus on one in particular and single it out from the others, he could remember his farda saying those exact words when he was but a small, skinny prince with no knowledge of anything but life atop a waterfall within the impregnable walls of Windmast Castle.

"Focus, Sebastian, focus."

And he did, he only had eyes for a particular podgy carp that was struggling to keep up with his brothers and sisters. But while the King focused on catching his supper he did not notice the shadows that moved from tree trunk to tree trunk. Slowly several Men appeared, dressed in black hooded habits. One

Man crept forward as five others followed, they remained hooded waiting for their leader's sign. He removed his shroud unveiling a coarse face smeared with white and black stripes, his beady eyes circled in blood red made him appear very menacing. He crept closer still, a streak of black hair hung over one side of his head, the other side shaven to the skin, etched with a tattoo of crows wings. He wore several crow feathers around his neck, his followers wore only one, this was obviously to show his authority.

King Sebastian had another unsuccessful attempt at catching the carp and reeled the blade back in again, the collection of assailants remained motionless. The leader held his hand aloft signalling for his followers to remain where they were. Sebastian regained his composure and went back to tracking the carp.

The leader lowered his hand and retrieved a black handled sword from his sheath and hoisted it into the air, torchlight caught the blade and it glistened in the gloom, Sebastian saw nothing.

The followers followed suit and retrieved similar weapons and worked their way ever closer to their target. The blade was hoisted in the air and hovered behind the King's head, it was positioned in a way that if the thrust were true it would take the King's head clean off.

The King's dagger was thrust again into the water, cut straight through a frenzy of bubbles and hit its mark, piercing the carp and with a swift tug of victory Sebastian retrieved the dagger and held it aloft by the length of rope as the carp flitted to and fro on the point of his blade. He called out a euphoric cry of victory just as the Man behind him swung his blade. He felt a burst of breeze at his cheek, steel flashed past him, dangerously close to his face. An axe hurtling through the air from across the stream, he turned instinctively away from it and heard it wedge itself into something hard, a gargling sound of death echoed through the woods, a sound he had become all too accustomed to in battle. He saw the Cult of Crypors leader drop the sword down the rocks and fall to the floor, an axe buried in his chest. It took Sebastian a moment to collect his thoughts, he could have been dead, should have been dead, but someone just saved his head. He glanced over in the direction that the saving axe came from, but saw nothing. The rattling and clanging of weapons brought him back to the impending doom that awaited him, the remaining five Cult of Crypor followers circled him, hoods removed to expose shorn heads decorated with black, white and red paint to form a menacing ghoul-like appearance by the light of the single torch. Sebastian removed the still wriggling speckled carp from his dagger, its slimy lips gasped relentlessly as it hit the rocks below.

"Supper can wait!" Sebastian grimaced, grasping dagger and rope in hand before spinning it around to fend of the advancing monks of menace. The group stalled, second and third thoughts swirling through their minds, before one of them screamed and launched himself at the King with a jagged sword grasped above is head. Sebastian unleashed the dagger (keeping a tight grip on the rope) it burrowed its blade into the face of the approaching aggressor. The sound of steel shredding through flesh and muscle was nauseating, but it was the cracking sound of his skull that caused the remaining Cult of Crypor to fall back. The lifeless carcass fell to the ground and Sebastian tried to retrieve the dagger by tugging vigorously on the rope, but it was lodged in the dead Man's skull and refused to do its King's bidding. Sebastian knew that this particular cause was lost and so did the Cult who growled at him with sadistic intent. They moved in ever closer and Sebastian was forced to abandon the rope and instinctively looked to acquire the hilt of Reignmaker. He realised that his sword remained sleeping by the campfire, his eyes met the bloodshot glare of the Cult members who smiled back at him with broken brown teeth.

"It seems you have me at a disadvantage." Sebastian announced as he looked to climb higher up the rocks to gain the higher ground, but one of the Monks had crept around and cut him off at the top of the rocks, in his hands he cradled a hefty bludgeon.

"And it would appear outnumbered!"

The King made eye contact with each approaching assailant, his eyes flitted back and forth to axe and dagger both lodged in their victims and the Cult leader's sword that was just out of reach. He readied himself to fight as best as he could with his bare hands and maybe even fight dirty if he had too.

"TO YOUR LEFT SIRE!" Came the cry through the trees and Sir Maximillious Mondt came leaping across the narrow stream, clad in white armour like a beacon of hope in the darkness, God's Hand clenched in his gauntlet waving it aloft.

"Mondt!" Sebastian gasped.

Mondt's long golden hair swirled behind him and a bright grin met the King's relieved glance.

Mondt's presence was enough to distract the Monks and Sebastian took advantage stooping down to reclaim the floundering carp and with such force swung it into the face of the monk above him, the half dead carp slapped the taste out of the startled Monk and caused him to drop his hefty bludgeon. As Mondt appeared in the midst of the three other Monks forcing them to retreat slightly, Sebastian grabbed hold of the Monk's belt and hoisted him into the air and sent him head first into the shallow stream. The horrendous sound of his skull exploding on the stream-bed was sickening and blood seeped into the water causing the school of speckled carp to flee and swim up stream away from flying daggers and dead monks. The Monks realised they still outnumbered the knight and the king and lunged forward to attack Mondt, three on one, but amazingly Mondt looked untouchable, every swipe of sword or swat of bludgeon, missed its target, it was as if Mondt was a ghost, so fast so fluent were his movements that by the time the Monks regrouped from their wayward attacks, two of them were already dead and one with a deep wound to his leg. Sebastian watched on as the Monk hissed with annoyance and discomfort and charged again on weakened leg wildly swinging the heavy bludgeon, it missed its mark as Mondt danced around him and with one true strike of God's Hand the Monk was headless. Mondt wiped the blood from his blade on his white surcoat, he stood calm almost mellow, his brow had no signs of perspiration and his breathing was neither heavy or rapid.

"It seems I underestimated your abilities, Sir Maximillious. Please forgive me and let me thank you for saving my life from these hoodlums." Sebastian announced as he stepped down from the rocks and approached him. Mondt knelt before him, bowing his head low.

"It is my honour to serve my King. I expect no praise for fulfilling a Knight's duty."

"Rise, Mondt." Sebastian commanded, to which Mondt did as he was asked, sheathing his sword safety back into its scabbard. Sebastian grasped his heavily armoured shoulder and looked the Knight in his chiselled face, green emeralds meeting pools of blue, both men emotional, Sebastian had nearly died and Mondt brimmed with pride.

"You shall kneel before no Man again, Mondt. If you will allow it, I can offer you a place as my Head Knight!"
Mondt collapsed to his knees, tears welling up, honoured by the King's offer.

"You have taken my breath, Sire." Mondt choked. "It would be an honour, but you have a Head Knight in Sir Winstone Vespa. I would not wish for him to lose his post for me. I would feel it dishonourable."

"Rise Mondt," the King smiled, "I said you will kneel before no Man again."
Mondt rose to his feet wiping away tears from his cheeks.

"Sir Winstone grows older, he knows this, but you may work along side him until the time comes that he wishes to step down. That's if you two can coexist without having another scrap." Sebastian smirked.

"Forgive my words at the tavern, Sire." Mondt blushed. "Too much ale and too much arrogance I feel."

"I forgive your words for they were folly. I know that you have never met Sir Winstone in combat."

"Actually that part was true!" Mondt laughed. "But it was I that was on the pleading end."

The pair laughed and Sebastian retrieved the speckled carp, and held it aloft.

"Would you join me in a carp supper?"

The pair sat in the clearing, Sebastian turned the carp on a makeshift spit as it cooked quickly over the rising flames. Mondt's white mare Karbia lay next to Dayboy, both of them snoring loudly.

"I had hoped to accompany you when you left Tendor, but the stable boy told me that you had left before cock crow. I'm glad that I chose to pursue you."

"Not as glad as I!" Sebastian chuckled, he held a large leaf out under the carp and used the end of his dagger to slice pieces of the fish onto the makeshift plate, the carps flesh broke away easily and white soft chunks fell onto the leaf, he handed it to Mondt who took it and Sebastian repeated the process again for himself.

"Who would have thought that I would be dining with King Hartwaker." Mondt chuckled as he stuffed pieces of carp into his mouth, he bounced the hot flesh around on his tongue as it tried its hardest to burn him.

"If only it could have been in a more grander setting." Sebastian replied.

"Oh I don't know." Mondt answered looking up at the sky. "Being in the company of Marda Nature has its merits. But I wonder where all the stars are tonight?"

They both surveyed the thick black sky, but neither had an answer.

"You handled yourself extraordinarily with those Monks, Mondt. Forgive me for presuming that you were only a tournament Knight. You have proven yourself to be much more than a jouster and sportsman."

"Aye, my passion lies within tournaments, but I have just not had the chance to be in many battles due to you keeping the realm peaceful for so long."

"Oh, so it's my fault is it?" Sebastian mocked and the pair laughed as they ate.

Mondt reached into his saddle bag that he was leaning on and retrieved a bladder.

"I almost forgot, I have ale." Mondt said and handed the bladder to his King. Sebastian took it, uncorked it and drank heartily, before his face turned sour and he swallowed hard.

"I see it is the Withering Tree's finest."

"Aye!" Laughed Mondt who took the bladder and took a swig too. "But I am used to pig swill disguised as ale. Your palate is much more refined I imagine."

"Aye, I must admit I am used to a much finer pig swill."

127

There was a silence between the two for a moment as each enjoyed their meal.

"I would like to accompany you on your journey, Sire." Mondt said. "I feel it my duty."

"I knew you would want to, but..."

"Please allow me to, Sire. You have already seen how treacherous the realm can be and you are not even in Dwarf country yet."

"I can see that you are passionate about your duties, Mondt."

"If it would please you, Sire. I wish to actually be part of a real adventure, instead of conjuring my own tall tales." He blushed at this, the arrogant persona that he displayed at The Withering Tree had vanished, presenting the Knight in a true light.

"As you wish," Sebastian nodded, "how can I deny your request."

"I will not let you or the crown down, Sire."
Sebastian smiled and took another swig of the bladder and immediately wished he had not.

"Let us bed down and be refreshed for an early rise on the morrow, for our journey to Hammillda is a long and tedious one."

CHÃPTÉR II

THÉ BÏTTÉR TÃSTÉ ÖF BLÃCK MÏLK

cross the desolate desert of Lunarc, where Man no longer treads, lies the barren land known as Grotte. It was given its name after the first Goblin, the evil tyrant that only existed to do the bidding of his master, Sloore. With the help of his Master he created an army of Goblins and crowned himself 'The Goblin King'. He marched against Man and Dwarf with the sole purpose to eradicate their species from existence and rule Maglore in their stead. Time after time 'The Goblin King' failed in his objective and on several occasions he felt the wrath of his Master. Until the infamous Battle of Grotte's Tusk where he was defeated by 'Red Cecil' himself, King Cecil Hartwaker, who from then on took the moniker of 'Goblin Slayer' for the rest of his days. Although it was not King Cecil that delivered the killer blow to end Grotte's existence, but his own kind that did the deed. Heavily wounded by arrow and steel, Grotte fled the battlefield for the safety of Sloore's Dwell, but his master denied him sanctuary and passage to The Shrouded Realm, he had failed once to often. Wounded and alone Grotte finally fell when his own Goblin army returned from battle, weary and sore they were consumed by hatred for their King and tore him limb from limb, gorging themselves on his black hollow heart and his dark entrails in a feast that lasted for ten days, before they returned to The Shrouded Realm.

On the edge of nowhere and nothingness, lies the entrance to The Shrouded Realm, a giant burrow dug in the earth that is said to lead to the very core of Maglore. Although Man has no wish to venture to such a desperate place of pestilence and brimstone, the place is mocked by many calling it 'Sloore's Nostril' or 'The Snot Pit', playful words of jest, but still these words spill from the lips of those that would not dare venture there.

The one that had become known only as 'The Dark Master' stood at the entrance to Sloore's Dwell, he remained covered in hood and cloak, was the reason for this garb part of his worship of The God, Sloore or was the reason to hide his identity?

A thick grey smog bellowed out from the hole and The Dark Master felt the warmth being emitted from it, he smelt the rancid pungency of rotting flesh and it aroused him. He entered undeterred by those mischievous Black Imps that clambered across the walls and ceiling of the gigantic cavern, as he continued on his journey into the darkness. The sweltering heat consumed him first, clogging the back of his throat but still he ventured on until he saw the amber glow of The Shrouded Realm. The air was close and thick with the heat of a thousand fires created by inextinguishable flames. Before he even saw the molten chamber of Sloore that erupted with several spewing geysers of lava, he heard the booming of hirs voice.

"Come forth my son." The words caused the cavern walls to shudder, was it the voice that caused the tremor or was it fear? The Dark Master walked slowly into the chamber and there sat Sloore, on a gigantic throne formed from volcanic rock. Hirs gargantuan frame filled the chamber, a hundred times that of a regular Giant, no longer did hirs appearance match those tales of folklore, an unsightly stomach sagged between hirs legs and two heavy breasts hung from hirs chest. The centuries of seclusion had not been kind, hirs skin wore wrinkles of burden on hirs fat face, but the horns remained sharp and proud protruding from his forehead, originally put there by Marda Nature as a warning to Adeve that hirs sibling was mischievous and should not be trusted.

Goblins scampered around at hirs fat feet, some chiselling away their master's jagged toe nails, others collected the shards into barrows and disappeared into separate caves with them, the purpose of the nail carvings were to be melted down by the fires of the Shrouded Realm and armour forged from its evil for the impending Goblin Army. Other Goblins herded Juugs towards the throne, an obese Cyclops waited, his fat flesh secreted in blood and sweat, the searing heat causing his bald head to pour, sweat cascading around a single circular eyeball fixed in the centre of his head. He held aloft a oversized cleaver and brought it down across the Juug's neck, the head fell to the floor and was immediately carried off into the shadows by Black Imps, the sound of them sucking the blood from it and then the horrendous crunching of bone was lost on The Dark Master for this was his upbringing and everything he saw was completely normal to his eyes.

"Come closer my son." Grumbled Sloore as hirs gigantic hand swooped down and scooped up the headless Juug and drained it of its blood, the warm plasma dribbled down the evil God's chin and into the fat crevices of hirs neck. Ze discarded the lifeless sack of the Juug onto the floor and again the remains were soon removed by the Black Imps who took it back to the shadowy crevices within the walls.

"Farda and Marda." He said kneeling before him.
Sloore wiped away the blood that was drying from hirs chin with the back of a clawed hand.

"LEAVE US!" Sloore bellowed and hirs words shook the cavern walls once more.
The Cyclops bowed and left, possibly thankful of the break from executing Juugs. Goblins herded the remaining Juugs away and others dropped the broken toenails before scampering away to the confines of several narrow tunnels. The Black Imps remained, as they were Sloore's children but hid in the safety of the shadows, thousands of yellow eyes watching intently.
The Dark Master looked up at his surrogate farda and marda and waited for hirs to speak.

"I remember the day you were brought to me, an insignificant Elfling, freshly born and of only one turn of the moon to your name. During The War of the United, when Elf and Dwarf stopped squabbling and put aside their differences to fight against the Goblin uprising. The Elf King, Argo

Calgaras sacrificed his castle, his family and his own race to save his own skin."

"I remember the story."

"Of course you do." Ze laughed.

"He opened up the doors of Windmast Castle allowing it to be besieged by Goblins. Calgaras had taken his army with him to forge a pact with The Dwarf King, Krandel Hammillaxe, leaving his people exposed. The Goblins slaughtered all the Elves that they could find, raped Elf wives, drank Elf blood and fed on the Elflings."

"Apart from you!"

"Yes."

"The Children of the Shrouded Realm found you in a crib in the highest tower of Windmast, your identity still remains a mystery. Were you of royal bloodline? Or a dirty secret kept hidden away?"

"It matters not."

"No, I guess it does not. Either way my Black Imps saw something in you, something that I still cannot. If you are the prophecy written in the stars I am yet to see any evidence of such a claim."

The Dark Master was glad that he still wore his hood so that Sloore could not see the blushing of his pale skin beneath.

"Yes, for years you suckled at my bosom on a diet of black milk and Man blood, it made you strong. But, I fear not strong enough."

There was disappointment in Sloore's tone and The Dark Master's head bowed in embarrassment.

133

"There are days when I think I would have been better off if your brothers and sisters had left you to die."

"I apologise for my failures Farda and Marda."

"YOU APOLOGISE!" Ze roared and shards of molten rocks fell from above colliding with the floor around The Dark Master, he did not flinch for he was used to Sloore's torturous words and bursts of hatred, his pale flesh was branded and scarred with constant reminders of his farda an marda's tormenting ways.

"You have been given great power and you squander it!" Sloore spat with annoyance.

The Dark Master grimaced under the shroud of his cowl, mutinous thoughts pricked his devious mind but he remained tightlipped.

"Your negligence hinders my return to power. I grow impatient."

"The scenario has not been without complications..." The Dark Master attempted an argument but was interrupted by the slobbering God.

"Complications that are due to your incompetence!"

The Dark Master's fists clenched tightly, his shape nails digging deep into his palms.

"The time has not been right." The Dark Master pleaded his case. "I have had to infiltrate the Mystic Circle for several years and learn all I can from them, this has taken time I agree, but it is all for the good of the uprising. They must not have any indication of my true identity else it will all be for nothing."

Sloore grunted, smoke and blood rising from hirs nostrils, but ze remained silent.

"I have had to wait for my astronomer to calculate the correct configurations of the stars. Stars that hold the future in their grasp. Stars that show the prophecy."

"I know all of this!" Sloore spluttered, a mass of saliva settling on hot molten rock below and sizzling liked cooked meat. "Your forked tongue manipulates words to hide your errors, talking as though others were to blame."

"I have tried my best. There have been many complications..."

"PAH!" Sloore erupted, the walls shook again under the sheer velocity of hirs voice and again shards of molten rock broke away and rained down on them.

"Your failure to rid the realm of its Light Bearer was but the final straw."

"But Farda and Marda, I achieved my goal. The dark foal Gri'ul was born of my own seed and even now walks the realm bringing with it a blanket of darkness."

"Fool!" Sloore spat. "You should have made sure that Unico was erased before you began your celebrations. With her foal Ulla still treading the earth there will always be light. The two Unicorns now walk the land, one bringing darkness, one light. If there is to be total darkness shrouding this realm, Ulla must be destroyed at any cost!"

Ze slammed a weighty fist down on the arm of his molten throne, causing an avalanche down its side, rock and brimstone travelling into pools of lava that bubble and spit around the

God's sacred cavern. A Black Imp scuttled out from the shadows, travelling across the ceiling of the cavern, jumping down onto his Master's shoulder and scampering to hirs ear, where it disappeared.

"My children bring me whispers from the outside world that the East remains in darkness, but the West continues its daily cycle. Man and Dwarf in the East believe that it is but the Season of Gloam come early. We are fortunate that they are so naive. We shall need complete darkness if we are to unleash the full power of The Shrouded Realm."

"Yes, Farda and Marda!" He reluctantly agreed.

Sloore's words had angered The Dark Master, he was tired of being treated like a child in such matters, he grew disenchanted with the whole affair. How can he be scorned by his farda and marda for making mistakes when ze himself continues to hide hirself in The Shrouded Realm because of hirs fear of Dragons? The Dark Master feared nothing or no Man, he believed in his own abilities, he could whisper and control Dragons, if it was his wish he could lead The Black Arrow, Demios to Sloore's Dwell and have hir melted into a pool of fatty flesh. He also had learned the conjuring ways of the Mystic Circle from the greatest Wizards and Witches in the realm, if he could possess Pagmai's source of power, The Orb of Quirinus, which was thought to be the heart of Sirod the Phoenix. If he had that in his grasp he would not even need an alliance with Sloore. The Goblins would follow who ever had power and the Black Imps could be swayed to changed their allegiance if threatened by Dragon fire, several packs already had become affiliated with

136

him by not relaying the information of Demios to Sloore. The Dark Master felt as though he now had the upper hand, not Sloore.

"You remain silent for too long." Sloore growled as ze leaned forward curiously, smoke bellowed from hirs nostrils and engulfed The Dark Master as he continued to kneel. "I wonder what theories form in the mind of a Dark Elf? You would never believe yourself to be above my reign would you child?"

"No!" The Dark Master was quick to respond. "Never."

Sloore sat back in hirs throne and stared at him.

"Then what does your dark mind conceive?" Ze asked, before pointing a gigantic talon in his direction. "I see the wheels turning inside, you are plotting. Devious critters The Elves, I should know that was one of many traits I instilled in your race during their conception."

"Only plots against Man, oh mighty Sloore." He bowed his head lower concealing an angry grimace. "I believe that it will be soon time to strike against The Mystic Circle and I believe we will have enough power to overthrow Man without a sky of black."

"If you believe you can then so be it. Make it happen!" Sloore said.

"I wait only a few days more to see the outcome of King Hartwaker's visit to the Mystic Circle."

"Why wait?"

"To see if Kelda's shrouding spell has worked. If they do not believe Hartwaker then we know that they have not seen

137

what is coming in the stars. I shall strike and they will be powerless. The Dark Reign shall be upon them."

Sloore smiled, it was an horrendous expression, everything wrong with the realm could be conceived by such a smile.

"Then go!" Ze said. "Leave me and do not return until the realm is mine."

The Dark Master bowed again before rising and leaving the stifling heat of Sloore's Dwell. As he stepped out into the air, he noticed that the breeze brushed his face with the first warm winds of Fervor, indicating the changing of seasons. He removed his hood revealing a pale, slender face, his features were as sharp as a blade. The Sun of Seylm pulsated in the West, shining on his hairless head, his ears were tapered into points and his magenta eyes twinkled with malevolence. Change was coming to Maglore and he would rise upon a Dragon across a sky of light and darkness and douse the realm in Dragon flame.

"They will call me The Harbinger of Darkness! They will cower before their Dark Lord..." He whispered to himself, forked tongue slithering through the contours of his serrated teeth as he gazed at the breathtaking landscape of two skies already at war.

"...The Dark Lord, Grimalkin!"

CHÃPTÉR 12

THÉ ÉÃGÉR CÚPBÉÃRÉR

ooka's throat was as dry as the Lunarc Desert, he paused from his recital to clear his throat. He surveyed the room as dozens of wide eyes stared back at him, frozen in anticipation of their teacher's next words. He knew from their almost hypnotised gazes that he had them trapped in his snare. A snare created through their own imaginations. Pooka felt envious of these children, he would have given anything to peek behind their eyes and witness what amazing images were being painted on the canvas of their mind's eye. A smile caressed his chapped lips realising that he was in total control of these children of Man and what a thrill that was he thought. He fancied himself a conjurer who knew the secrets of the trick that was taking place before their captivated eyes. He cleared his throat again, it was as if his throat had been filled with straw as if to bed down a weary colt. Thirst pricked at the roof of his mouth, his tongue tried and failed to muster up some kind of moisture that could possibly quench his thirst.

"It would appear my throat is dry." Pooka spluttered, he

coughed dryly and with each violent convulsion his long dangling ears wriggled amusingly like two hairy worms.

"I fear that I may have to put a halt to proceedings and continue this tale on another day." Pooka wheezed.

"NO!" Cried Jasson leaping from his seat. "I will bring you some water."

Before Pooka had a chance to reply Jasson had disappeared out of the great hall, the sound of his swift footsteps slapping the cold stone floor quickly as he headed to the kitchens.

"It would appear I am continuing with the tale." Pooka smiled, crooked yellowed tusks rising over his upper lip as he surveyed his class.

"Are there any questions why I wait for my eager cupbearer to return?"

"Pooka?" Xen rose from her seat with her dainty hand held aloft.

"Yes, my dear?"

"Our ears have been shielded from the horrors that occurred during The Dark Reign. I already weep inside for family lost in this time, family that you have already mentioned. Will there be more death and grief? I don't think my heart will be able to take such atrocities. Will it all be okay?" Pooka's mass of wispy eyebrows contorted in empathy for the young girl.   " W e are all sitting here now with a roof over our heads and food in our bellies are we not?"

Xen replied with a confused nod.

"I don't have any water to quench my parched throat, but we are okay are we not? We live do we not?"

The classroom nodded.

"The Scrolls of History tell us to embrace and remember when Maglore was taken back from the cold grasp of Lord Grimalkin. To rejoice in the realm being free again. But when we do this we forget what came before the war, we only remember that Maglore became whole again and forget who fell to set the realm free. It is not how the story ends, but how we get there that is important. When one is eager enough to take on such power that they do not care for the consequences then there will always be casualties."

Jasson burst through the doors, a golden cup grasped in one sweat cladded palm and the other wrapped around the slender neck of a golden decanter.

"Did I miss anything? You didn't start without me did you?" Jasson gasped heavily as he hurried towards his teacher and handed him the cup and decanted some ice cold water for him, his shaking excited hands almost spilling it over Pooka as he rushed.

"It's okay, I was just answering a question for your sister."

"Xen!" Jasson scoffed. "You and your questions!"

"That is how one gains knowledge Brother!" She snapped back quickly.

"As long as you haven't worn out Pooka, I need to hear more of this story." Jasson scowled at her as he put the decanter down next to Pooka and returned quickly to his seat.

141

Pooka drank quickly, relieving the cup of its refreshment in one huge consumption.

"That is much better!" Pooka announced, filling the cup a second time, sipping it and placing it at his side. "To answer your question Jasson, no I am not too 'worn out'. There is still many a tune to be played on this old lute!"

The class laughed and he raised a hairy hand to silence them.

"Now settle back down and I shall continue."

CHÃPTÉR 13
DWÃRF HÖSPÏTÃLÏTY

he dark shroud that hung over the East had heavily effected King Sebastian and Sir Maximillous' progress. They had slept much longer than they had intended too, the darkness manipulating their minds to believe that it was indeed still night and that they should be lost in slumber. When finally they had come to their senses and realised that this blackness was indeed peculiar, they had already lost three days of their quest. Several days followed that were also lost to the bewildered travellers as they wandered, disorientated around the Lupiin Forest, without the Sun of Seylm to guide their direction they were seemingly trapped in a never-ending loop. They wandered in a dark daze with only torch light for company and always seemed to return to their originally starting point, their steeds did not like the experience and finally showed their disapproval by collapsing in frustration and refusing to move a muscle. Maximillous finally had the idea of scaling a tree to see if the sun could bee seen from that vantage point. He removed his armour as to not hamper his climb and was quickly near the top of the tree, King

143

Sebastian even quipped that he was so quick in his ascent that he must be half Sprite.

The Knight known as 'The One' was not ready for the sight that met his eyes for when he reached the top and looked out to see the sky divided, the East was consumed by darkness, yet the West danced with colour, bright and flourishing like the palette of an artist. He almost lost his footing and fell to his death, but somehow he managed to compose himself and adjust his footing, for such a sight was too much for his mind to comprehend.

"You will not believe the vision that torments my gaze, my King." Called Maximillious from the highest branches.

"Pray tell, Mondt?" Sebastian called up through the labyrinth of branches and leaves. There was no answer for a time and Sebastian became worried, so worried in fact that he was about to ascend the tree himself to see what had happened to his new travelling companion. Mondt appeared suddenly through the cover of leaves and startled the King, who guffawed at his own skittishness until he saw Mondt looking pale in the face, like some undead ghoul under the flicker of torchlight.

"Mondt! What is it?" Sebastian demanded.

"The sky…" He searched for the words, "…it has been cut in half!"

Now that they were aware of their bearings they were soon on their way, finally leaving the claustrophobic confinement of the Lupiin Forest and towards Hammillda.

Hammillaxe Castle loomed in the distance, a fortress constructed by the hands of those that dwell there, Dwarves.

The high walls of Hammillaxe were made from black stone said to have been culled from the broken remnants of Adeve's Throne, tremendous hunks of mountain peak that had fallen during the great God's demise. The walls were said to be double the girth of any other fortress that had been built by Dwarf hands. The Dwarves had openly mocked those that tried to take their fortress, jeering them from in-between the merlons of their high parapets, almost encouraging them to succeed with their catapults and battering rams, but none ever did. The Dwarves would laugh heartily as the failed raiders would flee as vats of boiling oil and liquid steel would rain down on them from the cunningly placed gargoyles that protruded from the castle's walls.

It was indeed a menacing sight to behold and both Hartwaker and Mondt gave the structure the respect it deserved as they rode towards it in silence. That thick haze still covered the sky but the black castle was lit by a hundred or more torches that at least made their approach less painful. Both their colt's legs were weary and they had to spur them both on gently, reassuring them that rest and food awaited them.

The mighty doors had no need for the cover of a portcullis or even a drawbridge, because of course the Dwarves invited all challenges, but the gigantic doors were made with the same stone as the walls and unbreakable to any weapon or contraption that had been conceived and if any straggler should find themselves on the inside of the fortress they would no doubt meet the edge of a broad axe or the blunt end of a war hammer.

145

Mondt held the torch aloft, guiding their way through the gloom as they came to a halt where they would be easily seen by the castle's sentry.

"Pleasant place is it not?" Chuckled Mondt as the pair sat upon their tired steeds looking up at this formidable hulk of black stone.

"I thought that they would have had streamers and banners awaiting on our arrival." Sebastian jested.

"Are you sure this is wise, Sire?" Mondt asked. "Dwarves are not known for their hospitality at the best of times."

"No, it isn't wise at all, my friend." Sebastian sighed. "But I am way past the acts of a wise Man."

Torches flickered in abundance from the parapet of Hammillaxe Castle and the unmistakable grunting and grumbling of Dwarves could be heard from within its walls. Sebastian took in the surroundings, the mouth of the fortress was grim and uninviting to say the least, broad fortified towers had the carvings of several Dwarf Lord ancestors depicted in stone. Sebastian knew the faces of some from the Scrolls of History like Higgelhard 'The Rational', Caro 'The Forger', the Dwarf Knight, Herth Rockhorn who was known affectionately as 'The Whorer' and of course the only Dwarf King to ever reign over Maglore, Haggart 'The Arrogant'.

"A ugly band if ever there was one." Sebastian said, his words meant for his own mind, but slipped through his pursed lips.   "They all look the same to me." Shrugged Mondt, it was blatantly obvious that the Knight had no love for Dwarves.

146

Finally Sebastian hollered into the haze, hoping the sound of his voice would carry over the cacophony of rowdy Dwarves. There was no reply so he called again.

Still nothing.

"Sire, I do not think it right for a King to be calling for the attention of Dwarves! Let me carry this burden for you, I would hate to see you embarrassed." Mondt said.

"I am past embarrassment!" Sebastian chuckled. "My kingdom takes me for a fool and I have already been rejected by Man, Knight and Fairy. What is the laughter of a Dwarf to me now?"

He called again and this time there was movement from the turret above the great stone entrance, a torch quivered, slicing through that hanging purple haze that haunted the East.

"Who be bloody bawling?" Came a voice, cross in tone and rough in sound. "Can me not even have a muck in peace?"

Mondt sniggered and Sebastian grinned as a weathered round face, covered in greying, auburn hair appeared above them illuminated by burning torch light, he wore a glare of annoyance under a wild mass of hair.

"It is I, King Sebastian!" He calls again.

"A what now?" Came the response.

"Listen Dwarf!" Mondt cried in his annoyance. "You are addressing the King of Maglore! King Sebastian of the House Hartwaker! Have some damn respect!" "Calm yourself, Mondt." Sebastian murmured. "We don't wish to antagonise them. They need no excuse to be defiant."

147

"A King say?" Came the voice. "Me can't hear a blasted thing up ere, me ears are not what they was."

"Yes! It is I King Sebastian, I wish to parlay with Lord Dagyan on an urgent matter."

"Me still can't hear you! Blast me ears!" He grumbled. "Speak louder."

"This is ridiculous!" Scoffed Mondt with annoyance. Sebastian repeated his words in a stronger voice, his words must have carried far and wide for the ruckus from behind the walls hushed and even from the ground he could see the old Dwarf's eyes widen and his unruly eyebrows rise.

"The King be ere!" He exclaimed, turning away from the turret for a moment probably relaying the information to a fellow Dwarf to take the information to their Lord.

"Me thinks this is a joke? Some folly?" He called.

"No folly!" Sebastian replied.

"Me say bugger off to you, Dagyan has no times for fool's games."

"There are no games at play here." Sebastian unsheathed Reignmaker and held it aloft, Mondt made sure that the torchlight caught the whole of the sword, the strong broad blade of steel and the golden hilt shaped like the flamed wings of the House sigil, the Phoenix, its beaked head rising triumphantly from the sword's pommel.

"Look upon Reignmaker and see my words are truth." Sebastian knew that Dwarves were enamoured with weaponry and were masters in forging themselves. As Sebastian was brought up with stories of great Kings past, Dwarves grew up

148

on tales of great builders and forgers, they all knew the great forgers of Maglore, such as blacksmiths of Houses Neidhart, Lunggate and Bloodgaard and that the arms of House Hartwaker would be well known.

"Me say, tis the blade of the King." Came the reply, awe in his tone now as he gazed down on the sword that appeared to be a blade of flame as the torchlight bathed in its own reflection.

"A Bloodgaard forge, me can see that from ere, aye, good blade, good blade. Not be as good as Dwarf forge mind, but nevertheless…"

Sebastian sheathed his sword and the blade's reflective fire was extinguished.

"Open your doors and allow me and my Knight to enter!"

There was a pause and then the Dwarf replied with an almost lighthearted chuckle to his tone. "You be not going away be you?"

"Not without seeing Dagyan, no!"

He heard the Dwarf call in a commanding tone for those below to open the great doors. There was much noise bellowing over the walls now, anger bitter and grumpy groans and then there was the crunching of steel on stone and the doors slowly began to open.

"Dismount, Mondt." Sebastian said and jumped down from Dayboy.

"Whatever for?" Mondt replied. "We should ride through those doors large, proud and on the back of our steeds."

"We already tower over them in height, Mondt. Our size is a trait that Dwarf already despise of Man. Let us pay them the courtesy of not flaunting that fact."

"You pay them too much respect I fear." Mondt said climbing down from Karbia, his armour crunching as he hit the stoney, uneven ground. "That is one consideration you will not receive back I am afraid, Sire."

"Nevertheless!" Sebastian said and they moved toward the doors on foot leading the colts by their reins.

As they trudged through the doors of Hammillaxe Castle, seemingly dragging their steeds along with them, they were met by hundreds of eyes, the courtyard filled with short round fellows, most of them with beards of all colours and lengths. Sebastian took in the dark surroundings and sure enough they were as uninviting and miserable as the exterior of the fortress. Even the long grey flags that depicted the Hammillaxe sigil of the crossing of hammer and axe topped by a crow looked forlorn, and drooped rather than flew with pride. Behind the doors two towers of Dwarves stood aloft each others shoulders, responsible for removing the bolts from across the colossal door.

"A friendly welcome, what a surprise." Mondt whispered sarcastically.

The eyes that glared up at them from waist height and those that peered down at them from the towers and walls, twinkled in the torchlight like precious stones sunken into the craggy walls of a mine. These eyes were not friendly and the grumbles and groans from their owners had started to grow in volume as the visitors were inhospitably surrounded by these miniature mercenaries, all gripping axe and hammer in their rough, stumpy digits.

"I am King Sebastian Hartwaker." Sebastian finally spoke for the silence had been too long. "I am here to parlay with Lord Dagyan."

There was another unsatisfied grumble throughout the congregation of Dwarves that had now amassed into possibly every Dwarf that remained in Maglore. Mondt was eager to find a Lady Dwarf as he had heard tales of how ugly they were and that it was impossible to tell Lord from Lady in the world of the Dwarves. To his surprise the tales were indeed folly for his amazed eyes looked upon several Lady Dwarves, ripe and plump as they were, their faces held such flushed beauty and even the babes in arms bore more resemblances to their marda's than their farda's. He found himself smiling and then felt the point of a spear through a gap in his armour prick his buttock and he turned on the spot quickly to see an angry looking Dwarf with a head of white wildness and a chin beard to match.

"You be looking at me Lady, Man Knight?" He growled through teeth like broken stones.

"Get away from me Dwarf!" Mondt shouted angrily, swatting the spear away. "We demand to see Dagyan!"

"Easy now Mondt! Do not antagonise them." Sebastian whispered through clenched teeth.

"Sire, this one poked me in the..."

151

"I do not care where he poked you. Please just apply some decorum or we shall leave here without our heads!"

Some of the Dwarves heard the King's words and met his gaze with crazed smiles.

"Bugger you off now, bugger you off!" Came the call from the stairwell that led above the gate, the old guard that had let them enter came limping down to greet them. On hearing his voice the Dwarves mumbling disappointedly and dispersed.

"Be gone with you! We be havin' guests, that be no way we treatin' em!"

He limped towards them in a dress of heavy chainmail underneath a worn grey tunic with the sigil of Hammilaxe embroidered in gold thread.

"Me King, it be an honour!" The Dwarf guard said with a smile that contained only four teeth, he bowed his head in respect, then blurted. "Caught me with me chainmail up and me britches down. Me be having a muck me was!" He laughed and his whole body wobbled.

"How delightful!" Mondt scoffed, his face contorted with disgust.

The Dwarf laughed at Mondt's response and slapped him on his seat, his armour vibrated and made his eyes widen in surprise, Sebastian could not hide a snigger himself.

"I be seein' from your sigil you be 'The One', Sir Maximillious Mondt! Nobody be tellin' me you be so humorous!" The Dwarf cackled.

"You have our names!" Mondt snapped. "What be... I mean what is your name Sir?"

Sebastian sniggered again, it was fun watching the Knight get so flustered and a good folly was just what the King needed to break up the seriousness of his quest.

"I be Miglay. Miglay 'The Mindful' they say!" He said proudly. "Me be of House Hammillaxe, second born son of 'The Dwarf King' Haggart and brother to Dagyan 'The Defiant'!"

"Then it is an honour to meet you Lord Miglay." Sebastian nodded his head in respect.

"Bloody hell, be not botherin' with title be me! Just Miglay, that be me."

"Forgive me for I believe my grandfarda, Grayfall II was responsible for your farda's demise."

"Be silly not, a different time it be and different kings. We can never be held accountable for the sins of others."

"Wise words." Sebastian smiled and the two embraced hands and shook them vigorously.

"For a Dwarf." Mondt scoffed.

"Ha!" Miglay laughed and slapped him again on the backside. "You be truly humorous you be Man Knight. I shall be likin' to converse with you over ale and maybe a little boar?" Mondt's mouth watered and Miglay laughed again.

"I be showin' the King to my brother then we be doing some serious drinkin! What say?"

"Agreed!" Mondt exclaimed, salivating at the fact that ale and boar was on the menu.

"Right you bloody buggers!" Miglay shouted a voice that was now hard and commanding. "Be gettin' those doors closed and be feedin' these colts."

There was a flurry of movement all around them and the two towers of Dwarves waddled to the doors to push them closed, grumbling and moaning as they did so, but finally they were closed and each one at each level slotted in large steel bolts into brackets.

"Me be takin' your colts, Sire." Came a small voice up from the King's knee cap and a young Dwarf child looked up at him with a little smile lost in the centre of his round and podgy face. Sebastian smiled and flipped a coin to him he caught it and blushed with gratitude.

"Here you go lad." Sebastian said and handed him the reins to Dayboy, who was so tired and hungry that he would have gone just as easily if the reins had been given to that of Sloore himself. Mondt followed suit and the Dwarf child led their steeds away. Sebastian watched the child as he walked away and it made him remember Ern from The Withering Tree and then his own child, his daughter, Princess Vai-Ra who would one day be Queen. These thoughts meant that the folly had ended and it was back to the matter in hand.

"Ethel!" Miglay cried at the top of his voice and out of a door waddled a Dwarf maiden, fair of hair and flushed with beauty, she wiped her hands on a cloth.

"What be you hollerin' about now Miglay?" She sighed.

"Be takin our guest you be!" Miglay said pointing to

Mondt, who towered over him looking strong in his white armour.

"Oh!" Ethel blushed, fluttering her eyelids and thrusting her ample bosom in the direction of the Knights widening gaze. "My, my he be a Knight in shining white he be!"

Miglay rolled his eyes as she swayed across the courtyard and took the Knight by his hand.

"Be gone with you Man Knight, she won't be biting you." Miglay said.

"Well it not be hard if I does, I be promisin'." She giggled as she led him towards their banqueting hall.

Mondt looked bewildered as Miglay laughed and smacked him on the backside again, but this time he paid no mind as he was lost in the beauty's vast cleavage.

"I think he is in love." Sebastian chuckled.

"Now let's be seein' about you meetin' my brother." Miglay said and he led him to the keep.

Miglay led Sebastian down beautiful corridors, that were high of ceiling and decorated with marble and black stone through out, hefty armed guards watched as they passed with wary eyes, that were untrusting of a Man walking their sacred halls, an omen that meant trouble in their minds. Lavish paintings of the Dwarf Lords of the past hung on the walls, each one as brutish as the next, but Sebastian saw a proudness in their worn and lined faces, it was simple to forget that other species were proud of their own kind too, so easy was it to think just of his own kind that he forgot about the thoughts and feelings of other races and their ways of life. His first proclamation as King

155

was to allow the other races their own kingdoms and own rule, he still believed he was right to do so, he had no right ruling over ways of life that he did not understand, but in doing so he had also put the power back into the hands of Dwarves, Giants and Fairies and now he had already found that it was indeed a difficult task to ask them to join in a war that they will not believe is theirs to fight.

They walked through a hall of black stoned pillars that rose out of a mirror marbled floor reaching up to the high ceiling. The grand ceiling depicted famous Dwarf scenes from their history in beautiful oiled paints. Miglay's heavy chainmail rattled loudly as he limped towards large wooden doors at the end of the hall and they were met by two armed guards, who stepped out and acknowledged Miglay, untrusting eyes were all the guards had for the King of Man.

"Miglay, you be not enterin' now." The guard announced.

"Bullocks!" Miglay replied. "I be the brother of the Lord and you be knowin' your place you be!"

The guard looked embarrassed. "But Miglay he be slumberin now. Just eaten he has, now he be at slumber and then he will be whorin'."

"My brother be a routine stickler he be." He rolled his eyes and sighed. "I be not carin' if he be slumberin', shittin' or shaggin'!" Miglay scoffed. "Me friend ere has parlay with him, so be gone, go be havin' a flagon of ale on me."

The guards bowed and left, the crunching of their heavy armour could be heard around the entire hall until it dissolved into the distance.

"So you be tellin' Miglay what you be ere to see me brother about?"

Sebastian smiled, he liked Miglay, his bluntness was refreshing.

"I fear my words would alarm you, Miglay. They must fall on Dagyan's ears first then it will be left up to he who he tells."

"It be matterin' not." Miglay shrugged and winked a beady eye at the king. "I be listenin' at the door any ways."

Miglay laughed and flung open the door.

"Go, on me King. Follow the snorin'."

CHÃPTÉR 14
DÃGYÃN THÉ DÉFIÃNT

ebastian walked into a gigantic hall of marble, black stone and steel, the Hammillaxe sigil hung from tapestries and flags, the crow's eyes on each seemed to watch the Man King as he entered the great hall as the doors closed gently behind him. Torches burn brightly on the walls and made the marble appear alive as if liquid in its consistency, Sebastian could hear the loud, obnoxious snoring coming from the raised dais at the end of the hall. He strode across the marble that danced underneath his feet, his cape draped over one shoulder and his gloved hand leaning lazily on the hilt of Reignmaker. He was tired from travel and his stomach rumbled loudly, a sound that could rival that of Dagyan's snoring, but he ventured on in high spirits, he must have high spirits or he would have already failed his quest.

He must make Dagyan see the truth in his words, to make him see sense, and to make a Dwarf see sense was indeed an arduous task.

The sound of congested breathing echoed around the hall, like the sound of slumbering boar, Sebastian shared a smile too himself wondering if this was the boar that Miglay had promised Mondt for eats. He stopped at the foot of the dais' black stone steps that led to a throne that was made from the untreated rocks of the God's seat. The jagged shards of Adeve's Peak had beed manipulated into a throne, the seat wide to fit that of the widest backside of any Dwarf, the rock pieces breaking out in all directions behind the seat in an impressive display. A large cumbersome piece of weaponry leaned casually against the throne, the infamous war hammer of House Hammillaxe, forged from steel and black stone, broad axe on one side, blunt hammer on the other. Sebastian stared at the tremendous arm and knew that it had belonged to Dagyan's farda before him.

"Lungblower!" He whispered to himself, awed at the realisation that it was the weapon used to slaughter his granduncle Brode Hartwaker during the Dwarf Uprising. His inquisitive green eyes examined Lungblower, it truly was a weapon forged for destruction, a bloodthirsty piece that took a sadistic owner to wield it. Sebastian wondered whether Dagyan was as sadistic as his farda. He gazed at the slumbering pig and wondered whether this Dwarf was capable of performing the same barbarous butchery to take throne and crown. Sebastian's blood boiled and his eyes watered at the thought of the heartbreaking dark time that Haggart Hammillaxe unleashed upon House Hartwaker, not only for slaying King Brode and taking the throne and crown for his own but for the despicable deed in the assassination of the ten year old heir to the Hartwaker rule.

"Please Pooka!" Came a voice from the class, a dainty hand raised above the mass of heads. Pooka was interrupted from his tale by a student at the back of the class.

"Yes, Danell?" Said Pooka as he strained his old eyes to gaze upon a small girl, two timid dark eyes peeping out from drapes of long hazelnut hair.

"What happened to King Brode's heir?" She asked meekly.

"Oh a tragic tale, very tragic!" Pooka shook his head. "But I do not know whether it is the right time for such a story."

"Oh but it is! It is!" Came the enthusiastic response from Jasson.

"I do not know." Pooka pondered. "I am not sure such a tale is for such young ears."

"Pah!" Jasson groaned. "Again you are shielding us from the truth." And with that slumped back into his chair, folding his arms crossly.

"Oh please, Pooka!" Xen asked. "This is one tale I have never heard of and I have studied all the Scrolls."

"Not all the Scrolls my dear,"
Pooka smiled mischievously, it was a smile that held secrets and information.

"It is true that this tale has not been told to children, perhaps it brought night terrors to them in the past, but if you believe that you are all mature enough for such a story..."
There was a unanimous cry from the class which made Pooka smile. "Very well. Brode Hartwaker II was known as 'The King for a Day, his sad tale entitled..."

160

CHÃPTÉR 15
Ã CRÜÉL CÖRÖNÃTÏÖN

he War of the Two Kings was over and 'The Dwarf King' Haggart Hammillaxe sat on the throne in Windmast Castle wearing the crown of Maglore upon his cruel dome. After several years of war Haggart, had finally outsmarted King Brode and slaughtered him in his own throne room as his family watched on in horror and disbelief. While Brode and his brother Grayfall had been lost in their own strategies of how best to attack the advancing Dwarf armies that had positioned themselves in Winaldo and Trinpola. They were both blind to the attack that came from the castle's bowels. Haggart had combed the entire realm in search of a Dwarf elder known as Uggol Breakspeare, the architect and builder that was responsible for Windmast Castle's construction. The ancient Dwarf was the only living being that knew of the secret entrances to the inside of the castle, entrances that were accessible through the waterfall that cascaded down it's high rocky motte, a protective curtain of constant running water that kept its inhabitants safe from attack, but also made them oblivious to the secrets that were hidden within. With this knowledge Haggart led a small troop of his best warriors including his right hand, 'The Whorer' Herth Rockhorn, through the tunnels and were able to blindside Brode and his men in the great hall, taking the head of 'The Dragon Slayer' with one vile swipe from Lungblower.

With the King dead, his house fell into panic and the ones who were lucky enough to survive fled Windmast Castle, leaving Haggart Hammillaxe to crown himself King and celebrate by drinking the blood that flowed from Brode Hartwaker's headless corpse like wine.

Brode's brother Grayfall had taken control of the house and led all the survivors away from Windmast to the relative safety of Hive House in Tendor, which was House Vespa and the birthplace of the Queen consort, Lady Helgay, Unfortunately Lady Helgay had been taken prisoner by Haggart and legend has it was raped and beaten on a daily basis by Herth Rockhorn, the same fate awaited her daughter Mia. She was savagely raped and beaten and did not survive the ordeal, many believe that it was her own marda that put an end to her life in a dark dungeon cell, as to not let her go through any more.

The Hartwaker's had always had a strong relationship with the Vespa's and were taken in with open arms by Helgay's farda, Lord Christoff Vespa. Grayfall immediately made plans with the Lord's of several close Houses to take back the throne, but the ageing Lord Christoff proved of little use to them, consumed with anger and frustration that his daughter Helgay should be freed he rode for Windmast Castle with a handful of his own Knights, even against the objections of Grayfall who

162

had labelled his intentions ludicrous. Grayfall's warning's fell on deaf ears and Lord Christoff never returned to Hive House. The Knights close to him returned, with a tale of Lord Christoff's heart stopping and falling from his steed, dead, but the body could no be retrieved as they came under attack from a mass of Dwarf arrows and were forced to flee. One Knight declared that he stayed behind with the intention of waiting for the siege to cease and then reclaim his Master's body, but his waiting proved to be in vain for it was the Dwarves that recovered the body and it was said that his head was removed and placed on a spike at the border to Calgaras. Some have whispered that the words of these Knight's were false and that it were his own Knights that left him to die for they feared the wrath of the Dwarves.

The Houses were in disarray as morale wained and fear of the Dwarves gripped them, they all looked to Grayfall for leadership, he felt that it was not his place, even though he was a great strategist and war general, he was not the rightful heir to his brother's throne and could not betray the bloodline. The duty fell to a boy of a mere ten name days, the young Prince Brode, the only born son of Brode Hartwaker. But the boy knew nothing of warfare or even life for he had not lived himself and Grayfall reluctantly took control of the situation, but he would only do so if Brode were named King. Grayfall announced that the boy would be crowned, he believed that this would unite Man and lift their spirits if they had a King at their helm. And so a great coronation was planned to take place at Hive House in the beautiful gardens that surrounded it. It would be a celebration and an act of defiance towards Haggart Hammillaxe, besmirching his reign. When the Dwarf King learnt of what was to transpire he was furious, his crown and reign would be tainted if another King of Man was allowed to rise, he knew that he would not be taken seriously by the realm if this was allowed to happen, so he made plans to prevent the crowning of a new King.

On the eve of the coronation, Grayfall spent much time with his nephew, Brode, trying to put his young mind at ease and to answer any queries that the young Prince had, which were indeed many. Grayfall made the pledge to him that he would not let any harm come to him and that he would help him rule the realm with mind and sword until the time came when he was mature enough to make his own decisions.

The day of the coronation had finally come and the proceedings could not have been blessed with a finer day, the sky was clear and the Sun of Selym shone down awaiting the festivities. The flowers in the grounds were in full bloom and the family's nurtured hornets danced from petal to petal humming along pleasantly with the lute and flutes that welcomed guests. The guests came from far and wide and wore elegant garments, ate canapés and sipped honeyed wine from the Vespa's own vintage stock, seemingly obvious that Dwarves now ruled their lands.

Daughter of Helgay and twin sister of Mia, Lady Tessandra Lacey was in attendance with her husband Lord Paoul Lacey and their children Siilva, Kate and young twin boys Darios and

Matho. She looked beautiful with her mass of golden curls cascading down her white gown that was trimmed with the blue of House Lacey, but her face wore a forced smile for she still mourned her marda, farda, grandfarda and sister. She put on a brave face for her younger brother who was about to be crowned King and occasionally their were glimpses of love in her eyes as she watched her young twins chase butterflies and hornets around the fabulous grounds.

A majestic dais had been constructed in the grounds and the hornets buzzed around the golden throne that had red velvet cushions for seat and splat which had been finished elegantly with a flaming Phoenix in golden thread. A long white coronation carpet cut through the luscious green grass, leading from the keep of Hive House all the way to the dais, it was indeed a long walk, but Grayfall insisted that Prince Brode make his way past all who had come to join in the festivities, from Servants and Squires, to Knights and Lords. He had explained to his nephew that it is important to acknowledge all those that honour the crown especially in these dark times, for a King without followers is no King and by arranging the coronation in such a way meant that no Man or Woman of lowborn or highborn birth would feel left out and would think highly of the new King for taking their feelings into account.

Grayfall had worked tirelessly making sure that the guards had been doubled around the walls and gates of Hive House and had continued to inspect the guard throughout the morning to make sure they had their wits about them, Grayfall would not give Haggart any opportunity to strike. The ram horns of Lacey sounded and Grayfall hurried to take his place at the foot of the dais and await his nephew. He strode quickly down the coronation carpet, clad in a red tunic and his best leather britches and boots, his hazelnut hair and beard had been trimmed immaculately and even at his age of thirty seven years, flecks of grey had started to form through. In his hands he carried the arm of House Hartwaker, the family's broad sword known as Reignmaker. The mirrored steel danced in the sunlight like water and the golden hilt and handle that had been forged in the shape of a Phoenix spread its wings proudly. Grayfall acknowledged the crowd that smiled at him with subtle nods of his head, he was proud to the one to deliver Reignmaker to it's next heir, the sword that his grandfarda and namesake Grayfall I used to slay Argo Calgaras and usher in the Age of Man 136 years ago. The same sword that his brother Brode used to slay the Dragon known as Grosa 'The Bronze' in the battle that was named in the Scrolls as 'The Ballad of the King and the Dragon' which led to the title of 'Dragon Slayer' being bestowed upon him. Grayfall was proud of his family lineage and today he would be even prouder to see his nephew take the sword for his own. He stood at the bottom of the dais and smiled proudly at the mass of people that had gathered, his intuition was correct, the coronation had brought Man together, a unified coalition ready to stand against Haggart's rule. Just the thought of thwarting The Dwarf King's celebrations was enough to cause an arrogant smile to slice his handsome face, it was not an attractive expression, but he supposed that his intentions were honourable.

166

The lutes, fiddles and flutes continued to join the hornets and butterflies in their cavorting cacophony and the congregation waited patiently for the guest of honour. Grayfall took the time to soak in the warm atmosphere, an excitement that seemed to radiate from the crowd, it sent a shiver down his spine, the fine hairs on his flesh rose eagerly, he pushed his chest out and bathed in the euphoria. This gave him time to survey the walls of the great House one more time before the proceedings, the finely constructed merlons and embrasures cutting through the blue sky like the teeth of some stone built monster. There were guards aplenty all at their stations around the keep battlements. He looked to the towers and saw guards with ram horns grasped in hands at the ready in three of the four towers. The Northwest Tower was unmanned as it had been damaged by lightning strike during a storm a few months back and it had been deemed unsafe, it was currently undergoing some reconstruction. Grayfall's eyes flitted to the broken down tower convinced that he had seen some flicker of light, a reflection of the suns rays upon steel perhaps, he had no time to query the situation because there was a sudden blast on the ram horns and Grayfall's attention turned to his young nephew, who stepped out from the keep with eyes as round as plates, the young Prince looked terrified.

The guards from the towers continued to blast their horns in respect for the Prince and he made his way slowly down the white coronation carpet towards the throne. He wore white linens trimmed intricately with golden thread and pearl, the design that of flames rising on his tunic, the Hartwaker sigil ever present in magnificent design on his left breast and a white mantle, trimmed with durge fur seemed to swamp him and the young Prince looked lost underneath it as he struggled to pull the weight of it behind him. He gazed nervously into the crowd and saw the face of young Meena Forrestor smiling back at him, he knew her well for she was his betrothed. A pretty girl of 13 years with a riot of red curls that cascaded down her back. Her eyelashes fluttered bashfully, mimicking the movements of the audacious butterflies, Brode looked away quickly, his face consumed with blush.

Grayfall smiled as he approached and when Brode saw his uncle he smiled back, his plump lips quivered and his emerald eyes glistened with moisture, he stopped in his tracks as if his legs would not allow him to move any further, he lowered his head so that his Uncle could not see the tears that swelled up in those innocent young eyes, his thick brown fringe hung down his face and hid him from the crowd.

The poor boy was overwhelmed by it all.

The horns that were erupting to announce his arrival stopped abruptly and the crowd started to mutter amongst themselves. Grayfall stepped forward to greet the oncoming King to be and taking the sword in one hand lowered it down by his side and reached out with the other hand placing it on young Brode's shoulder and whispered some words of encouragement to him. Brode smiled, his eyes glistened and his round cheeks flushed, but he felt comforted by his uncle's words. Grayfall looked into his nephew's green eyes that flickered like dewy blades of grass on a morning breeze, two sets of eyes that were reflections of each other, a family trait of the Hartwakers.

"I know this is scary nephew," Grayfall whispered, moving Brode's fringe to the side, allowing his face to be seen. "But this is not for me that you do this, you understand why?" Brode nodded and wiped his eyes across the soft linen of his tunic's cuff, it was so soft against his skin and immediately soaked up his salty tears.

"This is your destiny!" Grayfall added. "This is your throne to take, not mine. It is what your farda would have wanted, what the people of this realm want. A true Hartwaker on the throne!"

"But what if I fail uncle?" Brode stuttered. Grayfall smiled and knelt down to meet him, tenderly he embraced him and whispered into his ear heartfelt words that even brought a tear to his own eye as he spoke.

"I will not allow you to fail nephew. For you to fail is only possible if I fail and I refuse to fail you. Nor will I allow you to be put in danger. You are my blood, my brother's blood and I will spill my own to protect you."

Their emerald eyes met again and sparkled at each other, matching smiles appeared, the family likeness was uncanny and in that moment Grayfall saw his brother staring back at him and it was all he could do to keep his composure. He stood quickly and turned to face the dais, gesturing towards the throne.

"Shall we make history, Sire?" Grayfall asked.

169

"Yes, Uncle," Brode smiled and he started to make his way up the steps towards the throne. A chorus of horns erupted once again as the heir started to move, the sudden sound startled Grayfall and he found himself looking to the towers and watched on as the guards blew their horns expertly, the broken tower winked back at him again, a shining reflection that confused him. A tool left by a labourer perhaps catching the glare of the sun.

Brode's majestic long white mantle trailed behind him and consumed the dais steps long after he had ascended them and when he turned and took his seat, the fur trimmed mantel swept across the steps and cascaded down the one side like a mighty snowdrift. The timing was impeccable, for the bellowing of the horns ceased as Brode sat on his throne. His hands shook, his palms thick with perspiration as he gripped the golden arms of the throne as if for safety, his quivering fingers followed the contours of the Phoenix and flame design that was etched into them. His fingers found the beaks of the Phoenix heads that protruded from the arms, he squeezed them tightly the beak pressing into his palms so much that blood was drawn. He surveyed the courtyard through squinted eyes, The Sun of Selym shone down on him with reckless abandon, everywhere he looked he saw the eyes of the congregation staring back at him. Even when he closed his eyes to cower from the suns rays he could still see those eyes and although there were smiles on their faces, there was judgement in their eyes.

Could he live up to the legacy of his farda?

Could he be what the people of the realm needed him to be? Could he be King?

These questions danced around his head and his eyes flitted around the congregation of family, friends and people he did not know, the pressure that he felt was like nothing he had ever experienced before, he was only of ten years! Only last Season of Algor was he playing with his wooden Dragon and Knights, how could he now be sitting on a throne about to be made King of Maglore. He was overwhelmed by nausea and sweat trickled down from his scalp. He gazed into the crowd of his extended family and cared not if they were there or not for he had lost too many dear to him. His beautiful marda, his loving grandfarda, his sister Mia, who he always argued and fought with but he would give anything to see her face again. He lost his favourite Knight of the House, his farda's Head Knight, 'The Knight of the Berry Isle', Sir Jude Holloway, who always took time for him and made him laugh with his japes. He would have given anything to have them here with him now. He felt the uncomfortable itch of tears scratching at his eyes once more and his head felt light as if he would fall faint at any moment, then he saw a rotund man waddling around at the foot of the dais and he managed to focus on him and the sickness and emotion seemed to subside.

"My Lords and Ladies!" The man announced in a croaky voice. Brode sniggered to himself for the man not only looked like a toad but sounded like one too. "It is indeed a glorious day and we praise Adeve and give thanks to The Sun of Selym for bestowing its warming embrace upon us."

171

He was Chancellor Charles Plume, his job was to counsel the King in affairs of politics, Brode cared not for what he had to say for he knew that his uncle would be taking that role upon his wide shoulders as well as being his Head Knight.

"Today we leave the sadness of the past few months behind us and we as Man move forward, united as one race, just as we have always done and prove to our enemies that we will not abandon our duties and let the realm fall into the grasp of evil."

There was a scattering of applause and Chancellor Plume nodded to the congregation in recognition, a wide smile stretching across his bulbous face, sweat trickled down from his receding hairline and his thick neck bulged over the tightness of his collar.

Ribbit! Thought young Brode and he tittered to himself, he may not like the chancellor and he and the other children may have made fun of him, but he brought a smile to his face and made him feel more relaxed about the whole bizarre situation.

"Today we shall crown a King." Plume continued, his croaks reverberated around the courtyard walls, Grayfall considered them again, they were strong and tall and heavily manned, but still that broken down tower pricked at his curiosity.

"One King for Maglore! A true King, A Hartwaker!" Plume cried and the congregation erupted in applause.

"Aye, a Hartwaker has sat on the throne for the last 136 years. That is the way it is and should be." He turned to face young Brode and his eyes widened as if he had been caught

172

doing something untoward by the chancellor, still only a child his reactions will be that of a child.

"Prince Brode, son of a King with the same name. Brode Hartwaker, 'Brode the Brave', 'Brode the Eager', Brode 'The Dragon Slayer!" The crowd applauded and Plume smiled. "By what moniker will you become known as I wonder?"

Brode's young eyes flittered from side to side, he thought he was being asked to pick such a moniker, but he had never thought of such things.

"But of course that is not for you to choose, the people of this realm that worship the crown will appoint a suitable name in time."

A squire walked quickly from the sidelines, he cradled in his hands a red velvet cushion and upon it sat a golden crown. Shards of sunlight collided with the gold and silver circlet and seemed to explode with light, it was so bright that many onlookers were forced to turn away or close their eyes. Brode seemed unaffected by it and stared at it as if hypnotised by its alluring beauty. This was not the crown that had been worn by the other King's that had gone before Brode, unfortunately 'The Dwarf King' Haggart had claimed that for his own. A new crown had been forged by the master forger of House Bloodgaard, Randal Bloodgaard. It is said that he worked for four days without sleep, in the sweltering heat of the furnace to construct what many said was his finest piece. Silver and gold had been expertly threaded like rope and was encrusted with vibrant red rubies, the same sort that were embedded in the hilt of Reignmaker.

"The crown!" Plume announced and the congregation bowed in respect for its significance. "Brode Hartwaker do you accept this burden? Will you wear this crown with honour and dignity? Will you breathe and bleed for the realm and the people within it? Will you be King?"

There was silence, it was if the whole courtyard had held their breath, perhaps they had Brode thought, but he took a moment to listen to the sound of hornets cavorting with the flowers and smiling he looked at Grayfall who smiled back at him.

"I do!" Brode announced in a tone that sounded to mature for his years and the congregation breathed a sigh of relief.

"And so it shall be!" Plume announced and bowed his head to his future King and held the crown in between his fat sweaty digits. "Who giveth our King his arm?"

"Tis I, Lord Grayfall Hartwaker! Brother of Brode & Harold, Son of Willem, sworn Knight of Maglore and protector of the crown." Grayfall said proudly as he stepped forward holding the family arm and bowed before the crown, before kissing it and then turning to ascend the dais steps towards his nephew that appeared to have been eaten up by his vast throne. Grayfall stood in front of Brode whose eyes twinkled with the innocence of youth, Reignmaker shimmered too, his face reflecting in the clear steel and still he looked to the broken tower behind the dais.

What is that? A shimmering shard of a labourer's chisel perhaps?

Brode could see his uncle was distracted and his brow furrowed with concern, but Grayfall caught this and was snapped from his musing and smiled at him affectionately.

"I give you Reignmaker," Grayfall said as he knelt before Brode, holding aloft the broad sword. "Wield it to serve and protect the realm, for it is not a weapon but a shield. Use it wisely."

Grayfall handed it over into Brode's dainty unblemished hands, the only swords he had ever gripped in his hands were wooden and meant for play. Brode could feel the weight of Reignmaker immediately, it made his arms ache as he held it.

"Put the blade at rest." Grayfall whispered and Brode let the point of the sword connect with the dais and he held it vertically next to him by its hilt that was nearly his own body length. Grayfall then unsheathed his own sword and lay it down at Brode's feet.

"You will have my own blade as long as you will it. Stormchaser is yours." He left his sword and stepped to Brode's right hand side indicating that he would be the King's Head Knight during his rule.

The horns erupted again and Chancellor Plume made his way up the dais steps the crown held out before him. He stood at Brode's left indicating that he would be his ear and mouthpiece during his reign.

"Knights of the realm," Plume addressed the congregation. "Who of you will lay down their arms for the King to be?"

Around fifty Knights stepped through the crowd and gathered at the foot of the dais, all manner of colours were prominent and a plethora of sigils burst proudly from their scabbards as they all unsheathed their arms and knelt on the coronation carpet giving their swords for the overwhelmed heir. He had never seen so many Knights and it awed him to think that they were their for him, so taken aback by it all was he that he almost dropped Reignmaker.

"YOU HAVE MY SWORD!" Bellowed the Knight's in unison, their proud proclamation reverberating around the walls of the courtyard.

Young Brode did not really know how to acknowledge such a gesture but smiled and nodded his head courteously at the gathering of knelt Knights.

Plume nodded towards the Knight's and then turned his attentions back to Brode holding aloft the crown above the child's head. The newly forged crown shimmered like a halo and he resembled the mythical creature that many believed lived in the clouds.

"Under the watchful eye of the Great God Adeve, we bear witness to the crowning of a new King!"

The Knights scooped up their swords and stood swiftly.

"Before the Realm of Maglore, I Charles Plume chancellor and counsel to the crown declare that Brode Hartwaker will be named your King."

The Knights took a tight grasp of their hilts and held them out before them, the blades quivering over the coronation carpet in anticipation.

"We honour those that have come before and those that will follow. We remember the blood spilt for the crown and

176

those that held aloft Reignmaker in battle and all those that sat upon the throne whether their tenure be short or long of length, it matters not for without these Kings of our past then we would have no future to build upon. Let us praise, 'The Just', 'The Man King', Grayfall Hartwaker 'The First'!"

There was a cry of 'HAIL!' from the Knights who thrust their arms into the sky in respect, before lowering them again.

"Robin Hartwaker 'The Unready'!"

"HAIL!" Cried the Knights and they repeated the praising process.

"'The General' Willem Hartwaker 'The Gallant'!"

The words 'HAIL' rang around the courtyard, the sun dazzled young Brode as he sat above all others, the swords rising up and piercing the blue sky with shimmering blades was indeed a spectacle.

"Harold Hartwaker!" Plume cried, there were several sniggers throughout the congregation, who knew that Harold's reign was indeed short and was known throughout court as Harold 'The Ungraceful' having fallen from a colt and breaking his neck. An act that ended his short reign and his life, but the Knight's hailed the unfortunate King nonetheless.

"And 'The Dragon Slayer', Brode Hartwaker!"

The cry of hail was loud and proud, and it seemed to rattled the stone walls of the keep, their was passion for the former King. Brode's eyes swelled again with tears at the mention of his farda's name, he too was proud and sad, he hoped that he could live up to his farda's name and legacy.

"It is with great honour that I crown you Son of Brode..." Plume cried loudly.

Brode's eyes looked up trying to see the crown above his head, which was impossible, but he saw the sun's rays bursting from it, the rays danced before him. Brode thought he could feel the heat of the crown hovering above his head as hornets whirled around him in rapid bursts, he could already feel its weight and the burden it would bring. But before fear and apprehension could consume him the words had been said and the crown was gently placed on his nest of hair the colour of tree bark.

"All hail King Brode Hartwaker II!"

"HAIL TO THE KING!" Were the words that were bellowed by the entire congregation and the Horns of Lacey burst into life once again. King Brode II sat wide eyed and the crown sat heavy on his head before his uncle leant close to him and kissed him on the cheek, whispering. "It is time to rise my King."

King Brode II nodded, his eyes wide and mouth gaping.

"Greet your people, Sire." Grayfall smiled proudly and the new King slowly rose from his throne.

King Brode II waved to his congregation and he noticed the mirrored tears in his sister's eyes, proud tears, then he saw Meena and her eyes were warm with love, he smiled at her and then he whispered to his uncle.

"I would like to say a few words."

"Of course, Your Majesty!" Grayfall replied and then held his hand aloft to silence the horns and the cheers. There was

178

immediate silence as if the courtyard had become draped in a shroud.

"Your King wishes to speak!" Grayfall announced proudly as he watched on as his nephew and new King stood holding the huge sword in his hand and the crown lopsided on his head. There was silence as they awaited his first words as King of Maglore and only the buzzing of the hornets flitting from flower to flower could be heard. Grayfall swatted at them as they moved swiftly past his face, he felt a large one that he believed in that moment must have been that of a Queen almost grazed his cheek, but he remained focused on the young King.

Brode opened his mouth to speak but no words came, the young King stood mute for what seemed the longest time and then from underneath the band of the gold and silver of the crown a bead of blood emerged and slid down his nose before dripping from its tip and staining the pristine whiteness of his furred mantle.

Grayfall reacted first but his motions seemed cumbersome, he seemed to impeded by his own judgement. He saw the fletchings of arrow flittering, the shaft still quivered from the sudden impact, his mind's eye must surely be making jest, there was surely no truth in this vision that haunted his eyes. Young Brode's grip on Reignmaker fell loose and his fingers squirmed as if trying to retrieve it, the sword fell and the blade sang as it collided with the dais steps. Brode tried again to speak but could not and now his mouth was filled to the brim with blood, it seeped down his chin and he spluttered, choking

179

on its metallic thickness. The young King could hear muted cries that seemed far away, he saw rapid movement as Knights ran towards him, the eyes of the congregation looked haunted now shrouded in crimson. Grayfall was the first to reach him but it was too late, King Brode collapsed and slid down the steps, the crown left him rolling down the coronation carpet where it settled and remained, stained with royal blood.

Someone called loudly "The broken tower! It came from the broken tower!" That was the last thing that met Brode's bleeding ears, he saw the blue of the sky and then his uncle's face, pale and full of shock. Grayfall's mouth moved but Brode could not hear the words and he smiled meekly at his uncle before he passed.

Grayfall held the child to him and shrieked with tears of anger, "Bring me this assassins head!"

The arrow had entered the young King's skull from the rear, unleashed from the broken tower by an assassin sent by Haggart. Grayfall held his nephew tightly and his tears became that of sadness as he sobbed for him, murmuring unknown words into his blood-filled ears.

"It is said that Grayfall held 'The Boy King' long into the night, some say for ten hours, and hour for each year of the child's life." Pooka looked out at his class and the majority of eyes that looked back at him for overflowing with tears. Although his flesh was leathery in appearance his sadness could be seen upon his brow, it truly was a touching tale, and he awaited the inevitable questions that would arise.

"So tragic." Xen sobbed, wiping her eyes. "Was the assassin apprehended? How was he executed?"

"The archer deserved to be tortured or what he did!" Growled Jasson, doing his upmost to fight back tears himself.

"Unfortunately the identity of the archer was never discovered."

"What say you?" Jasson gasped.

"A full search of the House and grounds was completed and Knights even rode for three days in each direction in search of the fleeing assassin, but none was ever found."

"Was it Dwarf or Man that was responsible?" Asked a tearful Danell.

"Who can say." Shrugged Pooka. "There are some tongues that believe that it was one of the congregation present at the coronation that was responsible. Someone that did not wish Brode to take the crown, but there is no truth to this, but it is possible as no trace of the assassin was ever found."

"Did Grayfall then take the crown?" Asked a child.

"No!" Pooka shook his head, his long dangling ears flapped from side to side. "Not immediately no."

"But why?" Jasson asked.

"Chancellor Plume had tried to persuade Grayfall to take the crown, which was now his right, but he would hear nothing of this. Grayfall as we all know would take the crown, but he had vowed that he would first avenge his nephew before he ever wore the crown. It would take almost ten years before Grayfall managed to dethrone Haggart Hammillaxe during the Battle of Deceit."

"It is heartbreaking to hear this tale, Pooka." Xen snivelled. "But I for I am glad that I have learnt this of my ancestor. I shall honour him with my prayers to the Great God Adeve tonight."

Pooka smiled as he waddled over to her, he wore a tunic which was embroidered with the Phoenix of House Hartwaker, he looked into her moist young eyes and he was proud to be apart of this House and teach the new generations of the realm's history, whether it be light or dark, it was information that was needed to be known. Yes, he felt very proud about his position, but that wasn't always so. He handed her a handkerchief, "Shall we return to our story?"

CHÃPTÉR 16
DÉFÏÃNT BY NÃMÉ ÃND NÃTÚRÉ

t pricked at Sebastian's pride to be in the same room as such a weapon as Lungblower, a Dwarf's weapon of hatred and disgust. But then remembered his conversation with Miglay and his wise words about not being responsible for the sins of those family members that had gone before us and he was right, he would truly be a hypocrite if he were to dwell on these thoughts.

Sebastian gazed at the trail of discarded food that lay on the dais steps like a harvest offering that could feed a poor village for a month. Tankards of ale were abandoned in small puddles of their own making, the bubbling remnants pillows as they lay unused like drunken fools after a rough night of drinking and whoring, flaccid and useless in pool of their own vomit. The snorting and grunting of the slumbering Dwarf Lord brought Sebastian back to the here and now and he gazed upon him as he lay slouched across the wide seat of the throne, draped in a hefty fur cape and topped with a silver crown, several protruding shards bursting from it, like the antlers of some gigantic stag. In truth he had no right to don a crown, nor did

Queen Oleander to wear her extravagant tiara, the crown should only be worn by the true sovereign of the realm and that right was Sebastian Hartwaker's. But he knew that when he had given them their own independence that the leaders of each would expect nothing more than to be treated like a King or Queen, but in truth they were only rulers of there own houses and their crowns of steel meant nothing in the grand scheme of things. Sebastian's mind wondered again and he believed that if he was not successful in his quest to unite the realm and he were to lose his life to this dark haze then it would mean war for his daughter. The Dwarves, the Giants even the Goblins would rise up and think the realm of Man weak without a King to rule and surely they would look to take advantage of such a weakness.

The rotund frame of Dagyan stirred and snorted again, and Sebastian stared at the slumbering mass that lay grumbling before him and laughed to himself, how it might be if he ruled his own kingdom like this. Daygan's face was worn and weathered like rock, his hair and beard long and black flecked with streaks of grey like forked lightning. Like many a Dwarf he wore braid in his beard, but saliva that dripped from his gapping maw meant any finesse from such stylings were lost. His rotundness was dressed in elegant velvet, of grey, trimmed with golden stitch, and two fur smothered boots made up his slumbering ensemble.

Sebastian grew tired of waiting and announced his presence with a sudden clearing of his throat, the sound carried around the high ceilings and reverberated through the steel armours that had been worn by the Dwarf leaders of the past, causing them to rattle as if applauding his arrival.

Dagyan stirred and grumbled, but did not wake. Then ungracefully he lifted his dumpy leg and unleashed an aggressive response of flatulence, which was surprising tuneful considering the instrument it was being played on. The sound was so loud and proud that it could have rivalled the Horns of Lacey for its grandiloquence. When the smell of secondhand meaty boar caressed Sebastian's nostrils he had had enough and this time he called the Dwarf by name and their was an authoritative tone to his words. Dagyan snorted and rose quickly as if woken from a nightmare, his beady eyes peered out from between narrowing slits that fought back the blur of sleep that had coated them.

"Who be that?" Dagyan grumbled, struggling to seat himself with some kind of dignity on his wide throne. "Who be wakin' their King while he be at slumber-rest?"

King! Sebastian thought, the voice in his head scoffed at the very thought of it, but he bit his tongue and allowed Dagyan to collect himself.

"You be answerin' me if you be knowin' what be good for yous!" Dagyan still sleepy eyed reached for the grip of Lungblower, his rough digits wrapping themselves tightly around soft leather.

"It is I..." Sebastian announced proudly, "King! Sebastian, of House Hartwaker!"

He watched as the Dwarf's fingers immediately relinquished their grip, but then for a second playfully tapped on its pommel as if he contemplated waking it from its slumber and using it to cut down the Man King and take the realm for his own. His thought must have betrayed him for his eyes darted to looked upon Sebastian and then withdrew his hand.

"HA!" Dagyan laughed, as he settled into his throne trying to look dignified, like he belonged there, high above the King of Man. He enjoyed sitting above Man, any Man, but even more so a King.

"Why you be ere I is askin' meselves? Why be a Man King... A Hartwaker be ere at me Hammillda?"

"I bring a message..." Sebastian started, but Dagyan's eyes grew wide with mania as if frightened.

"You be meanin' war! I be right I be!" Dagyan growled and leant forward in his dark stone throne, his weathered face scowling under the mass of black hair that covered his head and chin. "You be meanin' to be slayin' me why I be at slumber-rest!"

"No, not at all, Lord Dagyan..."

"King!" Dagyan spat violently, almost leaping from his seat, but thinking better of it.

"King of what?" Sebastian snapped in response, a glare of frustration to match Dagyan's, their stares locked stubbornly like the antlers of two virile Stags.

"PAH!" Dagyan scoffed, knowing his answer would be vague and he had no answer that would win him the argument. "You be just like your granfarda! A sneakin' bastard who be lookin' to strike when others be unawares!"

186

"No worse than what your farda did, Dagyan! At least my ancestors did not rape and murder women and children!"

Dagyan had no answer for that either, he was not his farda and he was no way Godly in his own conduct, but even he knew that the actions of his farda were unforgivable. Dagyan looked away from the King breaking the heated clash and scooped up a half-filled jug of ale that rested by his foot, he took a long swig and brought it to rest on the arm of his throne, bubbling froth dribbling from his mouth into his beard.

"I'm not here to talk about the sins of the past!" Sebastian said, "and I am not here to start a war with Man and Dwarf, far from it."

"Then why you be ere!" Dagyan murmured.

Miglay listened at the door, Sebastian's voice carried around the vast hall and found his ear that was wrapped around the keyhole, there was no distortion and he heard every word uttered of the Man King's fantastic tale. Miglay had heard of Man having such visions and believed that there were several members of The Mystic Circle that possessed this gift. Miglay was much wiser and knowing of the realm than his brother, leaving many to say that he should be the Dwarf to rule and not his drunken boar of a brother. Miglay had no wish to take his brother's birthright and cared not for rule, but his mind would be served far better in an advisory role if only his stubborn brother would listen to his words, unfortunately he did not. The more that Miglay heard of Sebastian's vision the more he believed it, he had the ability to judge a character and could discover a lying tongue with ease. Sebastian's tongue although it wagged with outlandish words, they fell on his listening ear as truth.

When Sebastian had finished his tale there was an abrupt silence, Dagyan's face was sullen, a mask of rigid stone gave Sebastian nothing. Had he taken the Man King's words as truth and was he deliberating what he could do to help him or had he taken the story as folly? Dagyan stroked his beard, seemingly deep in thought, a trait that was reminiscent of his farda before him, but he did not speak for the longest time. It was Sebastian that broke the silence.

"Dwarf Lord Dagyan, have you heard my words?" Sebastian asked. "Will the Dwarf Army align with Man for the good of the realm and to stop this coming darkness?"

Dagyan's face quivered behind his mass of hair and his large stomach began to tremble, his lips seemed to squirm as if he were chewing on a tough piece of meat that was being worked over by his craggy teeth.

"What say you Dagyan? Will you help us? Will you help Maglore in its time of greatest need?"

Dagyan irrupted in hysterics, spittle spraying into his beard as he laughed. The Dwarf Lord rolled around on the seat of his throne and clutched his shaking gut as tears ran down from his eyes. Sebastian was not amused by his outburst and believing he had the Dwarf's answer he turned on his heel to leave, but as he walked away from the dais, Dagyan spoke.

"You must be takin' me for the fool with such a yarn. It be just the Season of Gloam come early that be all."

Sebastian stopped and turned to face him once again.

"The only yarn is that you sit on a throne, Dagyan!" Sebastian spat aggressively.

"Bastard!" Dagyan growled and slipped off the throne and grabbed the handle of Lungblower and almost hoisted it in the air, when he turned to see Sebastian halfway up the dais with Reignmaker in hand and pointed at his bulbous nose that hung over his angry maw.

"I beg you to take Lungblower!" Growled Sebastian. "Hoist it above your head and bring it down with all the fury of your ancestors and see what will become of you."
Dagyan's fingers twitched around his hammer-axe.

"How be darin' you! You be showin' me the blatant bloody disrespect Man King!" Dagyan growled, but he did not lift Lungblower.

"I have shown you the same courtesies that you have bestowed on me, Dagyan." And with that Sebastian sheathed Reignmaker and walked away from the Dwarf, his back to him as he casually took each stoney black step of the dais in his stride. Dagyan saw his hand still wrapped around Lungblower and for a moment he imaged he had lifted it and swung it violently through the air and brought it down through the back of the King's head. He thought of other thoughts and realised that it had been many years since he had wielded the weapon, on closer inspection a thick layer of dust had actually gathered on its head and doubt fluttered inside his thick torso that he would never wield it again. His sweaty palm relinquished the handle of the hefty piece of steel and Sebastian spoke again, still with his back to the Dwarf.

189

"I come to you and you laugh in my face." Said Sebastian calmly. "You not only laugh at me and my people, but at the realm in which you live in. You mock our very existence. You worry about keeping your throne, but you seem to forget who allowed you to take seat there!" The words were spat with venom by the King, but also with truth.

"I not be listenin' to your cursed words any longer!" Growled Dagyan and he wobbled down the dais steps to meet Sebastian at its foot, Sebastian turned and looked down at him.

"The words I speak are truth. All of the words I speak are truth." Sebastian said proudly. "My grandfarda Grayfall II gave you your kingdom and saved your miserable life. He let you have your life and what have you done with it? Drink ale, eat boar and whore women!"

"HA!" Dagyan laughed again. "And what a bloody life it be!"

"A crown sits on your head, but what are you King of? Do not forget that I gave you your independence when I took rule over Maglore. I gave all the races their rights to make their own laws and look how I am repaid?" Sebastian walked away at a rapid pace.

"You be comin' here on a fool's errand Man King! With fantastic words that be that of bad dreams and bad ale me be thinkin'! Go back to Windmast there be no war to be havin' with anyone. Not anymore! You Man don't be wantin' peace me thinks, Me be thinks that you be on this quest to be startin' a war."

"If that is what you think, then you are a fool!" Sebastian made for the door, his rapid footsteps reverberated around the hall and then he heard Dagyan's mocking laughter once again and it angered him so, so much so that it stopped him in his tracks, hand gripping the Phoenix hilt of Reignmaker once again.

"I have never be likin' Man!" Dagyan spat as he worked his way back up to his throne, he snatched a half empty tankard with one hand and a leg of cockerel with the other as he made is ascent, swigging and chewing as he climbed.

"You be believin' that you be above all else." Dagyan added as he sat down on his throne once again, slightly out of breath. "Your kind always be thinkin' that. Thought you be above the Elves and you be endin' them." Dagyan pointed the leg of cockerel at the King. "That be why I not be trustin' your words. You be thinkin' about endin' Dwarves too."

Sebastian sighed, there was no reasoning with The Dwarf Lord, he was indeed known for his stubbornness, but with so many years spent in his own company it had made him wary of all others and their motives. The mind can truly be ones worst enemy.

"I have no more words for you Dagyan, for they fall on deaf ears." Sebastian sighed and continued on his way to the door, all the way his journey was accompanied by the mocking laughter of the Dwarf as he ripped meat from bone and threw thick stale ale down his gullet.

As Sebastian neared the doors, eager now to have his leave with yet another bitter taste in his mouth, they were suddenly flung

191

open and two women burst in. Sebastian was taken aback and they were startled to seem him there.

"Oh Sire, please forgive us." One of them giggled as they bowed low, their flimsily dresses plunged low to reveal their subtle breasts. The cotton of their garments were cheap and almost transparent, revealing a thick clump of hair between their legs. They stared at him seductively, there was no hiding what these women were.

"Whores!" Bellowed Dagyan.
The pair rose on hearing their patron's calls and smiled bashfully at the King as they ran barefoot across the cold stone floor towards the dais.

"Please be forgivin' the intrusion." Said Miglay who was standing in the doorway. "Whores be impossible to halt when they be havin' the smell of gold in their nostrils."

"You be comin' to me my beauties!" Laughed Dagyan as he sat on the throne, his posture welcoming to the two whores. Sebastian was not a whorer, never had been, even in his younger days as a Knight, he loved his wife and Queen dearly and had never once strayed onto the path of infidelity, but he was still a Man and his blood ran hot, so he watched on as they disrobed, unveiling their exquisite figures that were curved how nature had intended. The cold hall pricked at their flesh and immediately and they were smothered with gooseflesh, their delicate nipples protruding aggressively and sharp as though they would cut a Man who dared to touch them. One of the whores had skin the colour of olives and dark hair that wound down her back in a thick braid, the tip swayed from side to side as she cantered up the dais steps, almost pointing to her moving buttocks like the swaying of a pendulum, almost hypnotic. Sebastian found his eyes favoured the red haired beauty, hair like fire that flayed around in all directions as she moved, he gazed at her breast as they moved freely of her body. He gazed upon her pale flesh and craved to run the tip of his finger across the clusters of freckles that patterned her skin like the markings of some Ferals he had seen in the jungles of Tangotta.

"You be likin' what you be seein' Man King?" Dagyan laughed.

Sebastian was torn from his sordid stare, his face flushed with embarrassment as Dagyan continued to laugh, the pair of beauties climbing onto the great stone throne and straddling the Dwarf, they were twice his height and wrapped their limbs around him playfully as they kissed his leathery flesh. They cared not that his face were covered in bumps, welts and warts for he paid them for their time with thick golden Dollin, so they cared not what he looked like, or the stagnant meaty smell that seeped from his maw.

"The red head me thinks?" Dagyan smiled as the pair caressed his rotund belly, the darked haired whore working vigorously to untie his britches. He grabbed the face of the red head and turned it to face Sebastian her eyelids flickered at him enticingly. Sebastian saw that it was an hypnotic gaze that she had become proficient in and he had seen enough he turned and left, but not before hearing one last slanderous heckle from The Dwarf Lord.

193

"I may not be carin' for Man, but I do be lovin' your whore women!"

Miglay kept pace with Sebastian as he strode down the corridor away from the great hall.

"I be apologisin' for me brother's inhospitality. He be a bloody idiot."

"To call him an idiot is a compliment!" Sebastian growled.

"Please be slowin' down!" Miglay gasped, "I not be as nimble as I once be."

Sebastian slowed and then halted before the door that led to the courtyard, so many emotions attacked him from within, he was embarrassed.

"I thought this would be such a simple task, Miglay." He started. "I believed that notifying the Lords would unite us against an enemy that means to destroy us all, but yet they hear my words and cast them aside as deceit. They all believe that I am either mad or that I look to lure them closely and commit treachery upon them. Nothing could be further from the truth."

"I be believin' your words, Sebastian."

"You do?"

"Aye!" Miglay smiled, it was not a pretty smile but it was genuine and warm. "I be around a long time, maybe it be too long?" He chuckled and Sebastian smiled.

"I be tellin' if lies be spilt from lips and your words be of truth."

"It warms my heart and puts my mind to rest a little that there are some that believe in my words."

"I be hearin' of some who be havin' this gift of visions. You be visitin' the Mystic Circle? You be findin' answers there me be thinks."

"That is my next destination. Then I journey on to Kanka to parlay with Troggo Brockonbak, leader of Giants."

"I feel he be trickier to win round than Dagyan." Miglay scoffed.

Sebastian smiled. "You are a good Dwarf." He said and lay a royal hand on Miglay's broad shoulder.

"Aye, well, me brother be the bad apple it be true. I just be doin' what I feel right."

"Would you join me and Sir Mondt on our quest? I could do with someone of your intelligence at my side."

Miglay stroked his mass of beard as he thought long and hard about the King's proposal.

"That's if you can still wield that axe of yours at your age."

"HA!" Miglay laughed and slapped the King's rump. "I be a Floret chicken compared to some of these elder Dwarves, I be tellin' you."

"Will you join me?" Sebastian asked again, he could see the sparkle of adventure in the Dwarf's old grey eyes.

"Let me be talkin' with my brother. I be changin' his mind."

"I fear that once Dagyan has made his mind up about something it remains made. That is why they call him Dagyan 'The Defiant' is it not?"

195

"Aye!" Miglay chuckled. "That it be, that it be. But I be given the chance to try, aye?"

"Of course! If that is your wish."

"But if I be failin', I be joinin' you on the road." Miglay smirked, there was playful mischief in his grin, as just the thought of adventure had breathed life into his old bones.

"It would be an honour to have you join us." Sebastian bowed his head in respect.

"Enough with the bloody bowin'!" Miglay whined with slight embarrassment as he pushed the doors open and they walked out onto the courtyard, that dark purple haze greeting them again.

"I be no one."

"Nonsense!" Sebastian snapped. "You are Miglay 'The Mindful' are you not?"

"Aye."

"That moniker has been bestowed upon you for a reason my friend."

They smiled at each other as they made their way to the banqueting hall.

"I never be havin' a King as a friend before." He cackled. Raucous singing escaped from the banqueting hall and they realised that Mondt was in there.

"I fear we have neglected Mondt." Said Sebastian a wrinkle of worry on his brow.

"I dread to think what they be doin' to him." Miglay winced.

They entered the banqueting hall to witness a sight indeed.

"Bloody Hell!" Miglay gasped.

Sir Maxillimious Mondt danced on the table with a tankard of ale in his one hand and Ethel cradled in his other, his face nuzzling at her neck as she giggled. Hundreds of Dwarves surrounded the table jumping and dancing and singing merrily while throwing ale into the air as if celebrating.

"I see you have built bridges between Man and Dwarf Mondt!" Sebastian called, which halted Mondt's drunken exploit in the middle of some complicated jig.

"Sire!" He gasped taken aback and fell from the table, Ethel still clutched in his arms, he landed on several Dwarves knocking them over like they were skittles at a fair game that one might witness at The Deerheart Games. There was a groan from the other side of the table and the singing was changed to the boisterous laughter of a hundred Dwarves. Sebastian and Miglay hurried to the table to see Mondt lying on a bed of fallen Dwarves, his head buried in Ethel's vast cleavage.

"Me be thinks the Man Knight be underestimatin' the strength of Dwarf ale." Miglay chuckled.

Mondt appeared from underneath Ethel's bosom, his blue eyes swimming with the after effects of too much ale and he looked up at them smiling strangely.

"What have you got to say for yourself?" Sebastian mocked.

"Sire." Mondt snorted. "I think I'm betrothed!"

Ethel kissed at his handsome face rampantly and the Dwarves let out a loud cry and started singing again as Miglay and Sebastian laughed. It was all a very pleasant distraction, but

197

Sebastian needed to move on with his journey, it was decided that he would travel on alone and Mondt would join him after he had slept off the aftereffects of the engagement celebrations, Sebastian left Hammillda with only his trusted steed Dayboy for company. He could not help but feel that he had taken a step backwards on his journey.

CHÃPTÉR 17

MÖÛNT QÛÏŘÏNÛS

ayboy was confused by the constant darkness that hung all around him, he would snort and grumble (but there is nothing new there), shaking his head from side to side in his anguish. The colt was fidgety, every movement in the shadows made him apprehensive and several times tried to turn back for home, but his Master would not allow it. As Sebastian travelled his eyes started to adjust to the strange blackness that was draped over them, he could make out the Kayalian Mountains and see the castle of the Mystic Circle high above Mount Quirinus. The black mountain that homed the castle Quirinus was not like any other mountain, its rocky face had the skeletal remains of a huge Dragon embedded in it. The menacing bones of the Dragon known as Claarac remained frozen in time as the mountain has become her grave. For a time the mountain had been even more menacing, when Claarac had remained alive for a time, stranded in the rock. How could a Dragon become one with a mountain I hear you ask, well by magic of course!

During the infamous war that had become known as The Rage

of Man, Pagmai the wizard battled on the side of Man against Elves, each side had a Dragon, Lennoc the Red fought alongside Man and Claarac the White who had sided with the Elves. Claarac had dominated the first and second waves of Man's assault with her vicious black flame that turned those on the receiving end into pools of bubbling tar. That was until Pagmai broke off from his place of relative safety and took on the beast single handedly. Others thought him mad as they fled past him in retreat. Claarac had screamed in hysterics to see the old Wizard take a stance of attack far below her, she glided through the air like a white ghost, easily denying the archers of glory with her swift movements until she descended upon the Wizard, who began to glow with the power from the Orb of Quirinus. Claarac unleashed black flame that consumed him as she hung in the air, there was no way that anyone could withstand such an onslaught. Believing that the deed be done, Claarac extinguished her fires and waited with arrogance to witness the Wizard as yet another puddle of black tar, but this was not the case and her black eyes blinked with disbelief, for there stood Pagmai, unharmed and releasing the power of the Orb through the point of his sword, Hex towards her. The Power of the Orb was too much for Claarac and she was forced back violently. The velocity that she was driven back with was unprecedented, surely the Orb of Quirinus had never unleashed such power before? It was enough to send the Dragon hurtling across the realm from Tendor to Zalenta where she came to settle at Mount Quirinus. Her body was painfully pushed into the rock face leaving only parts of her to protrude, flailing and screaming for her freedom. It was there she remained on a diet of Cloud Skimmers and Trolls. The Trolls always starving, attacked her slicing off pieces of her to feed on. But that was long ago and now only the bones remain, but to our traveller in the darkness the sight of it was enough to send several shivers down his spine.

"It is not a shroud of darkness but a haze." King Sebastian had remarked to himself, his eyes focused to better understand his own words.

"Yes!" He exclaimed. "A haze, the colour of lavender. It circulates all-around us. This is no Season of Gloom come early as the Dwarves believe."

Dayboy snorted as if in response to Sebastian's revelation.

"No, this is dark magic at play." He murmured to himself.

The Sun of Selym was far behind him, but as it shone in the West, oblivious to the change of its pattern, the haze was not as black as pitch as it had been in the forest, somehow its powerful rays made that haze gleam wonderfully as though a million Sprites had come to his aid to guide his journey. The King could now see better and disposed of his exhausted torch that he held aloft. Finally after several days over plains and hills he had reached the rocky terrain that sat at the foot of Mount Quirinus.

King Sebastian dismounted and stretched his already weary muscles, there was a cacophony of creaking joints which both satisfying and distressing, another sign that he was growing older. He craned his neck to gaze upwards at the castle that sat upon Mount Quirinus, that hundreds of years ago was ruled by the conniving Elf Queen, Queen Evaa Quirinus. Since the eradication of the Elf race the castle has been home to The Mystic Circle, a collection of Wizards, Witches and Astronomers, those who had special gifts that set them apart from Man and Dwarf.

The castle itself was built of black stone that seemed to glimmer, was it enchanted or was it merely the texture of the stone that caused the effect? Several spiralling peaks reached up to the haze of darkness as if trying to slice through it and escape its sinister clutches. It looked as though it kept secrets concealed in its stone entrails, and it did, secrets that a mere mortal Man could never comprehend, dark secrets that were heard far and wide, carried on whispers to cynical ears.

The only positive that King Sebastian took from this suspicious structure was that torches burnt inside, illuminating the dark dwelling in its even darker surroundings.

"At least there appears to be someone home." King Sebastian quipped.

Dayboy joined him staring up the mountain, his long face wearing an expression of trepidation, he nuzzled at the King's hand as if for a caring gesture of reassurance. The King did not disappoint and lovingly stroke the colt's nose and mane.

"It will take a few hours journey to reach it and no doubt a treacherous one underfoot."

Dayboy snorted defiantly with new found courage that he would like to help carry his Master's burden.

"Ha! Brave Dayboy." Sebastian smiled. "You would never make

such a climb, too steep and unstable for your size and hooves I fear."

He fussed Dayboy and took his reins leading him to a nearby congregation of trees and shrubs where he could have shelter and be able to explore, no doubt in search of berries and shrooms to feed his always hungry stomach.

"I shall have to go alone this time my old friend." Sebastian announced, loosing the reins and removing the burden of the saddle before hiding it behind a small rock formation, so that it would not be seen by any passing thieves, his chainmail would just add to the burden of his journey, but he took a dagger and Reignmaker, just incase.

"I have heard many tales of Trolls dwelling in the mount's crevices. It would be foolish to go unarmed. I shall return as soon as I can, Dayboy." Sebastian said as he walked away from his Steed. "Do not stray too far, for Sir Mondt will be joining us."

He started to climb, he made the mistake of looking up and realising what a daunting task this was of his ageing and tired body. The intimating gaze of Claarac's dark empty sockets watched him and was enough to make him fault in his proceedings, he reached out and caressed the protruding bone of the Dragon and swallowed hard before contouring with his ascent.

As he climbed higher, he felt as though he was not alone.

"Trolls!" He whispered, with a quiver in his voice, he could already smell their scent of muck on the rocks. His eyes were weary and flitted around to dark crevices in the mountain

203

to see if any Trolls were peering at him with hunger in their needy eyes. Was it fear that halted the King, possibly for all Man fears something, for fear takes many forms.

From far below, Dayboy watched as his Master climbed and was smothered by the dark haze before lowering his head, nostrils sniffing at the ground for something to eat. He disappeared into the cover of trees.

As expected Sebastian found the climb treacherous, on numerous occasions he lost his footing and if it had not been for a strong grip he would have fell to his death and his quest would have ended, just like that. He knew that halfway up the mountain there was a safer pathway, a pathway that was carved centuries ago by Quildor Planesphere who made it his aspiration to link the Kayalian Mountain range through bridges and pathways making it easier for travel, it became know as The Bridge of Quildor. The great Man died on Mount Quirinus unable to finish his bridge that he planned to end in Brood's Reach.

After a few hours of strenuous labour King Sebastian was forced to stop, his body needed to rest so he made the decision to settle on a ledge. He situated himself in a seated position with his back to the rock face just in case he fell asleep. He ate a small amount of stale bread that he had kept in his pouch for such an occasion, the bread was dry and rough on his throat, his meal was accompanied by swigs from his boar skinned canteen, it was necessary to help the bread go down. He looked out at the West, a wash of vanilla and cornflower, glistening in the sun as he sat in darkness unable to determine the time of day or even what day it was, he no longer had any concept of time, there was just darkness. With his bread consumed he relaxed a little, resting his head on the rock face, the ledge was just big enough for him to stretch his legs out. He thought of home and his daughter, he could still hear her sweet laughter within his ear, a found memory to recall. Then thoughts fell on his wife, his Queen and he focussed on the band that wrapped around his ring finger of his left hand, his wedding band, he kissed it and sent loving thoughts to his Queen.

He gripped the handle of his dagger in the darkness, could Trolls be near by, hiding in the shadows, stalking him from hidden crevices cut into the mountain. He was too tired to even consider such scenarios for his eyelids were heavy and all he wanted to do was sleep. Sebastian had no knowledge of the length of his slumber because it was obviously still dark when he roused. The Sun of Selym was setting in the West, going on with its cycle oblivious to what was taking place in the East, ignoring it as if it were an unwanted bastard child. He stood and stretched, he staggered slightly, his head still a little woozy and realised he was on the edge of a mountain, quickly he stepped back and clung on to the rocks face for some kind of safety, where he found himself gripping the boney claws of a dead Dragon. He looked out at the realm that was being constricted by that thick haze and so many torches burning in several spots, small towns had lit torches to try and carry on with their day to day lives, this comforted The King.

"The good people of Maglore never cease to amaze," He smiled, "no matter what they are put through they continue to survive. War, famine, the Black Plague and now even through this strange darkness, they carry on."

Far below he could see a small flicker of amber glow, a Man made fire. Sir Maximillious Mondt had arrived and made camp, another sight that filled him with hope. At least someone had believed his words. He could have stood there forever and gazed out at the sliced landscape, like two jigsaw pieces from two very different puzzles. It was the disturbed gravel that he heard rolling down the side of the mountain that tore him away from his musing and immediately he went for his dagger, gripping its handle tightly in his chapped and rough hands, it would be too risky to unsheathe Reignmaker in such close surroundings.

Trolls.

This was his initial thought and became very aware that he was not alone on this mountain. He had heard many tales of Mountain Trolls, never nice tales either, they were believed to be no better than the vermin that climb from ships in the ports, bringing with them pestilence and disease. Sebastian must be on his guard for Trolls had been known to attack with rocks and their own excrement, giving them the unseemly moniker of 'Muck Spreaders'. Either flying rock or dung could cause The King to lose his grip of footing and would fall to his death where if legend is too be believed, his carcass would be stripped of its flesh and guzzled down greedily by the hungry Trolls.

Sebastian surveyed the area as best as he could, the dark haze did not help, he could see very little, if there were Trolls hiding nearby it would be impossible to see them. He readied himself and began to climb once again. His fingers and palms throbbed, the jagged shards of rock grating away at the sensitive flesh, but still he ignored the discomfort and carried on upwards.

He finally reached the pathway and pulled himself up, he rolled slowly onto his back, looking up to the castle that still seemed like it was days away, but the burning torches looked welcoming and acted as a beacon for him. Sebastian gazed at the palms of his hands and grimaced as he moved his fingers, they had become rigged and fixed into a clawed position, blood trickled from wounds and thin layers had peeled free. He rose to his feet, brushing dust from his clothes, they were worn and torn in places and he now resembled a beggar more than he did a King. He gazed back at the vast Kayalian Mountain range, The Sun of Selym had now safety nestled itself behind its summit in the East, it formed an uninviting silhouette of dozens of sharp peaks cutting through the glow like the maw of some hideous, gigantic beast. He was now on the trail that had been so painstakingly excavated by Quildor Planesphere all those centuries ago.

If he looked to the West it was obvious that this was where The Bridge of Quildor came to an abrupt end. King Sebastian wondered whether Planesphere's exhausted carcass had been devoured by hungry Trolls and it made him shiver. It did not take him long to find the slope that snaked its way around the mountain like some constricting Serpent leading the way to Quirinus Castle. The trail leading to the top of Mount Quirinus caused the muscles in his legs to quiver, he was physically spent, but at least this part of the journey was less strenuous than scaling the rock face. The Season of Fervor was in full effect and although it was warm he found himself praising the dark haze for it shielded him from a heat that would have added another discomfort to his journey.

As Dayboy and Karbia continued their blossoming relationship, which meant Karbia curling up next to the large stallion and Dayboy not complaining about it, Sir Maximillious Mondt tucked into a meal of freshly slaughtered peagle that he had roasted on a spit over his fire. While this was going on at the foot of the mountain King Sebastian had reached the top and stood adjacent to the black jagged castle, slender windows glared back at him like glowing amber eyes. There was no drawbridge of portcullis to protect the castle as no army could every make the treacherous journey to take such a stronghold, it reminded Sebastian of his own Windmast Castle that was to built in a similar vein. It made him think of home and his Queen and his child, he brushed the thoughts aside, he could not give time to such musing as it may hinder his quest and influence a change of mind and heart.

He stood in the vast courtyard, surrounded by torches, the breeze joined him from the snowcapped peaks of North Point and caressed his brow that was clad with sweat, it was soothing. He started towards the large dark door, his boots thumping hard on the courtyard stones, thousands of different coloured stones made up the courtyard and it was not until Sebastian focused on them did he realise that the lighter stones created a shape in the courtyard, a gigantic sigil of The Mystic Circle. A pale moon entwined with a golden sun. As Sebastian took in this magnificent piece of artistry he heard the sound of falling rocks again and he stopped immediately grasping the handle of Reignmaker turning cautiously on the spot. Several creatures moved quickly between the torches using the quivering shadows to conceal them. He could hear their gurgling growls and the sound of bare feet slapping on stone as these mysterious creatures cavorted in the shadows.

"Trolls!" Growled Sebastian under his breath.

It was as if they were waiting for such an invitation because they appeared from the dark crevices in droves. There were more than The King had feared and they quickly surrounded him, small in stature, these ugly hunched characters scrambled around him, seemingly in haphazardness, but Sebastian could see that with each chaotic flurry of movement they tightened their snare. Their bodies were naked and scrawny with various patches of thick dark hair that covered their modesties, long hairy ears swayed from side to side as drool dripped from their bulbous bottom lips.

With his back was to the door and castle seemed like his only place for asylum. He unleashed Reignmaker from its scabbard and the torchlight collided with the blade, shafts of light blazed in the gloom causing the Trolls to cower from its brightness, instinctively shielding their sensitive black eyes.

"Come for me creatures and I shall have all your tongues!" King Sebastian roared, using the light that reflected from the sword against them and forcing them back to the shadows, but as he did this to one group another would get closer and he was forced to keep alternating his direction. Sebastian cautiously crept backwards trying to put distance between himself and the Trolls (a tactic that Sir Winstone had instilled him in) he unfortunately lost his footing, tripping over one of the protruding stones of the courtyard and he fell to the ground dropping the blade in the process. That was the opening that the hungry Trolls needed and suddenly they emerged from the shadows with such speed that The King would have never thought possible of the crooked creatures. Gurgling roars of triumph erupted around the courtyard and spiralled around the peaks of the neighbouring mountains. Sebastian saw the look in their dark orb like eyes, it was not a look of vengeance and murder that he had seen in other creatures like the Goblins and Cyclops, but desperation. These creatures were hungry.

As they closed in on him, he saw their protruding ribcages and their wrinkled skin that looked as tough as old boot leather, they were smeared with all manner of dirt and debris and the long tangled hair that grew from their gaunt frames was matted with dried feces. The smell of them on the breeze was enough to make The King snap from his musing and he clambered for Reignmaker, but it was too late he was surrounded. He could see hope in their faces, hope that they could return to their families that were hidden away in the unexplored crevices of

Mount Quirinus with a limb or some other edible souvenir from The King.

Sebastian felt for these creatures, but although his sacrifice could feed the Troll population steadily for a moon's turn he could not allow it, his fingertips tapped relentlessly at the Phoenix's beak on the sword's pommel and finally he managed to grip the handle of Reaignmaker and pointed it at them. The torchlight reflected, send shards of light at the Trolls once again, but this time it was not enough, hunger had taken them and made them impervious to Sebastian's shield of light. They closed in slowly now, they conserved their energy knowing that their meal could not escape. Sebastian made it to his feet and gripped the sword tightly, swiping it wildly in front of himself, but still they inched forward, the scent of stale breath, dung and dampness consumed him and it took all his composure to hold back the nausea that bubbled up in the back of his throat.

"Damn you!" He screamed, "I do not wish to harm you, but I cannot be your meal."

The Trolls stopped and looked at each other, their large nostrils sniffing loudly at the air as if they were communicating, they looked confused and one of them grunted and they started to move forward again, a hungry circle around the cornered King. He did not know whether the Trolls could even understand his words but he tried again, knowing that if he shouted loud enough it would halt their process and why they were confused he may be able to make a run for the door to the castle.

"I cannot give myself to you, for I have important business here. Important business that will effect us all!"

They stalled again, but the Troll that grunted for them to continue before growled again and they moved within touching distance, he could feel unfamiliar fingers tugging at his clothes and just as he was swarmed by them there was a burst of blinding white light that appeared that sent the Trolls scampering to the safety of their dark dwellings in the gaps of the rock face.

"What is this?" Sebastian gasped, covering his eyes from the brilliant blaze of light.

"Do not be afraid King Hartwaker."
The voice was gravelly and unpleasant, but he felt no threat from the tone and as he turned to face the voice, the silhouette of a hooded figure stood before him, the light glowed around him and then finally dispersed.

"The Trolls?" Sebastian cried looking around at the deserted courtyard, nothing but the wavering flames of the surrounding torches greeted his glances.

"Do not fear, for they have gone." Said the hooded figure. "They have not been harmed."

"Good, I would not wish for pain or discomfort on such pitiful, primitive creatures."
The figure cackled, it was unpleasant to Sebastian's ears, it reminded him of the hissing of a snake and somehow it sounded familiar to his ears.

"They are easily startled but they may return. Shall we go inside?" The figure asked, a pale outstretched emerged from confinement of an oversized sleeve and drew Sebastian's attention to the open door.

Sebastian sheathed Reignmaker, glad that he had not had to use it on creatures that he now felt sorry for and not fear.

"Who are you?" The King demanded.

"Of course!" The hooded figure bowed his head in reply, before removing his hood to reveal a pale balding head, peculiar pointed ears and a jagged grin.

"You're an Elf!" Sebastian gasped.

"Tis true, Your Majesty, the last of my kind."

"I could never have believed such a sight if I had not seen it with my own eyes."

"My name is Grimalkin, Your Majesty."
Something flashed in The King's mind, a memory of some kind that was obscured by a lavender haze.

"Is something the matter?" Grimalkin asked.
Sebastian shook away the strange apparition from his mind's eye.

"Nothing!" He grimaced. "Days of travel and lack of food and sleep I imagine."

"Yes, the early cometh of Gloam is effecting all our sleep I fear."
Sebastian stared at those magenta eyes of the Elf, something familiar, something he could not quite find in the locked doors of his memory.

"Shall we?" Grimalkin said and again gestured to the door.

"Aye!" Sebastian said, and although something in his head screamed at him like a banshee to not trust this Man, this Elf, the warm glow of the castle's innards looked very inviting.

213

Grimalkin led the way and King Sebastian followed taking one final look at the courtyard to make sure there were no Trolls loitering. There was not, it remained empty, the sigil of the sun and the moon in the cobbles of the yard looked back at him with an upside down gaze, their smiles turned to sorrow. He entered and the door closed behind them, a heavy thud that echoed through the Kayalian Mountains.

CHÃPTÉR 18

Ã QUÉÉN'S BLÉSSÏNG

ueen Marie Ann Hartwaker held her little Princess close to her ample bosom as she eagerly suckled at her teat. The Queen was very pleased with how quickly Vai-Ra had taken to her breast as she knew that many Ladies of House Vespa had struggled to manage the suckling part of Mardahood and most had to make do with a nursemaid to bring the milk to the child. Queen Marie Ann did not wish this, she wanted to connect with her child and be the one to nurture her daughter. Many scholars had declared that sharing the birth marda's milk with the offsprings not only brings the nutrients that only the birth marda can produce but also shares their bloodline, many believe that the child learns about the family's history through these feedings. Queen Marie Ann wanted nothing more than to be the one to instill these wonders upon her child, she would not allow her child's soft lips to suckle on the exhausted sack of flesh of some nursemaid that has fed a hundred children before.

The Princess had seemingly had her fill and withdrew from her marda's nipple, milk trickled from her lips which made the

Queen smile warmly. She wiped away the excess milk with a thin cotton cloth and gazed into her daughter's tired eyes. Weary eyelids heavy from her fill, hung over sparkling emeralds.

"You will be a true beauty of the realm." Said Queen Marie Ann as she pulled her silk gown back over her sore breast. She held her aloft as the sunlight shone through the balcony window of the tallest tower of Windmast Castle, her royal chambers had never looked so bright and alive, but yet it felt deserted to her heart, she longed for her love to return from his quest, a quest that some had been so bold as to call it a fool's quest.

"You shall break many a heart I am sure." She smiled at Vai-Ra who gurgled a reply in some absurd language, cloudy bubbles forming in her tiny mouth before her stomach sounded like the roar of trumpets welcoming the arrival of His Majesty himself, and with that she let out a mighty belch, indicating that she had most definitely had her fill.

"Well!" The Queen laughed. "That is most unladylike! What would they think of you at court?"
The Queen stood and swaddled Vai-Ra close to her, swaying her gently from side to side, already the young Princess' eyelids sagged heavily. She kissed her on her forehead, brushing her nose across the mass of golden curls that sprouted out of her head in disarray, she inhaled her scent, the aroma of youth and innocence was intoxicating.

"I bless you with my milk, I bless you with the knowledge of my ancestors and I bless you with the strength and bravery of your farda. I know these are not traits usually bestowed upon Princesses, but if you are to be Queen as your farda wills, then you will need such blessings for whatever hindrances you may face." She whispered to the now slumbering child.

The Queen stepped out of the royal chambers and onto the balcony, the day was glorious and her nostrils were met by the sweet scent of pollen that caressed the air. The stone balustrade was wrapped in vines of cherry blossom and dozens of hornets flitted from flower to flower humming a pleasant tune.

"The Season of Fervor is most definitely upon us little one." She swooned.

The warmth from the sun's rays, the cheery hornets, the succulent smell of blossoms, reminded her of her youth and growing up in Tendor at the Vespa family home of Hive House. Their land was covered with flowers and hornet apiaries stood erected like little houses, her farda Lord Nathaniel would tell her that little houses belonged to Sprites and that the hornets came to visit to bring them gifts of pollen and nectar, so they may bake sweet little honey cakes. She closed her eyes to reminisce, it was easy for her to conjure up the memories with the smells of blossom and the sound of hornets all around her. She remembered sitting on her farda's knee and looking out at those little apiaries, pointed roofs rising above the mass of surrounding flowers. He told her that the honey was special, very special honey indeed, magical even, he said it was made by the Sprites that lived in those apiaries. She chuckled to herself in her dreamy state and remembered questioning him thoroughly on the matter, not believing, but so wanting to

217

believe that his words were true. But he always had an answer that would corroborate his story making it impossible to not believe him. As a child she had wanted so much to tiptoe through those flowers and gaze upon the Sprites that she believed were inside hard at work making honey and cakes, but she daren't, for she knew deep down that it was but a tale, a tale that she wanted to believe so very badly. If she were to gaze upon the inner workings of the apiaries and see only hornets she would truly be disappointed, so she chose to believe, to believe in magic.

A cold breeze suddenly swept across the balcony which took her by surprise and tore her away from her woolgathering. She opened her eyes and the chill had dispersed, it was bitter and cold as if it had come straight from the tip of Adeve's Peak. She gazed out at the realm, the landscape had never looked so beautiful, she could see the monumental Willow of Kalfahr in full bloom of glorious greens and yellows. She gazed upon Kanka and to the distant Hills of Brockonbak where the Giants resided, if she focussed she could see their heads rising sporadically above the treetops. Obviously the North was dominated by the Kayalian Mountains, but on a day so pleasant even they looked solemn.

The day was so clear that she could even see the sun's rays greeting Lake Salivia, sparkling like a million diamonds. A smile caressed her lips until her eyes met the East, a thick blanket of darkness consumed it and that made her shudder, she held Vai-Ra close and thought of her King and his words.

Words that no one seemed to believe, emotion began to well up inside her, if Sebastian was right, what did this mean?

There was a knock at her door.

"Come." She called, her voice cackled as she fought her emotions.

"My cousin!" Called Sir Winstone. "It is I, I have come to gaze upon the Princess and pilfer her youth."

He entered the chamber with all the enthusiasm and zest of a thespian stepping through the curtains and onto the boards of a stage. He wore an exquisite red tunic, trimmed elegantly with golden thread and the sigil of House Hartwaker, the flaming phoenix. He was taken aback to see that the room was empty his hand instinctively wrapping tightly around the grip of his sword, Shard.

"Cousin?" He called out.

"Come join us on the balcony Winstone." She replied.

Sir Winstone relaxed and strode through the soft drapes that hung on either side of the balcony and stopped in awe.

"Don't move!" He gasped in theatrical fashion. "Is there anything more beautiful than marda and her child embraced on such a delightful canvas of sun and sky."

"You tease, cousin." She laughs as he joined her, brushing her cheek with a kiss.

"Not at all, Marie Ann, I have never seen you look so radiate, so alive!"

He gazed upon the sleeping Princess.

"Beautiful!" He smiled. "A gift from Adeve if ever there were one."

"I will not argue against those words cousin, for they are the truest you have ever spoken."

"But I do have one concern."

"Concern!" She gasped, examining Vai-Ra as she slept, her eyes frantically inquiring what problem her child could have.

"She sleeps too much." He declared playfully, she gave a heavy sigh of relief and Sir Winstone continued. "I wish to play with her, take her riding, hunting and pick fruit. But she is always sleeping."

"Winstone, she is but a babe in arms. She is not ready for such adventures."

"Adventure is everywhere my Queen."

There was a silence that fell between them and the playful tone of the conversation had now disappeared, they both looked to the East and then gazed back into each others eyes.

"You worry about Sebastian?" He asked.

"I do." She nodded, eyes welling with moisture, he turned back to the dark East, and wrapped his rough hand around her dainty one.

"This darkness is coming." He said, his tone was grave. "Just like he said it would."

She nodded and tears fell from her eyes, Sir Winstone pretended he could not see, he could not deal with women when they cry, it wasn't that he was a stern Man, he was humble and caring, but having no wife of his own he did not know how to act around such emotions.

220

"The word from the East is that they believe it to be The Season of Gloam come early."

"But that is preposterous!" She snapped. "We have entered the warmth of Fervor! How can it be two seasons at one time?"

"I agree." He nodded, eyes locked on to the East. "The King's words were indeed true, but the people of the East no not of these words to do anything about it. I do hope he has reached..." He realised what he had said and not wanting to upset his Queen further he manipulated his words, "...his words, I hope they have reached the ears of the Lords and Ladies and that they believe. They can then fight against whatever this darkness is, but until then..."

"How was court today?" She asked, changing the direction of conversation. "I could not bear the burden of their worries and strifes today, for I have my own to worry about."

"As well as it could in the absence of their King." He replied. "I do not know how Sebastian does it every day, the throne is uncomfortable to my buttocks."
They laughed to slice through the trepidation of serious matters.

"There are worries of course, fear is gripping them, fear that their King is... that his words were indeed true. They are not blind they see the darkness in the East. They ask me of my counsel on what should the kingdom do, but I am merely a Knight and have no knowledge of politics. There are some that look to take the power and make the decisions, but I have been

221

left in control and I will not relinquish that honour until Sebastian returns."

"What do you tell them?"

"I speak to them as a Man of war and a Knight of many battles. I tell them that the walls of Windmast are impregnable, they shall not fall nor be taken by Man or Beast."

"And is this true? Is it impregnable or are they but the words of dead Kings?"

The Knight had no answer to his Queen, the castle had only been taken once by the Dwarves who discovered the secret passages that had now all been filled in. He honestly did not know whether Windmast would stand up to a full-fledged attack. The Queen walked away from Sir Winstone and back inside the royal chambers where she sat back into her nursing chair and stared at her bundle.

Sir Winstone stood in the doorway gazing on them both, his mind wandering to what could happen if the darkness came for them.

"I wanted to join him." He said.

"I know."

"He was adamant he went alone. Damn him! I could have helped him... protected him."

"You talk as if he has failed!" She snapped angrily.

Winstone swept across the chambers and onto the fine carpets that consumed the cold stone and knelt before her.

"You misunderstand my words, my Queen. I am guilty of doing nothing. Our King wanders the realm unaided and I blame myself for not being more persistent in challenging him. I should be with him on this quest."

"You are to protect us cousin, that is your lot."

"Aye!" He nodded, his eyes too were moist with emotion. "I just want to be of service."

"And you are." She smiled at him and brushed the tear that fell down his withered cheek. "You are sworn to protect me and the Princess."

"And that I will." He nodded, rising to his feet and turning away to hide his tears. "I will be held to my vows to the very end."

Again there was an uncomfortable silence between them as they both thought of Sebastian and wondered. He was Husband, Lover, Farda, Brother, Uncle, Cousin, Friend, Knight, King and Man. He was all these things to them, he was the realm and without him they felt lost.

Queen Marie Ann swallowed hard and asked the question that had been tugging at her heart since her beloved had left.

"Will he return?"

There was a moment of silence again as if the same question were on the mind of the Knight.

"Of course!" He announced and smiled broadly, "I know Sebastian as well as my own family, he gave his word he would return and return he will."

He stroked the golden curls on Vai-Ra's scalp and smiled.

"You will both see your King again I promise you."

CHÃPTÉR 19
THÉ ÉÃGÉRNÉSS ÖF GÖBLÏNS

s Sir Maximillious Mondt stoked the flames of his fire and settled down to rest his head a while, he was unaware of the eyes that scrutinised his every move, that salivated at every breath his broad chest took. From crevices in the rock face concealed by shadow watchful eyes paid close attention. The bowels of Mount Quirinus swarmed with Trolls, but these eyes were not glistening black orbs overwhelmed with hunger and desperation, these eyes were yellow and burned with depravity. These stalking eyes belonged to most despicable race in all of Maglore, Goblins.

"When will he sleep?" Hissed a voice like broken rocks, "I yearn to slit his throat and taste his blood on my lips."
There were three sets of amber eyes fixed on the unknowing Knight, gathered together in a cluster at a narrow gape in the mountain, they were quite well hidden.

"Nothing tastes better than Knight's blood." Gargled a deeper voice.

"Apart from royal blood, Sluug!" The sound of his long

moist tongue licking saliva from his fangs filled the cavern, "Yes! So much sweeter is the royal bloodline."

"It must be the pride that runs through their veins that makes it taste so sweet, Brood." Chuckled Sluug.

"You can keep your blood!" Scoffed the feline purr of the third Goblin. "I want is cock! Lovely with a bit of rock salt it is."

"Your craving for Man cock is becoming quite obsessive, Kraag!" Moaned Brood.

"Yes!" She hissed, eyes wide and her snakelike tongue wiggling like a worm on a hook. "He looks like he would have plenty to gorge myself on! Yes, indeed!" She caressed her sagging breasts with creeping talons.

"Let me take him now why he is unaware." Sluug asked, removing his humongous broad sword from its scabbard that was strapped between his gargantuan shoulder blades. "Let Guzzler be the blade to cut down this proud Knight."

"It should be my Geld that ends this mortal's life!" Snapped Kragg, swiftly unveiling her serrated short blade from her belt. "I'll skin his cock and balls and roast them over flame until they're crisp!"

"No!" Seethed Brood. "We cannot."

The two sheathed their weapons and grumbled miserably.

"Why not?" Sluug sulked, "I wish to rip his veins out and Kraag wishes only for the taste of Man cock!" Sluug leaned in close to Brood and whispered into his long pointed ear. "Surely you would wish to dip your tongue in his open throat and drink his valiant blood?"

225

Brood licked his lips emphatically as he imagined the piece of artistry that Sluug was painting, he looked almost lost in his malevolence and reached for his own weapon, a blunted axe cleaver called Craver. His eyes glowed with the lust for blood, Sluug and Kraag shared a hopeful glance, when Brood got lost in bloodlust it usually meant that Man cock was on the menu.

"No!" He snapped and hissed as he pushed the large Goblin away.

"You try to tempt me with your words. We have orders to obey and obey them we must."

"I say dung to the orders!" Sluug growled.

"Aye!" Kraag agreed. "It is only one Knight, he will not be missed."

"Aye!" Echoed Sluug. "Dung to orders!"

"Dung indeed!" Came a voice from behind them and suddenly they were illuminated by torchlight. Their scarred skin, the texture and colour of an olive glistened in the light, as did the Man armour they wore in random parts of their bodies, trophies from fallen foes of past battles. Their amber eyes widened on seeing their General standing before them and they collapsed on scabbed knees.

"General Feng!" Brood gasped, collapsing into a cowardly pool at his leader's feet. "They wanted to kill the Knight, but I told them no!"

"Stop your grovelling, Brood and rise! Stop wriggling at my feet, you are not a worm!"

"Yes, General!" He stood, quickly followed by his allies,

they stood as orderly as they could for a misshapen band of Goblin cutthroats.

The General stood broad and strong, his golden armour was amassed with hundreds of small spikes protruding from the shoulder plates and his horned helm. Clad in gold he glistened against the flames of the torch that he held in his clawed hand. The armour was worn and flaunted the riggers of many a past battle, as did the other Goblins, but Feng's had something that the others did not have, etched into the plates was a tally, an ongoing inventory of Man that he had slain in battle which he affectionally referred to as his Massacre of Man.

General Feng strode back and forth inspecting them as he did so, three very different soldiers garbed in animal furs, random fragments of armour and decorated in the bones of Man. Feng gazed upon the huge mass of torso and shoulders that belonged to Sluug, he stopped and looked up at him, glaring intensely at the Goblin's broken and scarred face, the furrowed brow of a simpleton.

"Sluug" Feng growled, Sluug straightened up as much as his bent spine would allow. "The largest of all the Goblin army! The Beast of Grotte who has pummelled the skulls of many a Man in battle!"

Sluug grinned a crooked smile of broken shards, as he gleamed with pride.

"They call you 'Vein-Ripper'" Feng spat, saliva spraying on the wide scarred chest of Sluug and dripping down the contours of his barrelled stomach. Sluug did not bat an eye as if being spat on was a daily occurrence, if anything he looked pleased.

"You will have chance to rip those veins of Man again and inhale the gore within their cowardly innards, I can promise you that!"
Sluug smiled wide and sadistic.

"But not today!" Feng announced and moved along to the next Goblin in the line, Kraag.

"Kraag, my sweet!" Feng hissed and she stared at him, almost seductively, like a whore in a brothel filled with Man with much Dollin to spend. A long slender tongue slithered out of her narrow mouth and flirted with the moisture on her lips.

"Tiny in stature and snake-like in stealth." Feng smiled at her and reached out with his clawed hand and caressed the oily flesh of her face, he like many had had the pleasure of her company many times. She playfully snapped at his hand, her vicious serrated fangs lurching like an animal trap.

"It is not playtime, Kraag." Feng grinned and she hissed in reply as if disappointed. "You will have your time to play soon enough! They call you 'Gobbler'!" Feng cackled, the sound fluttered around the cavern as if it were the wings of a Bat-Fiend.

"And tis true that many a Man has felt your barbaric wrath upon their ballocks! You too will have the chance to taste the flesh of Man's flaccidness again."
Kraag licked at her lips, almost euphoric, her eyelids flickered as she bit down on her bottom lip and drew blood with just the imagery of her General's words.

"But not today!" Feng hissed, her face fell again in disappointment.

Feng's eyes met the Goblin, Brood, he bowed again, almost grovelling to his General.

"Brood..." Feng hissed with contempt, the Goblin race were joined together in common cause, the War against Man, but that did not mean that they liked each other, they were tolerant of each others existence, "...they say, 'Blood-Licker' in your presence."

"Yes, my General!" Brood hissed, bowing again. "It is a honour to hear my name on your lips."

Feng grabbed the smaller Goblin by his throat and hoisted him. "I've told you to stop grovelling! You will gain no favour from me with false smiles and insincere words."

Brood gasped for air, his tongue whipped around in a frenzy as if looking to lasso the air he needed so desperately and his scrawny limbs wriggling in the forceful grip of Feng. Kraag and Sluug smiled sadistically at Brood's misfortune, it would not concern or distress them if their General ripped the Goblin's throat out there and then, for Goblin's cared not for each other, unlike Man they lacked all compassion for their fellow species. Feng let go of Brood and he fell in a heap, clutching at his throat as he struggled to catch his breath.

"Your mouth will one day be the death of you Brood!"

"But... General...what have I...done?" He gasped.

"You can't tell me that your presence here is due to Sluug or Kraag?"

"Well..." Brood started, but was interrupted by Feng.

229

"Whatever lies are about to trickle from your maw means nothing to me. You should all know better than to be here so close to a Knight. The King of Man meets with the Wizard above as we speak. Are you so foolish to risk so much for the blood of one Man?"

"But General, The King is here..." Brood sneered, "Think how he would taste on your tongue?"

Feng stared at him as he rose, contorted like a spider, he appeared to be all limbs as he approached the General. Feng looked on with confusion etched across his forehead.

"And why shouldn't the General of the Goblin Army be the one to slay the King of Man?"

Feng looked at Brood who seemed to contort around him like a python, then unleashed a large hand across the face of Brood knocking back to the ground again.

"Your words of persuasion will no work on me worm!"

"I'm sorry, General! I led them here yes, but only to look for food, a juicy rat perhaps or a mountain fox. It's been days since we have eaten."

Feng glared at him with absolute disgust, his strong hands gripped the handle of his sword known as Flesh-Stripper, the most famous sword in Goblin lore, the cruel serrated blade that was once held by The Goblin King himself, Grotte. How he came of it remains a mystery, the moist forked tongues of Goblins had wagged with many a tale, most believing that Feng was indeed the one who cast the killing blow to their King and who would dare try to take it from him?

Brood's yellow eyes widened with horror and he fell at the General's feet blubbering.

"He tells the truth, General." Kraag sighed reluctantly, the perverse part of her would have surely loved to see Feng shred through Brood's slimy flesh and end his life, but for reasons known only to her she intervened and saved the retch's life. Feng looked at her with disbelief visible on his face and was met by a pair of unenthusiastic nodding heads.

"Tis true General." Sluug grunted. "It was Kraag and I that wished to purge the Knight."

Feng nodded, believing their words to be true and Brood watched under a thick layer of sweat as Feng's grip fell loose, Brood breathed a sigh of relief that could be heard around the cavern.

"The Knight must not be harmed, not this day."

The bloodthirsty Goblins showed their distaste with the bearing of their teeth but respected the ruling that their General had put in place.

"We have waited too long for us to bathe in the blood of Man I know, I echo your frustrations. But we must listen to Lord Grimalkin, he has seen the prophecy told in the stars above, he tells me that the time is almost upon us. But until he gives me such an order, then we must remain in the shadows."

There was suddenly a sound of footsteps that attained their attention and they turned gripping their arms tightly. The sound got louder and louder, bare feet rapidly slapping on hard stone. Feng directed the torch in the direction of the footsteps and growled. "Who goes there?"

The sound stopped abruptly, and the torch caught the visitor, shaping a gigantic silhouette on the ceiling of the cavern, it was a disjointed shadow that quivered eerily due to the dancing flame.

"By Sloore! What is it?" Whimpered Brood.

"It's the snow beast of the mountains!" Sluug groaned.

"Impossible!" Feng scoffed.

The shadow moved awkwardly, watching them, stalking them, the sound of rocks being disturbed under feet echoed around them.

"It is!" Kraag seethed. "It is Snowka!"

"Who goes there I say?" Feng growled again, Flesh-Stripper was quickly unsheathed, jagged edges shining like the fangs of a Feral, eager to taste blood.

"It is I, General..." Came a squeak of a voice that hardly met their ears it was so unimposing and a small creature stepped into the light, "...Pooka."

There was a relaxing of arms and a unified snort of derision at the newcomer.

"It's the halfbreed!" Spat Brood.

"Spawn of the union of a Goblin and a Troll." Kragg seethed, "I spit on it!" And she did, and Pooka wiped the mucus from his tiny snout. They glared upon him as though he did not belong, and he did not.

Pooka stood garbed in nothing but an old sack, that was frayed and worn. He was waist high to a common Goblin, with long gangly limbs, his flesh was the tone of a fallen leaf of Yield and leathery in appearance.

"Well?" Feng growled, disgusted at the sight of the halfbreed that stood before him. "What is it?"

"Please, General..." Pooka murmured as he stepped toward them, the frightening silhouette behind him, growing less intimidating as he drew nearer and it shrank behind him.

"Spit it out, Runt!" Kraag hissed aggressively.

Long hairy ears hung in front of his face, his bulging eyes remained focused on his feet, watching as his long hairy toes wriggled nervously beneath him.

"I bring a message from Grimalkin." Pooka stuttered.

Feng strode towards the halfbreed and kicked him hard too the unforgiving floor of rock and dirt.

"How dare you, halfbreed!" Feng growled, the others watched on with wide eyes and a sadistic smiles.

Pooka cowered on the floor, his entire body physically shaking, this was his life and had been since he could remember, a half Troll, half Goblin had seemingly no place anywhere. He was rejected by the Trolls when his marda died and Grimalkin took him in as a slave, but the Goblins too rejected him and treated him ever so badly that Pooka would cry himself to sleep on many a night.

"You shall refer to our Dark Master as Lord Grimalkin!" Feng spat.

"Yes, General..." Pooka whimpered, "Forgive my tongue. I meant no disrespect to The Dark Master."

"Stand up!" He growled again.

"Yes, get up worm!" Hissed Brood, Feng turned and glared at him angry eyes of amber and Brood again cowered behind the massive Sluug.

"Yes, General of course!" Pooka said as he picked himself from the floor, his elbows scrapped and bleeding, "I do not wish to antagonise I..."

"What?" Sluug grunted.

"What is the word you speak?" Feng growled angrily and seized Pooka by his long delicate ears and hoisted him into the air as one would do with a coney they had caught.

"Is this some half breed tongue you mock us with?"

"No, General!" Pooka bleated, his face contorted with pain and embarrassment. "Just a word I discovered in a scroll."

"Aye, the Runt reads." Kraag hissed, "I have seen him with those scrolls."

"Pah!" Feng scoffed, dropping him unceremoniously to the ground again. "Reading of words? What good will come of that? Reading is a trait of Man! You're not a Man lover are you Runt?"

"He's a traitor!" Brood hissed.

"Let's pull his ears off and teach him what happens to traitors." Sluug groaned.

"Enough, rabble!" Feng cackled and his eyes met Pooka's large orbs moist with tears like two delicate raindrops, "I grow tired of this folly! Tell me what message has The Dark Master sent from above?"

"The Man King, Hartwaker meets with The Grand One, Pagmai at the mystic Circle." Pooka spoke rapidly.

234

"We know this!" Feng growled, growing increasingly impatient with every word that spilt from the half breed's mouth.

"Yes, of course." Pooka nodded. "Lord Grimalkin has said that the time is now to prepare your army."

The eyes of the Goblins seemed to twinkled with euphoria of the bloodbath to come.

"Is this true?" Feng asked. "Is this wise with the King so near?"

"The Dark Master has said this is the perfect time as guards will be lowered and the King will be unaware of the attack and helpless to stop us." Pooka said.

"Tis true." Feng pondered.

"You are to lead the attack on Kalfahr and send armies to Foxall, Trinpola and Tendor."

"What of Shantanga, Elken, Kanka?" Feng frowned. "And Hammillda & Voltora! What of those?"

"Shantanga will be seized by the Zwulf..."

"ZWULF!" Feng growled, spitting with hatred at the mere mention of the race. Pooka cowered under the General's wrath.

"Why are those retched Beast-Men involved? I was not told this!"

"I know not." Shrugged Pooka. "All I know is that these are your orders."

Feng slapped blood and saliva from the mouth of Pooka, who again found himself on the uncomfortable floor of the cavern.

"Insolence!" Feng growled.

235

"No, General!" Pooka whimpered. "The Zwulf have pledged their allegiance to Lord Grimalkin."

"Would you dare lie to me, Runt?"

"No, General! Never!" Pooka shook his head rapidly from side to side. "These are the words of The Dark Master, I only repeat them as I am told to do so."

"What of the other kingdoms?" Feng sneered. "Tell me, quickly!"

"Hammillda and Elken will be dealt with by The Children of the Shrouded Realm. Lord Grimalkin will release the Black Imps of Sloore upon them."

"Yes!" Feng hissed, a serrated smile caressing his chapped lips.

"But what of Kanka? And Valtora?" Brood asked. "Giants will not be defeated by Imps alone?"

"And Valtora has powerful magic protecting it." Kraag added. "How does The Dark Master plan to take the Fairy kingdom with Imps?"

"He will unleash a Dragon's fire upon them." Pooka whispered, just the words terrified him.

Goblin eyes widened with what appeared to be fear to Pooka, but he dared not say such a thing.

"A Dragon…" Feng gasped, unbelieving.

"But there are no Dragons!" Brood hissed. "He lies! Kill him!"

Feng unleashed the back of his hand into the face of Brood, silencing him immediately.

"The Dark Master is indeed all powerful." Feng said. "This Runt is a lot of things, but his tongue does not lie, I can see the fear in his eyes, they tell the truth. If Lord Grimalkin has a Dragon on our side then there will be no stopping us!"

The Goblins cackled like a pack of frenzied jackals, Pooka slowly pulled himself up and crept away, tears in his eyes and a pain in his heart, he did not wish to see Maglore become ash and bone, but who was he to stop these powerful beings, he was nothing but a half breed.

The Goblins glared out of the cavern and watched the Knight slip into a world of slumber as the fire shimmered off his armour.

"It would appear that Knight is on the menu after all." Feng cackled.

CHÃPTÉR 20
THÉ MYSTÏC CÏRCLÉ

rimalkin led King Sebastian up through the levels of the castle, through spiralling stairwells and dank twisting tunnels of dark stone, it was as if these corridors had been formed by a giant worm that had contorted here and there, leaving behind its damp mucus clinging to the walls. The castle was centuries old and had many secrets to tell, secrets that would make even the wisest Man reassess what they knew of the realm's history. The structure was Dwarf built, constructed from the dark shards that were carved from the mountain itself. It was an impregnable dark fortress able to repel any outsiders unwise enough to try and take the castle by force.

When 'The Elf Queen' Queen Evaa Quirinus lost her grip on the holding it was due to her lack of judgement in what friends she kept and being too trusting of them. King Argo Calgaras manipulated her brother G'nora to poison her wine in return for a Lordship and treasures beyond anything he could comprehend. G'nora did just that, all be it begrudgingly as he fought heavily with his own conscience when committing the deed, her words were unkind to him that particular day and in anger he let the poison slip into her goblet. As the poisoned wine dripped from her dead lips, so did the tears from her brother's eyes. He quickly fled Mount Quirinus, leaving the gates open for King Calgaras to stroll in and take whatever he wished, G'nora was consumed by guilt and has not been heard from in centuries.

Mount Quirinus is indeed another impregnable castle built by the intelligent Dwarves and it is true that any castle constructed by Dwarf hands has never been taken in assault. But it is the betrayers and assassins that already walk within the walls of these holdings that are mightier than any army that awaits outside.

King Sebastian was amazed at how unkempt the castle was, if it wasn't for the burning of torches in every corridor and the presence of his guide, he would have believed this castle deserted.

"I know what you are thinking my Liege." Grimalkin spoke, his crackling tone reverberating around him on the narrow corridor walls, it was all to close for him, it made his flesh crawl as if infested by lice.

"You do?" Sebastian scoffed, not sure whether he knew that he had thought better of such powerful beings like Wizards and Witches, never expecting them to live in such squalor.

Grimalkin cackled as if he had just read the King's inner monologue.

"The Mystic Circle no longer use the lower levels of the castle." Grimalkin stated. "Only the higher levels and the towers are in use on a daily basis."

"I see." Replied Sebastian who had just trodden in something soft that squelched under the sole of his boot.

"Possibly Troll dung, my liege?" Grimalkin suggested not even looking back. "They get in through narrow crevices on occasion, they cause no bother, they are only looking for scraps of food."

"Indeed!" Sebastian cringed as he wiped the boot aggressively on the jagged wall to remove what he could.

"We are almost at the Circle." Grimalkin announced as they turned a corner and was met by a distinct difference in the tone and decor. The walls were clean and lit well by the burning torches, flames that constantly changed colour, flames of enchantment.

"Fascinating!" Sebastian gasped, reaching out to touch the flame. "Bewitched flame!"

"Be careful my Liege." Grimalkin warned. "The fires indeed dance exquisitely, but they still burn like any other flame."

The pair turned onto a long corridor, a large double door stood at its end, the sigil of the Mystic Circle's Sun, Moon and Stars had been painstakingly carved into the thick wood and painted very precisely. The sigil could be seen on several tapestries that hung from the walls as well as magnificent oil paints of the circle's members, that appeared to be enchanted themselves. The eyes watched as they approached the double doors.

"Bear them no mind, my Liege, just more trickery." Grimalkin smiled, Sebastian did not like that smile. "First class wizardry, second rate artistry."

Although Grimalkin had been courteous and pleasant to the King, there was still something about him that he did not trust. Sebastian was halted by the inclusion of a piece that looked out place in this world of wizardry.

"A suit of armour?" He exclaimed, examining it closely.

"Ah, yes, the armour that Pagmai wore in battle at The Rage of Man." Grimalkin answered. "He served with your ancestor the great, Grayfall Hartwaker, if my recollection is correct?"

"Aye!" Sebastian nodded, still hypnotised by the armour that shimmered like water, it seemed to be alive to his eyes, "I never knew that he ever did battle or drew sword!"

"Only once, my Liege!" Grimalkin added. "The Scrolls of History tell us that he believed that Maglore would indeed be in more capable hands under Man's rule. The Elves seen as not to be trusted and selfish. So he sided with Man in battle, showing a good account of himself I hear, using staff and broad sword..." He pointed to the sword that was leaning lazily against the suit, a hilt of black, encrusted with amethysts that winked in the torchlight,

"...He called it Hex."

The suit of armour was black and was trimmed elegantly with the same gemstones that were fixed into the hilt and sheath of the sleeping sword. Floating above the chest plate was the helm, large flamboyant feathers of purple and lavender burst

241

out from its comb which would have done one of two things in battle Sebastian thought, looked magnificent as he sliced through Elves with magic and Hex or made him a target with such ostentation. There was no visor attached to the helmet, Sebastian speculated whether this was an act born out of stupidity or vanity, only one of the two reasonings seem to conform to his thoughts.

"No visor?" He spoke to himself. "Madness."

"Indeed!" Cackled Grimalkin. "But let us not forget that Pagmai would have been shielded by spells or surely would never have taken to the battlefield. The armour, I believe was of only cosmetic value."

The armour was indeed an incredible sight to behold, forged by a first class blacksmith for sure, it would have fit Pagmai like a glove, comfortable and durable. It had amazingly held its shine for centuries, it still flickered with signs of magic, a shimmer of lilac glowed around the plates and helm. Sebastian touched it, the chest plate was warm to the touch, not like normal steel which always seemed to remain cold.

"He was of course responsible for Claarac's Grave too, but I am sure you have heard that tale before."

Sebastian had heard of Wizard versus Dragon, but did not realise that it was Pagmai that was responsible.

"What think you of your Master's involvement in the war that eradicated your species?" Sebastian asked and for the first time there was no immediate answer from his guide and it was impossible to read this Elf's face for it seemed to hide wonders and horrors behind those enchanted eyes.

"It was a long time ago." Grimalkin said, "I hold no grudge."

Without another word Grimalkin pushed open the doors, it seemed to take such an effort for such a frail looking creature.

"Behold, The Mystic Circle." Grimalkin said with a contorted bow, gesturing for The King to enter, which he did with a subtle nod of appreciation. The doors closed behind him with Grimalkin remaining on the outside, Sebastian thought this odd as he did not join the rest of the Circle, at least he thought that he should be introduced. But he had no time to dwell on such matters because before him there was a long wooded table, etched in the middle with the Circle's sigil and amassed with food and wine. A group sat around the table and their merriment was interrupted by the slamming of the doors, then all eyes were upon The King, who gazed around the room before settling at the head of the table and the Master of The Mystic Circle himself.

"The Grand One!" Sebastian announced with a bow of his head. "Pagmai, it is a honour."

Pagmai sat at the head in a high backed chair that was carved beautifully with astrological signs, deep purple cushions fitted for comfort in the backrest and one could only presume the seat too. A frail vessel wrapped in a purple gown, decorated in tiny silver stars encrypted with amethyst and diamond. His skin hung loose from his old face like an ill-fitting tunic, a hairless head plastered with dried flakey skin, that glowed in the magical torchlight and a long white beard that was peppered with shots of grey hung from his ancient face, his

243

moustaches were painstaking braided and the ends disappeared out of view underneath the table.

"A King Hartwaker!" Pagami exclaimed. "Here?" His skin contorted and creased like worn leather, and suddenly Sebastian wondered whether he was going to be welcomed warmly. The old Wizard examined him with wary but wise eyes, his sclera no longer white but yellow and bloodshot from broken vessels, but life continued to dance in those eyes still.

"Please forgive my intrusion." Sebastian announced, "I must speak with you on an urgent matter."

Pagmai remained the same, he did not rise in the presence of the King and seemed unmoved by his unannounced arrival. Sebastian gazed around the table all eyes wounding him with their stabbing stares. Nine sat around the long table that seated eleven, two chairs remained empty, Sebastian wondered whether one of them belonged to Grimalkin. Two chairs at the foot of the table were empty, but even though he was King of the realm he knew never to sit in someone else's dwelling without an invitation. His eyes gazed around the table and greeted each representative with a glance. First on his left was a Smidge, a very rare occurrence for The King it had been years since he had laid his eyes on a Smidge. The species were no species at all, the looks of Man, but their growth stunted halfway, smaller in size and stature than a Dwarf. Genuinely these creatures were unpleasant natured and did not associate well with other species, but from the table full of bizarre individuals maybe he was wrong about them. The Smidge sat upon a stool, his feet dangling high above the floor that was covered with several rugs, he glared with ugly untrusting eyes at him, a mouthful of food, then the Smidge belched loudly and that was Sebastian's cue for his eyes to move on.

A jittery fellow met his gaze, a silk turban wrapped around his head and a long brown beard that clung to his chin, he was clad in a silk gown that shimmered in the light, and still he refused to make eye contact with The King, instead sipped at his wine slowly.

Sebastian was taken aback by the beauty that met his gaze next, an Elf Witch. Sebastian did not know whether he was more surprised of how radiant she was or that he had seen two Elves this day, he started to disbelieve the Scrolls of History that he had grown up reading, Elves were not extinct. Her skin was as pale as snow, almost transparent, long platinum hair adding to her allure, she raised an eyebrow at the King and he realised he had been staring for too long, and quickly his eyes flitting to the next seat and another Witch. This time a comely and buxom Lady, dressed in an emerald green gown like the Ladies of court would wear when taking part in an evening of Carole. Her ensemble was finished with a flamboyant tiara of wild flowers atop a bed of thick red curls. She almost smiled at him before lifting up an apple from her plate and staring at it until it became consumed with green flame, Sebastian gasped, but her attention was fully focused on the flame that rose from the apple.

His eyes met with Pagmai again at the head but still they looked at him insidiously, a female hand gently lay itself down upon the arm of Pagmai, this action caused a shift in

Sebastian's gaze once again and on a small chair next to The Grand One sat a kind looking Witch staring back at him. She was old but the years had been kind to her and her hair had kept its natural gold which was draped either side of her narrow face. She too wore the same colours as Pagmai, she gestured to him with the slightest of nods and Sebastian reciprocated the gesture.

The eyes that met him next were that of a dog's, brown and wondrous and full of questions, it sniffed the air, seemed to loose interest and settle on the lap of the Man in the seat, he stroked the dog gently and it seemed to go to sleep. The eyes of the Man were wild, they mimicked that of the dog's then seemed to change with each glance.

An Animan!

A species that he had never come across in all his years, for they were indeed rare, so rare in fact that many do not believe that such a creature exists, but The King believed for he was looking at one now.

How fascinating it must be for a Man to have the ability to converse with animals.

He looked like any other Man and wore splendid clothes and fair hair that sat at his shoulder, there was no way of knowing that he was anything but a Man apart from those eyes, those animalistic eyes.

Sebastian's eyes almost burst from their sockets in awe of the next member seated at the table of The Mystic Circle, one single eye winked back at him through a curtain of black hair, a pale and jagged gaunt face peeking out under the dark veil.

A Witch... a Cyclops!

After several moments she lost interest and focussed her attention on the bowl that sat in front of her, it looked like chicken broth and did look inviting to The King's hungry stomach. The one eyed crone retrieved a small vial from a long black shroud and held it between black clawed fingertips, of which there were only three, a synonymous feature of the Cyclops species. The crimson formula encased moved like oil, she removed the cork and poured it into the broth, her large eye fixed on the King through the process, the liquid mixed with the broth and bubbled in a frenzy, she took her hideous claw and stirred, her dark chapped lips jittered as she began some silent incantation. The carcass of the chicken rose up in the bowl and flapped its wing of bone and meat, Sebastian held the vomit that mutinied in his throat, what was this horrendous sight he was witnessing? The chicken (or what was left of it) left the bowl and started to peck around the table as if searching for corn, the crone cackled to herself. The dog's ears pricked up and it sat up quickly, Sebastian saw the Animan's eyes reflect that of the dog's again and whispered in its floppy ear, the dog barked loudly before bursting onto the table and dashing towards the chicken carcass, he snatched it up in his jaws and leapt from the table, disappearing with his prize underneath. The one eyed crone hissed at the Animan who returned a smirk in her direction.

What madness is this? These Wizards and Witches mistreat their gifts. They play children's games!

247

The rotund Wizard next to her laughed loudly, food and ale spilling from his maw and lodging itself in his bushy red beard, he held a hefty tankard in his large mitt and when he looked at The King he stopped and took a hefty swig of his ale.

The last seated at the table was an horrendous looking crone, luckily the majority of her face was hidden under a hood of black, she cackled cruelly as she eyed him with one milky eye visible under the shroud. Sebastian eyed her plate and noticed a large grey rat on it, still twitching with life, its entrails oozing out on the plate in front of her. Again the vomit bubbled up in Sebastian's throat, but as King of Maglore he had become accustomed to holding whatever wished to escape from his throat until he had thought of the consequences. He glanced away and then back at the plate and it was but a chicken leg, her eye twinkling mischievously.

She is but playing games with my vision, showing me what she wants me to see.

Suddenly the Smidge spoke, with a squeak to his voice but a face serious. "Why does it smell like Troll shit in here?"

The table erupted with raucous laughter and Pagmai rose spritely from his chair wearing a large inviting smile.

"I'm sorry, King Sebastian!" He laughed moving around the table quickly to greet him. "Just folly! Just folly!"

Sebastian was startled but gazed around the laughing faces and realised they had japed him and he chuckled along with them as they met him with respectful bows of the head and raises of goblets and tankards.

248

"I was beginning to believe that my presence was unwelcome here." Sebastian said.

"Nonsense!" Pagmai laughed as he approached, his glorious gown sparkling with life as had his armour in the hallway, a glowing orb hung around his neck on a chain of silver, it was mostly hidden by his mass of beard but Sebastian saw it winking.

"Hartwaker King's are always welcome at The Mystic Circle. We were expecting you."

"You were?" Sebastian asked.

"Of course! Yodel informed us days ago that you were on your way. We did expect you yesterday though, so we forgive your lateness." Pagmai laughed and slapped The King on his back.

"Forgive my husband." Said the Witch that sat next to Pagmai. "But he does like to play games with guests, royal or otherwise."

"Tis forgiven!" Sebastian laughed, "I would not be a true King if I could not laugh at myself."

"True words, My King! True words!" Pagmai laughed gesturing to the table. "Come, drink and eat with us and tell us why you are here."

"Pagmai are you forgetting something?" His wife announced.

"Ha!" He laughed again, "I get carried away. I have not introduced you to the Circle. Sit, my King, sit and drink!"

Pagmai returned to his seat and Sebastian moved towards the two empty chairs focused on Pagmai as he announced the names and prowess of the Circle.

"The Smidge is Grooble, my cup bearer. Grumpy little bastard and drinks more wine than he serves."

The table erupted again with laughter, Grooble just grunted.

"Yodel, our astronomer. I call him 'The Stuttering Stargazer'!"

The jittery Man, nodded nervously at the King and held up his goblet in respect. "M-my K-King!" He stuttered.

"Haras Lunarc, last of the Elf Witches." Pagmai announced. "Manipulator of the elements. Water and flame be her friend."

"Your Highness, it is a pleasure." She said softly, with a gentle bow of her head.

Pagmai said as he held out a hand towards the Witch on his righthand side.

"They call her Marda Nurture, the power of giving life to plants is her gift. A beauty indeed is Hyacynthia." She smiled alluringly, fluttering her soft pools at Sebastian, the flowered tiara bloomed as she did. She thrust forward her heaving bosom for all to see.

"Put them away Hyacynthia! This is the King!" Pagmai laughed and she blushed heavily.

Pagmai settled into his chair and grasped his wife's hand and kissed it.

"My wife, my soul, My Holleet!" He smiled, love and

magic sparkled in his wise eyes and Sebastian wondered which was the more powerful force, be it magic or love?

"It is an honour, My King." Holleet smiled.

"The honour is mine, M'Lady." Sebastian bowed as he found his chair, but did not sit until he had been introduced to all the circle.

"Ah!" Padmai cried. "This be 'The Whisperer', Gallian Grund!"

Grund smiled sincerely and was joined by his dog again, leaping playfully onto his lap. Sebastian saw his eyes mimic the dog's again and the dog barked a friendly greeting towards the King.

"This is Robin." Grund grinned, Robin barked again. "He bids you good tidings."

Sebastian smiled.

"Now don't look directly at Cragna Vanic!" Pagmai mocked. "The one eyed Witch of Brood's Reach. I'm sure you have heard ghost stories of her when you were but a small Prince?"

She hissed and Sebastian smiled falser, he had too heard the tales when he was but young and the crown was the last thought on his mind. The thought of even looking into that eye made him shudder with dread.

"You've already witnessed what she can do."

Pagmai grinned mischievously.

"Indeed!" Sebastian answered.

"This loudmouthed oaf drinking us out of ale is L'llak.

251

His abilities, apart from the obvious gorging himself on ale that is..."

L'llak used his powers to move objects and snatched Grooble's tankard from his hand and it drifted towards him where he grabbed it and emptied it before sending it back in the air to the sour faced Smidge. L'llak just laughed heartily, his massive stomach shaking up and down as he held his tankard aloft to The King.

"And yet another true beauty to Feist your royal eyes upon." Mocked Pagmai, "Kelda Wormtail."

She gazed at him with those marbled eyes and said nothing, Sebastian smiled courteously, but she was truly hideous.

"Although she does dabble in the dark arts we find she is useful to have around." He laughed. "She probably knows how each one of us in this room will meet our end."

Although Pagmai laughed there was truth in his words and Sebastian gazed upon her hideous face that cracked a sadistic smile indicating that Pagmai's words were indeed true.

"You honour me with such an unforgettable welcome." Sebastian said as he attempted to sit down and was met with resistance and then pushed off the seat.

"What trickery is this?" He gasped, turning around to see a male Fairy lost in the seat.

"Do you mind?" He asked. "Forgive my silence, but Pagmai believes that unsuspecting visitors sitting one me is hilarious. I would bear to differ."

The room erupted with yet more laugher and Sebastian

apologised and took the seat next to the Fairy, who was smiling too.

"I am Mingus Mothe, Your Majesty." He said, taking off and fluttering around the table to bow in front of the King, his turquoise wings fluttering frantically, fairy dust sprinkling the table as he flew back to his seat.

"Now, my King...Sebastian." Pagmi smiled, settling into his chair. "Before you tell us why you have blessed us with this visit, let us eat!"

CHÃPTÉR 21
Ã CÃLLÖÜS CÖLLÃBÖRÃTÏÖÑ

rimalkin drifted down the crooked stone steps like some ghastly apparition, his silhouette consumed the wall with the shadow of a reaper. Pooka's stunted legs struggled to keep pace with his master, especially being weighed down by a cumbersome torch, which was the reason for the haunting image that convulsed on the moist stone wall. Grimalkin wore a masterful grin across his pale and weathered face, a mask of some all-knowing being who concealed dark secrets that were for his ears and eyes only. He came to an abrupt halt where the stairs became lost in jagged hunks of rock, his bandaged feet disturbing several small stones that fell down into the bleak pit of darkness beneath. Pooka skidded clumsy behind him, somehow managing not to collide with his Master or engulf his dark robe with flame. Sweat leaked from the half-breed's brow, matting the thick, rugged hair that sat chaotically on his head.

"My brothers!" Grimalkin called. "My sisters!" His voice croaked menacingly as it echoed around in the darkness below. There was a grumbling sound beneath, movement in abundance and then flame appeared, hundreds of torches lit almost simultaneously breathing life into the deep cavern below. Grimalkin smiled, Pooka's torchlight caught the glimmer of deceit in his Master's eye and it shook him to his core.

"Yes!" Grimalkin hissed as the torches illuminated his army. All the horrors of The Shrouded Realm lay before him, bloodthirsty atrocities eager to do Grimalkin's bidding. The torches flickered rapidly, eager to caress these depraved creatures with its warming kiss, unveiling scales and fur, leather and steel. A mass of armoured bodies writhed impatiently, flesh moist and the colour of green tree sap, stolen and rusted weapons clutched in clawed hands.

"My Goblins!" Grimalkin addressed them and they replied with an enthusiastic cry.

Grimalkin surveyed them and saw that they were indeed ready.

"General Feng!" He croaked. "Step forward."

General Feng a brute in scarred gold, burst through the rabble of his own kind and removed his horned helm, revealing a grotesque head etched with several deep war wounds.

He knelt and bowed his head as he addressed his Master. "My Dark Master!"

"Rise, General. You need not kneel before anyone."

"You honour me with your words." Feng rose and stood proudly.

"What better General to lead the uprising than you Feng. Who here has spent more time on the battlefield? Who here has tasted more Man blood than you? Even your armour is embellished with the lives of Man that you have taken."

The Goblins roared affectionately for their Dark Master's words and the respect for their General.

"If any of you are apprehensive about going to war with Man..."

Pooka swallowed hard at his Master's words, he felt out of his depth and only here because no-one else would ever accept him. He hoped that Grimalkin would not notice his anxious demeanour. Fortunately for Pooka he did not, for his eyes were filled with passion and terror and were fixed on his army beneath.

"...look upon your leader! The ruler of Grotte! General Feng! A brave Goblin with a legacy built from honour and destruction, they do not call him 'Man-slayer' for japes and follies! He shall not shy from battle, but be the first on the battlefield and the last to leave with mace and sword bloodied with the warm entrails of Man!"

General Feng unsheathed his sword and held aloft its biting edge, before doing the same with a heavily spiked mace that still wore the dried rotting flesh of battles past. The Goblins roared again showing their respect to the greatest warrior of their species.

"Yes!" Grimalkin applauded. "Feast your eyes upon the arms of Feng! Man-Eater and Flesh-Stripper will do you all proud no doubt. The same sword that he took with force from King Grotte! Willing to do what was needed and deliver the killing blow. Would you Goblins take up your arms and follow General Feng into the bowels of Sloore?"

There was a massive roar of agreement and swords, spears, maces and hammers rose aloft, the steel shimmering like a thousand stars, all aligned with Grimalkin's dark vision of decay and destruction. Grimalkin smiled showing jagged, discoloured teeth, Pooka sighed with sadness, he would love nothing more to be able to stop this madness, but what could he do?

General Feng fell back into his own kind and was met with hefty slaps as Grimalkin's cruel eyes flitted across the cavern, as he was attracted to movement in a gloomy corner, there huddle thousands of Zwulf, a species formed like Man but their bodies covered in thick fur of various tones. They wore chainmail and various armoured steel, most of it rusted and the majority held large bludgeons in their furry mitts, steel spikes drove through the thick wooden arms to create menacing looking arsenal. Their faces were creased like leather, pierced with steel and copper through gaping nostrils and bulbous lips. Sharp teeth protruded upwards from their jaws, misshapen and crooked like the tusks of wild boars. These Beast-Men held Ogres on reins, the dimwitted species that resembled large grubs, small black eyes and a maw of needle-like teeth, blubbery torsos with pitiful arms sprouting out that are little or no use for anything, but large bugling legs, this was where their strength lay and that is why the Zwulf had always used Ogres as steeds for their quick movements across all terrain and because their small minds were easy to train. One Zwulf in particular stood at their

257

head appearing quite restless at Grimalkin's praise of The Goblin General.

"Let me welcome the proud race of Zwulf!" Grimalkin bellowed, the reaction was underwhelming from the other races, some even jeered their presence.

"Their leader, Purge 'The Grim'!" Grimalkin hissed and watched as Purge's bronze eyes, stared at him through a shroud of dark brown fur, his gruesome primitive face pierced with bronze and silver rings. "The King of the Beast-Men!" It appeared that the presence of the Zwulf was unwanted by the others that had joined Grimalkin's dark cause and the reasons were many. The Zwulf had been at war with Goblins for centuries, the races had never seen eye to eye and the battles between the two were both bloody and many, too many to comprehend. Purge has been open of his hatred of Goblins and has been stubborn when it has come to forming alliances with anyone, they are untrusted by many and unloved by all.

"Purge!" Grimalkin called out.

"Aye!" Grunted Purge, openly brash and ignorant, sure not to bestow any titles on the dark Elf, for he had been promised several privileges, but because he had yet to see them he remained stubborn.

"I hope the days of travel from The Isle of Beasts was not to taxing on you and your army?" Grimalkin said with a wry smile.

"Nay! The Zwulf are strong and eager, travel does not weaken us as it does other species!" He grumbled, his eyes were blatant as they flitted towards the Goblins, who were known for not revelling in travels across water. General Feng was quick to acknowledge the stab at his race and fired back quickly.

"I was beginning to think the Zwulf confined to their isle." Feng scoffed.

Purge's face contorted with anger, it's as if he had been craving the hostilities.

"And what know you of island life, Goblin? Nothing!" He spat. "Too afraid of water! Pah! Afraid to even bathe in it by the sight of you!"

Goblins and Zwulf growled at each other, shouting back obscenities to each other across the cavern as Grimalkin watched on quite amused by it all.

"What know you of bathing?" Feng cackled. "I can smell your matted hides from here! Do you lie with your Ogres often?"

Goblins erupted in laughter and Purge lifted his heavily spiked Bludgeon into the air to goad Feng on. The spikes were long and thick, flecked with rust and dried blood, in the Zwulf culture a spike was hammered into their wooden clubs for each life they had taken in battle, by the look of Purge's there had been many battles and many had fallen to its vengeance.

"Come closer Goblin!" Purge urged. "Let me introduce you to 'Retch' and it may greet you with a kiss on that pretty face of yours!"

Now it was the Zwulf who heckled the Goblins with their barking laughter.

"Enough." Grimalkin said firmly, his voice cut through the animosity like a hot blade.

259

"But my Dark Master," pleaded General Feng. "They do not belong here! History shows they cannot be trusted!"

"We are here to change history General!" Grimalkin replied, "I have cemented an alliance with Purge and his Beast-Men. They will help us take the realm and then that will be the end of it."

"Promises have been made!" Purge smiled, his broken teeth clicking together in his wide mouth.

"What promises?" Feng growled with annoyance. "What have you promised these primitive wretches?"

"Do not forget your place General!" Snapped Grimalkin. "My judgements are my own and I will not have my decisions scrutinised!"

"You have my apologies." Feng bowed, Purge enjoyed the Goblin General's unease with a hideous smile.

"Promises have been made to all!" Grimalkin announced. "Promises that will be fulfilled!"

"Purge 'King of the Beast-Men', will rule the Great City of Shantanga!" The Zwulf erupted triumphantly, violently slamming their spiked clubs against their wooden shields. A scowl of irritation quivered across the brow of Grimalkin, he had indeed made promises to all the leaders of each band that would fight for darkness. Grimalkin was annoyed that Purge had announced what spoils he would receive, this act could cause dissension with the other races.

"Is this true?" Feng growled.

"Purge tells no lies!" Purge growled at Feng, but he ignored him fixing his attentions on Grimalkin.

"Alas, I fear that Purge has spoilt my surprise!" Grimalkin slithered quickly as he knew he would need to keep Feng onside or else loose the Goblin army. "As I said promises were made to all and the spoils of war will be more than you could ever conceive."

"We know of the golden Dollin and jewels, but what of land? Land is power!" Feng replied.

"That is why Hammillda will be yours, Feng!"

"Hammillda! Dwarf land!" Feng gasped.

"It will be Goblin land soon enough." Grimalkin smiled and Feng returned the gesture with a bow of his head.

With the unrest settled, Grimalkin surveyed his terrors and settled on a small congregation of humongous beasts, sweating and dribbling, their gargantuan obese bodies, clad in leather aprons and rusted cleavers clutched in hands that had but three digits. Each of them with a single gigantic eye flickering back at him.

"The Cyclops of Brood's Reach!" He declared to a growl of satisfaction from the assembly. "Are they not fearsome and destructive? Do they not yearn for the same as all of us here?"

There was cry of agreement.

"Brutes that have fought along side The Shrouded Realm in many battles of the past, like the Siege of Elken End, and the Colossal Collision with the Giants to name but a few. We are honoured for you to fight along side us." Grimalkin bowed and they lifted their cleavers and gargled a grunting response.

Cyclops had always terrified Pooka, ever since Moote who was Sloore's executioner and chef tried to eat him. He cowered behind his Master's dark robes and hoped that one did not spot him and take a fancy.

Grimalkin glared into the dark walls, away from the shimmer of torches and searched for his other allies, there was an abundance of yellow eyes staring back at him from the shadows.

"There you are." He cackled. "The Children of the Shrouded Realm, The Black Imps of Sloore! You are a sight to behold."

There was a chattering sound from the shadows, thousands of jaws biting down frantically at Grimalkin's words.

"I know you long for mischief, but the time is almost upon us. It is time for The Children to play."

Chattering, growling and roaring met his long slender ears and it filled him with sadistic euphoria.

"Ferals!" Hey cried and was met with howls and feline shrieks as large furred creatures moved on four legs in the dim, unable to light torches, but no need to do so with such excellent eyesight.

"Bat-Fiends!" He cried again and was met with high-pitch screeches from the cavern's ceiling, where leather winged hulks hung, eyes red and piercing holes in the darkness.

"You will be steed and chariot for our fearless warriors, indeed a most important undertaking. Your speed and cunning will help us win this war."

Screeches, growls and yelps met his ears, it was indeed welcoming, but not as welcoming as the next sound that was heard from deep in the darkness of the cavern under Mount Quirinus, the grumble of a Dragon's empty stomach.

"Demios!" Grimalkin cackled. "Come forth my beauty, come!" Grimalkin spoke so tenderly as if addressing a pet.
There was heavy movement and the entire army of Goblins, Zwulf, Cyclops, Black Imps, Ferals and Bat-Fiends shifted with unease and made way for The Black Arrow. Demios grumbled and cared not for the army around him, torchlight kissed his black scales and they glistened like shards of obsidian, dancing and shining with each movement as he strode towards Grimalkin. Its stature so big that it almost filled the cavern and was able to meet Grimalkin face to face. Pooka slid even more into his Master's shadow not wanting to draw any attention from a hungry Dragon.

"My beauty!" Grimalkin smiled and caressed the gigantic beast's snout that was still warm to the touch, his pink eyes gleamed in his Master's presence, a look of love and trust.

"This is what will win the realm for us!" Grimalkin announced and the army erupted with cries of glory.
General Feng strode forward, seemingly the only one not aghast at the gargantuan black Dragon that stood next to him.

"A Dragon!" Purge gasped, The King of the Beast-Men's thick lip wavered at the sight of such a gargantuan beast.

"My Dark Master!" Feng called and the cavern hushed, Grimalkin gestured with a pale hand for his General to speak. "We are eager to drink the blood of Man and crunch their bones into the earth. But the orders we have received seem convoluted."

263

Grimalkin glared at Pooka from the corner of his eye and then his focus was solely with his Goblin General.

"It is a complicated situation General. We look to strike silently with speed and precision. With so many kingdoms to seize at one time, it is difficult. But we have the element of surprise with us."

"Is it possible to destroy all of Man in one fell swoop?" Feng asked.

"All of Man?" Grimalkin Laughed, the sound was chilling to Pooka's drooping ears and immediately caused his rough skin to sprout out in goose pimples.

"My General, I do not wish to destroy all of Man."
There was a gasp and voices conversed eagerly at these shocking words.

"SILENCE!" Grimalkin roared, it was the first flash of anger that the army had seen this day and immediately there was silence. Pooka had seen that anger many times and took a step backwards, the torch trembling in his long, hairy grasp.

"It has never been my intention to eradicate the Man race as they did my own Elf kind. No, the most powerful of their species shall be the ones to fall, the Higher Houses that offer us nothing but war will be eliminated as well as the others who believe they can rule the realm, like Giants and Dwarves. They will be the ones to be rubbed out!"

"But why not all of them, My Dark Master?" Feng asked.

"Tear their flesh from their bones, says Purge!" The Beast-Man roared. "Drink their blood, gnaw their bones to dust!"

"For once I agree with the Zwulf!" Feng scoffed.

Grimalkin lifted his pale hands in the air to silence them.

"Those that serve purpose may be saved, but only if they live under my rule. What is it to be a King if you have no slaves to do your bidding?"

General Feng smiled with understanding and bowed to his master.

"General Feng you will send armies to the West on the back of Feral and Bat-Fiend to take Foxall, Trinpola and Tendor. You will lead the assault at Kalfahr and with the Dragon fire of Demios you will engulf that Weeping Willow for all the realm to see. It will be a beacon of death!"

There was a buzz of excitement from the cavern.

"The Children of the Shrouded Realm with be released from the shadows to pillage Elken and bring with them Dragon fire to burn fiercely from Tudor Hall to Elken's End." So passionate were his words that he continued without a care for the cheers from his followers. "The Giants of Kanka will feel the wrath of Cyclops as they lead a ground attack on the Hills of Brockonbak and watch as the unexpected Giants are ambushed by Dragon flame raining down on then from above."

General Feng, did not share the cheers of his army, they were lost in the words of The Dark Master, but Feng was a strategist and something felt odd to his trained mind.

"The Kingdom in the Flowers will be consumed with Dragon fire. In the East the ancient House Hammillaxe and their fortress Hammillda shall fall at the hands of The Black Imps! Purge and the Zwulf will be free to invade the Great City of Shantanga, wreaking havoc on the ships of Man to stop any of them fleeing the port of Shang."

The Goblin army salivated with the mere thought of Man blood, but still Feng remained confused.

"The Mystic Circle shall fall to my hand and then I shall finally taste the power of the Orb of Quirinus. But only when the King has left."

"You shall not kill the King?" General Feng interrupted, Grimalkin was not angered, for he knew that Feng was the one that shared an equal intellect to his own.

"No, General! I want the King to see everything he loves die before he falls." Grimalkin hissed, eyes burning, forked tongue tasting his own saliva on the tips of his pointed teeth.

"Would it not be wise to take him now when his belly is full with food and his mind disturbed by strong wine?"

"He is but one Man." Grimalkin scoffed."What can he do?"

Feng nodded, but unspoken words danced in his maw, words believing that this was a mistake.

"When all our targets have fallen and smoulder in flame we shall meet at Windmast Castle where we will take the crown! We take the throne and we take Maglore. It will fill me with satisfaction to see the irony in the Hartwaker sigil burning in flames."

The creatures below him were now in a frenzy and were thirsty for blood and gore, but Feng spoke again with words that hushed the crowd.

"How do we take Windmast? It sits upon a waterfall and its thick stone walls are impregnable, many have tried and failed at this task!" Feng shook his head. "And you speak of Dragon flame as though we have it in abundance! But Demios as mighty as he is, can only be in one place at one time my Dark Master."

Grimalkin smiled at him.

"I can see that there is nothing that passes your astute eye, General. You truly are the right warrior to lead this charge. Your worries could be truth if you had knowledge of all, but you do not."

"No, my Master I do not." Feng shook his head.

"We shall take the castle with ease with the help of the Runt!"

Grimalkin moved aside to unveil the cowering half Troll, half Goblin that stood behind him, grasping the torch so tightly that the rough bark bit into his palms.

"The half breed!" Feng snarled, his sentiments were echoed by the Goblin army and several spat in his direction. "What good is he for anything?"

"He is good for eating!" Purge cackled licking his lips. "Come to me little one!"

Pooka swallowed hard and hid behind his Master's robes.

"The Runt is a reader, he came across some very interesting scrolls in the depths of the forgotten libraries of Mount Quirinus where he brought me information on the secret passageways to Windmast through The King's Fall."

"The passageways were closed up years ago my Dark Master, we have tried many times..." Feng attempted but his words were interrupted.

"There is one that still remains! The knowledge of it is only known by the King himself. The Runt will lead us through it and to victory!"

There was a roar from the followers again, some even called out Pooka's name as though he were a hero. Pooka was surprised that any of them actually knew his name and he did not feel much like a hero, it was guilt not pride that flowed through his veins and he wished he had never found the scrolls.

"What of the Dragon flame you speak of?" Feng called over the ruckus, it died again eager to hear their Dark Master's words. Grimalkin surveyed the room with his mistrustful magenta eyes and smiled, before turning away and climbing the steps back up towards Quirinus Castle.

"My Dark Master!" Feng called. "The Dragon fire? Tell us of this plan."

"You make a mistake in judgement General."

Feng looked at him confused.

"What mistake do you speak of?"

Grimalkin turned, his grinning face lit by the light of Pooka's quivering torch.

"Your mistake is that you believe that I only have one Dragon."

CHÃPTÉR 22
THÉ PÃTÏÉNCÉ ÕF Ã KÏNG

ebastian was relieved to break bread and indulge in Man food once again, the boar he had tasted at Hammillda was much too salted for his liking and he found although he was very hungry he could not finish the large helping that Ethel had so generously slopped in front of him. Pagmai and the other members of The Mystic Circle had listened to his story very graciously and they now talked quietly amongst themselves all but Hyacynthia whose mouth did not even quiver with movement, Sebastian believed that she had the capabilities to speak into the minds without the use of her tongue. For once in his life he felt inadequate as a Man, he was King of Maglore and he had reigned for 19 years. He had fought bravely in many battles and slain Man, Cyclops and Goblin and honoured for the slaughter but these beings that sat around this table had the ability and power to do more than he could ever dream of with just the blink of an eye and think nothing of it. He felt in awe of them, below them even, which was a strange way for a King to feel. Some might say that he feared them and he would not have been the first, that is why they lived as they did, in the solitude of a castle on a mountain range, away from all others. Sebastian felt sorry for them, it was Man and Goblin, Dwarf and Elf that had pushed these beings aside as being evil for their differences, their gifts. A thought entered his mind, he had no right to the throne when there were such powerful creatures as these, but knew that they had no want for rule and no need. But who could stop them if they ever wished to seize throne and crown?

Sebastian felt as though Cragna Vanic was staring a hole in him, but the thought was ridiculous as she only had one eye, which happen to be fixed on Pagmai as he mumbled rapidly in a whisper that he could not hear. The Witch to his right hand side however was a different matter entirely. He turned away from the remains of his delicious broth to be met by the beady-eyed gaze of Kelda Wormtail, her one marbled eyes seemed to follow his every movement even if her gaze was on the secret meeting that took place in front of his very eyes moving at ridiculous speed so that he could not make out what words were being uttered, it hurt is mind to gaze upon Pagmai's lips, quivering like the wings of a hummingbird. She looked as though she was frozen in time, she did not blink or even breathe, Sebastian turned away from her hideous face, he could not bear to look at her, but something made him glance back quickly as if she moved, no flickered, it was a strange occurrence and he found himself staring at her again as she sat motionless. He turned his attentions back to his bowl of broth and quietly emptied it of meat, potato and roots and then wiped the butt end of some black-bread around it, soaking up the thick onion gravy.

Robin the dog wandered over from the lap of 'The Whisperer' Gallian Grund and sat next to Sebastian.

"Are you hungry my friend?" The King asked the dog who looked up at him with eyes that looked as though they did not belong, blue and wise, almost Man-like. Sebastian patted Robin on the head and retrieved his bowl setting it down in front of the dog to lick clean.

"There you go my friend."

Robin just looked at it, tilted his head to one side and then stared back at Sebastian as if to ask why he had done such a thing as if the custom was foreign to him.

"Go on." Sebastian urged. "Eat up now."

"But Sire I have eaten my fill." Said the dog.

Sebastian almost fell from his seat in surprise, his eyes wide and his mouth hung.

"Do not be alarmed," The Dog said, "It is I, Gallian. Pagmai sent me to check if you were okay."

Sebastian nodded frantically.

"Aye, I'm fine thank you."

"I know these proceedings can take a while and Pagmai can be a gasbag when he wants to be. Would you like to take a walk in the hall?" The dog asked, bursting into the instinctive scratching behind his floppy ear. It appears that the dog had no idea that Gallian had invaded his brain and manipulated it and just continued on regardless.

"No, I'm fine here, thank you."

271

"As you wish." The Dog nodded and then trotted back towards his Master, he jumped on his lap, yawned and curled up falling straight to sleep, Sebastian noticed its eyes turn from blue to brown before its lids closed.

"Fascinating!" Sebastian whispered to himself all the while shaking his head in disbelief.

Mingus Mothe burst out from the confines of the conversation and fluttered over to The King.

"He can talk can he not?" He laughed as he hovered in front of the King's face.

"There is much to discuss." Sebastian answered, "I would like to be involved in matters of the realm."

"Of course." Mingus agreed. "I'll inform Pagmai that you grow restless." The Fairy swooped down and retrieved a thimble from his place at the table, flew across the table and scooped up ale from a tankard before returning into The Mystic Circle's frantic conference.

He saw Kelda flicker again as she sat motionless next to him, it sent a shudder down his spine to see those pearly eyes shining at him, he turned away again.

Why do you flicker and the others move rapidly as if possessed?

But to reason with the sights he had seen in this room was madness.

A jug of ale rose from the table and floated across to the King, it poured the thick honey ale into his cup and stopped as white froth bubbled up over its rim. Sebastian watched still amazed by the wonders all around him and looked into the conference to see L'llak laughing heartily back at him and raising his own cup. Sebastian smiled and raised the cup before taking a long swig, he was amazed at how cool it was as if it had been chilled in ice, yet more magic that he could never understand. The ale was sent to pacify him while he waited, he knew that much, the conversation was taking an age, he wondered which was worse a torture, waiting for Wizards and Witches to make a decision or parlaying Dagyan 'The Defiant'? At the moment both seemed just as frustrating, but at least here he had ale.

CHÃPTÉR 23
Ã CÏRCLÉ DÏVÏDÉD

rimalkin had made the arduous journey back from the bowels of Mount Quirinus while discussions were being made about King Hartwaker's dilemma. Grimalkin had been making his own preparations that would leave The Mystic Circle's response invalid, their actions (if any) would come too late, King Hartwaker's quest had come too late and his words were not even being heard, Grimalkin knew that The Man King had failed and in the flutter of a lilac torched he smiled sadistically. The wheels had already been set in motion and after today Maglore would never be the same.

"My Dark Master!" Came a cackle in the darkness, he gazed along the corridor towards the door to The Mystic Circle's meeting place and watched as a cloaked Kelda seeped from the shadows and joined him.

"Kelda!" Grimalkin said firmly. "You dare leave The Circle in the midst of such importance?"

"I am still there Master, I allow those fools to see what they want to see. I am here as well as there." She smiled a horrible smile, a mouth that homed only a handful of rotten teeth.

"And what news from within?"

Grimalkin was confident, maybe too over confident that his plans would come to fruition, a trait that Man called arrogance, but even with this confidence, nothing was ever absolute. He had attempted such plans several times before but had always been thwarted in their infancy, this time he knew it was different, he knew there was no-one to stand in his way, it was too late. But even still, he asked the question with a hint of apprehension.

"Pagmai talks and talks." Kelda hissed. "His tongue wriggles like that of a worm. I be wishing to cut it out and chew it up, it displeases me so."

"What words do they speak?" Grimalkin asked. "Do they accept Hartwaker's words? Do they believe they be the truth?"

"The Circle is split, Master." She replied. "Like how the Moon of Tenaj sometimes appears, only half shines and half in darkness. That is how goes the debate."

"His visions..." Grimalkin said more to himself than to Kelda, "They would take the visions seriously. Where others have disregarded them, they would embrace them."

"Indeed!" Kelda nodded, her eyes reflected the torch, glimmering eyes of hatred in the darkness.

"They will see what we want them to see just as you have with Yodel and his stargazing. We shall control the stars and the destiny of Maglore, not a Man King as his visions."

"Yes, my Lord!" Kelda grinned. "Are the plans in place for your war?"

"It is arranged." He said darkly. "Now you must return to The Circle before you are missed."

CHÃPTÉR 24
Ã WÏZÃRD'S VÉRDÏCT

e are decided." Pagmai announced as the meeting was adjourned. Sebastian studied the faces of the Mystic Circle, but they gave no hint of their decision. Pagmai caressed his beard slowly and then his ancient hands found themselves clasped around the Orb of Quirinus that peered out from his length of beard. He pondered for the longest time and even his own congregation seemed to grow restless at the awkward silence. Sebastian wondered whether the touch of the Orb helped him see things that had yet to happen, were visions of Maglore's future manifested before his eyes? Pagami remained in a trance for the longest time and it needed a nudge from his beloved, Holleet to bring him back to the here and now.

"So, we are decided." He said again, his voice a gravelling croak as if waking from a long slumber.

"You've already said that." Grooble scoffed as he swayed drunkenly on his stool. The others glanced around at each other, some rolling their eyes as if they were used to waiting for this great Wizard to bestow his knowledge upon them.

Sebastian noticed that they were all powerful in their own right but they had been so accustomed to Pagmai making their decisions or speak for them that they had lost the ability to speak for themselves.

"And what have you decided?" Sebastian asked finally, his agitation was clear for all to see.

"Hmm..." Pagmai mumbled to himself as if he were listening to the Orb that he held in his hands, could it be that the precious stone spoke to him?

The Man King could take no more, no longer could he wait. He was tired and cranky from lack of proper sleep, due to the dark haze he had lost track of all time and no longer knew his days or weeks, he demanded an answer.

"Pagmai!" Sebastian bellowed as he rose from his seat, his eyes flitted to Kelda for a split second as she seemed to burst back into life with snakelike movements, he paid her no mind and directed his gaze at the old Wizard that sat at the head of the table.

"I demand an answer!" Sebastian cried again and he could see that Pagmai released the Orb of Quirinus. The King watched as it retreated into the safety of Pagmai's thick white beard.

"Yes, I know you do King Hartwaker." Pagmai spoke, eyes now clear and locked upon him. "We have discussed your little problem."

"Little problem!" Sebastian guffawed. "This is no little problem! It effects us all! Everyone of us that dwells within the realm of Maglore is in danger."   "Yes, I have seen your visions through the power of the Orb of Quirinus. It has shown me what you fear, what you see, I know."

"And?" Sebastian snapped, "I need your answer, not your recognition of what I already know to be truth!"

"These things take time," Pagmai sighed, "we cannot just rush into them blindly, The Circle must know all the facts before we can act."

"I have no more time!" Sebastian thumped the table, tankards fell and drink was spilt, L'llak's magic burst into life and saved his tankard. It hovered over the shaking table and was swept rapidly through the air to find his grip, he sighed in relief and took a hefty swig.

"If you have no words for me that I would care to hear then I shall take my leave." Sebastian added. "Perhaps The Giants will be more accommodating."

"HA!" Cackled Cragna Vanic mocking him with her awful eye.

"I doubt the mighty Troggo Brokonbak would be as forthcoming as The Mystic Circle." Hyacynthia said softly, her voice was calming and it did help to soothe the heat that flowed through the King's veins.

"Aye!" Grooble slurred. "The Giant King has no love for Man or any other species for that matter."

"He will still hear my words!" Sebastian declare. "As have you all! Maybe he will bring forth an answer with more swiftness than The Circle!"

"I believe," Pagmai began again, "that is, The Circle believe that your words are true..."

"Thank Adeve!" Sebastian sighed.

"...but we believe that the visions are but folly."

"What?" Sebastian snapped, he could not believe his ears, ears that could now hear the jeering cackles of Kelda and Cragna.

"They are but night visions, just dreams, my King." Pagami said gently as if to ease the blow.

"It must be said." Holleet announced. "That these are not the thoughts of all The Mystic Circle. Some of us are open in acceptance of your fears." Gallian Grund, Haras Lunarc, L'llak and Mingus Mothe all gestured their agreement with Holleet. "But without the consent of all The Circle we cannot be of service."

Sebastian pushed away his chair and turned away from the table.

"Then there is nothing more to discuss!"

"Please, King Hartwaker." Pagmai tried to reason. "We mean no disrespect, but we are children of the stars. We honour the stars, The Moon of Tenaj and the Sun of Selym for instilling these gifts within us. So it is the stars that pass judgement."

"The stars! PAH!" Sebastian snorted in frustration.

"Tis true, Sire." Stuttered Yodel, "I have gazed upon the stars for many a day, there is nothing but tranquility seen in them for the forthcoming Seasons."

"And what of this dark haze that surrounds you all?"

"It is an early cometh of The Season of Gloam, nothing more." Yodel stuttered.

"Aye, it is known from time to time for Gloam to come early." Added Grooble.

"Aye, but never has it cometh so close to Algor." L'llak said with a shake of his bulbous head. "Never in all my days."

"Tis true enough." Added Haras Luanrc. "We all still feel the warmth of Algor."

"PAH!" Grooble swept away their comments with a drunken shake of his head.

"There have been warm Gloam's before." Hyacynthia swooned.

"Not like this!" Gallian Grund added, even Robin the dog shook his head in time with his master.

Voices started to rise as each member looked to add their opinion, Pagmai stroked his beard as the others discussed, his eyes locked on to Sebastian's.

Sebastian had heard enough.

"Enough!" He barked, and there was silence. "Enough of this bickering! You sound like children! You argue for you do not understand what is happening, that should be the horn that blows a warning surely? That such wise and powerful beings such as yourselves cannot see that something is wrong?"

"Without all the members agreeing, King Hartwaker, we cannot commit to help you, I am sorry, but that is the way of it." Said Pagmai.

"And the stars!" Yodel stuttered again. "We must obey the stars and they say nothing of this."

281

"Damn your stars!" Sebastian growled and was met by a gasp from Yodel, who seemed to sink into his seat with offence.

"You sit here oblivious to what transpires outside these walls!" Sebastian cried. "Something is coming! Are your eyes blind to it?"

The faces of The Circle stared back at him, some ashamed as they must feel that something is not right and should act, others taken aback having never being spoke to in such a manner before.

"It waits like a beast in the shadows!" Sebastian continued. "It hunts us using this dark haze as a shroud, we are walking into an ambush and I alone cannot stop this threat!"

The King looked emotional after his tirade, but Pagmai's face was stern and his decision left unchanged.

"I am of noble blood, royal blood." Sebastian said proudly, his eyelids fighting to hold back tears, "I have never bent a knee to anyone in my life, but the King's that have ruled before me. But I beg of you!" He lowered himself to a knee and bowed his head, "I need you, the realm needs you or it shall fester and shrivel and die only knowing darkness."

Pagmai stood, his face remaining stern, but his eyes displayed a kindness, a pity.

"You need not kneel before us King Hartwaker." He said softly and he gestured for him to rise raising two wrinkled hands that appeared out from the confines of oversized sleeves. Sebastian rose and composed himself, his tears did not fall but retreated back into those brave green eyes.

"Your pleas do not fall on a heart of stone…" Pagmai said in a caring tone. Several of the Mystic Circle looked on in anticipation, was 'The Grand One' about to change his mind?

"…But, you have my decision."

The words were heavy and those that wished to help The King bowed their heads abashed.

Sebastian composed himself again, he was too tired to be angry anymore.

"I thank you for your hospitality." He said with a bow of respect, "I shall take my leave."

As he turned to leave he was halted by Pagmai's words.

"I wish you well, Sebastian. I truly hope you find the answers you desire."

"Do you?" Sebastian scoffed.

"Of course!" Pagmai replied, "I hope you can lift this burden that you have placed upon your shoulders and know there is nothing to fear from dark dreams. It is always a difficult task to ask oneself to admit he is wrong."

"I pray to Adeve that I am wrong!" He growled.

His blood boiled again, he could feel his face glowing with searing heat, his hands clenched into tight fists. The doors opened behind him and it was enough to halt him before he unleashed his wrath upon The Mystic Circle. He turned to see Grimalkin standing in the doorway with a startled look upon his grotesque face.

"Please forgive my intrusion, Oh Grand One!" Grimalkin announced, "I believed you to be finished with your conference."

283

"Do not worry, Grimalkin." Sebastian snapped. "We are finished here." Sebastian left and strode with pace down the corridor, he scoffed at the suit of mystical armour that shimmered in the gloom and swiftly made his way towards the spiralling stairs to make his exit.

"My King!" Cried a voice from behind him, Sebastian did not slow his pace nor look to see who the voice belonged too, he had no more words to waste on The Mystic Circle. As he made it to the steps the voice was at his shoulder, he turned to be face to face with Grimalkin.

"Grimalkin!" Sebastian said taken aback. "You are surprisingly swift."

Grimalkin grinned at him, there was mischief within it and a strange glimmer in his eyes.

"I will take my leave."

"Of course, My King!" Grimalkin replied with enthusiasm. "May I be so bold as to offer you a swifter exit?"

"You may!" Sebastian scoffed, "I grow tired of this place."

"I too grow tired of these dark walls, but what can be done?"

"These walls will grow darker I fear."

"Indeed."

Sebastian glared at him with intrigue.

"You speak as if you know things Grimalkin?"

"Let me say this, Sire." His voice lowered to a whispering hiss, "I believe your words."

"Then why not go forward and tell your Master of this?

Your words may change his mind! Whispered words in dark corridors are no good to me."

"I understand your frustrations." Grimalkin lowered his head sighed. "But, alas I am not a member of The Mystic Circle, only an apprentice and I am not permitted to sit at their discussions. My word means nothing."

"Then there is truly nothing more that The Mystic Circle can do for me."

"I can help you on your way at the very least."

"So be it." Sebastian agreed. "But how?"

"The descent from Mount Quirinus can be as treacherous as the ascent. Let me make it a little easier for you."
Grimalkin's eyes twinkled strangely, his gaze caused Sebastian's flesh to burst to life with goosebumps. In the back of his tired mind he could hear a voice calling him, almost warning him. But The King seemed almost hypnotised by those eyes flecked with magenta and agreed to Grimalkin's proposal. So enthralled with those eyes was The King that at that moment he would have followed the Elf to the very top of the volcano known as Vollox and thrown himself into the liquid hot magma that bubbled in its bowels.

"As you wish, My King." Grimalkin hissed gently as he placed a skeletal claw upon the King's shoulder and whispered an incantation, bizarre words that Sebastian could not comprehend, an ancient tongue that he knew not, for a moment he felt suffocating darkness, the visions he had had consumed him and constricted around his mind like some hungry serpent, he was about to scream out and tell Grimalkin that he would rather take the treacherous journey down the mountain's face and risk the onslaught of muck and stones of the hungry Trolls that no doubt awaited him. But it was all over in a single beat of his heart and he found himself standing at the dying campfire that he had seen shining like a beacon when he came to rest a day ago, a fire made by the hands of the brave Knight, Sir Maximillious Mondt.

"I don't..." Sebastian attempted to speak, his voice trembling, but then realised he was at the foot of the mountain, he looked all around unbelieving of such possibilities.

"You are quite safe, Your Majesty." Grimalkin smiled. "It may take your mind a few moments to find its bearings but should not effect you further."

"Incredible!" Sebastian gasped, he glanced at his hands, wriggled the fingers that were rough from years of gripping a sword and chapped from the rigours of climbing Mount Quirinus. He groped at his tunic to make sure that he was still in one piece and that no part of him had been left in the castle of The Mystic Circle.

"These are indeed gifts from the Gods!"

"Nothing more than a parlour trick, Sire, I assure you." Grimalkin bowed to the King for his kindness. "My 'gifts' as you say, are but tomfoolery compared to those who sit on The Mystic Circle. I still have a lot to learn."

"Maybe you should sit at its head, for it would seem that its current leader cannot see further than his own pointed nose." It was a needless jape at Pagmai and immediately he felt ashamed for his outburst, he turned away to look for Mondt.

The fire had died and all that remained was the meatless bones of what appeared to be a peagle and a cloud of smoke that rose and disappeared into the dark haze that still hung all around.

"Where is Mondt?" Sebastian announced, "I see not him nor the colts?"

"Perhaps he has moved on, Sire." Grimalkin said. "What was your next destination?"

"Kanka." He replied. "To the Hills of Brockonbak to parley with Troggo."

"Giant country."

"Aye."

"Would your Knight have travelled there without you?"

"I believe not." Sebastian shook his head and stooped to retrieve a branch to construct a torch with. "He is an honourable Knight and he would rather die than go back upon his word."

As Sebastian struggled to make light, Grimalkin was at his side again, he seemed to glide without movement or sound. "Allow me, Sire." And with a click of his sharp fingers the branch burst into life, as magenta flame fluttered before him. The torch hovered in the air and it bathed their surroundings in its magenta kiss but there was no sign of Mondt.

"It would appear that you have a lost Knight, Sire." Grimalkin allowed himself a sadistic smile at the King's misfortunate, but did not let it show.

"DAYBOY!" Sebastian called and added a specific whistle that his steed would know. There was a crunching of dried leaves and Dayboy emerged from the cover of the small woods where he had spent the majority of his time since the departure of his master.

"There you are!" Sebastian said with relief in his voice, his quest and journey home would have indeed been an arduous task with a steed. "Come!"
Dayboy approached and enjoyed the attention from his master.

"What a beautiful beast!" Grimalkin grinned and Dayboy stopped in his tracks and he shied away from the Elf.

"What's the matter you old fool?" Sebastian quipped.

"Maybe it is the scent of Troll dung that is responsible for his restlessness. It does linger on the air."

"It does." Sebastian agreed as he tried to calm down his restless steed.

"I wish you good journey to Kanka then, Sire." Grimalkin said with a bow.

"That's if it is worth my time." Sebastian said in a moment of second thoughts, he seemed to ponder his journey, his entire quest.

"Oh!" Grimalkin grinned, but made his response appear as surprise and the reply brought Sebastian back to the now.

"Aye, I grow tired of the rejection." He sighed and scooped up the saddle and dropped it over the wide back of Dayboy, who had settled now but still eyed Grimalkin with caution.

"That is understandable, Sire. To have no support from the kingdoms that you gave independence too must come as personal blow to your pride and your spirit."

"Indeed!" Sebastian chuckled as he fastened the saddle in place. "True words."

"I may have the forked tongue of a dark Elf, but the words that spill from it are the truth."

"I appreciate your help, Grimalkin, your presence is truly needed on The Mystic Circle." Sebastian said as he mounted Dayboy.

"You honour me, Sire."

"If it were you that I came to see then I may be leaving this place in higher spirits and a cavalry of Wizards and Witches to help my cause."

"It grieves me that I cannot help you more."

"Come Dayboy, let us go…" He paused for a moment as he looked into the distance, back into the West, it was dark their too, but different, the stars shined brightly as if calling to him to return and the Moon of Tenaj shone like a pearl in the darkness, "Home."

"Home?" Grimalkin asked. "What of your Knight? What of the Giants? What of your quest?" Grimalkin asked, his voice trying to sound sincere.

"I am sure I can catch up with Mondt, wherever he may have got to? And head back to Windmast, for this appears to be a war that I will have to fight alone and I should be there to protect my Queen, my Daughter and my people."

"If only the other Lords and rulers were as righteous as yourself, Sire."

Sebastian extended his hand and Grimalkin's eyes widened with astonishment.

"You honour me with your royal hand?"

"I do."

They shook hands and Sebastian smiled down at him. "When we next meet, I hope I was wrong, wrong about everything."

Sebastian and Dayboy galloped away to the West, the magenta torch followed them, keeping pace with the quickness of the stallion as it floated along side them, leaving Grimalkin shrouded in darkness.

"Are we foolish to allow him to leave Dark Master?" The voice sounded like the screeching of a hawk and Kelda appeared from nothing to be at his side.

"You question my judgement?" He sneered.

"Never Master! Just the words of a curious old hag, nothing more!"

"He is brave and honourable, strong and resilient."

"Then why let him leave?"

"He is not yet broken."

"But even still he is just a Man." Kelda scoffed. "What can he do to stop you?"

"You underestimate the heart of Man. We need to wound him first, only then will his heart be tender enough to break."

"As you say my Dark Master." Kelda hissed.

"What of The Circle?" He asked.

"They bicker like children. The King's visit has them divided."

"Good!" Grimalkin smiled hideously. "Then it is time."

"As you say." She cackled and disappeared into a cloud of

vapour leaving Grimalkin alone to watch Sebastian gallop away into the West.

"When we meet again King Hartwaker, I will reveal just how right you were." He hissed in the darkness and in the beat of a heart he was gone.

CHÃPTÉR 25
Ã CÖÜRÃGÉÖÜS QÜÉÉN

ueen Marie Ann was the wife of King Sebastian Hartwaker, a strong woman who did not shy away from her duties as Queen and marda. Even before she had wed the King she had been very hands on with all political matters when she was but a girl, helping her farda Lord Nathaniel Vespa with his duties of running Hive House. She stood behind the doors to the great hall with Vai-Ra held in her arms, she was a happy child, carefree and rarely shed tears, she was a content little Princess who wanted for nothing.

Queen Marie Ann wore a high necked gown of amber, trimmed with red embroidery, the design bringing together the colours of both her beloved houses Vespa and Hartwaker, bound together in silk and thread as they had been for a hundred or more years with blood and marriage. She smiled at Vai-Ra who clung to her farda's crown still, she had barely been without it since he had left for his quest. The Queen smiled at her child, her full attention given to the child as it had always been, she had forgotten that she was supposed to be addressing the council and answer their question's on their King's quest, questions that she knew she had no answers for but her time spent with her farda and watching and learning from how Sebastian dealt with awkard inquests had put her in good stead that she would be able to handle them. There would be panic within the council and words that may slander or call for a new leader in the King's stead but she would hold firm and warn her tongue from forming words that may be misconstrued.

Her cousin, Sir Winstone joined her at the doors, she did not notice him, for in her child's eyes she saw Sebastian's and she would gaze open them and talk to them as if he were there with her.

"Give me courage my King." She whispered, in the reflection of those beautiful flecks of green she saw Sir Winstone behind them.

"Cousin." She said.

"My Queen," He bowed.

"I did not hear your steps approaching."

"I am still as nimble as a Feral cousin, even for my age." He chuckled and then smiled at the Princess before contorting his face into that of a playful Troll's, immediately causing her to laugh.

"You may well be silent and swift but you are still late." The Queen quipped.

"Forgive me, I shall try not to stop off at the kitchen for a scoffing of sponge pudding and a goggle at Neeta's bosom."

The pair shared laughter and both sets of eyes fell on the Princess again, they both saw her farda within her and a sullen silence quickly sliced the merriment.

"Will he return, Cousin?" She asked glassy eyed, a moment of weakness was not what she need before a council meeting. "It has been many a day now and it remains black in the East and I fear for his safe return."

"He shall return Cousin. I have given you my word and he has given his, that should be more than enough."

"But still, I fear."

"Tis natural for a Queen to miss her King while he crusades."

"But this is different."

"True are your words, but I have heard news that he travels not alone any longer."

"Pray tell!" She gasped.

"Aye!" He smiled, jubilant that he could bring her at least something that quench her thirst for knowledge. "Two travelling Knights stay with us on their way to Locklow Reach. Sir Dustin 'The Lion', Son of Laymon and 'Tall' Tom Tolos, told me over ale how the King was spotted in a small tavern in Tendor."

"The King in a tavern?" She said taken aback. "Whatever was he doing in a tavern?"

"Food and ale, a bed to rest for the night." He shrugged and his armoured shoulders crunched with the gesture. "Apparently he made quite the scene, telling all who would listen of his quest."

"They must think him mad!"

"Most did." Sir Winstone chuckled. "But one Knight did not and he has joined him on his mission."

"Blessings from Adeve!" The Queen sighed. "And what is the name of this loyal Knight? He must be honoured on their return."

"A tournament Knight, 'The One' Sir Maximillious Mondt!"

"I have heard of his success at several Deerheart Games."

"Tis true, he is a Wizard with a sword. I'm sure that he will keep our King safe."

She smiled with relief. He smiled too but he told her not of how Tolos and Droggon had mocked Mondt for his fantastic tales and that although he was a great tournament Knight he had never proven himself in battle and bloodshed, Sir Winstone hoped too that Mondt was as good as he told everyone he was.

"Take the Princess why I am with the council." Marie Ann said handing the child to him. "She always grows impatient at such tedious affairs."

"Of course!" Sir Winstone cradled her and bounced her up and down playfully. "We will have such fun, shall we not wee Princess?"

Vai-Ra giggled and it was infectious, that they all started laughing, she opened the door and floated into the great hall, those that sat around an oval shaped table stood immediately and bowed to the Queen, the doors closed behind her and Sir Winstone was left holding the most precious bundle in the kingdom.

"So what shall we do little one?" He asked of her, she just continued to gnaw on her farda's golden crown.

"How about some sponge pudding?" He whispered.

CHÃPTÉR 26
WHÉN BLÏŊD ÉYÉS SÉÉ

agmai sat slumped in his chair at the head of The Mystic Circle, frustration boiled up inside him as the rest of his congregation unleashed a verbal tirade at each other. Venomous words were spat and angry glares cut through the atmosphere as The Circle continued to argue about King Hartwaker's dilemma that he had brought to their door. As items were thrown magically across the table and then deflected by equal magic, and Robin the dog growled and yelped, paws on the table and his bawling aimed at that those that saw the coming of the darkness theory as folly. Mingus Mothe fluttered around from each member to let his thoughts be none to their faces, they swatted at him with annoyance, but Yodel curled up on his seat, hands over his ears stuttering for them all to stop, for he was not one for confrontations. The only member that did not take part in this frenzied argument was Grooble who remained collapsed under the table in a drunken slumber. Cragna Vanic cackled loudly as she enjoyed the argument that erupted before her, tears falling from her bulging eye from her excessive laughter. Kelda flickered again in frozen animation, was she ever truly there?

Did the others even know what she was fully capable of doing?

Pagmai grew more and more visibly annoyed, his ancient fingertips prodded at his temples as if the procedure would make all their quarrelling disappear. His beloved, Holleet, placed a sympathetic hand on his shoulder, he felt her energy, her warmth, her love and his annoyance subsided for a time, but still the argument continued. It had all gotten out of hand and the final straw came when L'llak sent two jugs of ale hurtling through the air towards Mingus Mothe who expertly dodged them with his exceptional flying prowess. The jugs unfortunately continued whizzing through the air and were tipped up unceremoniously over the heads of Haras Lunarc and Hyacynthia. The pair sat drenched and L'llak whined with apology, as the two sodden Witches rose from their seat. Haras Lunarc conjured up a gust of wind that dried her off immediately, as the pair readied themselves to unleash their power at L'llak who magically whipped a shield away from its decretive position on the wall and brought it to him for him to cower behind. Robin the dog left the table as fire brewed in the eyes of Haras Lunarc and her hands glowed with gloves of flame. Hyacynthia's floral tiara drooped from her wet red hair, she removed it and whispered to the damp petals, they quivered and become as sharp as blades and hovered in the air pointing at L'llak who trembled behind his shield.

Pagmai exploded from his seat, light and smoke and flame erupted all around him as though he were a living, breathing volcano, he hovered in the air above his place at the table, eyes glowing, mimicking that of the Orb of Quirinus, that hung around his neck.

"ENOUGH!" He bellowed in a voice that may have come from Sloore himself, it was enough to halt the bickering and the room became silent as he hung there in the air. The members of The Mystic Circle returned to their places like remorseful children, their eyes gazed up at him and they quivered with angst, to gaze on Pagmai so was a rare occurrence, it was recognition of how powerful he was and no one wanted to push him past this dark version of himself. Pagmai seemed to settle and the theatrics dissolved leaving The Grand One to sink gently back down into his seat.

"That is more than enough." He sighed. "The Mystic Circle has already settled on a verdict. The majority ruled in favour of Hartwaker's plight being that of dark dreams."
Gallian Grund attempted to speak and then met the tired eyes of Pagmai, his show of power had taken much from the old Wizard and he wished, not to anger him further and declined from adding more words that would no doubt fan the flames.

"Yodel has spoke tirelessly of the stars and what they hold and they show nothing of this coming darkness. We have always made our decisions using the stars and that will not change."
The rest of The Circle nodded in agreement, they knew this but something about The King's tale had felt true to some of them, he spoke with such heart and passion that it could not be the words of a liar.

299

"The King is a fine man." Pagmai announced, "I wish him no ill feeling, but how can we help a Man fight against his dreams?"

Pagmai looked around the table looking for an answer, but he knew that there were none to come.

"There are no answers, for we cannot help with hauntings of the mind. There is nothing that Wizard and Witch sorcery can do when it comes to such matters as this, Man must defeat those inner demons himself."

The doors flew open and Grimalkin wandered in, seemingly without a care to his name.

"Grimalkin!" Pagmai growled. "What is the meaning of such an intrusion?"

"Oh my apologies, Oh, Grand One!" Grimalkin hissed, bowing in mockery of his master, "I know I am but a lonely apprentice and my presence is forbidden at the meetings of The Mystic Circle. I know I should return to the kitchens and prepare your suppers. To sweep your halls and polish your trinkets and decorations."

"What is this Grimalkin?" Pagmai seethed, "I am in no mood for insolence."

The doors slammed behind him and a dark haze filled the room.

"Deaf are your ears," Grimalkin cackled in chant, "and blind are your eyes, open and see the darkest of skies."

"Grimalkin!" Pagmai cried and rose from his chair, "I demand to know what game you play here?"

Grimalkin moved ever closer to the table, surveying all the eyes that watched him with bemusement shimmering in them.

"The words from your lips drip nothing but lies," Grimalkin continued his eyes were glowing with lavender glare, "for the darkness comes forth and the Dragon it flies!"
The walls suddenly became alive, yellow eyes as bright as the Sun of Selym shone in the gloom of the haze.

"Hear the Children of The Shrouded Realm play," Grimalkin cackled, "as they sing and dance in Maglore's decay."

"Tis mutiny!" Cried Gallian Grund and he took the body of Robin to bound across the table and launch at Grimalkin. Grimalkin held out a clawed hadn't which held Robin by its throat, it yelped and then with a swift flick of the wrist his brittle bones snapped and he fell lifeless from the Dark Master's grip and onto the table, his body limp and lifeless. Gallian fell back into his chair, breathing heavily and holding his own throat, he was covered in a layer of sweat and when he attempted to rise, he realised that his neck had too been shattered, the weight of his head rolled and hung at his chest and he fell to the ground dead.
Cragna Vanic suddenly dissolved into a puddle of black tar and was gone, her nose well attuned to danger and made her leave while she could. The others tried to rise but they were seized by the jagged arms of The Black Imps, their mouths silenced by horrendous three fingered hands, obstructing them from any spells that may pass their lips. Mingus Mothe was grasped tightly by a dark hand. Kelda's persona still remained flickering glaring at them all in that blank frown stare. Pagmai

instinctively brought forth a shroud of energy, shielding himself and Holleet from attack, Black Imps touched it, felt its power and were engulfed in flames, rapidly burning up into nothing but ash.

"Why are you doing this Grimalkin?" Holleet asked softly. "We took you in and nurtured you, treated you as one of our own."

"I was treated as a slave." Grimalkin snapped.

"You were like a son to me, Grimalkin!" Pagmai groaned, tears dancing in his old eyes. "All this would have been yours one day."

"All of this will be mine, but I will have it today Grand One!" Grimalkin cackled loudly.

"You dishonour us with your conduct, Grimalkin!" Pagmai sneered.

"Your words are wasted upon my ears." Scoffed Grimalkin. "For centuries the Children of the Shrouded Realm have waited in the shadows for their time and now is that time. You have all been over indulgent with your power, selfishly keeping it to yourselves, afraid that someone may take it and use it against you." Grimalkin grinned and true evil formed on his face, a face that The Mystic Circle had yet to see, the true face of Grimalkin.

"You never thought of looking past your own narcism to see that I was here to do just that. I have learnt from you Grand One! I studied all of you! You gave me my power, The Mystic Circle's ignorance is to blame for what will transpire as you sat oblivious around your table debating this and that, trivial matters that matter not! What mattered was the realm and under the rule of Man it has fallen into rot and decay. A firm hand is needed to rule this and that hand is mine!"

"Traitorous pig!" Shrieked Mingus Mothe and the Fairy glowed a furious shade of red and burnt through the Imp's hand that held him. The Black Imp clutched the burning stub where his hand had been and could do nothing as Mothe cut through the air like an arrow leaving an archer's bow, a red dart hurtling towards Grimalkin's face. Grimalkin smiled and with reflexes that were too fast for the naked eye he reached out and caught the onrushing Fairy in his hand.

"So very predictable," Grimalkin sighed and stared at the Fairy that struggled in the Dark Master's grasp, the burning trick incapable of penetrating the dark magic that protected his pale flesh. "How amusing that the one who looks to fight for you is the smallest? If only the rest of you had such courage!"

"Release him Grimalkin," Pagmai announced, "release them all and I will give myself over to you without squabble." Grimalkin smirked with malevolence and held Mothe out in front of him by his wings. In his heinous fingertips he held the poor defenceless Fairy as if he were examining him, there was still fight in Mothe and he continued to struggle courageously.

"Fairies have always fascinated me," Grimalkin grinned, "so very beautiful,   so very delicate..." and with that he wrenched his hands viciously, tearing the colourful wings from his spine. "...so very... pointless!"
Mothe screamed as he fell on to the table writhing in agony, his wings turned grey and lifeless in Grimalkin's clutches, they

turned to debris and stained his pale fingertips as he sneered with revulsion and watched as the ashy remains crumbled around the bleeding carcass of Mothe who looked up at the Dark Masters and died, the flamboyant glow leaving him barren and grey. There were gasps of anger and pain from the members of The Mystic Circle and the shields that protected Pagmai and Holleet quivered as if feeling the pain of the fallen Fairy.

"NO!" Pagmai shouted, the agony in his tone was evident.

"Stop this Grimalkin!" Holleet pleaded.

"No one else needs to die, Grimalkin." Pagmai pleaded. "Let your brothers and sisters go."

"Brothers and sisters? PAH!" Grimalkin spat with hatred. "None of you bear me any love."

Pagmai's teary eyes looked at L'llak, Hyacynthia, Haras Lunarc and Yodel, he knew if he unleashed the power or the Orb of Quirinus then Grimalkin would surely call for his Circle's execution.

"Let us discuss this...please!" Pagmai pleaded.

"The time for discussion ended an age ago." Grimalkin said dismissively, The Black Imps tightened their dark grip on their captives.

Holleet's eyes passed anxiously around the table and her gaze met the frozen stare of Kelda Wormtail. In the melee none of them had realised that she had not been involved or been seized by The Black Imps.

"Kelda!" Holleet said. "It would appear that you have been in collusion with Grimalkin."

"My beloved, what are these words that you speak?" Pagmai asked, he was confused by it all and his mind was struggling to process all that had occurred.

"It is obvious!" Holleet sneered. "He could not have acted alone and she sits their unaffected by what transpires. Kelda, answer for your sins!"

There was no change to Kelda's cold gaze, but around her an aura flickered.

"She is but an apparition!" Holleet gasped.

"We have been tricked." Pagmai added.

"I would wager that this is not the first time." Holleet agreed.

"Very perceptive!" Grimalkin mocked. "It has only taken a century for the pendulum of realisation to sway in your favour." His words dripped with sarcasm as he scoffed at their incompetence. "It is so very easy to manipulate those whom cannot see past their own ego. Your eyes gazed upon the visions that I wanted you to see. You heard words that I allowed you to hear. You gazed upon stars that were but sorcery."

Yodel's eyes grew wide and filled to the brim with tears, somehow he managed to break free from the grip of The Black Imp that held him captive.

"No!" Yodel cried, "I have failed The Circle." He weeped openly and staggered forward, leaning on the table to keep him from fainting. "This is all my fault."

The Black Imp attempted to seize him again, but Grimalkin waved him away back to the shadows, the walls were now consumed with the amber glow of eyes and their seemed no escape for The Mystic Circle, Grimalkin's dark grasp was all round and it constricted with every second that passed.

"Do not blame yourself, Yodel." Pagmai pleaded. "We were all blind to this treachery."

"I-I won't stand for this!" Yodel stuttered and he grasped a large knife from the table, its blade dripped with the meat fats of a cockerel that had been carved earlier.

"I-I will not die a c-coward!" He hollered and charged Grimalkin, who swiped the air with a clawed finger, magenta energy split the gloom and sliced through the onrushing stargazer, it cut him in two pieces and each piece fell to the ground twitching rapidly as his innards doused the rugs beneath.

The members of The Mystic Circle weeped for another loss, L'llak, Hyacynthia and Haras Lunarc had no energy left to struggle as they were frozen by the horror that had taken place before them, it would do them no good either way for the multiple Black Imps that clamped them tightly would not allow it. Grooble, the Smidge remained in a drunken sleep beneath the table, oblivious to Grimalkin's wrath. Pagmai and Holleet weeped openly, the shield of energy that flickered around them seemed to lose its power again and Black Imps were able to see an opening and step through it before Pagmai focussed again and the shield strengthened again slicing limbs from the bloodthirsty Children of the Shrouded Realm, their limbs burning to ash and consuming them to nothingness only to be replaced by yet more Black Imps that emerged from the shadows.

"KELDA!" Holleet cried, tears cascading down the contours of her ageing but pretty face. "Please put a halt to this madness!"

As she pleaded to Kelda, she remained frozen like a statue as if in a trance.

"Grimalkin must have control of her mind." Pagmai growled, anger had replaced his sorrow now and he knew he would have to fight.

"On the contrary Grand One! Kelda has championed my cause since it were conceived."

Pagmai and Holleet stared at Grimalkin, emotions fluttering in their old eyes, eyes that were supposed to have been all seeing, all knowing, how could they be so blind to this?

"I told you that you were blind!" Grimalkin sneered. "You were only allowed to witness what I conjured."

Kelda had appeared behind Holleet and Pagmai, again blind to her presence. She had bided her time for the moment when the shield was at its weakest and then revealed herself. The eyes of the captive Wizards and Witches doubled in size as they tried to warn Pagmai and Holleet of Kelda's presence within the safety of their shield, but it was to no avail, they remained unaware of Kelda's location.

It was too late.

Kelda smiled sadistically, her marbled eyes bright with wonder as she revealed a jagged blade from the confines of her dark and tattered cloak, the fingers that held the handle were as sharp as the shard itself, but still her movements were muted as she crept ever closer to Hollett, lights reflected from the surrounding energy to the blade and she licked away spittle that hung from her remaining teeth.

"It did not have to be this way, Grimalkin." Holleet cried, still pleading, Pagmai had moved past tears and looked to unveil the Orb of Quirinus from the confines of his long streaked beard. Grimalkin caught sight of the Orb and he too salivated, Kelda longed for death and grief and he yearned for power and control, a truly heinous union. Grimalkin saw the tears shimmering in the eyes of the captives and smiled and with a gracious nod of his head, Kelda made her move. Kelda's long clawed fingers were around Holleet's throat before she could even acknowledge her presence and before she even had time to fathom what was taking place, the makeshift blade hacked through the flesh of her neck, slicing muscle and tissue and opening her throat. Holleet uttered no other words only the constant flow of blood left her now as she clutched at her throat frantically, her fingers tips glowing with the flicker of magic that still remained as if she were trying to seal the wound. But there was no magic powerful enough to heal a cut throat. Pagami turned and saw her fall, through unbelieving eyes, she seemed to wear a dress of red as the blood consumed her.

"Holleet?" Pagmai murmured and he fell at her side and cradled her in his arms. He too tried to mend her wounds with his magic fingers to no avail. "No, my beloved, no, no, no..." He chanted and then heard Grimalkin's horrendous laughter that seemed to surround him like a wall of vile mockery.

"Grimalkin!" Pagmai seethed, looking around him and noticing now that he was no longer protected by the shield and Black Imps crept ever closer, their serrated teeth chattering as they approached him. He lowered Holleet's lifeless body to the ground as the last of her blood left her body, her eyes remained open and staring, but there was no life there, no magic.

"You wrong me!" He growled, he looked older than he had ever looked, as if his beloved's assassination had taken a part of his life-force too. "You wrong The Mystic Circle and you wrong the realm! You will pay with your own death for this outrage!"

"You will not kill me!" Grimalkin laughed again. "You do not have it in you to do what needs to be done. You never have!" He added with venomous spit as Kelda appeared in her body at the table once more and she rose slowly, shuffling over to her Dark Master's side.

"A Wizard's duel it shall be!" Pagmai announced. "To the death!"

Grimalkin pondered these words.

"All I ask is that you let the other members of The Circle go free. There has been enough needless blood spilt this day."

"So it shall be!" Grimalkin nodded. "But I think I will have your friends remain were they are until the duel is over." Grimalkin knew that they had seen what had taken place and the element of surprise is what would win this duel for him, he

309

would not risk The Grand One's friends ruining this moment for him.

"So it shall be." Pagmai actually smiled as he stood as upright and proud as the old Wizard could and his withered hand disappeared into the mass of his beard that was now stained red with the blood of his one true love. The smile soon departed as he rummaged frantically behind his beard, searching for something that was no longer there.

"I have told you more than once that you are too blind to see past your own nose, Pagmai." Grimalkin cackled and Pagmai looked at him in horror as Kelda handed her Dark Master the Orb of Quirinus.

All hope seemed to drift away and his body went limp, he did now truly look his age. The Orb of Quirinus believed to be the heart of Sirod the Phoenix that rose from the remains of the fallen God, Adeve and destroyed the Dragon brood before returning to the realm leaving only the Orb. It was said to be the most powerful object in Maglore and now with it in the hands of pure evil, Pagmai was left with no hope. The Grand One obviously had magic running through his veins and a vast amount of knowledge on the stars and planets, the Orb increased all these elements and without it he could feel that power leaving him.

"Cheap parlour tricks!" Pagmai growled as he lent on the table for support as the Orb's power left him withered and almost empty. He had held the Orb for so long that he had not realised that he had become so reliant on it, was he truly this old, this weak without it?

310

"Without The Orb of Quirinus that is all you will be capable of!" Mocked Grimalkin as he watched his old master age rapidly before his malicious eyes, his flesh tightening around his bones, he looked gaunt like a weathered corpse.

Grimalkin took The Orb of Quirinus in his pale hands and exhaled with euphoria as he felt its power.

"The power..." He wheezed, "...it is divine!"

Grimalkin began to glow with this newfound strength, thoughts in his mind hurtled at ridiculous speeds, the potential to this force seemed to have no bounds.

"I am a God!" Grimalkin hissed and cackled, his voice was as sharp as a Knight's blade and it sliced through the gloom with menace.

"It's power will be your downfall." Pagmai whispered as he pulled himself back to his feet, somehow standing in defiance with only the gifts he was born with to confront this Dark Master, this Lord of Darkness.

"Nonsense!" Grimalkin spat, "I feel its power flowing through me, there is nothing or no one on this realm that can stop me now!"

"The power grows as does your ego, Grimalkin." Pagmai said, struggling, but managing to pull himself onto the table where he stood again defiant and challenging. "This is one duel that you have not won yet."

Grimalkin laughed, the Wizards and Witches that watched on weeping for all that had happened and for what they knew now would be their fate.

"You are either very foolish or very brave, Pagami!" Grimalkin scoffed almost choking on his own vanity as he floated up onto the table, still clutching the glowing Orb in his hands, he kicked away the dead wingless carcass of the fallen Mingus Mothe. The Children of the Shrouded Realm's teeth chattered excitedly and as Kelda watched on she seemed almost aroused by what would come and she slowly licked Holleet's blood from the shard that took her life.

"I am neither brave nor foolish," Pagmai replied, "I am duty, I am obligation, I am still The Master of The Mystic Circle and I shall shield who remain until I breathe no more."

"Which will be any moment now!" Grimalkin mocked and playfully threw the Orb into the air before catching it again, his clawed fingernails clicking impatiently on the Orb's pebble like texture.

"That is no toy you handle, Grimalkin!" Pagmai snapped, it seemed to take all his energy. "Prepare to duel!"
Grimalkin grinned again Pagmai's weary eyes met the glazed eyes of his Circle and suddenly dropped to a knee, clutching his chest.

"This is all so needless, Pagmai." Grimalkin laughed. "Your time on this realm is through, just die now and be done with it."
Pagmai's hands quivered over his chest and his eyes met those of his fallen beloved who still stared up at him from a bed of blood.

"My love, I will see you again." Pagmai whispered and as Grimalkin clutched the Orb close to unleash the killer blow,

Pagmai's fingers quivered and sparked with yellow energy. As Grimalkin forced the power of the Orb towards Pagmai in a flurry of magenta rays that burnt the air, Pagmai unveiled energy of his own that was suddenly domed around him like a transparent shield, the Orb's energy struck his shield and the castle shook, everyone except The Grand Wizard and the evil Warlock lost their footing and fell to the ground. The force was so much that the energy hurtled towards the wall and reduced it too rubble, a gaping hole opened up revealing a view of the eerie haze that hung over the East. Hefty chunks of castle wall fell around the chamber and crushed some of The Black Imps that squealed painfully like a boar being led to slaughter. Pagmai held the shield for as long as he was able and there was a second eruption and this time the collision sent Pagmai and Grimalkin hurtling off the table. More rubble fell and Pagmai looked over to his Circle, L'llak lay dead under chunks of dark stone, Hyacynthia crawled across the floor, dragging behind her legs that had been shattered by the falling debris, but The Black Imps were on her and their chattering teeth tore into her flesh, blood sprayed up from them and they suckled on every drop before it hit the floor, she screamed loudly until death silenced her. Haras Lunarc panicked not knowing what to do, her damp eyes met Pagmai's and he told her to flee as she unleashed several balls of fire from her fist that turned Imps to ash where they stood as she made her way to the hole in the wall. More Black Imps attacked and she used her other fist to unleash water that washed away the attack sending her assailants spilling out of the hole in wall and down the

313

treacherous mountain face. She ran for the gaping ruins were a wall once stood and was almost free when Kelda was on her back and plunging her shard into her chest, she fell just yards away from the exit and as blood spurted from her wounds her fiery hand reached up with one final act of defiance and gripped Kelda around the throat, she shrieked in pain as the hand burnt away her old haggard flesh and she pushed herself away from the dying Elf Witch, her hand flickered with fire and water and then she was gone, leaving Kelda to hiss at her corpse as a handprint blistered her throat tattooing her with a painful souvenir. Grimalkin rose up through the rising plume of debris, his face glowing with the heat of his rage, he clutched the Orb tightly in his palm as if it was an extension of his arm, Pagmai staggered to his feet at the other side of the table and looked around at the death and blood that lay on the floor of the chamber.

"Look where duty has taken you, Pagmai!" Grimalkin seethed. "It has only brought you death and blood!"
The Black Imps consumed the dead, gnawing at their flesh and suckling the blood from their veins and Pagmai knew that it was over.

"Let it be done!" Pagmai could see no way out of the situation so he stood tall and waited for Grimalkin to take what life he had left away from.

"It shall be!" Grimalkin hissed and aimed the Orb directly at him and it glowed wildly as if it had been longing to be used for destruction. He unleashed its power but at the last moment something tugged on his leg which changed the trajectory of his energy and it destroyed another piece of wall. Grimalkin looked down to see the drunken Smidge emerging from underneath the table.

"You drunken fool!" Grimalkin seethed as Grooble clutched at his robes pulling himself up.

"What have you done, Grimalkin?" He gurgled. Grimalkin slapped him away with a pale sharp hand.

"Release me!" He growled.

"You have slain them all!" Grooble wept. "Why would you do such a thing?"

"Foolish Smidge!" Grimalkin laughed. "For power!" He added driving The Orb of Quirinus into his peculiar shaped face and held it their as its energy burnt straight through his flesh and bone.

"Why else would I do this?" Grimalkin smiled as he released his magical grip on Grooble and watched as the faceless Smidge fell dead to the floor.

"You will not win, Grimalkin!" Sneered Pagmai who was now stood on the ledge of the broken wall and now encased in a glowing aura that sprouted yellow wings of energy, "I shall see to it!" And with that Pagmai threw himself out of the castle.

"No!" Grimalkin growled and he arrived at the broken wall in time to see a yellow bird that glowed like the Sun of Selym as it glided calmly through the dark haze.

"Pagmai lives!" Kelda hissed, still nursing her blistering flesh of her throat.

"But for how long?" Grimalkin scoffed. "He has no power, he is of no concern."

315

"You underestimate his magic, Dark Master." Kelda said and then cowered from his sudden gaze, believing he would strike her.

"You dare?" He screeched.

"I meant no disrespect my Dark Master, I live to serve you and worship you!" She fell pleading at his bandaged feet. "Pagmai is wise and knows many tricks. You should not forget about him so quickly, I fear."

"As you say." Grimalkin said after pondering her words. "He heads South, no doubt to seek refuge at the Tower of Solitude in Lunarc."

"Should we act?" Kelda asked cautiously as to not aggravate the already irate Warlock.

Grimalkin pondered this, knowing that he had important plans to put in to motion and gazed upon the mass of Black Imps gorging themselves on the bloody corpses that were lay strewn on the floor of the chamber.

"My brothers and sisters!" He announced, The Black Imps looked up from their meals, eyes burning amber, teeth stained pink with blood, their narrow nostrils twitching at their master's words. "Children of the Shrouded Realm, yes, enjoy your meals, you have earned such spoils, but I have need of you all!"

They rose up and their twisted bodies cracked as they contorted themselves to hear his words.

"Take word to your cousins that lie sleeping beneath the sands, whisper words of evil and stir them form their slumber.

316

Have them take the Tower of Solitude and slay any that stand in their way!"

Their teeth chattered in response and they could already sense that there would be blood and entrails waiting for them at the end of such a quest.

"Have them take the Wizard Pagmai! Devour him, but bring me his head!"

They shrieked and clambered out of the hole in the wall in droves and crawled down the mountains as if they were half arachnid. Grimalkin watched as they disappeared into the darkness and he smiled.

"Is it time, oh Dark Master?" Kelda cackled.

"It is time!" He hissed. "Give word to General Feng to assemble the army."

"It shall be so." She cackled and vanished in a black haze. Grimalkin was left alone and he kicked through the rubble of the chamber, he looked on without guilt or mercy at the remains of the dead that lay scattered in pools of blood. He reached Pagmai's chair and kicked away the corpse of Holleet that lay next to it and sat in the seat at the head of The Mystic Circle. He smiled at the table covered with the remnants of supper and hefty blocks of stone and rubble.

"Finally!" He hissed, turning the Orb in his fingers sensually. "But this is no throne for a Lord of the realm."

Using his new influx of power, he turned his attention to Holleet and with a twitch of his fingers her dead corpse floated into the air and hovered over the table in front of him, he gazed into her soulless eyes and caressed her chin with a black talon.

"Oh sweet Holleet, the marda I should have let you be." He sighed. "But alas you were not worthy." He sneered and took his claws and dug them into her face, tearing away the flesh and scalp leaving just her skull, dripping with blood. He wrenched her skull from the grip of its spine and held it cupped in his palm as though it were a chalice. Holleet's floating headless corpse fell unceremoniously onto the table and he stared at the dead eyes that hung from the dark sockets on stringlike nerves.

"If I am to rule, I shall construct a throne of my own."

CHÃPTÉR 27
THÉ FÃLLÉN ÖNÉ

ebastian had made good time from Zalenta taking the North route through God's March and now the crystal clear waters of Shanoli Creek sparkled invitingly ahead. After the constant travel of the past few days, Dayboy was showing noticeable signs of fatigue, his thick muscular hide had become tacky with sweat and he panted for refreshment and nourishment. Sebastian dismounted and praised his brave steed for his effort in getting them this far in such a short time, but now he must allow the colt to rest or he would be good for nothing but filling for a rider's pie. It took a while for his eyes to adjust to the brightness of day having been consumed by the dark haze for the past days, however many days it has been for time had lost all meaning to the King. The morning sun rose into a sky of cornflower, Sebastian felt relief and was comforted by its warming embrace, he turned back to face the West again still that shroud lay upon it, he was glad to leave it behind him but also apprehensive about his next steps. For when he crossed the creek he would have an important decision to make, should he travel to Kanka, to the Hills of Brockonbak and parlay with the Lord of the Giants, or should he travel home to Windmast Castle and be with those who believe his words. His heart was being tugged on by two competing entities, love held one end and pulled him home to Windmast Castle, and honour held the other half tightly too, he felt he had an obligation as King of Maglore to at least meet with the Giants, even if the words he received were not the ones that he required. As Sebastian pondered his thoughts Dayboy led himself to the creek and drank eagerly, lapping at the cool water with his thick, dry tongue. Sebastian followed and removed Dayboy's burden of the saddle and other additions that he had carried for so long.

"What to do?" He asked himself aloud, maybe he hoped for a reply from Dayboy, it would obviously never come, but even he believed that his loyal steed would choose Windmast over yet more travel.

"A King's duty is never without hindrance..." His words drifted away as something caught his eye up ahead, over the creek in the distance, in the centre of a vast acre of wild grass that stood long and strong like thousands of broad swords of green all reaching up to touch the sky, there was a shimmering of steel that dazzled him, the Sun of Selym's rays colliding with this mysterious object that called to him.

"What is that?" Sebastian said, Dayboy was usually alive to such things and it was often he that spotted things before Sebastian, but the colt paid no mind to his words or his strange object that called to him, he was too busy attempting to drink the Shanoli Creek dry. Sebastian placed his hand over his brow to block out the shining sun and focus on whatever it was that intrigued him.

"Steel...armour..." Sebastian murmured, he had witnessed many a suit of armour shimmering in the rays of the sun before, many a battle waged under the unforgiving heat of Selym's watchful eye.

He scampered through the shallow creek, the cool waters relieving his Juug leathered boots from the thick layer of dust that had coated them from constant travel. As he drew closer, through the long wild grass he could see that a Knight sat upon a colt, his posture appeared slightly slouched as there was no helm visible.

"The armour is treated, it is pale, almost white..." his words lingered "...like that of Mondt's..." as he drew closer he realised that the mare that he sat upon was indeed Karbia.

"Mondt!" Sebastian called a smile curling his lips, he was excited and thankful for familiarity. "Where have you been Sir Knight? Consummating one's engagement with the lovely Ethel?" He bellowed, but there came no reply and on closer inspection he noticed that Karbia looked weak and sullen, her body language was one that had been burdened for far too long and was on the verge of collapse.

"Mondt?" Sebastian called again, his pace quickened as his scythed through the tall grass, something was wrong, he began to run, the muscles in his legs burning, they were tight and pleaded for Sebastian to halt this unwanted vigorous activity, they pulled until ache rippled through his legs,

Sebastian was halted suddenly but not from the searing pain in his legs.

"M-Mondt..." Sebastian whispered his eyes wide and his lips aquiver with the horror of such a sight.

Sir Maximillious Mondt sat upon the weakened mare but he was not slouched forward in his saddle as the King had first thought. The Knight sat up straight without his head, blood smeared the Knight's collar and white armoured plate.

"No!" Sebastian whispered, emotion taking his brow and contorting it with pain of loss. Blood-flies buzzed around the wound of misshaped flesh where his handsome head had once sat proudly, soon the crows and ravens would come to eat their fill of the Knight's carcass.

Sebastian's gaze met Karbia's and she looked back at him with pleading, hurt eyes, they spoke to him, longing for death. Sebastian would do what needed to be done, but first he had to bring the matter to an end, to have closure on the ordeal and to be sure that this headless Knight was in fact 'The One', Sir Maximillious Mondt, who so valiantly protected him from the attack of the twisted brothers of the Cult of Crypor, for believing his words that many scoffed at thinking he was mad, a Knight that stood by him and travelled with him into the dark haze and the unknowing, a true Knight of the realm.

"I must see," Sebastian said, "I must know for sure." The words came but he already knew, this was Mondt's armour, his steed, his sword, 'God's Hand' the ivory pommel shaped like a fist, the fist of Adeve shimmered in the bright light. The helm sat in the lap of the Knight, its visor closed concealing horrors within, the realisation of the Knight's murder. With the visor closed the ordeal was still yet to be finalised even though he knew what he would find. Sebastian's hands quivered as he reached into the lap of the headless Knight that still towered above him on the back of the brave mare, he felt the white steel at his fingertips, even under the heat of the sun's rays it was cold to the touch, but inside the head would be sweltering and cooking in its own meaty juices. He opened the visor and was met by those handsome blue eyes staring back at him, the light had gone out of them, no playful sparkle was there and his lips that smiled so often and told long tales of adventures never had were now chapped and dry.

"By Adeve, who did this to you!" Sebastian seethed as he fought back tears, he had seen many dead eyes stare back at him, friends and family members lost in battle, but this touched him tenderly for this Man gave his life to follow him on his quest, believed him when many did not and saved his life in the bargain.

Blood-flies settled on the Knight's exposed face and nibbled at his pale flesh.

"You will have a King's funeral." Sebastian said as he turned away from Mondt's dead stare, "I will build the pyre myself, it's the least I can do."

He stroked Karbia's nose and whispered in her ear words that she had been longing to hear. "Go now brave steed, you have served your Master well, but go now."

323

As he walked away back towards Dayboy, he heard the clatter of armour as Karbia collapsed to the ground, the headless Knight tumbling into the long grass.

CHÃPTÉR 28

DRÛMS ÖF WÃR

ord Grimalkin strode through the rubble of the broken wall of Mount Quirinus, he wore the dark armour of Pagmai, an aura of magenta energy kissing the enchanted steel. He wore the black blade of Hex at his side and in his gauntleted hands he held a staff of dark steel, the likeness of Demios 'The Black Arrow' had been forged at its head, its slender scales and wings wrapped tightly around The Orb of Quirinus. He crushed debris under the force of his heavily armoured feet, kicking away bulky fragments of black stone. He felt the soft caress of the breeze that seeped through the dark haze, and displayed a horrendous smile that exuded arrogance and menace. The Dark Elf walked through the gaping maw left in the wall, debris of rock continuing to fall around him as he exited the castle and headed towards the edge of Mount Quirinus, the warm breeze consumed him but he did not falter or change his stride, even though half the castle lay in ruin behind him. He could hear the stir of his disciples at the foot of the mountain, steel rang out as the mass shifted impatiently below, the grunts, groans and growls of several different species came together to create a horrifying cacophony. Grimalkin's armour shook with each pretentious step as he finally reached the mountain's craggy lip, he looked out at the assemblage of creatures below and the roar from them was deafening as it rose off the breeze to meet his ears, Goblins and Zwulf roared and shields were drummed loudly. Below there were hundreds of torches burning brightly, unveiling the hordes of evil that awaited the arrival of their Dark Master. Some warriors even smashed fists against their armoured chests to show their appreciation at his arrival. The Bat-Fiends screeched and launched themselves into the air, flying up to greet him as if it were a rehearsed display. The large Cyclops' held cleavers and clubs aloft and roared through broken teeth, their bulging eyeballs strained with veins, intense as if at any moment they would explode, some even clashed heads as was their tradition when greeting each other. The Ferals growled and shrieked in a rowdy parade as they paced back and forth and lifted themselves onto their hind legs. Even the Orges reared up and skipped around defiantly in his presence. The glowing yellow eyes of The Black Imps glistened in the darkness in their thousands as if Grimalkin were staring at the mysterious stars above. The mountain top was suddenly attacked by a strong gale, so much so that even Grimalkin had to adjust his footing and force his staff into the rock to stop him from spilling over the lip by these vigorous swipes of air.

The rabble that stood below fell in silence as gigantic winged beasts sliced through the dark haze and Dragons appeared. They watched on in awe as three Dragons swept through the gloom, each one bigger than the next.

"Laasp!" Grimalkin smiled as the smallest of the three, whisked through the gloom, weaving its slender yellow body quickly around the peaks of the Kayalian Mountains to display its speed. It landed on a peak of the mountain range on strong back legs, its armless snake-like torso joined his long neck as it reached up to his Master and flapped its wings, before squealing loudly and releasing several rapid blasts of white, yellow flame.

"The quickest of all Dragons!" Grimalkin hissed with sadistic pleasure. "As swift as a hornet in yellow scale."

There was a peculiar roar that sound like the call of several creatures amalgamated to create the sound, all the calls of the animals it mimicked could still be made out.

"Ah, Tazak! The call of the hunter, 'The Grey Shadow'!" Grimalkin grinned. "The Dragon from the deepest jungles of Tangotta! Release your cunning and your swiftness!"

It twisted and turned silently through the haze, it's smokey scales shimmered like dull steel, but it emitted no flame, for Tazak did not have that ability. Instead thick smoke whirled from its pulsating nostrils forming a cloak around him, a technique it used while hunting in the dense jungles of Tangotta. Tazak had all but disappeared to the eyes of the army below, all wondering warily where the beast had gotten too, it burst from the smog only a short distance from their curious eyes surprising them with its mouth wide unveiling its rows of severed teeth as long as a Man's leg, the sight was enough to send some Goblins and Zwulf to the ground in fear, before the beast reared itself up and swooped back into the air again erupting in its horrid hunter's cry before perching on a mountain peak.

Then came forth one of the largest Dragons known, its size was double that of Tazak, its wingspan alone was an astonishing sight, each leathery wing the size of a Man made galleon. Its huge scales thick like armour and as black as the sky he flew in, a shimmer of magenta caresses each scale, it made them look as though they were alive and moving on their own accord, this was the Dragon know as 'The Black Arrow', this was...

"Demios!" Grimalkin grinned, the look on his face displayed both sadism and what could be called love. Was it even possible for this evil Warlock Elf to love?

Demios glided around the peaks of the mountains before settling onto the courtyard of Mount Quirinus so he could be nearer to his Master. Demios' huge talons crushed the cobbled stone as its mighty bulk touched down, unsettled boulders from the rock face and sending them hurtling down towards the ground. Some Goblins were crushed under this avalanche, but all the army did was roar with adulation for the mighty beast. Demios returned the gesture with a huge fire display, magenta and pinkish flame erupting from its massive maw, the powerful flare of fire cut through the dark shroud and for the first time in several suns the East looked bright again, but it was of course only a brief occurrence as it was gone when Demios had decided to extinguish his power.

"How beautiful you are Demios, how powerful!" Grimalkin said to himself, but the connection he had with the

Dragon was strong and Demios unleashed a deafening shriek in response.

Kelda appeared at his side to oversea the congregation, she appeared again from the shadows like a ghastly apparition, behind her G'nora the Dark Master's astronomer shuffled carefully through the rubble and remained behind them, reluctant to get to close to the edge.

"A phenomenal force, my Dark Master." Kelda hissed.

"Indeed they are." Grimalkin said proudly.

"I thought you spoke of more than three Dragons..." G'nora spat, immediately holding his mouth having not meant to say such words out load.

"Fool!" Kelda hissed at him and removed that jagged blade from her dark cloak. "Let me rid you of this burden, Oh Dark Master! My blade has already tasted blood once this day, I beg you to allow me to spill the astronomer's for his insolence!" Grimalkin did not even turn to address G'nora, his eyes were fixated on his army, the vision he had conceived centuries ago had finally come to fruition and he had no time for trivialities.

"Master?" Kelda said as she toyed anxiously with the blade, G'nora slowly began shuffling backwards, trying not to fall over the debris.

"Leave him, Kelda." Grimalkin replied.

G'nora breathed a sigh of relief and he remained where he was, Kelda gave him a glare with those milky eyes of hers and reluctantly made the blade disappear in the blink of an eye.

"There are many a Dragon stargazer!" Grimalkin spat. "But I only have need for one more of them at this time. Mighty

Maddox the Green could not join us here, his massive size means he lacks the ability to fly well, but he awaits the army to join him in Elken End."

"Forgive my insolence, Master." G'nora stuttered and once again swallowed hard when he caught Kelda's gaze, he truly believed that one day she would kill him, he hoped he would not have to look into her hideous face when she did the deed, that would be the last vision he would want to take with him to the other side of wherever the dead reside.

Grimalkin stood proud in the enchanted amour, that glistened in the haze, the colour and texture of ink. He gripped the staff in his hands, the sound of each rivet in the steel gauntlets crunched as his fingers tightened around the shaft. The Orb of Quirinus was sensitive to its new Master's touch and it glowed with power, its brightness was enough to silence the mass congregation with a mere twinkle of its energy, the creatures below were bathed in its light but did not shy away from it as they would sunlight. Instead they embraced it as if a God stood before them, some even dropped to their knees on the hard surface, stone and gravel digging into their flesh and tearing it. In many ways it was a God that appeared before them, Grimalkin was their new deity and they would cast themselves into the bowels of Vollox if it pleased their Dark Master.

He had the power of the Orb and power was control, power was rule.

The silence was breathtaking, even the mighty Dragon beasts did not stir as all ears waited patiently for the words of Grimalkin. He smiled as he took in the recognition, he wore a

330

mask of pure arrogance on his pale, gaunt face, who else in the realm could bring silence to such an assembly? In his cruel magenta eyes there was no-one that could, he believed that not even the mighty Sloore could have achieved what he had. A thought drifted across his mind's eye, a mind that was now linked with The Orb of Quirinus that seemed to see all there was to see, the thought was dark and treacherous but he cared not. Why should he hand the realm over to Sloore? He held the power and the armies and the... Dragons! Sloore would never rise from his dwell for fear of the Dragons and their destructive fires, Grimalkin could reign unopposed by Man or God.

"My children!" He hissed loudly, his voiced swept over the mass like seeping gas, seemingly touching the ears of all below personally. "The time is now. Too long have we waited in the shadows of Maglore. Too long have we hidden in holes and caves, treated like outcasts by those who believe themselves worthier to power and fortune, of crowns and thrones. I say no more!"

The congregation below erupted from their silence with an unruly cry for blood, but with the raise of his palm, Grimalkin brought them to silence once more.

"No longer will we hide. No longer will we be kept away from what is rightfully ours. This realm is just as much yours as it theirs, I say! Man, Dwarf, Fairy and Giant with their golden halos sitting upon their meaningless chairs, growing fat and believing that they are all so powerful. I AM POWER!" The armies smashed their arms together to create a loud drumming

331

hum of steel on steel that reverberated around the mountains that surrounded Zalenta.

When the humming had dissipated Grimalkin spoke again.

"I am Elf." He announced proudly, "The last of my race."

As these words left Grimalkin's lips the hooded figure of G'nora twitched uncomfortably, this response was not missed by Kelda, who eyed him with suspicion.

"The darkness came before anything, before the creation of sun and moon there was only darkness. You all know that Elves were the first of Adeve's creations to conquer and rule this realm, it is my given right that I Grimalkin, 'The Harbinger of Darkness', 'The Dragon Whisperer'... 'The Last Elf!', should rule! Like the darkness, my race came first and the right is mine to rule and rule it I shall under a shroud of darkness as it was meant to be."

The congregation below erupted again in response to their Dark Master's declaration. The fur covered Ferals roared in a feline frenzy, displaying their smooth tooth-like sabres that protruded out over malicious grins. The blubbering grey flesh of the Ogres wiggled uncontrollably as they vigorously stamped their massive legs, cleft feet kicking up dust and stones, so much was their excitement that even the mighty Zwulf handlers struggled to hold them still by their reins. Bat-Fiends screeched loudly as they scampered up the rock face, their hooked claws gripping the jagged stone, wings swept back and quivered in the breeze like a capes made of leather. Grimalkin's eyes danced with anticipation of what would happen when he released these brutal weapons of destruction upon an unsuspecting world. It was the Dragons' display that was the loudest and most flamboyant, Laasp and Tazak's talons gripped the peaks of the mountains, carving hefty chunks of rock with ease as Demios' massive claws crushed the cobbles of the Quirinus' courtyard as easy as shredding wheat. Collectively they spread wings of yellow, grey and black that sliced through the haunting mist. Tazak unleashed his hunter's cry again that sounded like every creature that there ever was and smoke rose from his gapping nostrils as yellow flame and magenta flame burst from the widening maws of Laasp and Demios. The jubilant Dark Lord smiled at the performance of his dark followers and held his hand out to them as if he were humbled and unworthy of such devotion.

"You honour me with your gestures."

There was suddenly a ruckus and the army parted ways, opening a wide path. There were mumbles of confusion and then whispers, then nothing but silence and something moved through the darkness along the path that had been laid before it.

"What is it?" Asked a bewildered G'nora as his old eyes squinted to see what it was, he saw nothing but a shadow moving slowly across the stone and gravel.

"Fool!" Hissed Kelda with annoyance. "The Dark Master's daughter returns."

"Daughter?" G'nora murmured to himself.

"My spawn! My seed!" Grimalkin cackled with delight. "My Gri'ul."

The black Unicorn strode towards the mountain, walled in

either side by Goblins, Zwulf, Cyclops, Black Imps, Ogres and Ferals. She did not falter under their sadistic gaze because she could sense their apprehension, she saw fear in their eyes. Her hooves scraped across the harsh soil and stone, burning her prints deep into its dry earth. It was as if the land of Zalenta had not seen a rainfall in many months, it was true that since the dark haze had shrouded the East there had been no rain at all. Her crimson mane and tail dripped like blood, her red eyes shimmered in the torchlight like two precious rubies and the obsidian alicorn protruded from her head proudly like a Princess' tiara.

"Our honoured guest!" Grimalkin bellowed in excitement. "My spawn, my child!" He hissed with sadistic euphoria. "The Shadow Bearer!"

Gri'ul came to a halt at the head of all the armies, still they stared at her in disbelief, the majority of them had never cast their malignant eyes upon a Unicorn and did not believe in their existence, until now. The songs and tales that they had heard of such creatures gave them a very different outlook, they believed them pure and light and being of the light they brought hope to those that had nothing. This creature that stood before them was nothing like the tales and songs, black as pitch with wild hair that seemed to leak from her skin and hooves of red fire that singed the ground she walked upon. Even the Dragon's considered her with curiosity, Laasp and Tazak fidgeted uncomfortably, but the mighty Demios displayed no such signs, an inquiring glance was all the Unicorn received from the one they called 'The Black Arrow',

334

for Demios feared nothing and no one. Gri'ul bowed to her Dark Master, her farda. She had travelled to the four corners of the East bringing with her the shroud of darkness, unable to cross U'lenka she would repeat her cycle again and again in the East, her timeline passing more quickly than usual Unicorns who walked the whole realm. She waited patiently for her farda's next words.

He gazed upon this mass of malevolence that he had created, centuries of preparation, of cunning and deceit and finally he was ready to unleash them on Maglore. He gripped his staff tightly and The Orb of Quirinus pulsed, vibrantly like a heart filled with life, with his other hand he ran steel tipped fingertips across the pommel of his new arm Hex, desperate to unsheathe it and have his followers gaze upon its enchanted black blade.

"All the pieces are in place!" He began, his voice was stern and serious and all knew now it was almost time. Anticipation swelled through the mass horde as layers of bumpy gooseflesh broke out on the green flesh of the Goblins, the pinkish skin of the Cyclops and even the fur covered limbs of the Zwulf although they hid it extremely well.

"Even the stars in the black sky whisper a prophecy of a Serpent taking the realm and leading it justly! Yes, my children it is time. Let the games begin! Listen to my words for I am your Lord of the Darkness and this is the beginning of a new era!" Grimalkin hissed before announcing each race with respect, a cry erupting from each race that spilt from his lips.

"HAIL LORD GRIMALKIN!" Came a roar of various tones, that sounded bitter and twisted, howling and shrieking, but it was like music to Grimalkin's ears.

"The Goblins of Grotte! The Zwulf from the Isle of Beasts! The Cyclops of Brood's Reach! The Black Imps of The Shrouded Realm! The Ferals of jungle and forest! The Bat-Fiends of cavern and cave! The spawn of Selym and Tenaj, The mightiest beasts in the realm, my Dragons!"

The army cheered in a bloodthirsty frenzy, constant drumming of shields and stamping of feet echoed through the mountains.

"Follow 'The Shadow Bearer' safely to the borders of U'lenka and then march forward and take what is rightfully ours! Spill the blood of Man, drink it down greedily, crunch and snap their bones, gnaw on their flesh and rip out their hearts!" Grimalkin screamed, now overcome with centuries of hatred and eagerness to share his message. "Burn their homes, rape their women, poison their waters, rip babes away from their teats and trample them into the dirt. It is our time and we must take every advantage to achieve our goal. Man will die, Kings will fall and the darkness will rule all!"

The army erupted and they began to march to the West, The Zwulf to the East coast and Black Imps disappeared into holes and caverns to pass quickly underneath the realm. Tazak and Laasp rose high into the air and disappeared through the haze. General Feng was the first to mount his steed, a huge Feral of light fur, flicked on its rear and legs with bronze stripes, its massive back and head was armoured in battered gold to match its rider. The beast's dark eyes burned with hunger and saliva dripped from his jagged maw as Feng dug his heels into its side and the Feral grumbled loudly before setting off at the head of the march.

Purge would not be bettered and pulled a fellow Zwulf from the largest Ogre available, The Beast-Man unceremoniously fell to the ground and his brothers of war mocked him, but he remained floored and bowed to his leader, allowing him to mount the cumbersome Ogre that was saddled in leather and had been painted for battle in blacks and reds. Purge gave an almighty roar and held aloft his heavily spiked club as his followers cheered with him. Purge glared at Feng who sneered and spat at the floor, as they both marched in opposite directions. The armies fell in behind their leaders and the sound of thousands of marching feet was rhythmical as they all fell in time. Some other Goblins mounted Ferals and charged ahead eager to get on with the slaughter, some even took Bat-Fiends as their ride and cut through the air ahead of the march and the riders. Grimalkin watched on like a proud farda as Gri'ul led the Goblin army East. As the mass of soldiers started to leave a small figure stood quivering in their wake, the half Troll, half Goblin known as Pooka stared up at the castle where his Dark Master stood, tears welling in his round dark eyes. The whole ordeal had been too much for Pooka, he cursed himself for ever finding the secret entrance that was hidden under the falls of Windmast Castle. He had always believed that he would never see battle, what good would he be in such a situation? But here he was drafted for war with an oversized helm plonked on his misshaped head and a dress of rusted chainmail that consumed him, making it difficult for him to even move.

What was he to do?

If he ran they would find him and when he had served his purpose they would no doubt kill him. He hoped that after he had shown them the entrance that the Dark Master may praise him or even reward him with his freedom, but what was freedom in a world that is no longer free?

Goblins pushed him aside as they passed him, he felt rooted like a small tree, unable... unwilling to move.

"Here Runt!" Came the unmistakable grunt of the gargantuan Goblin, Sluug as he dropped a small axe into the halfbreed's hairy hands. To Pooka the axe seemed immense and he almost toppled over from its weight.

"W-what do I do with it?" Pooka stuttered swallowing hard because he knew exactly what they wanted him to do with it.

"Try not to kill yourself!" Cackled Kraag who joined them looking eager to flay Man cock in her gold and silver armour.

"Don't worry," Hissed Brood appearing from out of nowhere, coiling around Pooka and making him almost jump out of his chainmail. "We will take good care of you." His long tongue flickered like a snake, Pooka heard the words from his lips but did not believe them as his amber eyes said something quite different.

"Now march!" Sluug growled and kicked the half breed

in the backside sending Pooka tumbling to the ground in a clatter of steel.

The Goblins marched on laughing to themselves as Pooka struggled to lift himself from the tough soil and gravel.

"Keep up Runt!" Brood called. "Or Kraag will eat your cock!"

"Aye!" Laughed Kraag, "I do enjoy a small snack before battle." She glared at him and licked her lips.

Pooka stood mortified, but slowly he followed them, he wished that he had never been born.

Grimalkin said nothing for the longest time as Kelda and G'nora waited patiently behind him. Demios stirred with impatience on the courtyard, eager to get involved in the war that would end Man.

"What happens now?" Spurted G'nora, again forgetting his place and regretting his tongues wavering once more.

Grimalkin looked over his shoulder at his astronomer, annoyance in his eyes having been interrupted from this monuments occasion.

"Tidy this place up!" He growled. "And make it fit for a King!"

Grimalkin suddenly struck the rock beneath him with the end of his staff and he and Kelda disappeared leaving G'nora alone staring at the room that was full of destruction and the decaying bodies of the fallen Mystic Circle. He sighed heavily before beginning to remove the fallen rocks.

Grimalkin and Kelda appeared from black smoke that evaporated as soon as they arrived on the courtyard of Mount

Quirinus, Grimalkin was met by Demios who nudged at his Master looking for affection, he did not have to wait long for his Master was in a very pleasant mood. Grimalkin caressed the gigantic Dragon's slender nose with fingers that were encased in steel and he smiled at the beast.

"Are you so in need of my touch Demios?" Grimalkin cackled.

Demios screeched and stretched his thick neck up to the sky and released a long blast of pinkish flame that cut through the haze.

"Magnificent!" Grimalkin murmured. "Think how glorious it will be to see the castles of Man engulfed in his flame."

"It will truly be a sight to behold, Oh Dark Master!" Kelda replied.

"I sense apprehension in your voice Kelda." Grimalkin said as he continued to caress the thick black scales of 'The Black Arrow'. "Speak now. Keep nothing to yourself."

"Pagmai, 'The Grand One' still lives." She stuttered. "And the Hartwaker King! Is it a mistake to leave these leeches alive?"

Grimalkin turned to her and smiled, staring tenderly into her glazed eyes.

"My dearest Kelda, I understand your reluctance to go ahead with the plan while they live but there is no reason to worry yourself. Pagmai is almost depleted of his powers, it has taken all he has to escape my clutches, but he will head for the Tower of Solitude in the Lunarc Desert, this I know. He will try to rest in the seclusion of the desert and gain strength, and think of ways to stop this from happening, but it will be too late, he is too weak. But I have already sent word for the Sand Sleepers who dwell beneath the hot sands of the desert to rise up and take the old wretch."

"Sand Sleepers!" Kelda licked at her chapped lips with her forked tongue, hissing with pleasure at such a heinous act. Grimalkin gestured for Demois to lower himself, which he did and Grimalkin climbed onto the back of the magnificent black Dragon, positioning himself at the nape of the beast's neck, Demios stood back up and wriggled its wings in preparation, his lengthy tail quivering with anticipation. Grimalkin grasped one of the many protruding spikes that could be found on the wide back of the creature and sunk the sharp tips of his steel sabatons behind the thick scales to act as stirrups.

"Your work is not yet done Kelda." He said holding the staff tightly in his free hand.

"Whatever you wish of me shall be done." Kelda bowed as low as her crooked spine would allow her.

"You will infiltrate The Kingdom under the Flowers. Lift the magical vale of Valtora and allow Laasp to burn their puny nation."

"It shall be done, my Dark Master!" Kelda grinned eagerly.

"But now I must go and take what is rightfully mine." Kelda still stared at him.

"More to say?" Grimalkin asked.

"What of the King?"

"I can see that I shall have no rest until I have put your mind at ease." Grimalkin cackled. "If it pleases you, unleash Laasp on the King when you are done with Valtora."

"Yes, Master!"

"Now I go to take back the realm in the name of darkness!"

Demios lifted into the dark haze above with slow powerful thrashes of his wide wings forcing his massive bulk upwards and Grimalkin gripped tightly to his steed. Demios' wings worked harder and faster and with each swipe of the air, Kelda fought to stay upright and not be blown from the mountain. Demios rose into the haze, there was an eruption of pink flame that lit up the sky and bathed Grimalkin on the back of the beast's back, shimmered on his dark armour, The Orb of Quirinus glowed brightly as if it was to act as a torch to guide their journey. The flame died and they were gone away to the West were the Sun of Selym was making plans to set, for when it rose again there would be a new ruler of Maglore.

CHÃPTÉR 29
Ã MÏNDFÙL WÃRNÏNG

ing Sebastian had removed his tunic and the setting sun glistened against the sweat of his bare chest, thick brown hair had become matted together and his back was already showing the effects of sunburnt flesh. He had had to search far and wide for enough wood to build the funeral pyre, a lot was needed to first cover his friend's dead Mare, Karbia who had fallen as soon as her burden had been lifted from her strong shoulders. He had decided that he would burn Karbia with her Master as she too was as brave, strong and loyal as any Knight of the realm and deserved that farewell. As he placed the last of the wood around Karbia he stared at the headless corpse of Sir Maximillious Mondt, the Knight known throughout the realm as 'The One'. His spine screamed as he stretched out his muscles and wiped the sweat from his brow.

"My fallen friend I will do right by you." He said drowsily. "You are deserving of a royal funeral and I shall let everyone know of your courageousness and loyalty to the crown. They will sing songs of your deeds forever more, I swear it!"

343

Sebastian looked for Dayboy, but he had wondered off in search of food, the large colt was disturbed to see his trailing companion lying dead in the long grass while blood-flies sucked out the moisture from her dark hazel eyes. Colts were known to be fidgety around the dead, the wisest of Man had said it was the stench of death they disliked, Dayboy's sense of smell was impeccable so Sebastian could only imagine how his steed's senses were besieged. He would let the colt morn, there was nothing he could do to help in any case, colt's were not known for their building abilities.

Sebastian took a deep swig of his water and watched as the Sun of Selym started to make its descent, he was glad to see it leave, as its Fervor heat had not been pleasant to grind in. The Season of Fervor was for having garden parties and picnics, to enjoy sweet cakes and breads, fine wines and ales and for young ones to make daisy chains and discover love. It was not for building funeral pyres for headless Knights.

He had taken the liberty to wrap Mondt's head in thick cloth as to preserve it from pests as best he could. He focused on the body first, another arduous task that he had been putting off if he was honest, the pyre probably did not need the excessive amount of wood needed, but he told himself it did, all he was doing was adding more time between him moving the Knight's body. He lifted it from under his armpits, his weighted armoured limbs fell limp, the weight of the lifeless body and suit of armour combined was fantastic, Sebastian had never moved anything so heavy.

"I am thankful that I made the pyre around Karbia and did not attempt to move her!" He chuckled, he had too, he spoke to Mondt as if he was still there, if he had not then he would not have been able to get this far.

He dragged the body towards the pyre and blew away the blood-flies that were swarming around him buzzing at him in annoyance for having their meal interrupted. He made the mistake of looking at the wound, the bloody mess that once homed the attractive face and the golden curled head of Maximillious Mondt. He wretched at the smell that seeped from the wound, a mixture of rotting flesh and the smell of blood, that to him always reminded him of steel being forged. He had smelt blood and death before, many times, sadly too many times to even begin to count, that was the way of battle and war, the stench of blood and gore always harboured ghastly memories that one would try to forget. He saw Mondt's windpipe wrapped around broken shards of spine, useless like a dead snake, never to breathe again, meaty chunks of muscles and flesh quivered like the grub that was served for dogs and again it caused him to wretch. He lowered the body down to the ground and decided that he would drag it to its destination by its legs.

"I heard many a tale of 'The One' Sir Maximillious Mondt." He said as he struggled to moved the body. "Was it true that you once hand reared a long hared Feral and when it came of age you rode it in the Deerheart Games?"

345

There was of course silence, but he had reached the pyre and was now positioning Mondt's corpse upon it, Karbia lay peacefully beneath.

"I imagine it was." Sebastian laughed, sweat streaming down his face and was immediately soaked up by his beard like a sponge, "I can just imagine the look of horror on Lord Reginald's cantankerous face when you rode in on a Feral to take part in his precious games." He laughed again, shaking his head in disbelief. "Was the Feral white?" He asked no-one in particular. "Yes I imagine it was white, with bands of golden stripes rising up its legs. And a golden mane to match its rider no doubt!"

He placed the body onto of the pyre and took a moment to catch his breath and again wipe his sodden brow.

"That is the story I shall tell my friend." He said as he scaled down the pyre and headed towards the head that lay wrapped up in a bundle of cloth along with Mondt's helmet and sword. "Of course there is some flare and folly in these stories, that's what helps them become legend. But if that is what I have to do to see you remembered by the realm for future years, then that is what I shall do. This will be my story and whatever tales I hear of your colourful past I will give my seal of approval. A royal seal for a dreamer and an adventurer, how about that?"

He untied the cloth and removed the head. Mondt's Crystal blue eyes flickered back at him in the waining sun, for a second he seemed alive and Sebastian fought back tears for a Man that died only because he was aiding him, doing his duty and serving his King.

"The real adventures are what we have shared these past days, however many they have been because of that damned blackness, I have no idea of days and times." A tear ran down his cheek disguising itself as sweat and joining the other droplets as they hid in the thick bush of beard. "Saving the life of a King shall be your crowning glory, I shall see of it my friend."

He climbed the pyre and placed the head in its rightful place and returned for his helm and sword.

"Your sword, God's Hand!" He said placing it on his chest and then draping his armoured hands across. He stepped back and held the helm in his hands a single golden feather rising from its steel comb.

"White armour," He said, "very difficult to forge I hear." He touched the thick golden feather between his dirty fingers. "You know my feelings on feathers," He chuckled, "but for 'The One' it all added to the mythos, and no visor, of course you would want everyone to see that handsome face of yours as you strode into battle."

He sighed and looked sadly at the helm watching as the golden feather fluttered in the early evening breeze.

"For the ones who have committed such depravity there will be no lenience. I shall take their heads myself in your name. Your name will be avenged I promise you."

He stepped down with the helm in hands and turned to his friend who lay ready to be put to rest.

"I shall keep this helm my friend and it will take pride of place in the great hall of Windmast." He stroked the feather

347

and for a moment he thought of home and his family, Dayboy's braying in the distance stirred him away from such thoughts and to the task in hand.

"Now to make fire and put you at peace my friend."
Dayboy again let out an agitated whine and Sebastian turned his attention to his massive colt that dug frantically at the ground with his blunt hooves, his mane flitting from side to side as he shook his head frantically.

"What is it Dayboy?" The King asked and looked past the steed to see a figure staggering towards them. The King tried to focus but the sun was settling down for its rest now and everything was bathed in colours like burnt citrus. The figure moved as if delirious, small in size but wide and solid in stature.

An Ogre?
Was the thought that first nestled into the mind of the King and although a creature of very little intelligence, mostly used as steeds or pulling farmer's ploughs these days. But there was no telling what one might do if hunger had taken it. The King was on guard and unsheathed Reignmaker in one well practiced swoop.

"Who goes there?" He called out, the figure seemed to halt for a moment, sway on the spot and move toward him with more pace. Dayboy trampled the soil and moved away from the oncoming stranger, Sebastian gripped the handle of his sword tightly, he flesh chapped and splintered from a days work. The stranger seemed to disappear under the cover of the long grass that took the King by surprise, it was no Orge at such a puny

348

frame. Grass moved from side to side vigorously as whatever it was continued to drive towards the waiting King.

"WHO GOES THERE?" The King bellowed and positioned his feet in the soil, stance wide and the tip of his steel pointed towards the quivering grass. It grew ever closer and Sebastian could stand the suspense no longer unleashing a swipe of the broad sword, the attack was never meant to wound or kill but as a warning which it did, removing the tips of several blades of tall grass as if it were a harvesting scythe.

"HALT I SAY!" Sebastian growled and the stranger fell out of the grass at his feet, turning over slowly to reveal an old Dwarf that was bleeding heavily from several various wounds.

"Miglay!" Sebastian gasped as the Dwarf rolled his rotundness onto his back. His face was spilt with lacerations and blood had dried around his nostrils and mouth, seeped into his beard and caused it to stiffen.

"M-my King!" Miglay spluttered, "I-I be so happy to be findin' you safe."

Sebastian dropped Reignmaker to the soil and moved quickly to the Dwarf's side, where he cradled his bulbous head.

"Speak to me Miglay!" Sebastian spoke frantically, the wounds that he saw were like many he had seen in battle, wounds that refuse to heal.

The Dwarf coughed and choked on dried blood, he seemed to have had thirst take him as he lay there wheezing. Sebastian reached for his canteen and poured water into the dry maw of the broken Dwarf, he lapped at it the way a dog would, eager to

349

taste it, most of it ran into his beard and dripped out pink as it mixed with his own blood.

"What is this Miglay?"

"Y-you be right my K-king, you was bein' right a-all the time y-you be." Miglay stuttered, grabbing the canteen from Sebastian and drinking again eagerly. Sebastian took the time to take in the Dwarf's wounds, for a moment he thought that the water he had consumed would spurt from them he was so severely injured.

"D-Darkness came," Miglay spluttered.

"I have never been more sorry to be right." Sebastian sighed heavily and he held Miglay tightly. "What happened?"

"B-Black Imps it be."

"Black Imps! The Children of the Shrouded Realm!" Sebastian scowled angrily. "So Sloore is behind this."

"W-who can be sayin'." Miglay shrugged, he winced with the pain of the such a simple gesture.

"What of your brother? What of Dagyan?"
Miglay shook his head.

"All I be knowin', now be dead." Miglay groaned sadly. "Our torches be extinguished and they be tearin' through us in the darkness. We not be standin' a chance, they be comin' from the shadows they be, they be killin' us all."

"I weep for your loss, Miglay." Sebastian sighed sadly with pain and anguish in his own eyes, "I cannot comprehend what you are feeling."

"I be feelin' like Troll muck, that what me be feelin'." Miglay chuckled before wincing again from the pain. "Who ever be thinkin' that laughter be bringin' so much pain." He smiled, his crooked teeth stained pink, his lips and eyes quivering with the realisation that it was his time.

"Just rest now, my friend." Sebastian said, trying to sound southing in his tone, telling him that everything was going to be just fine, even though they both knew that this was the end.

"Who would be thinkin' Miglay would be the last of the Dwarves." He laughed again and tears fell from his weary eyes. "But I be reachin' you in time, did I not?"

"You did Miglay. You are the bravest of all dwarves for such a perilous journey under such duress. They shall sing songs about you for many moons I shall make sure of it."

"Ha!" Miglay laughed. "Make sure they be drinkin' lots of ale when they do!"

"You have done more than you can ever know Miglay 'The Mindful', I shall avenge you as I will Mondt."

"Mondt is dead!" Miglay gasped. "We were to be brothers in marriage!" He chuckled and burst out in a frenzy of laughter and coughing, thick black blood and bile seep from his maw.

"I shall honour you both." Sebastian said through most eyes and quivering lips.

"I must be tellin' you more..." Miglay cried out in pain each word he spoke was agony.

Dayboy pounded the soil with his hooves and neighed relentlessly.

351

"Easy now, Dayboy!" Sebastian scalded him. "Miglay is our friend."

"It be not me that be causin' him jitters..." Miglay broke off again, groaning and bleeding.

"What is it?"

"There b-be..." Miglay's eyelids flickered and his breathing stopped.

"Miglay? Tell me!" Sebastian held him tightly.

Miglay's eyes open one final time and with blood on his lips he muttered a word that chilled Sebastian to the core.

"Dragons..."

CHÃPTÉR 3 ☉
THÉ TÖWÉR ÖF SÖLÏTÜDÉ

agmai fell through the large open window of the Tower of Solitude, he was completely exhausted from the long arduous task of flying from Mount Quirinus to the Lunarc Desert. Somehow he had just enough energy and magic left to reach the old tower and he collapsed into a heap on the cold stone. Four large windows were cut into the stone to give views of all four corners of the realm and the roof had been covered in glass to make stargazing easier for the astronomers that frequented the tower. All around him hung parchment and tapestries depicting the location of the stars and what astronomers called planets.

Pagmai had always thought it was fascinating that Man, Elf, Giant and Dwarf had no knowledge of planets and stars. Many still believed the stars to be the Angels of Adeve positioned in the night sky by the fallen God to keep watch until hirs resurrection, a belief that has been endorsed by the Adevian Monks.

Those of royal blood were brought up to believe that the stars were the souls of the fallen Kings of the past, but there are others who remain wary of the stars, still believing them to be the spirits of ancient Dragons who were waiting for the right moment to invade Maglore and claim the realm for themselves. Pagmai believed that the stars held incredible powers, each one homing a sleeping Star Child. A Star Child was a warrior encased within a star that could be summoned in extreme times of war to bring balance, there were thirteen of these Gladiators of the Stars who all had different abilities and attributes. Alongside The Mystic Circle's astronomer Yodel, they worked tirelessly to explore these theories and believed they were on the verge of discovering how to release them from their translucent cocoons. Planets that potentially homed other lifeforms in other far off realms astonished and excited him, he often thought that if Man knew of such places existence would they be so quick to initiate these wars amongst themselves? When the realisation was that they may wear a crown or sit upon a throne here in Maglore but it meant nothing in the greater scheme of life, that they were nothing but the smallest speck in the universe. Those were Pagmai's thoughts when studying astronomy but his thoughts lay elsewhere today for he quivered on the floor, his weary bones wrapped in his velvet gown as he wept aloud, he wept for Holleet. Tears ran down skin that now seemed to merge and become one with his skull as he muttered his true love's name over and over again, his heart had been shattered and the splinters that remained stabbed at his vital organs like poison tipped daggers.

"Now is not the time." He murmured he realised that this was not the time to mourn, if he did not act quickly then all would be lost and he would not have the luxury of mourning the fallen. He slowly pulled himself from the ground, his weary limbs creaked as they struggled to hold him upright. He staggered over to a table that was consumed by rolled up parchments, burnt out candles and all manner of astrological equipment. He leant on the table using the structure to help keep him on his feet as he pointed a boney finger towards a candle, the wick smouldered sporadically as it struggled to ignite. Sweat streamed down his gaunt face, anxiety consuming him as he fought to perform what was usually a menial trick. He concentrated and finally the candle burst into life, he collapsed into a chair adjacent to the table, breathing heavily and sweating profusely as candlelight flickered around. A broken shard of reflective glass lay on the table, he lifted up and manoeuvred it to catch his reflection.

"Am I so old?" He gasped, without The Orb of Quirinus in his possession his true age was shown for the first time in centuries.

"I have taken the power of the Orb for granted." He sighed sadly, lowering the glass, he no longer wished to gaze upon the ancient looking Wizard that he did not even recognise.

"What can I do without the power of the Orb? Who am I?" He asked himself. "What am I even capable of doing now? Do I have any power left?"

He stared around the room and his focus settled on a crooked staff, crafted from old wood, its lifeless demeanour reminded him of how he looked and felt. He reached towards the staff and closed his eyes, focused, his lips quivered rapidly under the mass of white beard as he chanted mystic words that were as old as time itself. The staff trembled, tapping against the stone wall and floor and then suddenly lifted into the air and flew towards him, instantly he gripped it tightly and rose to his feet. Using the staff to help escort him to the East facing window that looked out into to the dark haze. He saw flames rising through the haze, somewhere a kingdom burnt and Pagmai knew that Grimalkin had been true to his words and that he had wasted no time in executing his plan.

"You have shown your hand, Grimalkin." Pagmai growled angrily, "I too must act if I am to counter your malevolence, even if it means the end of my own life."

He gazed down at The Lunarc Desert below the warm white sand bathed in the haze giving it a tint of lilac, the sand began to move like the rigorous waters of the Crimson Sea.

Hands of bone emerged from the sand reaching and grabbing at the thick warm haze, folds of dead flesh dangled from the ruptured arms that gripped the surface and heaved rotting bodies from sweltering desert graves.

"Sand Sleepers!" Pagmai wheezed as hundreds of the undead desert dwellers rose up in force and started to stagger towards the tower. The Sand Sleepers' faces were grotesque, rattling jaws hanging from fractured skulls that were layered with loose pieces of flesh. They groaned as grains of sand filtered through their hollow corpses draining out from every orifice like a broken hourglass. The moving carcasses gripped the craggy rock face of the tower, even being so high up Pagmai could hear the sickening sound of their boney fingers scraping on the rock.

"The window for opportunity is closing, there is no time to waste." Pagmai said as he waddled away from the window, leaving the Sand Sleepers to climb up the tower.

The Grand One made his way to the centre of the room where he used the staff to help lower his withering frame to the floor where he gazed up to the sky, even through the dark haze that shrouded the East he could make out the shimmering of the stars.

"Grimalkin knows not the true power of the Orb of Quirinus for if he did he would know that he holds in his hands the ability to summon Sirod the Phoenix." He sighed wishing that he still had the Orb, not for the youth and power that came with it but with it he could end this whole ordeal.

"That is a secret that I must take with me to the other side when I pass. If Grimalkin learns that he could unleash Sirod upon the realm then Maglore is indeed doomed."

He sat for a moment, his body had never felt such agony, his bones weathered on the verge of shattering and turning to dust.

"What do I have left?" He asked of himself, "I will give myself to the realm if I could be gifted enough power to stop Grimalkin."

His old eyes flickered across tapestries that depicted famous battles and scenes from the realm's past, they settled upon a worn and tattered tapestry that depicted the final battle that had been entitled 'The Rage of Man', the only battle that he himself ever took part in. He stared at his younger shelf clad in the enchanted black armour, holding aloft the black bladed sword, Hex and through it unleashed the power of the Orb towards a huge white Dragon that hung in the air. Man battled Elf and another huge Dragon, scales of red dominated part of the scene, unleashing flame on the Elf army. There was a twinkle in his old eyes, a glimmer of hope and a smile creased his lined face.

"It may well take everything I have, but I have to try." He closed his eyes and lost himself deep in thought, he needed to fall into a trance to conjure the words to call an old friend for his help, a friend that he once travelled the realm with in search of a place to call home, where those born with special gifts could belong. Without his old friend The Mystic Circle would have remained a dream.

"I call upon you my old friend one more time." He murmured, the sound of scraping bone echoed around the tower as the Sand Sleepers moved ever closer. The trance took him and he felt as though he was floating through the stars and planets.

"Is this death?" He asked the stars that he floated past, but there was no response.

"My old friend can you hear my pleas?" He called, his voice echoed through the vast space, but he heard nothing in reply.

"I am in great need of your help for a final time. My time grows short and my life wains, my time on this plane is almost at an end."
Nothing.

He was almost woken from his reverie with a sudden loud crash as Sand Sleepers had broken through the entrance of the Tower. There was said to be one thousand steps in the tower and for the Sand Sleepers it would take time for them to climb, but it was still time that this old Wizard did not have to waste.

"My friend!" He called, his voice echoing strangely, "I beg of you, hear me! Lennoc I need your help."

There was silence and as Pagmai began to loose his grip on this trance, he started to fade out from this and return back to the room in the Tower of Solitude, his eyelids flickered and the stars glimmered as the room came back into view and as he collapsed on the cold stone floor quivering and sweating, sapped of all energy, believing now that this is how it would end, he heard a strong gruff voice of his old friend.

"I hear you Wizard."

With those words Pagmai's eyes grew wide, there was still hope, if his friend could find him in time, for the old Wizard no longer had the energy to prise his weary old bones from the floor. The groans of the Sand Sleepers drew ever closer, from each window they could be heard clattering against the sides of the tower. Their stuttering steps ascending the spiral of stairs behind a flimsy wood door, it was only a matter of heartbeats before they would be upon him.

Somehow Pagmai managed to roll himself over onto his back, his gown now appearing too immense for his delicate frame, he gazed up at the stars that still burned brightly through that haze as if they were a sign.

359

"If there is light, there is hope." He murmured and closed his eyes and fell into a deep sleep.

CHÃPTÉR 31
FRÖM PÉTÃLS TÖ ÃSH

gaunt black coney moved slowly through the tall flowers of Valtora, there were patches of fur missing from around its neck as if it had been heavily burnt. Its torso and mangy coat that it did have was in disarray, as if it had been attacked. It seemed cautious as its long hind legs crunched through old dead leaves, it smelt the air and its scarred nose twitched exposing two broken teeth hidden underneath its muzzle. There was a sound of rustling in the distance coming closer to it, its drooping misshapen ears, lifted and listened intently. It heard many small voices, the crunching of light armour as though a tiny army was on the march, and then the rapid flutter of wings. The black coney seemed to smile, if that was at all possible and its marbled white eyes glistened, eyes that looked like broken glass. It carried on through the flowers, above a mystical layer of dust glittered like a million stars above its head, it paid no attention and carried on into the dense cover of The Kingdom under the Flowers.

"Halt!" Came a tiny voice and the coney stopped dead in its tracks, those eerie eyes staring at an archway made by two

361

droopy daffodils as a Fairy, clad in rose gold armour whizzed through on vigorous lilac wings. He held a spear in his hand as he approached and immediately lowered it when he saw that it was but a hare. Other soldiers suddenly appeared like magic, from the cover of petals, leaves and foliage, an army surrounded the coney and all suddenly looked incredibly disappointed.

"Tis only a coney!" The soldier that found it groaned, and there was an unanimous outcry of annoyance.

The Fairy army worked tirelessly to protect their kingdom and took their oath very seriously, but it was incredibly rare for them to actually battle. Usually it was but travelling strangers that tripped the alarm accidentally, not even knowing that the kingdom existed and were encouraged by the army who were always on call to find another route, which they did for the feisty Fairies could be very persuasive with a sharp spear in their hands. They hovered around the coney, that did not move a muscle, did not twitch with panic as most its kind would in the situation.

"What is it!" Came a call that reeked of arrogance. "Why have we stopped?"

Prince Valian arrived on the back of his own coney, both him and his steed, elaborately dressed in turquoise silks, and silver armour. He was accompanied by two royal guards saddled on quails.

"Tis but a coney that tripped the alarm, Your Majesty." Said the Fairy who found it, hovering down to meet his Prince.

"Call that a coney?" Valian scoffed, his face creased with disgust at the black creature that sat motionless staring down at him. "Looks to me that the creature has the mange!"

"We could kill it and take it back for Queen Oleander. A great feast would be had of a coney this size." The soldier said.

"How dare you!" Valian spat. "You would serve this flea-bitten mongrel to your Queen?"

The soldier fluttered lowly, and dropped his head.

"Forgive me, Your Majesty." He moaned. Some of the soldiers found amusement in this.

"I would not touch such vermin. It makes me feel dirty just looking at the damn thing. Chase it away from here."

"As you wish, My Prince." The soldier fluttered back up towards it and thrust his spear at the coney, but it did not move. He prodded it with the tip of his spear and still the coney did not stir.

"What is wrong? What is taking you so long?" Valian called impatiently.

"It does not move!" Shrugged the solider.

"Well?" The Prince looked at his army of Fairy soldiers hovering around nonchalantly. "Help him!"

They suddenly burst into life and hundreds of colourful wings hummed swiftly as they wielded spears and swords and began poking the creature, blood seeped from the small wounds, but still the creature did not stir.

Suddenly Valian heard a familiar voice coming from the flower tops that swayed serenely above their heads.

"Oh dear Brother, are you having problems?"

363

Prince Ekim swayed drunkenly out from behind the petal of a poppy and grinned at him obnoxiously.

"Ekim!" Valian hissed. "You are banished from Valtora! Seize him!"

Ekim laughed uncontrollably, falling back into the poppy, his legs flaying out in jest.

"I would love to see your soldiers try." He scoffed. "They cannot even see off a coney, how are they to take me?"

"I'll take you myself!" Valian sneered, hand on the hilt of his sword, that was known as Proboscis. A sword that was so clean and pristine it was blatantly obvious that it had never seen battle or tasted blood of any kind.

"Please Brother, we all know that you could not best me with your blade on your best day."

Valian's face blushed as red as the poppy that his brother mocked him from, but he knew that he spoke the truth, before his exile Prince Ekim was commander of the guards and great swordsman and an exceptional strategist.

"Even as merry as I am I could still take twenty or thirty of your best soldiers."

The soldiers stared at him but none of them moved, they knew his words to be true.

"But I do not wish bloodshed, never have. Especially against my own kind." Ekim smiled, the grin of a tired but happy drunk spread across his face and he swayed from side to side kicking his legs merrily like a child.

"If you are to be no help Brother, then I suggest you take your leave and leave us to get on with our own business." Valian snapped.

"Oh yes, very important business this!" He giggled. "The Kingdom under the Flowers is indeed in good hands."

"Stop your mockery and leave us, drunk!"

"Come now Brother," Ekim sighed, "there is no need for such nastiness I shall take my leave and bid you all farewell." He stood on the petal, staggered from side to side and his wings quivered sporadically, but even they seemed drunk and tired.

"May you rid the kingdom of all its mangy black coneys." He laughed and then fell from the flower into an unconscious mess.

The soldiers laughed at his drunken fall.

"You see my soldiers, that could have been your next King! How embarrassing it would have been to serve under such a drunken fool." Valian chuckled and the soldiers continued to laugh raucously, completely forgetting about the coney that still stood motionless, unconcerned by its weeping wounds. Prince Valian leapt from his extravagant saddle that was fixed snugly to his coney steed and strode towards the motionless black coney.

"It would seem if one wants something doing in this kingdom then one must do it oneself." He scoffed arrogantly, his wings fluttering gently helping him skim across the soil and leaves as if to touch down on the earth would sully his fine jewel encrusted boots. He hung in the air in front of the coney and gripped the handle of Proboscis tightly.

"I am your Prince, I am your next ruler." He bellowed, so that all his soldiers could hear him, "I lead by example and I shall be the one to take this creature."

Some of the soldiers smirked with the sheer ridiculousness of Valian's words, he spoke as if he were about to slay a Dragon, not a flea-bitten coney that does not even appear to be hostile.

"Although I would not allow my marda's royal lips to touch such foul vermin, I shall slay it and it shall be taken back to the city for a great banquet." Boastfully he smirked. "The people of The Kingdom under the Flowers will see my kindness and will feast upon this poor creature for many moons."

"There has been no moon for several weeks now." Whispered one solider to another.

"His delusion grows." Replied the other soldier. "There is talk of the Season of Gloam come early, but I fear that the Man King's words may have been true after all."

Prince Valian unsheathed Proboscis and swiped needlessly at the air.

"Pay the price for your trespass vermin." He scowled. "Let none of your kind enter the Kingdom of Valtora to spread your filth and eat or vegetation. By order of Prince Valian I condemn you to death!"

He plunged the sword into the coney's torso, it lodged in tightly and the coney did not move, Valian struggled to retrieve the blade and fluttered around impatiently as his soldiers sniggered at such a performance, finally the blade slid free and he fell backwards in the air, but with his ability to fly quickly saved him anymore embarrassment by rectifying his stumble.

Blood poured from the coney but still the creature did not move.

"What trickery is this?" Growled Prince Valian. "This must be some folly?" He glared at his smiling soldiers. "This is some trick! Who is responsible for making me look like a fool?"

"He is doing a good job of that by himself." Whispered a soldier and his friend fought to hold back sniggers.

"Whoever has staged such a sham will pay dearly!" He cried, his face and wings glowing vibrantly with anger and embarrassment, "I shall have your wings for this!"
There was a cackle of laughter that rose up in the flowers, the plants seemed to quiver with unease from the foul sound.

"What is that?" Valian asked, still with his sword in hand dripping with blood for the first time in its existence. The sound of hideous cackling filled their ears as they looked around in bemusement. The black coney suddenly began to quiver and convulse sickeningly. They watched in awe as it seemed to close in on itself as if turning inside out, black bile and blood spat out from the contorted monstrosity and the Fairies watched on in perverse horror, as they could not tear their gaze away from such a spectacle.

"Make it stop!" Valian gagged, cupping a hand over his mouth as if he would vomit at any second, but the soldiers were just as sickened as their Prince and had no idea of how to react. As quickly as the exhibition had begun it stopped and the strange carcass of the coney lay in a pile of blubber in the soil. The quails became restless and the Prince's steed took off at full speed through the heavy foliage. At seeing this the quails reared

367

and removed themselves of their riders and fled as if they sensed the same thing as Valian's steed.

"Foolish little fairies!" Came a hideous voice from the pool of fur and flesh that bubbled before them, the shape started to change again and the fur and bile became cloth and flesh as the crooked form of Kelda emerged from the coney skin appeared from the confines of her cloak.

"You have bigger problems than a coney infestation I fear!" A broken smile cut across her hideous face and her marbled eyes shimmered with mischief. Before anyone could react to what they had seen, Kelda reached out as quick as a flash of lightning and gripped Prince Valian in her slender talons.

"Unhand me hag!" He cried and on seeing this the soldiers surrounded her with the tips of spears pointed at her. She licked her lips at the defiant Prince who struggled in a vain attempt to get free.

"My marda the Queen will hear of this outrage."
Kelda erupted into a mocking croak of laughter as she squeezed him tightly, causing him to grimace.

"Seize her!" He groaned to his soldiers in a last ditch attempt to see himself free, but as they moved into action Kelda waved her free hand, shrieking an incoherent word of ancient tongue and the Fairy soldiers froze in midair. They hung motionless their wings still, only their eyes seemed to be alive, darting around frantically.

"Little Prince..." She hissed, "...royal blood make the best spells."

With those words she ripped the Prince's head from its shoulders, popping it like a cork from a bottle of fine royal wine. Those eyes of the watching soldiers grew wide and fear took hold of them as they witnessed the head of their Prince fall to the earth below, a look of absolute shock frozen upon his face. His bloodstained blade, Proboscis, slipped from his lifeless hand and stuck into the soil below him as Kelda gripped him tightly. Kelda shrieked with that horrendous laughter of hers and gazed upon the frozen Fairy soldiers, those glazed eyes giving nothing away. She reached out and tore the delicate petals from various flowers and let them fall before her, chapped lips quivering in chant, words unknown to the ears of this age. She then plunged a pale talon into the moist soil below and retrieved a large earthworm, it wiggled in her pincer grip to no avail and then she crammed it into her mouth and she began to chew loudly. The sight and sound was enough to make the Fairy soldiers vomit, but they were unable to move a muscle. She hummed a tune that sounded quite pretty, an old ballad entitled 'Marda Nature's Gifts', not an apt melody to accompany such foulness. When the earthworm had been chewed to a pulp she spat it out onto the layer of petals below, some of the poor creature had not been fully gnawed and still attempted to squirm. Kelda began her humming again and lifted the headless carcass of Valian up and held it under her long slender nose where she exhaled the blood within, with her snakelike tongue she licked at the wound, tasting its purity and flavour as a royal may test a fine old wine.

"Royal blood is always preferred." She hissed, her eyes meeting her captivated audience before cackling loudly. Above her in the purple haze Laasp swept across the sky shrieking impatiently.

"Yes, yes!" Kelda snapped. "All in good time."

She turned the Prince upside down and watched as the Prince's blood gushed down and covered the petals and chewed up remains of the earthworm.

"Every drop be precious, yes!" She hissed again and shook him vigorously to make sure that every drop was used. She then tore the wings from the Prince and discarded his dead carcass to the floor. She cupped the twinkling wings in the palms of her hands, there was still magic within them and they changed colour rapidly, showing all colours of the spectrum.

"The magic will soon be gone." She said and crushed them up into fine grains in her hands before turning to the horrified soldiers. "You Fairies have always taken your power for granted. You fly and you twinkle and you look all nice and pretty." She spat at the ground disgusted by her words. "This is what you are as a race, vain and arrogant! Your true power is not what flickers on the outside, but what is hidden within. You are all more powerful than you ever imagined."

She grinned horrendously at them and licked her lips.

"And now it is too late!"

She sprinkled the powdered wings onto her concoction and mixed it with the long slender claw of a fingernail and whispered those ancient words once more, the mixture glowed and then erupted in a cloud of smoke shrouding everything and

370

everyone. The Fairy soldiers could see nothing but could hear that disturbing tune being hummed again. As the smoke cleared they were released from their frozen prisons and fell to the ground, Kelda was gone, they would have sighed with relief, but the realisation of the old hag's spell was blatantly clear for them all to see. The flower tops were no longer shrouded in its protective enchanted haze, the kingdom was exposed and they gazed up at the slender Dragon as it glided out of the dark sky. With there eyes wide they took to the air and made for their city, they had to warn their Queen, they had to reach their people in time and warn them before it was too late.

Laasp swooped down low, he unleashed a flurry of flame that consumed them and melted them in their armour. The flames engulfed Valtora, turning the flowers to black ash in minutes, no word ever got back to Queen Oleander and moments later their tiny screams went unheard by any ear as the Fairy kingdom fell.

CHÃPTÉR 32
THÉ YÉLLÖW HÖRNÉT

ebastian had spent the evening digging a grave for poor Miglay, he had buried him standing upright as the way of Dwarf burial. Most Man were buried these days to feed the realm, a ritual that rests them lying down so they may gaze upon the stars forever more. Royals were burnt so that their souls could join the Kings within the stars, it was also believed that when their souls passed through cloud that they replenished the rain to help the crops grow. Dwarves on the other hand believed that they should be buried standing up with axe in hand for when they are reincarnated and can leap from their grave and straight into battle. Many would say that reincarnation was ludicrous but was it anymore ridiculous than joining Kings in the stars? Sebastian had dozed throughout the night, the heat of Mondt's pyre had kept him warm through the night's chill, but dark thoughts had poisoned his dreams. Miglay's warning of Dragons had caused unease and soon it was time for the Sun of Selym to rise once again. He sat up and glared at Mondt's pyre that was all but burnt out, a plume of thick black smoke escaping from the black bones and armour left behind. He rubbed at his tired eyes and they were met by the grave of Miglay that he had spent most of the night digging, he had hoped it all a bad dream, but alas his aching muscles were enough to inform him that it was no dream. He rose, stretched and wandered into a cluster of trees to relieve himself, as he did so he wondered where Dayboy had gotten too, he had become incredibly anxious as if it could sense something.

"Dayboy!" The King called as he shook himself dry, his brow contorted when he heard nothing, it was peculiar for his steed not to come when commanded, so he called again louder. Still no sign of him and then his tired mind was stabbed at with an ice cold thought, a dark morbid thought.

Dayboy is dead!

It was too much to even consider, could his luck be so that he lost two friends and his steed at the same time?

"Dayboy! Where are you?" He called again, anguish in his tone now. He breathed a sudden sigh of relief when he saw the large colt burst from a gathering of trees and charge towards him.

"Where have you been?" Sebastian chuckled, but his face soon lost its smile when he noticed that Dayboy did not mean to slow down and continued at some pace passing him, and almost knocking him to the ground from the shear force of his charge. Dayboy's eyes flashed with fear, a look that Sebastian had never seen in his noble steed before. Dayboy came to a sudden halt at the campsite and thumped at the ground with his front hooves neighing frantically. Sebastian met the scared creature and stroked at his nose to calm him, but he snorted wildly and used his nose to nudge the King's belongings as if he wanted them to leave posthaste.

"Okay, okay, we shall make leave."

Dayboy shook his head up and down as if in agreement with his Master and Sebastian quickly dressed and fit Dayboy with his other belongings, he stowed the helms of both the fallen, the white steel of Mondt and the thick bronze helm of Miglay. He still could not believe that the Dwarf kingdom had fallen, and that Black Imps were responsible. The sighting of any of The Children of the Shrouded Realm in these times was a rarity, usually their numbers would be small and stay close to the cover of shadow, taking livestock or lonely travellers. He thought of how many Black Imps it would have taken to bring down the Dwarves and his mind could not conceive such a number. All he knew was this, that if Sloore's children had been unleashed in force then it was time to return home and ready Windmast for an attack.

"I shall be waiting for you Imps." Sebastian groaned to himself as he mounted Dayboy. "We shall be ready."

As soon as his backside touched the leather of the saddle Dayboy was gone at a quick canter away from the camp towards the West. Sebastian turned towards his fallen friends and said a quiet farewell one more time.

"Thank you, your sacrifices shall not be in vain."

Dayboy's pace quickened and his head shook from side to side again frantically.

"Whatever is the matter?" Sebastian snapped, trying not to be sharp with the animal, but so much had happened in such a short space of time that it was difficult for him to process all his emotions and he immediately regretted his reaction. There was a unearthly scream that left the clouds of darkness like a sudden strike of lightning and Sebastian tugged hard on Dayboy's reins to halt him, Dayboy did reluctantly and when Sebastian turned the colt around to face that dark haze once again, Dayboy could not stand still even with his Master's calls and yanks upon the reins.

"What in the name of Adeve!" Sebastian gasped as he stared into the East, the scream came again. In the distance he saw flames burning brightly. Sebastian heard Miglay's dying words again and could not bring himself to believe that Dragons had returned, but then out from the clouds of darkness came Laasp.

"Dragons..." Was all that Sebastian could whisper and he could feel Dayboy's gigantic body shake beneath him.
The Serpent's body was long and sleek with thick back legs and a wide wingspan. Its wings spread out as it glided towards the King who sat frozen upon his colt. Its features were slick and pointed and its yellow scales glistened in the rising sun of dawn. Sebastian unsheathed his sword, if ever there was a time that Reignmaker's wield be true it was today, the sword had tasted Dragon blood once before and had been victorious, was this another tale of a King slaying a Dragon?
Laasp was incredibly quick and it changed the shape of its wings and hurtled towards Sebastian with reckless abandon,

small bursts of flame flickered from its nostrils and hunger gleamed in its eyes. Sebastian knew from seeing the bones of Selym, Tenaj and Grosa in the Dragon's Graveyard of Rotunda that Laasp was small for its kind, but it was still four or five times the size of his stallion Dayboy and believed it big enough indeed.

"Be brave Dayboy!" Sebastian screamed as he held aloft Reignmaker just as Laasp swooped towards them, Dayboy reared on its back legs, sheerly out of panic and the Dragon snapped at the King with its row of razor-sharp teeth but met only the cold steel of Reignmaker. Momentum was not the King's friend however and they fell to the ground, as the Dragon whizzed above and turned around in the sky for another run at his prey which was now grounded and right for the picking. Luckily Sebastian fell from Dayboy and the colt did not fall upon him or it would have broken him. Dayboy squealed and rolled to its hooves and galloped away leaving Sebastian alone to peal himself up off the ground. Before he could even gain control of his thoughts Laasp came down at him again and Sebastian was sent sprawling to the ground, the huge talons of the beast's back legs almost scything him in two.

"Adeve be with me!" Sebastian groaned as he pulled himself up again, trying to grip his sword but again the Dragon was upon him, this time a whip from its slender tail sent him sprawling into the grass and sword-less. Sebastian hit the ground hard and winced, his body already ached but the impact from Laasp's tail hurt worse than anything he had ever endured. Luckily for him he had fallen into the cover of the overgrown grass and he thought to himself that this may buy him some time so that he could regroup and hopefully find his sword. He crept through the grass like a Feral hunting its prey, the irony being that he was in fact the prey and being stalked by a much deadlier predator. His hands had remained ungloved due to the warmth that had risen rapidly with the day and his fingers caressed the hilt of his dagger nestled safely in its scabbard at his side. He scoffed at just the thought of using a dagger to defend himself against a Dragon, what good could a blade so small do?

He caught quick glimpses of Laasp as it soared through the sky, swooping low over the long grass and causing it to quiver in its wake.

"Where is that damn sword!" Sebastian murmured to himself, his eyes flitting around through the slender blades of green, searching for a glimmer of steel and gold. There was no blade to be seen and he had noticed from Laasp's deafening shrieks that the Dragon was growing restless and if the beast was of as knowing of mind as a Man, it would be time to smoke out its prey.

The Yellow Hornet hung in the sky for what appeared to be an eternity, the rising Sun of Seylm kissing his yellowy scales making them come a live as it eagerly surveyed the acres of grass that lay beneath, its eyes focussed, waiting for any movement. Sebastian was fascinated by its strength and speed of course, but it was its finesse that awed him. As the Sun rose slowly it spread its rays upon him and for a moment he was blinded by glare, glare of shining steel and gold.

"Reignmaker!" Sebastian gasped and looked through the blades of grass to see his family arm calling to him. Frantically he moved through the grass, trying to stay as low as possible as he made his way towards the blade, but he had rushed his movements and that was all Laasp needed. The Dragon's incredible eyesight had noticed the frenzied twitch of grass and screamed into the sky in triumph, it had him. Laasp flew up higher, cavorted swiftly with the clouds and then turned towards the earth once more, hurtling towards Sebastian at audacious speed, wings tucked behind his torso, tail as straight as a jousting lance, beak sharp and pointed towards its target. It unleashed a burst of bright amber flame that danced yellow and white as it engulfed the grass where Sebastian had just been. The King felt the sweltering heat from the flame as it burned through the dry grass with ease. Sebastian scrambled again towards the direction he had seen the sword, but the fire had started to spread and thick black smoke had begun to fill his lungs and hinder his vision. He coughed and spluttered, his eyes leaked, all while the flames licked at him like the tongues of a thousand snakes. The grass became overwhelmed by Dragon fire and Sebastian had to leave its cover, he dove from grass and landed in a soft bed of soil, he looked back to see the entire field massacred by the fire, but there to his left protected by a cluster of hard to burn stems and nettles lay Reignmaker. He did not have to look to know that Laasp would be there and when he heard its war-cry again, he knew that it was descending upon him, he had to make for the sword to stand any chance, but as he did Laasp was upon

378

him and swiped a hefty talon across his back, it ripped through his fine tunic and its sharp tip pierced his flesh down his spine. Sebastian called out in the sheer agony and fell to the floor only a few feet from the blade, even with his head down to the ground in grimace, he knew that the Dragon was already manoeuvring in the sky to descend again and this time would finish him off.

Fire had now devoured the foliage around Reignmaker and he could see as he crawled towards it that the blade had begun to glow from the blistering heat of the flames that caressed the long steel like they were whores sent from The Shrouded Realm to arouse it. His fingertips touched the Phoenix head pommel, amazing still cool, the gold seemed to repel the heat, but as he reached to grab the hilt and relieve it from its furnace, Laasp was again upon him, relentless. It gripped the King with its talons just as he managed to grasp the blade's hilt, but Laasp liked to play with his food the way a cat does a mouse and he tossed Sebastian into the air, this motion disturbed the blade and once again it fell from his grip. Man and sword hit the ground at the same time. Sebastian winced and called out as pain shot through his body, Reignmaker became lodged blade first in the soil, the earth seemed to bubble from its heat. Still Sebastian crawled towards the blade, he believed it was his only hope for survival, his only chance to get back to Windmast and see his Queen and his daughter. Finally Laasp landed casting a huge shadow over the grounded King, he turned around to meet the beast and growled at it.

"TAKE ME THEN DEMON!" He bellowed. "TAKE ME!"

Laasp stalked forward and screamed his own warning, its mouth only feet from the King's face, razor sharp teeth filled its maw and the heat it gave off was like a blacksmith's furnace. Sebastian was hypnotised by the smouldering maw of the beast and blindly he still reached towards Reignmaker, finger tips frantically caressing the ruby encrusted gold hilt, but unable to take is eyes away from the bubbling glow of magma that would erupt at any moment. Laasp screamed and his throat gargled with fire before unleashing it just as Sebastian drove his dagger up through the lower jaw of the beast. Laasp shrieked with pain and was forced to recoil spurting flame into the air missing its target as the blade of the dagger split its tongue and almost piercing the roof of its mouth. It flailed around in pain flapping its wings and swinging its long neck from side to side in a futile attempt to removing the blade. Sebastian moved quickly and finally gripped Reignmaker in his hands, he did not need time to think and he drove its heated blade into the rearing Dragon's gut. The King's blade sliced downwards through the soft tissue of its underbelly as if he were at a royal banquet and sliced tender fowl from its bone. Laasp backed away dumfounded on unstable legs shrieking with pain as it flapped its wings wearily and its hot bowels fell from the gaping wound on a tide of blood. Sebastian rose from the ground, Reignmaker still gripped in his hands, the blade thick of blood with steam rising from the heat of Dragon fire.

"Hartwaker's always rise!" Sebastian growled and as he was about to charge and unleash the killer blow, Laasp's black eyes rolled back in its head and collapsed into the burnt grass. Sebastian lowered his sword as the creature's tail whipped in a frenzy and its wings took one final attempt at flight and then became limp and cloaked the fallen beast like a death shroud. Sebastian approached the Dragon as smoke left its nostrils and blood seeped into the burnt black ash that was once grass and he stood triumphantly over its large corpse and breathed a heavy sigh of relief falling to his knees and dropping his sword to the ground. He knelt exhausted by the rigours of his quest as blood seeped through the disturbed soil and ash, circling the King as he tried to take in what had just happened, his body ached, the wound that ran down his back stung, but there was nothing that he could do about that now.

"Dragons..." he murmured staring at the heaving mass of fire and destruction that lay before him, the blood puddling in front of him, he caught his reflection and a rippling red image of his face glared back, with tired eyes and the gaunt features of struggle.

"I wonder..." He whispered dipping his finger in the warm blood. He knew of the lore of Dragon blood and that the Scrolls of History had documented that there was knowledge and wisdom running through the veins of the Serpents and if drank then it would unleash the answers to the questions that they desired. He watched the thick plasma drip from his fingertip and he wondered whether there was any truth in these ancient findings.

"Perhaps it is all folly and nothing more, but there can be no harm in it."

He tasted the blood and immediately his mind's eye became warped, his vision distorted as the blood raced through his body looking to unlock the knowledge he required, the knowledge of the darkness. He saw through the eyes of Laasp and watched on as Grimalkin emerged from the broken remains of Mount Quirinus clad in Pagmai's enchanted black armour and spoke to an army of malevolent creatures that screamed for war. He watched on as Laasp's fire consumed the Fairy kingdom of Valtora and heard thousands of tiny voices cry out as they burned to death. He saw Goblins, Black Imps, Beast-Men, Ferals, Cyclops, Bat-Fiends, Ogres and...

"Dragons!" Sebastian gasped and fell on to his hands and knees, breathing heavily and sweating profusely. He vomited and his head felt heavy and scattered, it took him several moments to gather his composure and he looked up at the sky which was already turning to night.

"How long have I been lost in these thoughts?"

He rose slowly and collected Reignmaker, the blade now cold, he did not clean the blade before sheathing it, there was no longer time for such etiquette.

"Grimalkin means to take the realm." Sebastian gasped. "All of it in one foul swoop! The only hope I have is if I can reach Windmast in time."

There was movement in the wooded area to his rear and he turned quickly hand on the hilt of his sword again.

"What now!" He growled, growing increasingly tired of the constant surprises. "What beast or demon comes to test me now?"

Slowly Dayboy trotted out from the cover of the trees and Sebastian sighed heavily with relief.

"Dayboy!" He chuckled.

The colt cautiously ambled over towards his Master who scowled at him grudgingly.

"And where did you get too? Coward!"

Dayboy nuzzled his face and licked him, the playful scowl disappeared from his face and Sebastian laughed returning the sentiment with a loving stroke.

"I cannot say that I would not have fled if I had four strong legs like yours."

He embraced Dayboy for the longest time, he needed to know that love and affection still existed in this world.

"We must make for Windmast posthaste." He said mounting Dayboy. "Grimalkin's dark army has us at a disadvantage and ahead of us by a days travel."

Dayboy snorted and trotted around in a circle.

"We must travel at pace, Dayboy. Do you have what it takes to see us there?"

Dayboy neighed and reared up on his hind legs majestically before bringing his bulk down again and taking off towards West, towards home.

CHÃPTÉR 33
CÖMÉTH THÉ DÃRKNÉSS

he Sun of Seylm slipped into slumber once more, marking the end of another day, Queen Marie Ann stood in the flower garden at the rear of Windmast Castle trimming the royal roses.

"Another day leaves us my little one." She said with sadness in her voice as she turned to Princess Vai-Ra who sat in a crib gnawing on her blanket, the King's crown grasped in her podgy hand, she had hardly put it down since she had been given it. The Queen missed her King so very much and had spent the majority of his absence in the garden, planting and pruning, but mostly trimming her beloved roses that were now in full bloom and looked glorious. The rose vines were very strong and of great length, each one with an abundance of protruding thorns that had already claimed several drops of royal blood from the Queen's dainty fingertips. She had told her child that blood was good for the plants though, it helped strengthen their defences. As she gazed at her little daughter that giggled to herself without a care in the world, she could not help but smile. She still wore the Queen's dagger, The Maid of

Honour at her hip, its golden hilt and scabbard was encrusted with both diamonds and rubies and went well with most her dresses. She had been told by her cousin Sir Winstone Vespa to keep it with her at all times, especially with her King away, it was an unpredictable time and House Hartwaker found themselves on edge.

"Yes, another day closer to the return of your farda." The vines contorted around the wooden trellis' and up part of the castle wall, decorating it splendidly in pinks, whites, reds, yellows and golds. The Sun seemed to hang just above the castle's outer walls for the longest time, allowing Queen Marie Ann to soak in its last dose of warmth. She took in the smells of the evening, but there was something that seemed odd to her senses. The scent of flowers, grass and the dampness of the falls was apparent as usual, the smell of scented soap and powder floated up from the Princess, it   pinched her nostrils gently, there was no other scent like that of a clean baby, but on this night there was something else that came with it, a distance scent of...

"Burning..." Queen Marie Ann pondered this for a moment or two, the smell was pungent, like burning wood. She heard distance calls and steel on steel rang out, echoic and distant.

"What goes on?" She wondered aloud, still Vai-Ra continued to keep herself entertained by soothing her raw gums on the soft cotton blanket. There was a shrilling sound that cut through the air, again it was distant, but to the Queen she knew what that sound was, the screaming of woman and it seemed to travel up the King's Falls and spiral around the gardens like some shrieking apparition before fading to nothingness. Her eyes widened as she looked at the glowing light that still hung above the walls of the castle and realised that it was not the setting sun but...

"Fire!" She murmured.

All of sudden she felt nauseous with the realisation of what was transpiring, the glow now appeared to flicker and there were sounds of marching, steel on steel, shrieks and howls, the flapping of wings, growls and screams and the smell of burning was now all that could be smelt, no longer did the sweet smell of rose petals caress her nostrils, nor the beautiful pure scent of her daughter's flesh, all that there was now was war.

"It's an attack!" She stuttered and swiftly moved towards Vai-Ra, scooping her up. The little Princess was not happy at the sudden act and it scared her and she whined accordingly, but her complaints fell on deaf ears for the Queen had other thoughts, dark thoughts of blood and destruction, thoughts of death. Cradling the grizzling Vai-Ra close she made for the entrance to the keep where she was suddenly met by Sir Winstone Vespa. He was clad in his chainmail, armour and had sword in hand, wearing an anxious look upon his face.

"Cousin!" He exhaled, and the anxiety seemed to leave him at once. "When I could not find you in your chambers I feared the worst." He added and stroked Vai-Ra's soft cheek with his gauntleted hand, she laughed as the gold steel tickled her.

"Are we under attack?" She asked.

Sir Winstone sighed heavily. "They have taken Trinpola, Foxfall, Tendor and Kalfahr. The fire you see comes from the mighty Weeping Willow of Kalfahr, they have burnt it down!"

"Who have?"

"Goblins, Ferals and Bat-Fiends! I hear stories of Black Imps and Cyclops too and…" Winstone stopped as if to take a deep breath.

"What? Tell me Cousin." She asked frantically.

"There is talk of Dragons." The words lodged in his throat causing him to choke and splutter.

"Dragons!" She whispered all the while Vai-Ra became more and more restless and her moans became whimpers. Queen Marie Ann instinctively held her close and swayed from side to side.

"They march on us now as the Willow burns as if it were a beacon to the creatures of The Shrouded Realm to join them." He shook his head in disbelief. "Sebastian was right, damn it! By the Gods of the Mountains, the Earth and the Seas, he was right!"

"The darkness cometh!" She murmured.

"That is why we must get you to safety my Queen." He grabbed her hand and tried to lead her through the flower garden the other way, away from the keep. "You must flee. I will see you safely out of the castle and return to fight."

"No!" She barked defiantly and tugged her arm free from his grip "I shall not leave my home, I shall not leave my people."

"But my Queen…"

387

"My King will return, you will see and I will be here for him on his return. I shall not flee."

"As you wish, Cousin." He bowed before her. "Then you must remain in your chambers."

She nodded and again tried to calm Vai-Ra down who had now started to cry, unsure of what was going on she could no doubt sense the anxiety in the air.

"Let us move, we do not have much time to get you to safety." Winstone said as he made for the keep door bursting through clutching his blade, Shard in his hand and moved swiftly up the spiralling staircase that led to the royal chambers in the Royal Tower.

"Why do we hurry so Cousin? Surely the fortress is impregnable and these dark beings may not gain entry."

"Quickly, I say quickly." He said ignoring her question and continuing on their climb up the stairs, torches protruding from the wall cast dancing shadows on the stone and they scared the Queen, who cradled Vai-Ra tightly to her bosom, perhaps too tightly for the child began to cry hysterically.

"Cousin..." She asked again, but still he ignored the questioning.

Five guards came bolting down the stairwell and Winstone nearly had their heads on the end of his blade. Everyone flinched from surprise and as the Queen still questioned the Head Knight, he spoke only to the five guards in a frantic state.

"Are there any guards still at the royal chambers?"

"Aye, Sir, there be three."

"Good!" Winstone nodded. "You men go to the Great Hall and await my presence, send word to strengthen the walls with archers and ready catapults and boil the oil!"

The guards nodded and then were on their way down the stairs.

"Cousin!" She called, "I will not be ignored!" She grabbed him half way up the stairs and spun him around, he nearly lost his footing on the steps and went hurtling down them, but he managed to steady himself on the wall and he stared at her.

"Is this castle not the impregnable fortress it was said to be?"

"No!" Winstone barked back.

"What?" She looked at him horrified. "How is this so?"

"There is one secret entrance that runs through the falls that was never barricaded, the Goblins have learnt of this and..."

"And what? Tell me!"

"They are already within the castle walls." He murmured, with sweat dripping down from his receding hairline and lips all of a quiver. She had no words but followed him to the chambers where he gave orders for the guards to guard the doors with their lives, she ran into the chambers still holding the hysterical babe to her heart and looked around bewildered, the room had never looked so empty, where was her King, she needed him.

"Stay here and do not open the door to anyone but me." Said Sir Winstone snapping her from her musing.

"You mean to leave me alone?" She whimpered, all of a sudden fearful of what could happen, but fear more for her child than herself.

"The door is heavily guarded and I will station more men on the inside and outside of the keep's doors. Stay away from the balcony and keep safe."

"You cannot leave us Cousin." She cried.

He touched her face as tenderly as he could with his gauntlets on.

"You will be quite safe." He inhaled the scent of soap from the Princess' blonde curls, that stopped her crying for a moment as the bristles of his beard tickled her, "I need to be with the Men they need direction and I am no coward to hide in a tower."

"Then what of me? You take me for a coward, Cousin?" She spat venomously, it was an unfair retort and she knew it. She knew that he had his duties to attend to, but she felt so alone, so scared.

"Of course not." He snapped. "You are one of the strongest people I have ever known. But you are a Queen and your duty is to take care of the Princess as mine is to take care of this Kingdom."

"Of course." She said her head dropping.

He lifted her head up by her chin and smiled at her. "It matters not what happens to me, if I live or die, I do my duty and the same sentiment goes for you my Queen."

She nodded and kissed her cousin's cheek.

"I shall protect the castle, my guards will protect you and you protect that child, that is the way of it."

"Yes."

"You have your Maid of Honour, yes?"

"Yes." Her quivering hand touched its rose shaped pommel, hoping that it was there.

"Good!" Sir Winstone said. "Keep it close."

He bolted from the room bellowing to her over his shoulder. "Keep this door locked and bolted. I shall return I promise you."

The door slammed shut and she quickly turned the key and ran the heavy bolts into place. She held Vai-Ra tightly and collapsed to her knees in tears.

CHÃPTÉR 34
LÉNNÖC THÉ RÉD

agmai gazed up at the stars as the Sand Sleepers slowly crawled in through the open windows of the tower, they groaned with hunger raucously as their cragged teeth dripped with saliva, they scrambled over each other, their crooked contorted limbs reached for the floored, defenceless Wizard.

"I can hear you." Pagmai whispered.

The Sand Sleepers caved in against the door and the constant thumping of the old wood sounded like the impending doom of a war drum.

"I can feel you." Pagmai said with a smile on his weathered face and tears in his eyes.

The door began to splinter and break and the deep black sockets of the undead glared at him eagerly, tasting his scent on the warm breeze.

"Come..." Pagmai whispered. "Come closer, for the hour is nigh."

The craving to taste fresh flesh was too much for the Sand Sleepers and the door gave way and dozens upon dozens of the

392

unrestful collapsed into the room, clambering slowly over each other to reach their victim first. The undead at the windows broke their own brittle bones to enter the tower, but it did not stop them as they crawled in like long limbed arachnids. They came towards the fallen Wizard from every corner now and the end appeared to be so close he could reach out and touch it.

"Hello, Lennoc!" He announced.

All at once the glass roof of the tower erupted in an explosion of dense red flame, glass rained down around Pagmai, shards of it stabbing at the Sand Sleepers shrivelled flesh, some of them flailed after being engulfed in flame. Again red fire attacked the tower and the Sand Sleepers that were climbing its walls fell back to the sands from which they came. Flame hurtled through the door burning through all in its wake as it devoured the mass of undead that were snaking up the spiral staircase.

"You took your time." Pagmai laughed.

Pagmai smiled as a gargantuan red Dragon perched its heavily load on top of the broken tower as it looked down at his handiwork of Sand Sleepers smothered in flame, contorted bodies violently twitching.

Lennoc 'The Red' seemed to grin at the Wizard, its size rivalled Demios, resembling his brother 'The Black Arrow' although his head was rounder and was topped with two long slender horns with a stunted snout.

"Thank you my friend, it has been a long time." Pagmai said and Lennoc then showed us a trait that was not known of any other Dragon, when he spoke the words in the common tongue.

393

"I was wondering when I would be called upon to save your old neck again." Lennoc growled, the sound was loud and rough, but the tone was lighthearted.

"I thought saving you and your Man friends at the Rage of Man was my debt paid for the next several centuries." The Dragon scoffed.

"Is a debt every truly paid my friend?" Pagmai laughed as the Dragon's large front claws scooped up the fragile Wizard and cradled him gently.

"It would appear not, Wizard."

Lennoc started to ascend into the air on his massive thick wings that looked as though they had been woven with leather, and flew away leaving the tower in flames, twitching with the quivering corpses of the Sand Sleepers.

Lennoc rose into the sky, holding the fragile Wizard delicately in his claws and made for the West as the Sun was setting on Maglore. Pagmai watched as the Tower of Solitude and all its secrets burnt in flame, it was a bittersweet moment, he was heartbroken to see so many parchments and scrolls turn to ash, secrets to be lost, he thought it may take centuries before these findings could be reproduced and discovered by others. But he was glad to see the Sand Sleepers sprawling around in the flames suffering and still hungry. As they distanced themselves from the burning tower it looked ever so small and useless, but it burned raw like a torch in the desert, a beacon he thought, hopefully it will warn people to stay away.

"Where would you have me fly Wizard?" Asked Lennoc in his loud, gravelly tone.

Pagmai turned his attentions away from the tower and towards more pressing matters.

"Go North-west to Kanka."

"Kanka?" Lennoc replied confused. "Is the fight not to the West-coast?"

"It is but we are in no shape to fight just yet."

"Speak for yourself, you old dog!" Lennoc chuckled. "There is plenty fight left beneath my old scales."

Lennoc took the moment to spin in the air and dive down to the ground rapidly before gliding back up and spiralling several times.

"Please refrain from doing that." Pagmai groaned, green with nausea. Lennoc did nothing but laugh unleashing a long burst of red flame, Pagmai could feel its warmth and strangely it gave him chills. Remembering the last time he had felt Dragon fire at the Rage of Man battle and his enchanted armour had fought back the fury of the white Dragon known as Claarac and its peculiar black flame, it was something he did not wish to relive. Without the enchanted armour he would have been cooked to a crisp, magic Orb or no magic Orb.

"So why Kanka?" Lennoc asked steadying his flight to a gentle glide.

"To be more precise we need to go to the Hills of Brockonbak."

"Giant country!" Lennoc grumbled, as he had no love for Giants. When you are a gigantic predator like a Dragon then you attract giant huntsman, "I think I would sooner stay in exile."

Lennoc had spent most of his days in the pit of a mighty volcano in the Kayalian Mountains known as Vollox, there he had become forgotten and that was how he liked it. Lennoc had grown tired of Man, Dwarves, Giants and Elves and their pity squabbles and wanted nothing to do with any of it. So he exiled himself and lived peacefully in the safe confines of Vollox, for who in their right mind would ever go exploring in a live volcano?

"The journey is a must!" Pagmai announced, "I understand your hostility towards the Giants. I know they have tried to hunt your kind in the past. But this is a very strange time and alliances need to be formed if we are to fight this darkness."

"Forming alliances between races that hate each other is not a simple task Wizard."

"It is not." He sighed. "If I had listened with an open ear and an open mind to King Sebastian, we may not be in this situation."

There was a silence for a moment or two as guilt pricked away at Pagmai's pride, his thoughts turning to the King of Man and he hoped that he was safe, for if any Man was brave enough to lead a coalition against this darkness it was him.

"The Giants are the strongest force in the realm, to have them fight on our side does give us an advantage if..." Pagmai again drifted off and his thoughts turned dark.

"If what?" Lennoc asked, the booming tone like a gong being played in his head.

"That is if Grimalkin has not beat us to it."

Lennoc veered off towards the North-west and started asking questions of his own.

"Who is this Grimalkin you speak of?"

"He is an Elf..."

"An Elf!" Lennoc interrupted. "Impossible! There are no Elves left in maglore."

"I assure you he is an Elf, and he was my apprentice."

"You mean you educated him in the mystic arts?"

Pagmai nodded his head sadly. "Yes."

Lennoc said nothing, his silence was scornful and judgemental.

"You are right to cast blame at me my old friend. I was blind to see his treachery, maybe I was too arrogant to see the spider weaving a web of dark deceit under my very nose and for that I do not have enough apologies. The Mystic Circle is in ashes and its members dead, my friends dead... my love..." tears welled up in his old eyes and it was Lennoc's voice that soothed him with its sincere tone.

"My thoughts are with your lost loved ones, but matters need to be attended to now. We cannot cry over the past, it is the present that holds the key to the future, that is where we must focus our energies."

"True words my friend." Pagmai replied, closing his eyes tightly to lock in the tears, if they could survive this war he could grieve later.

"Do you have any knowledge of Grimalkin's plan?"

"All I know is that he means to take the realm for his own which would mean overthrowing Man first, but there are a number of various Man kingdoms with armies to fight against his Goblin Army, unless..."

"Unless what?"

"He has more than just Goblins bent to his will."

"The Children of the Shrouded Realm?"

"Indeed!" Pagmai agreed. "There is always the possibility that Dragons have joined his cause. It would not surprised me to learn that he has also mastered the art of the Animan too and whispered words or deceit to your kin."

"My brothers and sisters," Lennoc sneered, "fools! All of them!"

"Foolhardy they may well be, but hungry for flesh and power they are and the damage they could do under Grimalkin's command is inconceivable."

"Would it be possible to take the realm in a single stroke?"

"I do hope not."

They approached Kanka and their fears were realised as the Kanka Woods and beyond burned in magenta flame.

"Demios!" Lennoc sneered, knowing that his brother 'The Black Arrow' was the only Dragon who could conjure up such flame.

"We are too late." Pagmai sighed as they swept through the smoke that rose from the land of Giants.

CHÃPTÉR 35
HÃRTWÃKÉR'S ÃLWÃYS RÏSÉ

ebastian Hartwaker rode Dayboy hard through Tendor towards Calgaras, the massive colt had run flat out and was now covered in a thick layer of sweat that clung uncomfortably to the fine hairs of its muscular torso. Sebastian had never pushed his steed so hard before, he had never had to, but everything depended on him reaching Windmast Castle in time. Sebastian had been sure to stay close to the river that ran through the various kingdoms, known to all as Serpent's Tail for its bizarre meandering curves, the water flowed fiercely from The King's Falls to Lake Salivia as if it were an angry snake eager to strike.

He made sure that they paused at several intervals for Dayboy to take on water, before pushing on again, he cursed himself each stride for treating his steed in such a way but needs must and he whispered words of apology and encouragement in the ear of his noble steed every step of the way. It was a strange time for The King, his mind could not register that he had slain a Dragon, the last known Man to achieve such a feat was his granduncle Brode Hartwaker I and that was more than one hundred years ago. Still they sang of that triumph, his name had been etched into the Scrolls of History and the stories of the realm's folklore. There was a fragment of the King's mind that wanted to rejoice and celebrate the colossal triumph, wondering if his name would become etched into Maglore's history like his granduncle 'The Dragon Slayer'. These thoughts betrayed him and they were replaced by guilt and shame, how could he daydream about his name being sang for generations to come for slaying a Dragon, when his family teetered on the edge of annihilation. There was still much to do if he were to be remembered at all, if he could not save his Kingdom then he would be remembered as a failure of the people, not a slayer of Dragons.

Night had draped itself over the West like a blanket being placed over a dead corpse, the King knew that he could be too late, that Grimalkin's army were already a few days in front of him, but he would not concede, he could not.

Dayboy had started to flag, so again Sebastian tugged on the reins and brought his thundering steed to a halt, he dismounted, stretched his legs and back and allowed Dayboy to take in as much of the stream as he wished.

"Easy Dayboy, good boy, drink up quickly and we shall be on our way again soon."

Dayboy blew air and mucus from his nostrils before lapping at the water eagerly, he was a clever colt and he seemed to understand what was needed of him and why. Sebastian took the opportunity to disrobe now and add his vest of chainmail that his Queen had been so insistent on him taking with him.

He knew not what he was riding into so he redressed accordingly. The mail touched the souvenir that had been left from Laasp a gaping wound that left untreated would surely become infected, he winced at first but then the cool steel rings became soothing to the wound. It had been some years since he had felt the uncomfortable garb against his flesh and he had forgotten how much the damn thing weighed, but this was no time for the arrogant complaining of a monarch. Thousands of gold coloured rings shimmered under the Moon of Tenaj's icy kiss, and he placed his tunic back over the mail, crimson red embroidered with the sigil of his House, the golden Phoenix. He ran his coarse fingertips over the exquisite stitching that had been hand sewn by his Queen as a name day gift, it made him smile and he cursed himself for having the audacity to find anything to smile about. His belt went on quickly and he adjusted his scabbards, the dagger sheath remained empty, it had saved his life and remained a misshapen and melted piece of steel in a dead Dragon's maw. He unsheathed Reignmaker, its blade tacky with a layer of Dragon's blood, the smell stung his nostrils and he dipped it into the writhing current of the Serpent's Tail to cleanse the blade. Dayboy had quenched his thirst and Sebastian knew it was unwise to let the colt rest or else he would be hard to get started again, so sheathing his sword that dripped with the remnants of the river he mounted Dayboy and they took off again and full pace.

As he travelled he thought of many things, his friends at court, laughing and sharing follies over fine wines and good food, his lips dry at the thought of meat and wine and he licked at them hoping to find the rich, sweet taste of wine or the salted meat of a boar, but he found nothing. His stomach grumbled to him pleading for something, anything, but there was no time for such luxuries as food and drink.

Sir Winstone's face flashed before him and good times on hunts and on crusades, his boorish lust for women had made for plenty a tale, he missed him. He thought of his brother's with sadness, both King's, both gone and tears welled up within his eyes. New friends he had made on his quest the young stable boy, Ern, who was so kind and helpful. Sir Maximillous Mondt who had saved his life and Miglay 'The Mindful' both of them giving their lives for him, the guilt was overwhelming for such tragic losses. He wondered whether any of The Mystic Circle had survived, when he tasted the blood of Laasp and saw through its black eyes he saw Mount Quirinus in ruin and an army too large to be repelled by the few that dwelled there, even if they were Sorcerers. A dark thought sneered in his mind telling him that it was their own fault that they had fallen, that they should have believed his words and taken his warning seriously. He dismissed such darkness, cursing himself for even thinking such hideous thoughts. He saw through the eyes of the yellow scaled beast again as its flame burned through The Kingdom under the Flowers and thousands of defenceless Fairies screamed out in pain, how many more would have to fall before Grimalkin was satisfied. He pondered a treaty and handing the crown over to the Dark Elf if it meant his people and his family would be kept safe, but he knew such thoughts were folly, Grimalkin would slay all who threatened his rule.

He imagined his Queen cradling his daughter as she suckled, the sunlight illuminating her in their bed chambers, it was a beautiful memory and he made sure that it lingered on longer than any other. Vai-Ra's laugh, he remembered holding her aloft and vowing that she would be Queen. The laughter turned to mocking laughter in his head and then the realisation sunk in again of what was happening, they would realise now that his words be true and there would be no mocking laughter now.

"King Sebastian was right, they will say." He sneered, he did not wish to be bitter, but if only people had listened to his warnings, things may well be different. He felt the Phoenix shaped pommel of his sword dig into his side and that reminded him again of his family, of his House, the Hartwakers and the Phoenix.

"Hartwaker's always rise." He murmured to himself, it made him think of Sirod the Phoenix and he wished that he had the ability to conjure up this mythical beast, so that he may rid the realm of darkness once more, if only he knew how to summon it.

Dayboy's wheezing breaths was enough to bring him back to the here and now, he pulled on the reins to slow the weary colt and let him settle into a gentle canter, before smothering him with affectionate pats and strokes. Dayboy neighed again and Hartwaker realised that his steed was not meaning for them to stop but to notify his Master that they were sat on the outskirts of Tendor and had now reached the entrance to Calgaras. Sebastian brought Dayboy to a full stop and shared water from his decanter to the thirsty colt before looking out at the postern

403

that surrounded the Kingdom of Calgaras. The wall was not as high as the one that surrounded the actual castle but was high enough and solid enough to keep out intruders and was also equipped with a gate and portcullis. A small ravine had been dug around the wall's skirts which sometimes became filled with rain water.

"I see guards!" He exhaled with relief. "Maybe we are not too late after all."

He felt more relaxed as they moved closer towards the gate, the torches were all lit and illuminated, the four guards that were on duty, all of them clad in the House Hartwaker royal armour and colours, pristine gold coloured steel armour and an arrangement of red plumes that protruded from their helms. As he neared the gates he realised they were wide open and the portcullis raised and the drawbridge laid down invitingly.

"That is odd!" Sebastian said to himself aloud, it was customary for the gate to always be locked up and the guards on duty to open it and close it. It was especially strange for it to be wide open now that the sun had gone down, more precautions were always taken at night. He also knew that more guards should be on duty during these hours. He arrived at the bridge and Dayboy's hooves thudded heavily on the solid wood which announced their presence to the guards above. The guards turned slowly to see the King glaring up at them, the torchlight was at there backs and their faces were hidden heavily by shadow. Sebastian could have walked straight through but he would be amiss to not discipline their careless transgressions.

404

"Hello there!" He called up to them, he heard quiet voices whispering, it brought a frown to his brow and Dayboy stepped back from the bridge uneasily, it was always best to listen to a colt's intuition.

"What is it boy?" He whispered to his steed. "You sense something is wrong too?"

"Who goes?" Called a voice, the pitch was strange and it was not a voice that The King recognised to be one of his guards.

"I should ask you the same!" Sebastian said hand wrapped around the handle of Reignmaker.

"This is the Kingdom of Calgaras, home to House Hartwaker and The King!" The voice shrieked. "State your name and business!"

"Why would I do that when I can walk straight in?" He barked back, he looked into the darkness of the gate's maw, the torches had been put out and the portcullis smiled at him sadistically. Sebastian would not be passing through there he knew that much. He heard movement above and disgruntled whispers, whoever was guarding the gate were not his Men and they bickered about something, perhaps that had forgotten to raise the bridge and the portcullis was meant to be guillotine to The King when he entered.

"Who are you I say!" Sebastian growled and torchlight caught the guard's faces. Long noses and gaunt features were illuminated, skin as green as olives.

"Goblins!" He growled.

"ATTACK!" One of them shouted and the four appeared between the merlons of the parapet with bows homing the sharp steel of arrows, the twine taut, quivering eagerly to be released.

Sebastian yanked on the reins and Dayboy reared up as four arrows rained down upon them. Before he could turn the large colt around, four more arrows came in rapid succession and one sliced across the exposed neck of The King, slicing away a layer of flesh and causing him to fall from his colt. He cursed himself, hand at his neck to check the wound, there was blood on his fingertips, but luckily for him the wound was not deep. Another four arrows came fast, Sebastian danced away from one and unsheathed Reignmaker to swipe one out of the air, the other two disappeared behind him. Sebastian stooped down and grabbed a large rock launching it towards them, it hit one square in the face, it would slow them down for a moment while he backed up out of their range.

"Come Dayboy, let us regroup."

Sebastian moved, but he moved alone and that is when he saw his steed, his friend still on the floor, his gigantic torso riddled with arrows, blood seeping from the wounds and discolouring his beautiful golden coat.

"No..." He grumbled running to his side. "Dayboy, no!" Tears welled, but the brave steed's dark eyes had already glazed over. Arrows came again falling around him, this time they were tipped with flame. Sebastian rose up in sheer anger and took his bag that contained the helms of his fallen friends and swung it around his head before launching it at the Goblin

406

archers, it hit one Goblin with a loud thud and he fell into the other leaving only one archer with all his senses. He opened the satchel that hung from his fallen steed's saddle and took the wooden binturong and stuffed it inside his tunic, he was adamant that his little Princess would have a gift on his return. He lifted his sword and ran towards the drawbridge, arrows of fire burned swiftly as they passed him, the other archers regain themselves and joined in, more arrows came but still Sebastian stormed on. He refused to be stopped until one single arrow got through dislodging a weak link in his chainmail and driving through his shoulder. It dropped the King to his knees on the edge of the drawbridge as the burning arrow had burned straight through him and erupted from his back, still the arrowhead flickered with flame and spat with the moisture of his blood. He grimaced and dropped his sword to the wood of the drawbridge and grasped the shaft of the arrow, just his touch sent pain surging through his body and he felt warm vomit rise up the back of his throat.

The Goblins cackled at the fallen King's misfortune and mocked him openly, then one of them informed the others of a problem.

"He is out of position for a clean shot."

"Tis true!" Hissed another.

"We could go down and finish it up close and personal?" The Goblin licked his lips and removed a jagged dagger, torchlight danced on the blade as they laughed. Sebastian grabbed the arrow and tried to pull it back through where it had entered, but the pain was overwhelming and he screamed violently.

"No one can hear you Man King." Said the Goblin, as he came walking across the drawbridge toying with the dagger, the others hung from the parapet to get a better view, all smiles and cackles. Sebastian reached around for his sword, found it and gripped the handle again, trying to use it as a crutch to help him to his feet.

"They're all dead, Man King."
The Goblin stood over the King, feeling powerful and exuding arrogance.

"No!" Sebastian dropped his head, tears spilling from his eyes, he knew that Goblins were liars but the words hit a nerve, what if he was telling the truth.

"Oh yes!" He hissed dragging the blade of the dagger gently across the greasy scalp of the King, as if toying with his food before he ate it.

"Your Knights, your people, your Queen..." He stopped to cackle and raise the dagger in the air, meaning to plough it into the top of the King's skull, "...your child!"

"Vai-Ra!" Sebastian exhaled and realised that even if this Goblin spoke the truth then everyone responsible for such an act would die. Reignmaker was gripped tightly and swung upwards and drove it under the Goblin's chest plate, brutally destroying his internal organs. The Goblin's yellow eyes grew wide and he dropped the dagger and staggered back allowing the blade of Reignmaker to slide out from his body and he watched as thick black blood seeped out of him. He collapsed dead and Sebastian winced with the sheer effort of it all, dropping the sword again, this time the blade thick with Goblin's blood.

"What goes on?" A Goblin called from above. "We cannot see?"

Sebastian reached for the dropped dagger and launched it towards the nosey Goblin, the blade sunk into his face and he fell dead. The remaining two Goblins shrieked and one of them called to the left of the drawbridge. The portcullis hurtled down quickly as if the ropes holding it had been severed, the sound rumbled through the maw of the gate like a roaring beast and then the drawbridge started to tremble. Sebastian could feel the solid wooden drawbridge moving underneath him, he glared at the fletch of the arrow protruding out of him and he grasped it tightly in his fist and closed his eyes before whispering the words that had been said by many a King before him, "Hartwaker's always rise!" And with that he snapped the wooden shaft of the arrow, he groaned through gritted teeth and blood left his wound to stain the chainmail as the head of the arrow dropped out behind him. He grasped Reignmaker and then rose as did the bridge beneath him. As it became steeper his boots started to slip and before he could lose his footing he repositioned himself on the edge of the drawbridge. As it lifted vertically he rode it slowly as it made its way back underneath the battlements where he remained for a few moments in the shadow of the parapet's lip.

"Can you see the Man King?" A Goblin hissed.

"No!" Replied the other. "Perhaps his bones have been squashed against the portcullis and bridge."

"Yes!" The other hissed and they laughed until they heard a whistle in the darkness, their amber eyes met with confusion etched upon their hideous faces and together they looked through the merlon. Reignmaker rose up with an aggressive swipe and split one of the Goblin's face wide open, he backed away holding the greenish flaps of skin that was once his face as warm black blood ran through his fingers. The other Goblin backed away and discarded his bow before unsheathing two daggers. Sebastian emerged through the gape in the merlons, sword in hand dripping of Goblin blood and as the torchlight bathed the King's face the Goblin shook terrified by his menacing eyes that bore a hole in him. They were the eyes of a Man that had nothing left to lose.

"My blade has tasted Goblin blood." Sebastian growled. "And it would appear that the taste agrees with its refined palate!"

The Goblin swallowed heavily as Sebastian dropped onto the battlement. He flicked the sword around expertly and droplets of black blood flicked at the cowering Goblin, daggers trembling loosely in his grip.

"It seems that Reignmaker is ravenous tonight!" And with those words Sebastian attacked with heavy blows that the Goblin matched with his daggers, somehow blocking the thrusts and swipes from the heavy broad sword, but he did not attack himself, his eyes gave away his thoughts, he was just trying to survive. Sebastian managed a stiff kick to the Goblin

410

that sent him colliding with the wall of the parapet. As the Goblin collided with the thick unforgiving stone, he was forced to drop the daggers and he whimpered for his miserable life as he looked around frantically for a way out of this situation. There was a shriek from The King's rear and he turned just in time to see the Goblin (whose face was split in two) charging at him. The King quickly positioned his feet, stood his ground and dropping his shoulder launched the Goblin up an over the parapet, hurtling towards the empty ravine that surrounded the walls. If it had not been for the heat of Fervor then he would have been saved by water, he was not so lucky and his bones broke like twigs under the impact. Sebastian turned to see the floored Goblin back on his feet with a flaming torch in his hands waving it aggressively in front of him.

"Keep back Man King or I will burn you!"
The King began to laugh and mocked the Goblin who looked at him with bemusement consuming his yellow eyes.

"What type of Man is not scared of fire and flame?" The Goblin asked as he swiped the torch at The King that seemed unfazed by the flame and did not move.

"A mad one!" Sebastian growled and stepped forward towards the fire, the Goblin threw down the torch and immediately it engulfed the debris lying around the battlements, it did not take long for it to rise higher. The Goblin backed away to the wall, letting the flames create a shield of safety around him. For a moment he truly believed he was safe from this Mad King of Man, until Sebastian walked through the flames. The fire licked his skin and melted his chainmail, but he

411

did not show any emotion other than anger and hate towards the Goblin.

"I am a Hartwaker!" He shouted at the Goblin, "I am a Phoenix born of flames!" And with those words he drove Reignmaker through the chest plate of the Goblin, the heat of the blade melting through with ease, skewering him. The angered King lifted the flailing body into the air above his head a roared at him. "AND YOU WILL DIE OF FLAME!"

He drove the skewered Goblin into the flames and watched as the fire consumed his writhing body.

Sebastian stood and waited for the flames to die and the shrieks to disperse, the burnt creature that lay before him was satisfying to the King, a contorted mess of melted steel and broken bones. He looked out towards his castle and his Kingdom, flames of orange rose from the Southwest from Elken and Trinpola. The Northwest was a wall of magenta flame which engulfed the woods of Kanka and the great Weeping Willow of Kalfahr. Then his castle, remained seemingly untouched by flame, he knew this was because they had had no need assault the walls with flame or they had known the secret entrance through the King's Falls. He gazed upon his Kingdom and made a vow.

"If the lying tongue of Goblins turn out to be truth, everyone will pay the price, I will send as many of these demons back to The Shrouded Realm as I can! I may even join them!"

CHÃPTÉR 36
THÉ LÃST GÏÃNT

hen Lennoc 'The Red' touched down in Kanka it was too late. The Kanka Woods that surrounded the Giant kingdom in the Hills of Brockonbak were alive with magenta and pink Dragon fire, the fire of Demios and the flames danced with each other scornfully mocking the limbs of the great trees beneath them. Lennoc held out is claw and delicately Pagmai stepped down, using the staff he had acquired from the Tower of Solitude to steady him. Carefully he shuffled through the singed grass, the smell of burnt flesh filled the air and Pagmai had to fight back the urge to vomit. He hoped he wouldn't vomit for he believed himself to be so frail it may end his life to exert so much energy.

The Hills of Brockonbak was named after the last Mammocolt in existence, a humungous colt like creature that was the steed to Van Crok, the first known Giant. Brockonbak's size was immense and the steed towered over even the tallest Giants of that time. These hills were a place of peace, but now it was cluttered with the gargantuan carcasses of fallen Giants. Most of the Giants lay piled on top of each other and Pagmai wondered how these behemoths were ever moved, let alone picked up and piled on top of each other. Some of them had stood twenty feet in height, the largest species to walk the realm on two legs, a majestic, powerful and proud race like no other now lay disgraced, their entire race in ruins.

Pagmai's eyes leaked with agony to see the pain etched into their huge faces.

"Such a tragedy!" Pagmai sighed, as he stared into the open eyes of one fallen Giant, his eye as large as watermelons, he used his whole hand to close each lid and stroked the rough flesh of the Giant's face.

"My brother should pay for this." Lennoc seethed as he trudged around in disbelief that an entire species had been wiped out within the blink of an eye.

"Demios follows only the orders of his Dark Master, my friend."

"PAH!" Lennoc scoffed. "You speak as though he is not to blame for this."

"He is not."

"PAH!" Lennoc snorted aggressively in disagreement of the Wizard's words.

"I will not say that your brother is not evil in its purest form, but would Demios have committed such heinous acts without Grimalkin pulling on his reins?"

Lennoc did not reply but fumed with anger and he continued to traipse through the ash looking for survivors.

"He would take elk and boar, juug and heifer, occasionally Man if they were unarmed. Your kind had grown

414

wary of Man for they have armour and steel and the ability of making their own fire. That is why you have all been in exile for so long."

His words were true but Lennoc did not like them and chose to ignore them.

"No, Demios is not to blame..."

"HE IS NOT BLAMELESS!" Lennoc roared interrupting the Wizard, flame sizzling in his maw, spitting from in between his clenched teeth, plumes of smoke escaping from his flared nostrils.

"No, he is not and he shall be dealt with in due course. My words are not meant to offend you old friend, but make you see clearly and not be blinded by personal retribution. Grimalkin is the head of this Kraken and his tentacles control all. It is his head that needs to be severed for this carnage to cease."

Lennoc opened his jaws to speak again, whether it was to argue or agree will never be known for his sensitive ears heard something that halted his words.

"What is it?" Pagmai asked.

"I hear something..." He paused tilting his monstrous head to hear better, "...crying. I hear the crying of a child."

Lennoc marched away quickly following the sound, Pagmai followed as quickly as he was able. Everywhere they looked were the corpses of Giants, built around them like the high, impregnable walls of some abominable fortress, a sadistic fortress of flesh and bone.

The Hills of Brokonbak were overwhelmed with large circular

holes where the Giants resided, they had never had need to build houses of wood or castles of stone. They had always dug their homes deep under the hills were it was said their communities had vast caverns and chambers to interact socially. It had been many years since Giants had been seen out of their holes, some say that it was safety, others whisper of an uprising and they were waiting for the right time to take the realm for their own. In truth if the Giants had planned an uprising there would have been no one to stop them, except perhaps a coalition of Dragons, so if the latter words had been truth they would have led such an uprising centuries ago. War was not what The Giants wanted, they wanted peace and to be left alone but always found themselves being pulled into the battles and arguments of Man and Elf, Dwarf and Goblin.

The sound of crying grew louder from what appeared to be the widest of all the holes scattered throughout the hills, at its entrance sat the largest Giant ever known, 'The Giant King' Troggo. He sat slouched over, gripping the largest sword ever forged, it went by Grave-Digger and its blade was taller and wider than any Man. Troggo wore a vest of Feral fur that was thick and matted with blood and as Pagmai and Lennoc came closer they realised the blood was his own and great Giant sat dead.

"He's gone." Sighed Pagmai, Lennoc nodded sadly.
Troggo still clutched Grave-Digger in hand as he sat at the entrance in one final act of defiance to protect his home. Pagmai moved in closer and sighed. "The Giants have fallen."

"He guards his hole to the very end." Added Lennoc.

"Yes." Nodded Pagmai. "His home, his family."
The child's cries came from Troggo's home, echoing around the tunnel and filling the air.

"The cries! Could they be that of Troggo's offspring?"

"I did not now that they had birthed a child." Pagmai said. "But it would appear that there have been many goings on that my eyes have been blind to."

"We must enter and help this child." Lennoc insisted.

"Of course!" Pagmai agreed. "But I shall enter alone, the sight of a Dragon could scare the child."

"Ha!" Lennoc snorted. "You have been without a mirror for too long Wizard, your face is no oil painting."
Pagmai smiled at the Dragon, trying to find some kind of light in all this darkness and he loved that about him. Pagmai attempted to enter the hole but suddenly Troggo's limp hand fell in his path, the massive Grave-Digger fell from his grasp and thundered against the earth.

"Troggo still lives!" Lennoc cried.
The Giant lifted his gargantuan head, the movement seemed to be too much effort as he grimaced under an impressive mass of dark hair and beard. His face was burned in places and flesh blistered hideously as deep lacerations had taken much flesh and muscle making his appearance almost unrecognisable to Pagmai.

"Troggo, speak to us." Pagmai asked tenderly, as he patted the limp hand that hand fallen before him.

He tried to speak, but his eyes rolled back in his head and all he could muster was gurgled sounds before blood spilled from his mouth and caught in his beard.

"Is your child within?" Pagmai asked.

Troggo gurgled again, but his huge eyes made contact with Pagmai's, letting the Wizard know that he had understood.

"Let us take your child and we may keep your kin safe." Troggo's eyes flickered and rolled again and he dragged his hand way from the entrance to allow the Wizard to enter. With this act he had also given Pagmai his blessing to take his child for he knew that he and every other Giant had fallen.

"Ke…" Troggo spluttered, struggling through spit and bile in his mouth and throat to try and speak.

"We are here Troggo." Pagmai said. "We are listening."

"K-ken-dal…" He coughed and more blood joined the letters as they spilt from his mouth.

"Kendal." Pagmai nodded and patted the Giant's hand delicately.

"A boy!" Lennoc said. "A strong name Troggo."

Troggo smiled for a moment and then he was gone.

"Rest now Giant, rest now." Pagmai whispered.

The weary Wizard shuffled on frail legs into the hole. The walls were lined with many torches and they flickered at him, guiding him down the long tunnel towards the sound of the child's cries. The cries had become whimpers as if the child had become scared, crying no longer did anything for him as no-one seemed to be coming to his aid.

"I am coming Kendal." Pagmai said, "I am coming little one."

Pagmai cast his weary eyes over Troggo's home, wooden furniture stood three, maybe four times his size, the Wizard was awed, and it takes something extraordinary to awe a Wizard. In the corner on a chair sat Troggo's mate, Amily, in her thick arms and nestled to her massive bosom she cradled their Son Kendal.

She was dead, dried blood seeped from a wound at her throat, but still she clung to her child a marda's will, instinctively protecting her babe, even in death. Her broad shoulders were draped in a patchwork blanket, each individual square was as big as the Wizard, a real sight to behold as the varied coloured squares were wrapped around marda and Son. Pagmai could hear the child sniffling.

"Be still little one." He said as he approached and tugged on the blanket, breaching the folds and unveiling the Giant child.

"Not so little I see." Pagmai smiled.

Kendal's round, dark eyes glistened with moisture, but there were no longer any tears as he stared at this little Man with a long white beard before him. Kendal was about the size and weight of a sack of taters and Pagmai thought for a moment if he could manage such a load in such a weakened condition. The child reached out to him with a podgy hand, sausage like fingers wiggling frantically at the Wizard. Pagmai was suddenly overcome with emotion, it made him think of Holleet, they had always wanted to conceive a child but were unable to. They had

419

all the power in the realm, blessed with such magical gifts, but sadly they could not conjure up a child of their own. Ironically Grimalkin had been like a son to them, they took him in and taught him everything they knew, which turned out to be a mistake, doubt stabbed at his innards like shards of glass.

"I failed to be a farda to Grimalkin and look what he has become!" Pagmai wept.

He could not hold himself accountable for what Grimalkin had become because he was already that before he joined The Mystic Circle, but still all guardians of the young blame themselves when it all goes wrong.

Could he be farda to this Giant child? Or would he fail him like he had Grimalkin? Kendal made up the Wizard's mind for him as he reached out so much that he tumbled out of his marda's grasp and slid out of her lap into the waiting arms of Pagmai. He caught the weight and somehow held him in his arms, somehow he had found some inner strength from somewhere, could this child be what saves him from himself?

"My, but you're a heavy one Kendal." Pagmai smiled, with tears rolling down his face. Kendal gurgled and yanked on Pagmai's long white beard. The Wizard did not know whether to laugh or to cry again, but he smiled warmly at the Giant and instinctively began to sway with the huge bulk in his arms and that was all it took to send the child into the land of slumber.

"Yes, rest now Kendal. When you wake you shall be safe."

Pagmai exited the hole with the slipping Kendal cradled in his arms.

420

"Fardahood suits you Wizard." Lennoc smiled as well as a Dragon with a mouthful of razor sharp teeth can. Pagmai replied with a smile.

"You seem to have colour back in your cheeks."

"Yes, maybe it is because I have love in my heart and purpose in my life." He stared lovingly at the child that slept soundly, tiny bubbles of saliva forming on his lips.

"Then the child has saved your life." Lennoc replied. "You shall honour him by doing the same."

"Of course." Pagmai nodded, not taking his eyes from Kendal, he was smitten.

"Where to next?" Lennoc asked. "It would not be wise to risk Kendal's life by heading to Windmast."

"No, you are right." Pagmai said staring out at the West, a burning landscape of Dragon fire, where magenta and orange flames seemed to fight against each other for supremacy.

"I fear we are too late and I will not risk the life of this little one, the last of his kind."

"The same could be said for you, for you are the last of your kind." Lennoc replied, readying himself for take off.

"I do not even now what kind I am anymore. Whether I possess any power..." He shook his head, "...I do not know. But it matters not, the only thing that matters to me now is the survival of Kendal."

"Then we go into exile?" Lennoc asked.

"Yes, to the Island of Zodiic."

"I am not familiar with such an island?"

"It is small and remote, hidden between the isles of Berry and Guile. We should be safe there from Grimalkin's clutches, until…"

"Until?"

"Until the prophecy of the snake is fulfilled."

"You have spoken about Grimalkin and his Serpents being the prophecy that will save the realm." Lennoc said slightly confused.

"Aye, a prophecy that Grimalkin has arrogantly misinterpreted. A Serpent and a Snake, although similar in many ways are very different creatures."

"So we are waiting for a Snake to rise?"

"That is what the stars tell us and who are we to dismiss their wisdom."

CHÃPTÉR 37
THÉ ÖLD FÖÖT ÃND MÖÚTH RÖÚTÏNÉ

ebastian had crept through the secret entrance under The King's Falls unnoticed, he had chosen to enter the same way that the Goblins had entered, believing that they would have the walls well guarded if they had been able to take the keep or word could have reached those at the castle to be aware of his presence having slain their guards at the first gate of Calgaras. The King could take no chances, has he entered the kingdom, he had hugged the shadows as he made his way to the falls, trying his hardest not to look up at the majestic castle that burnt in thick orange flame. Steel rang out and shouts and screams filled his ears and the retched aroma of burning flesh caressed his nostrils. He could not bring himself to stare upon the castle if it had already fallen, he could not take it if that were so. Lucky for him he was a King and a Man that used his heart to make his decisions, if it were left up to his mind then he may have already conceded. He had seen Dragons, one the colour of smoke soaring silently through the night, swooping down on the kingdom and rising again with claws full of his people. An enormous land Dragon, with emerald scales ploughing through the inner walls, swiping his heavily spiked tail at the defenceless guards and bathed the kingdom in hot orange flame, but he had enough of Dragons for one day.

The tunnel was long and very narrow and moss clung to it in an abundance. There was a thick layer of moisture gripping the misshapen stones, the tunnel would have usually have been as black as pitch, but on this day it was lit up by several torches that the infiltrators had discarded during their invasion. Sebastian knew that they would not be astute enough to expect anyone else to pass through this passage and felt comfortable in the knowledge that there would not be a band of Goblins or Imps ready to ambush him when he made his exit into the great hall. His body was torn and weary, wounds bled and his clothing and hair was soaked through from entering through the relentless cascade of the waterfall, his chainmail felt like it had doubled in weight but he was driven, he would not stop, he had to reach his Queen.

"Get back you bastards!" Growled Sir Winstone Vespa, as he stood alone in the great hall fending off two Goblins at once. One of them was armed with a slender serrated blade, the other was the sinister Brood who held his cleaver, Craver close. The great hall of Windmast Castle that was normally filled with music and merriment and the rich smells of cooked meats and fresh fruits now presented a depressing gloom of death and decay. Banqueting tables and benches were over turned, broken and some smouldering in flame in disarray and the bodies of several Knights, guards, maids and servants as well as a handful of Goblins and Black Imps too. The Head Knight remained stubborn as he swung the broad blade of Shard into the peculiar shaped head of a Goblin, his skull caving in under the force of the blow, the blade sunk into the Goblin's head so much that it became stuck and Winstone hand to place his foot on the Goblin's neck to prise it loose. Brood backed off having witnessed this and hissed at him.

"Come on then you ugly bugger!" Sir Winstone roared, his face marked with several lacerations, his tabard torn and frayed. "Make your move and endure the same fate."

Brood hissed again and attacked, Sir Winstone was a seasoned Knight and knew all the tricks, dirty or otherwise and Brood was trying them all, there was no honour in the way that a Goblin fought. Sir Winstone managed to parry and unleash an onslaught of attacks himself which left the Goblin reeling. Slowly Brood backed off and warily circled the ageing Knight. Sir Winstone kept his old eyes on the stalking Goblin.

"Have you had enough Goblin?"

"Shut your mouth old Man!" Hissed Brood.

"Just tell me if you have because I have plenty of your brothers and sisters to slay and you are waisting my time with this little dance."

Brood attacked, Sir Winstone parried again, span around on the spot and put the pommel of his sword into the Goblin's back, knocking him to the ground. Brood slid across the stone floor and backed away cautiously.

"Had enough?" Sir Winstone chuckled under heavy breathes, he was not as young as he once was and the battle was starting to take its toll on him physically, mentally he was still a Man of youth and feared nothing, but time moves on quickly and the grey hairs that flecked his receding hairline told a different tale.

Suddenly there was the sound of many feet slapping against stone from outside the great hall, bare feet, Goblin feet. General Feng led a troop of ten Goblins into the hall, all with various weapons clutched in their clawed hands, each one was adorned with fresh portions of Man flesh and moist with crimson. The cowering Brood smiled wickedly and stood up as he was joined by his brothers and sisters in arms.

"Now what say your tongue old man, it hangs limp and quiet now does it not?" Brood mocked, licking his lips with anticipation.

"Nothing has changed." Sir Winstone replied. "Only the smell, that has worsened somewhat!"

Even with the odds against him he remained defiant and gripped his sword tightly with both hands.

"Foolish Knight!" Seethed General Feng, his heavy mace in his hands with flaps of fresh flesh hanging from each spike, his armour already decorated with more marks to add to his tally of scalps.

"Perhaps!" Sir Winstone smiled, the wounds on his face gaping as he did so, releasing a fresh flowing of blood. "But there is only one way to find out, General."

"You will fall like all the rest of your kind, Knight! Your legacy will only be remembered as another mark on my armour!"

"I think not!" Came a voice from the throne that sat high above them all on its dais.

All eyes turned to see King Sebastian Hartwaker standing next to his throne, gripping Reignmaker in his hand.

"The King!" Brood hissed in astonishment.

"Sebastian!" Sir Winstone smiled.

"Sir Winstone, how goes it?" Sebastian called to him down from the dais.

"I will admit my King that things have been better." He smirked.

"I leave you alone for a few turns of the moon and look what happens to my Kingdom."

The two smiled at each other trying to make light of the terrible situation when all they really wanted to do was embrace each other and share their tears of anguish.

"My King, you look like Troll dung!"

"I feel like it Sir." Sebastian smiled.

"Don't just stand there gawping at them, kill them!" Feng screamed and just like that the mood changed instantly.

The Goblins split off into two groups, Brood led half of them and attacked Sir Winstone, who parried their initial blows pushed them off and climbed onto a table to have a better vantage point, there he could see their attacks and make himself a harder target to strike. The others made for the dais as Feng barked orders but not leading this particular charge, he knew that The Man King had the higher ground, which gave him the advantage, the General would let the fodder do their job of wearing Hartwaker down. Feng followed close behind those that headed towards the King and he watched as they fearlessly ascended the steps of the dais. Feng licked his lips with anticipation what a scalp the King of Maglore would be, the tally would surely take pride and place upon his armour and his head would make an excellent gift for his Dark Lord.

"Remember to take their heads for The Dark Lord!" Feng roared.

Sebastian fought with reckless aggression, their was fire in his eyes, he had nothing to live for if not for the survival of his family and his people, the castle could crumble, it could burn to cinders, for castles can be rebuilt, but the lives of his people and family were but mortal, flesh and blood that once drained could never be recreated. Sebastian met two Goblins simultaneously and Reignmaker greeted their jagged blades with a discourteous swipe that sent them staggering back down the steps, The King's blade, broader and made of stronger steel, steel that had already sliced through the scales of a Dragon this day. Sebastian screamed at them like a banshee, their amber eyes glistened in fear, but a growl from their General sent them dashing towards him again. Sebastian parried the attack of one Goblin, jumped over the swinging blade from below and took the sword arm of another. The armless Goblin shrieked with pain and then Sebastian took his head, which was sent hurtling down the steps and coming to rest at the clawed feet of General Feng.

"You asked for heads!" Sebastian called sarcastically, Feng glared back at him to see another head leave a member of his army and the King greeted another with a stiff kick to the face which broke its slender nose and shattered its jagged teeth, sending the Goblin sprawling into the other two and falling down the steps of the dais.

Sir Winstone drove his blade into to skull of a Goblin and swiped the bloody blade across Brood's chest, slicing through his old, inferior armour, Shard's sharp tip cutting through his green flesh. Brood staggered back and let the others attack the Knight. A swipe of a Goblin blade tore through his thigh and Sir Winstone fell from the table as searing pain burnt through his leg.

"Winstone!" Sebastian called as he countered yet another Goblin attack.

"I am okay!" He called through clenched teeth, pulling himself up to his feet as three Goblins ascending the table to stalk the fallen Knight.

"Are you sure you are okay, old Man?" Sebastian called again.

"You worry about your own bloody goblins!" Winstone snapped as he swung Shard viciously in front of him, scything across the surface of the table, two of the Goblins swiftly hurdled it, but the third was too late and the blade cut through the flesh and bone of his feet and sent him sprawling into his fellow mercenaries which caused them to spill onto the floor. The ageing Knight limped around the table and put the footless Goblin out of his misery by slamming Shard's tip into his throat.

"Come forward you bastards!" Winstone growled, "I am not biased by what body parts I take!"

429

The Goblins scrambled to reassemble, trying to get behind Brood, who swiftly slid back behind them for cover.

Sebastian felt the tip of a blade caresses his face, close enough to trim his beard, which had now grown full and untamed. His eyes had been on his friend and he had not been focussing on his own battle, it was enough to bring him back to his own problems and he planted a punch in one of the Goblin's faces, before smashing the pommel of Reignmaker into the side of another's skull, shattering bone under the incredible force. The sword sliced through the other Goblin from shoulder to hip and the she slid down the steps reeling in agony like a fish out of water. The distraught Goblin reached out to Feng who snarled at his soldier, sneering in disgust at her weakness before driving his mace into her face and then watched her dismembered carcass quiver frantically under the impact. Feng growled at Sebastian who stared back, hatred in both their eyes burning into each other, Sebastian did not even acknowledge the remaining Goblin who snuck up at his rear, but he span into action with a swift flick of his sword and burst through the fiend's stomach and watched on as his bowels and entrails poured out from its hot pit and collided unceremoniously with the dais before cascading down the steps.

Sebastian and Feng's eyes met again and The King descended towards Feng who waited at the foot of the dais. Steel met steel as sword met mace, the blade of Reignmaker shivered under the weight of Man-Eater and fresh viscera sprayed between them from such a heavy and aggressive collision.

"I shall try not to damage your pretty face too much, Man King. Lord Grimalkin wants it as a souvenir!" Feng grunted as they held each other closely, locked by mace and sword.

"A Lord now is he?" Sebastian growled, struggling to hold back the powerful thrust of the Goblin General. " A Lord of deception and decimation is no ruler worth following!"

The General kicked at the King's knee and he buckled under the impact causing him to fall back under the weight of the heavy mace. Feng reared back and brought down a hefty club with the mace, but Sebastian met it with a defensive parry, but several more blows from Mane-Eater saw Sebastian stumbled backwards on his heels.

"Maybe I shall rename her King-Eater when we are through!" Cackled Feng as he closed in on the fallen King who was now scrambling on his back up the steps behind him. He delivered another thunderous strike with the mace, but Sebastian rolled away and its spiked head turned the marbled steps into rubble. Sebastian drove a fist into the General's face flooring him.

"She is heavy and sluggish, maybe you should rename her Pig!" And with that he unleashed another fist that broke several of the General's jagged molars.

Sir Winstone slid Shard through the gut of one Goblin but took a wound on the arm that broke his chainmail and shredded his flesh deeply. Winstone growled with pain and paid the Goblin back in kind with a vicious head butt that burst his crooked

431

nose before driving Shard up into his midriff. Only Brood remained and he continued to back away from the Knight hissing like a trapped viper, slowly Winstone limped forward, his limbs soaked in his own blood.

"Cowardly Goblin!" He barked. "You bark and you hiss like some vile animal, yet you have no pride, no honour!" Winstone hoisted his sword into the air which seemed like such a strenuous act before howling like a banshee, he was surely willing up the might to deliver the killer blow, but Brood was truly a coward and fled the scene before the blade could fall upon his malformed skull. Winstone was relieved, he was all but emptied of his energy and let the sword fall to, its point chipping a piece of marble from the floor, before he fell against the bench. He breathed heavily, cringing uncomfortably from his wounds, he turned to see two Goblin feet still on the bench and he sneered. The sound of Sebastian's sword connecting with the back plate of Feng's armour sang out loudly and brought him back to the matter in hand, the fight was far from over.

"The bleeding can wait!" He winced as he pulled himself back to his feet and clutched the handle of Shard tightly in his ageing hands.

Sebastian drove the Phoenix hilt of Reignmaker into Feng's wrist causing him to drop the mace and then met his gut with a swift kick that sent him sprawling across the floor, putting distance between the Goblin and his mace.

"I am coming Sebastian!" Winstone called which distracted Sebastian for a moment, allowing the Goblin General to rise to his feet and unsheathe his horrendous serrated blade, known as Flesh-Stripper and viciously swipe it across the King's exposed thigh.   Sebastian staggered back to the bench where his friend stood.

"Let me take this braggart in honour of my King." Winstone announced proudly limping forward.

"No, Winstone, the fight is with me!" Sebastian groaned, but before he could react his Head Knight had ignored his words and charged at Feng, who parried the ageing Knight's tired strikes and tripped him to the floor looking to drive his blade into his face.

"Time is precious for an old Knight and your time is up!" Feng grinned and hoisted the blade in the air but Sebastian interrupted the execution with a heavy charge, sinking his wounded shoulder into the side of the Goblin, sending him falling to the floor again knocking his horned helm from his head and his sword from his grip. Feng's head was a mass of scares and welts from savage battles of the past. Sebastian picked up Flesh-Stripper and swung the two swords in his hands playfully, almost mocking his fallen foe.

"You are grounded, General. Concede and I may be lenient with your sentence." Sebastian spoke loudly, the voice the tone of a King, of a ruler.

"What do you mean 'lenient'?" Winstone gasped as he stood slowly next to his King. "Our Kingdom lies in ashes and you wish to be lenient with this slug!"

"It is still my Kingdom and my rules, Winstone." Sebastian snapped, "I will not become horrors like these

433

followers of darkness, justice still has a place in this realm and if the best he can hope for is to spend the rest of his miserable life in a cell then so be it!"

Winstone lowered his head not liking to disagree with his King, but he came from a different time and believed that a life should be paid for with a life.

Feng shuffled forward on his knees bent before Hartwaker. "You are indeed a merciful ruler, King Hartwaker." He groaned as if he were wounded badly.

"I still hold the crown, I still rule Maglore, I am still the King! And my words are final."

"Your words are dung!" Feng growled lifting the mace that he had manoeuvred his body to conceal and launched it towards them, Winstone pushed his King out of the way, sending the blades spilling to floor in a cacophony of steel and marble. The mace collided with the stone wall behind them, dropping unceremoniously behind a pile of broken benches.

"Curse you!" Feng screamed and charged the unarmed King like a stampeding wild animal, but Sebastian was quick to see the attack and mannered his body so that when Feng connected with his hip and was able to use his momentum against him and send him spilling over the table to the unforgiving marble floor below. As they gazed over the table, Feng lay unconscious a seeping wound now carved into his head.

"We should slit his throat where he lies." Winstone spat.

"And where is the honour in that?"

"The time of honour has ceased to existence I fear."

"Not as long as there is still air in my lungs and a rhythm in my heart." Sebastian smiled, clutching the Knight's shoulder tightly causing him to wince.

"I misspoken when I said you looked like Troll dung." He grinned mischievously.

"Oh yes?" Sebastian chuckled, even the pleasant quivering of laughter caused him pain throughout.

"The truth be that you smell like Troll dung too!"
The pair shared an embrace and laughter as fire burned the walls of the castle and the distance sound of weapons clashing rang out, it was a moment that Sebastian never thought he would have again and it gave him some hope.

"Tis just like old times!" Sebastian grinned,
The moment was quickly quashed by the heavy falls of feet at the entrance to the hall as a humongous Cyclops appeared with club in hand and saliva dripping from its misshapen and broken smile, its huge eye blinking frantically in anticipation to get his mitts on two pieces of fresh meat. He groaned and guffawed as he bent down to enter the great hall.

"Why do these old times never seem to be pleasant?" Winstone scoffed.
The Cyclops squeezed its tremendous bulk through the entrance of the great hall, its large mitts gripped the stone clad frame of the door and forced its cumbersome bulk through it, its wide frame disturbed the hefty chunks of stone and as it squirmed under its arch, the force taking most of the stone wall with it.

435

"It would seem that we have never had any times together that have not been full of blood and chaos." Sebastian said with a sigh.

"I concur!" Winstone scoffed. "What is more pleasant than slaying a Cyclops?"

They smiled at each other as the massive one eyed creature grinned at them, tightening its grip on the huge club in its hand, its portly physique covered in protruding warts and growths, its modesty only covered by a loin skin made from a dozen heifers. The Cyclops was confused as the two puny Men did not greet it with cries of terror, as it was usually accustomed. Instead the pair stood unfazed and brimming at the creature excitedly. Not understanding this greeting, the Cyclops did the only thing it knew how to do and roared at them, smashing a fist against the wall which brought hefty lumps of stone down around it, but still they remained defiant. The single hairy eyebrow that resembled a fat little creature that you find crawling around flowers and digesting leaves, wriggled over it's bulging eye in confusion and then frustration. With one final attempt to infuse horror in them it hoisted its club above its head and swung it in a frenzy, cracking wooden beams that ran across its high ceiling and ripping the flags of Hartwaker House from their proud positions in the great hall's rafters. The golden flamed Phoenix on a blanket of red wrapped around the club as if trying to wrestle the huge shaft of wood from the beast's grip, but it was to no avail and the club came down thunderously in front of the two Men that refused to display their fear. The misshapen head of the club ploughed into the marble floor and uprooted it as if it were merely soil and pebbles. The Cyclops roared again, saliva seeping from its wide maw like the falls that cascaded below Windmast castle itself. The King and the Knight were still unfazed as they looked up at the beast unimpressed, they remained so defiant because they had dealt with Cyclops many times before, Sebastian himself had singlehandedly disposed of two at Freedom Place in the Lakes of Freedom at the home of House Forrestor in Zalenta. They were dimwitted beasts used for nothing more than for their strength and the destruction they could cause, when left to their own devices a good Knight could outsmart one quite easily.

"Well, what shall it be today my King?" Winstone asked gripping Shard tightly, hoisting it up on guard. "The old foot and mouth routine?"

"Yes, I think that will suffice." Sebastian nodded and brought Reignmaker up to meet the blade of his Head Knight, the sound of the steel rang out in the hall and the cyclops did not like its high pitched chorus, it shook its head rapidly to rid its ears of such irritation. King Sebastian from House Hartwaker and the ageing Sir Winstone, Head Knight from House Vespa strode out again together to rid the kingdom of pure evil, surely if they stood together darkness did not stand a chance against them. Sir Winstone strode forward as the Cyclops lifted his massive club once again, only to drop it and cry out in pain as the Knight drove his blade in through the top of his foot, so deep was the stab that the blade sang as it hit marble below. Sebastian dodged the falling club and used it to

437

run up as the cyclops instinctively bent down to tend to its foot, but as it lowered itself as far as it could, Sebastian leapt from the club and thrust Reignmaker up through the jaw of the Cyclops. The beast stopped dead in its movement and the point of the King's sword forced the Cyclops eye to leave its socket. The eye detached with a sickening snap from its optic nerve and hit the marble floor with a squelching sound before rolling away under a broken table. The two removed their swords and watched on as the eyeless beast stood frozen in its last moments, the two valiant slayers said nothing, just waited. They seemed to wait for the longest time until Sir Winstone broke the silence. "They have usually fallen by now?"

"We should have had a wager on how long." Sebastian laughed and then the dead Cyclops collapsed.

With a troop of Goblins vanquished and the Cyclops fallen the two friends finally had time to take a moment, to catch their breathes and to embrace. It had been so long since they had seen each other and both had been through so much, their were tales to tell, but now was not the time.

"I am glad you are by my side my dear friend." Sebastian smiled, releasing the Knight from a tight embrace, "I thank you for defending the kingdom in my absence and being cousin, uncle, friend and protector to those I hold so dearly."

"I fear that I have failed you my King." Winstone sighed, dropping his head in shame as he could not come to meet his friend's eyes. In that moment his wounds seemed to grieve him and his sword became heavy in his hand as if for the first time he felt as though he should release it and renounce his Knighthood.

"I am no longer worthy of praise." He added turning to look through the ruined entrance to the great hall, his old ears listening to the crumbling of stone, the singing of steel and the screaming of those unfortunate souls trapped in a suffocating cloak of Dragon fire, flesh and bone cooking in their own armour.

"And what would Windmast have been without your presence, Winstone?" Said Sebastian as he placed a hand on the ageing Knight's shoulder, he winced as he did so but the King held it there and gave it a tender squeeze.

"Look around my King!" Winstone hissed with emotion, tears welling in his eyes, "I take great pity to know that I was the one in control of this supposedly impregnable walls of Windmast Castle when it finally fell."

"You are much to hard on yourself." Sebastian chuckled and tried to make light of the situation. "There is still a bit of wall over there by that broken stained glass."

"Please do not mock me my friend, for my heart hangs by a fraying thread. The great hall that has stood strong for so many centuries for your family, falls into ruin as we speak. The Hartwaker crest falls from the walls all around us, I am no fool, I see the meaning of such an omen."

They both turned to watch the quivering sigil of the last remaining Hartwaker flag hanging above the entrance as the castle walls shook from the impact of the Dragon's attack on its outer walls. The flag became unhooked and drifted to the bloodstained marble of the hall.

"The last flag has fallen." Winstone whispered.

"Listen to my words, Winstone." Sebastian said firmly. "It is stone and mortar that breaks and burns, not our flesh, not our hearts. We still remain with sword in hand and until that changes we shall fight on."

Winstone's moist grey eyes turned to meet Sebastian's twinkling emeralds.

"But what hope do we have?" Winstone asked.

"Where there is light there is hope my friend." Sebastian smiled. "Even now the Sun of Selym rises to bathe the West in its rays, we need to be defiant as the sun and continue to rise. The East has been lost to darkness, we cannot change that now, but we can hold on to the light that we have and rise up with it!"

Winstone grabbed the handle of Shard tightly, he no longer felt like letting it fall.

"Our priorities have changed." Sebastian said. "We can no longer hold the castle, we would be fools to try. We must leave Calgaras and regroup, taking as many of our House with us as we can find."

"Aye." Winstone cried.

"I shall head to the Royal Tower and hope that I am not too late to save our future. You must search for survivors and tell them to head to the coast and to Locklow Reach. They should be safe enough there on King's Island."

"Yes, you are right." Winstone laughed. "You are always right, you bastard!"

"Hartwaker's always rise, my friend." Sebastian said with a grin.

"Aye!" Winstone cried, lifting his sword into the air. "The Phoenix always..." His words were lost and his eyes grew wide, his grip became loose around Shard's handle and it fell to the marble in an earsplitting din. Sebastian stared at his friend as his eyes turned to blood and tears of crimson fell from those kind and brave grey pearls.

"...rises..." He hissed and then fell face first to the marble, the heavy spiked mace of General Feng driven into the back of his skull.

"No!" Sebastian whispered and knelt at the side of his fallen friend.

"This time the Phoenix shall not rise." Feng hissed from behind him and Sebastian was on his feet again with sword at guard. Blood seeped from a heavy wound on Feng's head, another scar set to form, another war wound to tell tale of.

"I shall be the one to extinguish its wings of flame." Feng growled and turned his sword over in his clawed hands.

"BASTARD SPAWN OF SLOORE!" Sebastian screamed and readied himself for what could very well be the last duel that one of them would ever take part in. The two strode forward to meet each other and steel met steel with aggressive thrusts by both, fire burned in both their eyes, each unwilling to conceive as each of them rained down vicious blows on the

441

other. Their swordsmanship and expertise were equal, it would only take an error from the other for this duel to end, but neither looked as though they were wavering and continued their private battle over rubble, broken tables and benches and even over the blubbering carcass of the slain Cyclops. It was the kind of duel that would be turned into tale and song, but there were no eyes to witness the dance, no ears to hear the music that their instruments of steel conjured, no tongues to fan the flames of such a story. It appeared that nothing could bring a halt to this epic bout, until the walls shook again and the marble on which they stood trembled, causing them both to lose their balance and fall backwards, creating distance between the two. As they quickly rose on flooring that broke up into shards of black marble, orange flame erupted through the large window frame that once homed and exquisite stained-glass, the pair crouched low to evade the ceiling of Dragon fire, its heat was sickening, but the pair still glared at each other from underneath its sweltering shroud and then it dispersed, leaving them to both rise again and ready themselves to fight once more. But it was not to end in a King at the end of a Goblin's sword or vice versa for the gigantic tail of Maddox 'The Green' erupted through the great hall demolishing all in its path. The Dragon's tail was armoured thickly with green scales and heavily spiked at its tip, Sebastian and Feng were forced to dive out of harms way as it hurtled through the hall, wiping out the walls and ceiling in one fell swoop. Debris fell and the Dragon trudged away to reek chaos on some other part of the castle leaving a huge pile of fallen stone separating the two combatants, each one's route to the other obstructed. Sebastian rose from the rubble still clutching Reignmaker in his hand, his body covered in a layer of dust and debris, he gazed around what was once his great hall and sadness gripped his heart and squeezed it tightly. He looked around for the body of his fallen friend, but he saw nothing but a mountain of broken stone. There was no time for sentiment and emotional woolgathering, he needed to reach the Royal Tower and hope that his efforts were not in vein.

CHÃPTÉR 38
ÃN ÉYÉ FÖR ÃN ÉYÉ

ueen Marie Ann could no longer ignore the curiosity that welled up inside her, she had to find out what was happening and ignoring the wishes of her cousin she prepared herself to approach the balcony. She had placed Princess Vai-Ra in her cot, she remained oblivious to the chaos that surrounded them and continued to grip her farda's crown and suckle upon the cotton cloth that seemed to bring her so much comfort as her teeth threatened to break through her gums. But what was taking place around Windmast Castle could never be ignored by the Queen. Her hands trembled as she stroked them across her Daughter's plump cheeks, her own cheeks were lined with tears that had been constant since her cousin had left them. She stared at the wavering curtains that quivered in the breeze like ghostly apparitions taunting her, they seemed to warn her away, but still she disobeyed the omens and shuffled across the carpeted floor until her bare feet met the coldness of stone. The sudden change in temperature sent a shiver up through her body, yet another sign to leave well alone, there was nothing good that could come from her peering over the ledge of the balcony, but she was going to anyway.

"By the Gods!" She gasped as her moist eyes were unbelieving as she gazed upon the horrors that were transpiring in front of her. She had heard the shrieks and screams of dying Man, constant collisions of steel and smelt the fouls stench of smouldering flesh, but to cast her eyes on such sights was all too much and she staggered back and collapsed onto the floor of the balcony, tears streaming as she sat shaking her head so vigorously that her hair became loose from the confines of her tiara and hung in front of her face.

"What monstrous..." She wept, but could not even find the words to finish her sentence for there were none for what she had seen. The castle walls shook as if hit by something gargantuan and for a moment she had hoped and thought of the Giants, maybe they had come to the aid of Man? She scrambled across the cold stone and again braved herself to gaze over the ledge only to be gripped by yet more horror as she witnessed Maddox 'The Green' thrash his gigantic tail through her beloved great hall.

"No!" She spluttered and collapsed down to the stone once more, another Dragon of smokey scale flew past her silently, the current from its wings attacked her face, she became frozen with fear.

"Dragons... please tell me these are but illusions, please!" She snivelled and shook her head slowly, she was unable to take in such things for she had always been protected

445

from the real terrors of the realm. Protected by her farda, her cousin, her King.

"Farda always said that war was not meant to be seen by the eyes of a Queen," She sniffed, "he was right!"

Maddox roared and Tazak shrieked, she could feel the heat of Dragon fire in the air even in the relative safety of the Royal Tower.

"How long will we be safe?" She asked herself. "How long before the foundations of the tower are destroyed by one of those beasts or their fires cook us?"

It was all too much for the Queen, she had always been strong, but she realised now that there was falseness in her strength, for she had been blind to the real realm.

She felt weak.

"Stupid girl!" She cursed herself for her naivety. "You cannot protect your daughter from this!"

There were heavy footfalls from the other side of the royal chambers door and she froze. Screams and cackles, steel on steel, steel on stone, steel through flesh.

They were at her door.

It was only a matter of time before the Goblins came through the door, their numbers would outweigh the soldiers guarding her chambers and soon they would come for her and the Princess and then darkness truly would be upon them. She heard the playful gurgles of Vai-Ra and it was enough to snap her out of whatever self-pitying muse she had been caught up in and scowled.

"You will protect her!" She snapped and rose to her feet, her hand gripping the Maid of Honour at her hip. "If that is your destiny then so be it. I will not let them have her."

There was a sudden shuffle of feet outside the door and she heard the clang of armour and stone as if someone had fallen down the spiral steps that led to the tower, it quickly dissipated and then there seemed to be nothing, only the vile sounds from outside the window. Then came the sudden thrusts against the door, the bolts shuddered in their brackets, refusing to give way, but for how long could they keep it up under such sudden impact. The sound became rhythmic as the invaders used tool and weapon to ram the door. Queen Marie Ann stood defiant and waited for them to come, she did not feel scared anymore for her instincts had taken over, her instincts to keep her baby safe, a marda's instinct.

"YOU ARE NOT GOING TO TAKE HER!" She screamed at the door that rumbled in front of her, rattling on its thick iron hinges, for the moment they were safe, but for how long would it last. Then she heard something that made her flesh crawl, the sadistic cry of a creature that could only have been spawned in Sloore's Dwell. She turned to look out of the balcony and she was met by two terrifying eyes of magenta burning into her, a Dragon as black as shadow, it glared at her and opened up its wide maw. Queen Marie Ann was entranced by the pink and white molten fire that appeared in the back of its throat like a living breathing volcano, magenta flames danced on its tongue as it readied to unleash the contents of its

447

throat directly at her. Her eyes grew wide and drifted for a moment to see a pale figure mounted on the nape of the beast and realisation swamped her, she ran towards the baby's cot and scooped up her child to her bosom before Demios released his blazing onslaught upon the tower. Queen Marie Ann fell to the ground, turning her body at the last moment before impact to protect her little Princess. The Queen's spine rattled viciously as it took the brunt of the collision with the unforgiving stone, even if it was covered by a layer of fine carpets. Magenta flames ripped through the chambers, engulfing the curtains that now danced like ghosts of fire, it ate through tapestries and devoured the drapes and sheets that were fitted on the royal four post bed. She lay on the floor cradling Vai-Ra, her eyes gawping frantically at the flames that flickered above her head and then they were gone, all but the ones that still attacked her soft furnishings. There was another sickening scream from the dark beast and it came down awkwardly on the balcony, destroying the beautiful cherry blossoms that had tangled itself around the balustrade and taken much care and nurturing by the Queen to grow such a marvellous sight, it was all gone in an instant. The stone structure struggling to contain its weight and the ledge broke under its bulk, leaving most of the balcony demolished. Demios' claws dug into the stone wrenching several chunks of it away before it became safe for him to mount. His wings spread wide to balance itself and then when he felt comfortable enough with his perch he folded them back in on himself.

Queen Marie Ann watched all of this take place in bewilderment, she had no words and her only thought was to protect Vai-Ra even though the tides were turned heavily against her.

The chamber was bathed in a subtle pink glow now from the flames that slowly ate away at anything that would allow itself to burn, none of it felt real to her, not anymore and still the banging continued at the door, blades and maces chipping away at the thick wood.

"Good boy, Demios!" Came a voice from out on the balcony. Queen Marie Ann stared out through pink flames and saw The Dark Lord, Grimalkin descend down from his steed, his black armour shimmering like water, but his skin was as pale as snow and his features were that of a race not seen in her lifetime.

"An Elf!" She gasped.

"My Queen," Grimakin bowed as he entered the royal chamber, Demios snorting behind him as if announcing his Master's arrival, "even with fear squeezing all hope from your heart you remain perceptive." He held his staff proudly in his grip, The Orb of Quirinus pulsating with power.

"An Elf is correct," He grinned sadistically, "The only Elf left in existence thanks to your kin!" His words were bitter and dripped with venom, a grudge still held tightly to all of Man for what they did to his kind. His face returned to how it had been before, the false smile and probing eyes returned and he strode towards her, the base of his staff slamming down on the chamber's singed carpet with each casual step. Queen

449

Marie Ann pulled her child in even closer, she could feel the chill of the crown's gold against her chest, still gripped in the Princess's hands, it was soothing to her against the sickening heat that dominated the room.

"Ah, the sweet babe swaddled in its marda's arms. The little Princess..." His words drifted into a hiss.

"Do not touch her!" Queen Marie Ann barked, her throat was coarse from the plumes of smoke that hung in the air. "If you hurt her I will kill you!"

"I do not plan to hurt a curl on her head of spun gold." Grimalkin smiled, his face was solemn as though he had been accosted for being thought of as a murderer of children. "It is not for me to harm the helpless babes of Man. They are not to blame for the sins of their ancestors."

She stared at him as she rose from the floor, still clutching the Princess closely, Vai-Ra's tiny digits stretched out and wriggled frantically for her comfort cloth that lay out of reach on the floor. She began to grizzle and the Queen swayed her gently from side to side to soothe her, not realising she was in-need of her cloth, for her eyes did not leave those magenta jewels that shimmered with malevolence.

"Tell her everything will be okay. Tell her that her heart will not break and that tears will not turn to blood." His voice became but a whisper, a growl in his throat as it formed the words. "Tell her all the lies that Man tell! Lying tongues do not protect the defenceless! Let them cast their eyes on the truth of what will happen not swaddle them in a blanket of meaningless words of hope!"

"What do you want from us?" Marie Ann barked, trying so hard to keep her tone aggressively, but it wavered and she felt like breaking down and weeping.

"I want what is rightfully mine!" He hissed and pointed towards the golden band that the Princess held in her tiny hands.

"You have no claim to my husband's crown."

"I have every claim!" Grimalkin screamed, his eyes seemed to glow and pulse in anger and in time with the Mystical Orb as if the two were now one, "I am the offspring of Argo Calgaras! The Son of the Elf King, left for dead in a cradle centuries ago, nurtured back to health at the teat of Sloore! I have God's blood running through my veins and a royal heart to pump it around my body. I am the rightful heir to the throne of Maglore and I will take what is mine."

Demios exploded from the balcony and debris fell from its claws down into the constant flow of the King's Falls as the creature flew away.

"He grows tired of our discussion I fear." Grimalkin cackled. "He seeks death and destruction, not words."

"You will have to kill me before you get your evil hands on this crown."

"If that is your will, so be it."

Grimalkin reached out to her and The Orb of Quirinus began to glow, the power seemed to flow from the staff and into his body, allowing the Warlock to fulfil his heinous acts of power. His fingers twitched and the Queen began to float up into the air, she screamed in astonishment of what was happening, her toes wriggled and clenched as if trying to grip the carpet below her feet, but it had soon become out of her reach as she hung in the air.

"What are you doing?" She cried.

"I am taking my crown." He replied matter-of-factly. "Either you give me the crown or I will take it and you will die."

"No!" She growled in defiance still fighting this invisible energy that had full control over her.

"It is not worth your energy to fight my Queen, you cannot win. Give up the crown and I will be lenient with you." He moved his hand and she followed, he turned her weightless body around in the air, a hungry feline playing with an injured rodent. She clutched Vai-Ra tightly so she did not fall as she was turned in the air, a fall from this height would surely damage the child. Vai-Ra continued to grizzle and tears had started to form on her eyelashes but she would not let go of the crown just as her marda refused to relinquish her grip on her. As the Queen and Princess floated higher and higher, Grimalkin walked underneath them and looked into her face, she could smell the foul stench of stale fruit on his tongue, he smiled at her but his brow furrowed in concern.

"Look at her my Queen, the sweet naivety of youth, she knows nothing of what goes on here, she has no knowledge of pain and destruction, of war and blood, of death and loss. Let her stay pure, give me the crown and I promise she will not die by my hand."

"What good are promises from you!" She spat. "Your dark deeds have haunted my King's dreams for many a moon, your lies and deceit to claim this crown are shameful. How could I ever trust words that dripped from lips like poison."

"You have no choice." He smiled, "I can slit your throat here and now and let your babe fall from your limp dead grip, to her death. The choice is yours."

Tears well in her eyes and she squeezed her child tightly.

"You promise you will do her no harm?"

"What threat is a babe to me? You have my word that I shall not lift a finger against her."

She closed her eyes and she nodded.

"Good!" Grimalkin smiled and he lowered them both back to the ground, she felt relieved to feel the carpet touch her toes once again and she held her child out in front of her, tears ran down her face and Vai-Ra looked at her confused.

"Can you give me the crown?" She asked, but Vai-Ra just gurgled and spluttered before lodging the crown back into her mouth and gnawing on it.

"She does not understand!" Grimalkin snapped. "She is but a child, just take it from her and give it to me or I will intervene!"

"You said that you would not harm her!"

"And I will not, but you are trying my patience."

She grabbed the crown and tried to prise it from Vai-Ra's grip which was surprisingly strong.

"Give it to marda, come on now." She pleaded with tears rolling freely down her face, Vai-Ra clutched it with two hands and fought against her marda with shrieks of annoyance.

453

The sound of the child's screeching stung the dark Elf's delicate ears and he had seen enough.

"Enough of this!" Grimalkin hissed and with a flick of the wrist he unleashed a ball of energy that spiralled pinks and purples through the air and knocked the Queen to the floor, her grip went loose and she let go of the Princess and Vai-Ra fell towards the floor.

The Queen hit the floor first and called out in anguish for her child who suddenly stopped a hands width from colliding with the floor of the royal chamber. Vai-Ra giggled and dribbled, reaching a free hand to brush the carpeted floor below as she floated above it controlled by The Dark Lord. Marie Ann breathed a sigh of relief and moved forward to take her child, but the child floated upwards and then away from her marda, where she hung in the air still grasping the crown tightly, situated between the Queen and Grimalkin.

"Please..." Queen Marie Ann stuttered, frozen with her arms out stretched as if any moment the child would tumble back towards the floor, "...do not harm her. I beg of you!"

"It would seem that you still do not trust me." Grimalkin sighed as he moved his hand and fingers around gently in various motions, each action rotated the floating Princess, who appeared to be enjoying the magical jaunt.

"I have not harmed the babe, just like I said I would not." He pulled the child in through the invisible force that consumed her and looked into her sparkling green eyes, he smiled softly. "Beautiful eyes she has, I have seen these eyes before." He smiled.

454

"No!" The Queen's voice quivered as if something had become lodged in her throat.

"They are the same eyes that belong to the King."

"You have seen Sebastian?" She gasped, and hoped that the evil Warlock would not tease her of his whereabouts.

"I have indeed."

"Is he..." She could not bring herself to ask the question, "...did you..." Still she could not ask such things.

"Kill him?" Grimalkin said and then shook his head. "No. Fortunately for me I met him at The Mystic Circle where his warnings were ignored by those fools, fools that now lie dead."

The Queen's eyes doubled in size, the droplets of tears magnifying the sorrow that was within them, what would Maglore be without magic to protect it?

"I am thankful that they did not believe his words for I would not have looked forward to meeting him with steel on steel. I have heard of King Sebastian's heroics and expertise with his trusted Reignmaker. I however lack the abilities in swordsmanship to rival him."

"His he alive?" The words bursting from her uncontrollably, unable to keep them in any longer, she had to know.

"I do not know." Grimalkin sighed.

"You lie!" She sneered.

"I have not told you anything but the truth, why should I change that now?"

She moved forward again to see her child, but Grimalkin moved her closer to him again, swirling her around in the air, which caused her to erupt in childish laughter, before bringing her to a halt.

"Please do not try that again." Grimalkin's tone had become more serious.

"Where is my King?" She sobbed holding herself tightly, feeling so helpless.

"I did not lie when I said I did not know. The last I heard was when I unleashed 'The Yellow Hornet' upon him."

"A Yellow Hornet?"

"It's name is Laasp, a Dragon my dear. A swift and violent creature unleashed to turn his brave bones to ash."

Her lips quivered and she felt faint, almost losing her balance she fell against the bed post for support. She lent on it and sobbed, the once majestic mahogany had now been charred black and the smell of burnt wood caressed her nostrils. It was a scent that reminded her of Sebastian's brother's funeral, the first of such events that she had witnessed, a royal funeral pyre of a dead King. It made her remember Viktor's chubby face being engulfed in flames and as she turned away from the scene she had heard whispers in the crowd that he had been no worthy King to rule the realm. Had her beloved Husband already fallen?

Had his royal funeral already taken place at the hands of a Dragon?

"I have heard no word about the King or the Dragon." Grimalkin said. "The King may have been lucky or he may be dead. It matters not, it is too late now to change what has been done. Darkness will reign and I will take that crown."

The invisible force took hold of Vai-Ra again and pulled her in towards him closer. Queen Marie Ann finally understood the realisation that it was not the child that he was controlling, but the crown! Only her unrelenting grip on her farda's crown had saved her from spilling to the floor. As the babe floated ever closer to The Dark Lord, Queen Marie Ann knew that she must risk her life or die having tried nothing. She gripped the handle of her dagger still sheathed at her hip and launched herself toward the Warlock, unleashing the Maid of Honour she swiped it down across Grimalkin's pale face. He shrieked in pain and staggered away from the blade which had cut deeply into the top of his skull and tore the flesh away down towards his hairless brow, where the tip of the steel had sunk in deep behind his eyeball and pried it from its socket. The magenta eyeball twinkled as it fell to the ground and rolled away, the blade continued its journey down his cheek until it fell from Marie Anne's grasp, as did the child from the magical clutches of the Warlock. The Queen threw herself to the floor and caught the falling babe, Vai-Ra was no longer enjoying the ride and tears had started to come in floods. The Queen backed away towards the charred bed with Vai-Ra and crown nestled once again to her bosom, it was then that she had realised that the banging on the door had stopped, how long had they given up trying to get in she did not know, a glance at the door showed gapes within the wood as blade, mace and axe had worked its way through it. In the distance she heard the singing of swords but then Grimalkin's cries of frustration and pain interrupted her untimely musing.

The Dark Lord clutched at his wound and blood seeped from his useless socket down his black enchanted armour, it seemed to move the blood around and absorb it, feed off it.

"You bitch!" He seethed with a fork-like tongue that flicked blood and stained his jagged teeth pink. "You will pay for this. Both of you!"

CHÃPTÉR 39

RÉÏGNMÃKÉR

The King strode with purpose through the fragmented halls of his castle, his flesh tacky with sweat and blood, his tunic stained with dust and ash. He gripped Reignmaker in his hand tightly, squeezing at its hilt with authority as he passed rooms that were once familiar and welcoming and now appeared barren and broken.

Sebastian had no time to mourn over broken stones, melting steel and burning wood. His pace quickened, the soles of his boots struck the floor with determination as he heard the sound of armour shaking as Goblin soldiers appeared. He never gave the situation a second thought and did not break his stride as they charged towards him, wielding all manner of weapons that dripped with the flesh and blood of his people. He cut through them easily, the superior steel of Reignmaker dominated the old, rusted blades of the Goblins, shattering them like glass on impact before he pierced and slashed through their sickly coloured skins, leaving them to quiver and die in puddles of their own blood. It mattered to him not that some were lucky with their attacks and cut away rings of his chainmail under heavy blows or sliced his flesh, nothing mattered to him now but finding his Queen and his daughter. A force ran through him that seemed to make him impervious to pain and he walked away from a dozen dead Goblins in the direction of the tower, all the time walls exploded with the impact of Maddox's gargantuan tail and bursts of raging orange flame.

The King would not be stopped.

In his mind he saw the faces of those that had fallen on his behalf, a Knight, a Dwarf, a steed, a friend. Their names would live on in history, he would make sure of that, no matter what happened tonight the realm must remember those who gave their lives so bravely to protect it.

Another ruckus of armour shook in the corridor, the sound reverberating like a buzzing of busy hornets heading straight towards him, the sheer sound of the movement caused Sebastian to halt his proceedings, he knew that this was a mass of bodies moving quickly together, heading in his direction, he would have to stand and fight this time, dig in his heels and divert whatever came towards him. He breathed a sigh of relief as his tired eyes saw a troop of his own soldiers emerging from the haze.

"The King!" The leading solider roared, the words seemed to give the others a lift and they roared in triumph, they would fight better if they could witness their King with them on the battlefield. But Sebastian feared that they would not appreciate his words to them.

"My King!" The soldier said as they arrived and bowed before him.

"We do not have time for such formalities soldier." Sebastian said with a shake of his head and gesture of his hand for them to rise.

They looked around at each other in confusion.

"My King, we long to fight by your side, what will you have us do next?"

"I would have you retreat."

"Retreat!" Gasped the soldier, as if the word were slanderous. "We have never been taught to flee a battle, my King. If we leave then surely the kingdom will fall."

"Get a hold of yourself Man, the kingdom has already fallen!" Sebastian growled.

His soldiers looked around dejected and bemused that their King would call for them to retreat.

"But..."

"What is you name soldier?" Sebastian asked interrupting the confused soldier.

"Peter, Your Majesty, of House Callu."

"I knew your farda, a good man."

"Aye, he was." Peter swallowed hard contemplating whether to say what was dancing on his tongue, but he did. "He died fighting for you, not running."

The other soldiers looked at each other unbelieving of what Peter had just said.

"I mean no disrespect, my King..."

"I understand your frustrations Peter." Sebastian sighed as he placed a hand on his soldier. "You have been always taught to fight. That your honour shall be dented if you were to turn your back on battle. I too have lived by this philosophy for many years, but I tell you I was wrong to instill this ideology on you all."

"But, what kind of Men are we to not fight against evil?"

"You misinterpret my words, Peter. We fight, we will always fight, but it is knowing when something is lost and when to regroup. It is all very well to stay and fight with your passion, but sometimes we should fight using our minds."

"I do not understand such things, Your Majesty."

"I have only just understood it myself. If we stay and fight we will die. I would rather you flee to safety and be able to fight another day, when the odds are not stacked in the favour of evil."

Maddox's tail hurtled through the wall again and with a vicious swipe destroyed several of the soldiers as Sebastian and the others scrambled away from the falling stones and hid behind a mass of broken wall.

"There is no time left to argue strategies Peter, we must be away from here, before our future is lost."

Peter gazed upon the massive green Dragon trudging past them as they hid.

"There is no way we can fight against such atrocities." Sebastian sighed.

"No!" Called a deranged soldier from the troop, "I am no coward! I shall not die a coward!" He raised his sword in the air and stood. "Who is with me? Who will fight?"

"Aye!" Came the call of three other soldiers and they charged forward towards the departing Dragon. Peter felt the pull to join them, but Sebastian grabbed his arm tightly. The Grey Shadow, Tazak swooped down silently, shrouded in a thick plume of smoke and scooped up the soldiers in its claws and ascended back into the sky. Peter and the other soldiers looked on in utter disbelief.

"This is not a war we can win!" Sebastian said. "Do you understand?"

Peter nodded his head.

"Then what do we do?" Peter asked, his eyes seemed lost as did the remaining soldiers, fear had taken them now. Sebastian rose from behind the concealment of the rubble and the soldiers followed suit, they looked around jittery of looming Dragons and blood thirsty Goblins.

"Find as many survivors as you can and make for the coast, to Locklow Reach, then attain the royal ships and settle on King's Island."

The King started to move away from them towards the direction of the royal tower.

"But what of you my King?" Peter cried.

"I must save my family."

"Let us aid you in this burden."

"No, this is my concern. Your concerns lie with helping the survivors of the realm to seek refuge on the King's Island. Get them to safety."

"As you wish." Peter said bowing low and they headed off in the other direction.

463

"Peter!" Sebastian called, and the soldiers halted and turned.

"Yes, Your Majesty?"

"Go to what is left of the great hall and where the throne sits there is a tunnel which will lead you out through The King's Falls."

"A secret tunnel?"

"Aye!" Sebastian nodded. "Now go! And be safe!"

"And you my King!"

Peter led the soldiers away to where Sebastian had come from and the King ran quickly towards the tower.

He arrived at the foot of the stairwell and found a mass of dead guards, faces of Men he had known well staring back at him with dead eyes. Sebastian's heart sank to see his royal guards left piled on top of each other unceremoniously to rot on the cold stone. A bleak thought gripped him that if they were dead, then what had become of his Queen and his little Princess. But as he stood lost in grief he heard the echoing sound of thumping spiralling down the tower's stairwell.

"They have not yet broken through!" He gasped. "There may still be time!"

Moisture that danced across his eyelids disappeared as determination took over him and he headed up the twisting steps that coiled up towards the tower like a snake made from stone. The thumping of steel on wood stopped and he realised that they had heard his footfalls and he readied himself with Reignmaker held aloft as he continued to climb the steps at speed. Goblins appeared and he cut through them one by one in a blind rage, determined to reach the royal chambers and see his loved ones again. In such a close proximity the King used everything he could to dismantle the on rushing Goblins. Fist, foot and head collided with Goblin skulls, bones breaking on the sudden impact and Reignmaker cut through their limbs sending them sprawling down the stairs in a new pile of bodies. The door was in sight at the top of stairs at the end of a small corridor and one Goblin remained in his way with a spear gripped in his hands. As the King stepped foot at the top of the stairs the Goblin charged him but Sebastian sidestepped off the wall and manoeuvred behind the onrushing Goblin leaving the momentum to see the spearhead lodge into the wall and snap in half send him sprawling down the steps headfirst, his slender neck snapping violently on the unforgiving stones steps. Sebastian turned to the door that was filled with cracks from the fury of the Goblin's weapons, he could see a light of magenta flickering from within, a strange colour of flame that he had witnessed before. Even in his earliest night visions he had seen this flame and now it was quivering wildly behind the door to his bedchamber.

"Grimalkin!" He growled and he hurtled towards the door and crashed against it with his broad shoulder, the wound in his back had matted with dried blood but on impact split and fresh blood flowed from the wound again. He let out an uncomfortable groan, but he knocked the bolts from the door and found himself in the royal chambers. Queen Marie Ann hung in the air, her hands clutching at invisible claws that were wrapped tightly around her throat. Grimalkin held his hand

465

aloft squeezing tightly, Vai-Ra lay on the carpet, grasping the crown and flailing frantically, she did not appear to have been harmed.

"RELEASE HER!" Sebastian roared and he was met by the Warlock, who wore a grimace and left eye socket that flowed with crimson tears.

"Ah, the King returns to his castle." The Dark Lord grinned.

"I said release her, NOW!"

"As you wish." Grimalkin launched her across the room and she collided with the bedpost before falling to the floor.

"My love!" Sebastian called to her as she looked up at him with tearful eyes.

"You came back to me my King."

"I said I would." He moved forward towards her for an embrace, but Grimalkin sent a ball of magenta energy whirling in front of him, blocking his path before it erupted on the stone wall.

"What a touching reunion," Grimalkin hissed, "it seems like such a pity to intrude on such a scene, but needs must." Sebastian turned to him and gripped his sword with both hands readying himself for whatever the evil Warlock had to throw at him.

"I am the scalp you crave, Grimalkin!" Sebastian barked. "Let my family go to safety and you may have me to yourself."

"As tempting as that is, it is the crown I desire, I care not whether you and your family live or die. But I must admit

466

the thought of your skull taking pride and place on my Throne of Bones is rather enticing."

"Then take me in battle Elf!"

"You would like that, would you not?" Grimalkin cackled. "We both know that you are far superior with a blade than I."

"Coward's words." Sebastian spat.

"If that is what you want then so be it." Grimalkin held out the staff that cradled the mighty Orb of Quirinus and the staff floated in the air before the orb detached itself and flew around the room before settling on the chest plate of Grimalkin's enchanted armour. The discarded staff fell useless and unwanted to the floor as the Orb sunk into the black armour, the two powerful objects becoming one.

"What is this sorcery?" Sebastian asked.

"You are superior with a sword Man King. You would not begrudge me taking precautions. If you can achieve a killer stroke then it will be over."

"It will take more than enchanted armour to keep you safe from me Elf!"

"We shall see." Grimalkin smiled sadistically as he unsheathed the slender black blade, Hex.

The two circled each other slowly and cautiously, Sebastian made sure to keep himself in between The Dark Lord and his family. Queen Marie Ann slowly dragged herself across the floor towards Vai-Ra, her entire body aching from Grimalkin's dark embrace, her throat heavily bruised by slender fingers that were never there. She scooped up the child and again held her

467

to her chest, hoping that her heartbeat would bring comfort to the perplexed child, it had all become to much for the little one and she moaned with annoyance.

"Take the Princess and leave us Marie Ann." Sebastian commanded through gritted teeth, his eyes burning a hole in the dark Elf who's empty eye socket continued to weep with his thick dark blood.

"No!" She weeped, "I will not leave you to fall to the hands of this evil monstrosity!"

"I will take his head my love and bring it to you as a gift!" He seethed, all the while Grimalkin glared at him arrogantly. "Now go!"

She rose to leave, her body broken carrying her and child slowly on limping legs, but the door was suddenly consumed with shadow, a shadow that then spread across all for corners of the royal bedchamber, leaving only the wide open balcony free from its dark grip.

"I think not!" Grimalkin laughed.

"You want me you Serpent, then take me." Sebastian roared. "Let them go free!"

"They may stay and witness your demise, maybe afterwards if I am feeling lenient I may let them live, but there is the matter of my eye." He glared at the Queen, "I may need compensation for that. An eye for an eye perhaps?"

Sebastian screamed and burst into action bringing Reignmaker's broad blade above his head and driving it down towards Grimalkin, who only just managed to manoeuvre Hex into place to deflect the blow. The Warlock's legs almost buckled under the force of the attack and his eye grew wide with surprise, he had not foreseen this. Hartwaker was relentless and brought swing after swing down like heavy rain over Grimalkin who did all he could to defend himself, slowly he fell to his knees cowering under the protection of his black blade. Sebastian thrust his blade into the Dragon hilt of Hex and flicked it out of Grimalkin's grasp, disarming and leaving him cowering on his knees.

"It is over!" Sebastian said, his breath heavy and his words escaping staggered. "You fight better with your tongue than with a sword, Elf!"

Reignmaker's point glistened as it hovered in front of Grimalkin's pale face.

"It means nothing that you have bested me with steel. I said you would." Grimalkin panted heavily, his eye flitted towards the fallen Hex and his fingers quivered.

"Without your magic, your Dragons and your Children of the Shrouded Realm, what are you?" Sebastian asked. "You are nothing!" He raised the sword above his head to unleash the killer blow, but suddenly Hex glided through the air and sliced at the King's exposed torso. The serrated black blade bit through the bloodstained chain mail and found flesh and bone before removing itself floating in the air and as Grimalkin stood it returned to his hand.

"Sebastian!" Queen Marie Ann screamed and now Vai-Ra started to weep loudly, she did not like the strange black shadows that were hugging the walls tightly.

Sebastian's arms immediately brought the blade down, its point striking the floor and he grimaced in pain as blood leaked to from his fresh wound like water from a cracked dam.

"You say I am nothing, but I am more than you can ever imagine!" He cackled, as the Orb in his chest plate glowed frantically. "While you listen to your gut, or follow your heart, I do not. You wield your swords and throw your spears with muscle and vigour. I use none of these things, for my weapon is my mind and there is nothing you can do to stop my plan. A plan that has taken centuries to perfect. I have anticipated every outcome, there is nothing you can do to surprise me."

"We shall see about that!" Sebastian growled and again lifted the sword that has been wielded by every Hartwaker King of the past.

Grimalkin's eye turned to the Queen and child, his pointed nose contorted like he had smelt something sour, the sound of the child's moaning annoyed him so.

"Shut the mouth of your brat, Queen!" Grimalkin barked. "She shrieks like a harpy! The little bitch makes my ears weep!"

"How dare you!" Sebastian growled again and moved forward, his body screaming at him to stop, drop the sword and rest, but he listened not to the pleas of his body.

The shadows started to move and amber eyes appeared, hundreds of them like stars glistening in a night's sky.

"Ah, my children have come to witness your demise too."

Faces of Black Imps appeared from the shadows hissing at the King and Queen.

"Then they can weep for you when I remove your head!" Sebastian cried and swung the broad sword towards Grimalkin, who staggered back away from its advance, back towards the balcony.

Sebastian continued to unleash an onslaught of thrusts and attacks, the broad blade connecting with the enchanted armour, which absorbed the blows, blows that would have dented normal steel and done considerable amount of internal damage to its owner. But this dark armour was of a different caliber, every blow from Hartwaker was met by a quiver of magenta energy. It was as if the King was battling against water and each strike was unable to slice through causing only ripples. Grimalkin smiled arrogantly, even though the blows were heavy enough to force him back on to the balcony and all he could do was defend, he felt no discomfort or wounds from the attack.

"You are a fool to waste so much of your energy when you know that it has no effect, Man King!"

Sebastian's shoulders hung low and his breathes were heavy, he despised himself for agreeing with the Warlock, but his words were true, he could not break through the enchantment with mere sweat and steel.

"Your armour is truly one of a kind." Sebastian sighed. Grimalkin smiled again, lowering his defences which is what the King had been waiting for.

471

"But your jaw is still only made of bone!" And with that he drove the pommel of the sword into Grimalkin's face. Teeth snapped and fell from his maw like bloodstained shards of hail. He staggered physically fazed from the blow, so disorientated that he fell backwards onto the broken balcony. There was a quiver from the shadows as if The Black Imps all moved at one in sentiment with their Dark Lord, they surrounded the open balcony like the curtains that hung there before they had been destroyed by fire. For a moment Sebastian could not see the Warlock.

"Do not hide behind your brood Grimalkin!" He growled. "Face me damn you!"

Sebastian crept forward obviously wary of what lay in store for him behind the shroud of shadow.

"My King!" Queen Marie Ann called. "Please be careful."

He nodded in reply.

"There is nothing that this treacherous snake could do that would surprise me."

Marie Ann cradled Vai-Ra closer swaying her still did not seem to settle her, the child still yearned for her comfort cloth that could not be seen.

Sebastian swiped at the wall of shadow with Reignmaker, the blade cut through the shroud and sliced through the skeletal figure of a Black Imp, it shrieked out in pain and fell at his feet, it's yellowy eyes burning before it was engulfed into black flame, leaving behind its final shape as a layer of smouldering ash. Sebastian held aloft the sword again and the eyes of the

472

shadowy wall gleamed and they hissed at him, not wanting the same treatment they parted unveiling the broken balcony that had been destroyed under the immense size of Demios. Grimalkin sat sword-less and floored, sliding backwards towards the edge, his socket still bleeding, his arm outstretched pleading to be spared by the oncoming King.

"Please, spare me King Hartwaker."

"It is too late for such pleas now Elf. You must pay for the atrocities you have inflicted on my realm."
Grimalkin reached the edge and instinctively looked over to witness the rapid surge of The King's Falls as it continued down the castle and mount to join Adeve's Vein.

"Stand!" Sebastian commanded as Grimalkin sat quivering, his black armour flickering with magic as he made no attempt to move.

"I said STAND!" Roared Sebastian as he retrieved the black blade from the cracked stone of the balcony and threw it down in front of Grimalkin, "Pick up your weapon and meet me with some kind of dignity."
Grimalkin grasped the hilt of Hex and slowly rose to his feet, careful not to lose his footing and take a spill over the edge and end up being caught up in the unforgiving current of the falls. Sebastian unleashed another swipe of his sword that was blocked by Grimalkin and the two danced along the craggy edge, chunks of stone became disturbed and fell into the falls far below them. Their swords became linked together by their hilts and the two found themselves face to face, they growled at each other and as Sebastian yanked his weapon free, Grimalkin

sliced the air with a swift attack that cut through Hartwaker's hand, severing two fingers from his left hand. He called out in pain as his little finger fell to the floor and blood erupted from his hand, the other finger happened to be his ring finger and he could only watch as it hurtled over the balcony and was taken by the falls. Still burning with anger he unleashed a relentless attack on the Warlock, blow after blow scrapped across the enchanted black steel of Grimalkin's armour and the King no longer cared whether he was making an impact or not, he wanted to punish the Warlock and show his superiority over him that he refused to stop his relentless attack.

Rage exploded through the veins of the King and he disarmed the Warlock again, continuing to bring blow after blow down on the Elf's wrist even though the sword had left his grip as if he were a woodsman hacking firewood. Sweat dripped from his forehead as he screamed through clenched teeth, but still he could not make a mark on the armour, Grimalkin sat trembling from the velocity of each strike but he remained unarmed.

"Damn this armour!" Sebastian panted as he pulled back leaving Grimalkin grounded again. "Damn all the magic!" Grimalkin began to laugh at him, it was a mocking sound that made the King's flesh crawl and his face blush with the embarrassment of his bruised ego.

"Perhaps without your magic you shall be easier to dismember!" Sebastian growled and with that drove the tip of his blade into Grimalkin's chest plate, trying to prise The Orb of Quirinus from its bewitched confines. Grimalkin's face quivered and his mouth hung in awe as the blade started to

474

dislodge the Orb from his armour. Sebastian screamed as the Orb's power travelled through the steel and forced the King back. He hung lethargic, his breathes stuttering from such a forceful show of the Orb's powers, he lent on his sword for support as he heard the annoying sound of Grimalkin's arrogant cackle once more as the evil Dark Lord rose from the ground and took energy from the Orb in his own hand and allowed it to take the form of a ball of flame.

"Perhaps it will be magic that will be your downfall Man King."

"I shall never give up." Sebastian panted.

"When will you realise that you cannot fight against magic with steel?"

Sebastian had been taking Grimalkin for a fool, allowing him to believe that he was beaten physically, Grimalkin had dropped his guard and closed the gap just enough for Sebastian to strike and that is just what he did, with an almighty swing of Reignmaker, the blade whistled through the air and sliced through the exposed pale neck of the evil Dark Lord, taking his head in one quick stroke.

Grimalkin's head bounced across the balcony and came to rest before his body even acknowledged what had happened, it shimmered again in that strange mystical way and then fell to the stone at the King's feet.

It was over, King Sebastian Hartwaker had slain the dark threat to the realm, much to the displeasure of the shroud of shadows that surrounded him, their cries were of weeping children with tears of venom. Sebastian dropped his sword and finally his body had given up on him, giving him everything and that little extra to rid the realm of this evil monstrosity. He gazed at the headless corpse that continued to twitch with flecks of remaining magic that still haunted the suit of armour. Sebastian had no words for the corpse, there was nothing left to be said and even if he had the words, they would be wasted on the ears of the dead.

He staggered away towards his family.

Tears ran from the Queen's eyes and she smiled lovingly as her husband collapsed into her arms, a broken Man, he wept.

CHÃPTÉR 40
THÉ BLÃCK CRÖWN

y King." Queen Marie Ann whispered as she kissed her fallen King. He wanted to tell her of the brave men that had fallen for him. The handsome young Knight, whose future was a bright one and surely would have been filled with real adventures 'The One' Maximillous Mondt.

A wise and gentle old Dwarf, that could have been the one to bridge the sanity between the two races, Miglay 'The Mindful'.

His faithful steed, Dayboy who was so brave up until the very end and her cousin, his best friend, the Head Knight to House Hartwaker, Sir Winstone Vespa, the tears flooded out from the King and he did not have the words to give them the respects that they so deserved.

"You do not have to speak my love." The Queen shushed him as she stroked his hair that had become matted with blood and sweat. "It is over now."

Sebastian smiled at her and he lifted himself up, kneeling before them, Vai-Ra giggled and held out the crown towards him as if offering it to its rightful owner.

"Usurpers will try to claim the crown for themselves, but even she knows who the rightful ruler of the realm is." Marie Ann grinned, her eyes sparkling beautifully with tears.

"I bring a gift for the babe." Sebastian winced as he reached into his tunic a retrieved the beautifully carved binturong and handed it to Vai-Ra, she immediately took it in her hand and now had two toys to play with, the other being the crown of the realm.

"The crown will be yours one day little one." Sebastian said with a smile as he reached out and caressed her plump cheek with a rough fingertip. In that moment his moist eyes were filled with relief and love.

His vision became blurred and his brow contorted with confusion, there was a sickening crunch which caused his eyes to lower them to gaze upon his chest, as the bloodied steel of his own sword was driven through his back and exploded out of his chest.

"Oh no, Man King," hissed the voice of Grimalkin from behind him as he heaved the blade back through his body, causing the King's royal blood to cover his kin, "the reign of Hartwaker ends here!"

Queen Marie Ann gasped as she tasted her husbands blood on her lips and she frantically tried to hold him upright.

"No, my King, no!" She cried as Vai-Ra looked on with bewildered young eyes, twinkling with innocence.

"I-It can not be..." Sebastian stuttered as he turned around slowly to see Grimalkin standing over him with his

Reignmaker clutched in his evil hand as it dripped with his own blood.

"I have told you that you cannot defeat magic!" Grimalkin cackled, and his laughter was mimicked by the wall of shadows as The Children of the Shrouded Realm appeared from the darkness, their amber eyes a glow with satisfaction.

"B-but...how..." Sebastian asked, blood seeping out of his mouth and down his beard, his Queen wept for him, for her, for the realm.

"Your eyes gazed upon nothing but theatrics. They saw only what I wanted them to see." Grimalkin smiled as Kelda seeped out from a dark corner of the tower and the headless carcass of Grimalkin disappeared.

"You look confused Man King?" Kelda wheezed, her face was smug as she approached as crooked as and cragged as the castle in which she stood. "Which is the greater? The pain in your chest or your wounded ego?"

"You bitch!" Marie Ann spat, Vai-Ra now cradled in her lap as her hands frantically tried in vain to stop the constant flow of blood from Sebastian's wound, her hands thick with crimson.

Kelda hissed at the Queen and moved swiftly in thick black smoke and cloth until she appeared behind her with her favoured blade at the Queen's throat, a handful of her hair clutched in her wart covered claws.

"Your skin is so soft!" Kelda wheezed, "I wonder how it would taste?" Her tongue flicked out and licked the Queen's cheek. "Salted by tears, how very disappointing." She sighed.

479

"Please..." The Queen begged as Sebastian faded away before her, dropping into her lap and reaching for his child.

"This is not the time for pleas, my Queen. The time for niceties has come to an end. Remember I gave you the choice to give me the crown and live." Grimalkin spoke with authority.

"B-but..." She tried to intervene, but there was nothing else she could say that would change what had happened here or what was still to happen.

Kelda gripped her even tighter, the jagged blade peeling back a layer of her flesh from her throat and already blood was seeping onto the blade.

"You chose not to do so and then have the audacity to attack me!" Grimalkin added. "There will be consequences for such actions." And with that he nodded in gesture to Kelda who's smile was that of a child who had received a brand new toy to play with and she moved the blade from the Queen's throat and drove it bluntly into her eye. The Queen let out a bloodcurdling scream as the old hag removed the blade which was now topped with her moist eye that still appeared to be weeping. She collapsed onto her husband's slowly dying carcass as she clapped her hand over her eye and more blood wept through her fingers.

"How lovely!" Said Kelda who licked the thick, oily moisture that surrounded the eyeball, before sucking it from the steel and chewing on it. She moved away from the Queen and lifted up the babe in her arms. The child began to cry again at the sight of Kelda's hideous face gawping at her.

"All this babe seems to do is shriek." Grimalkin groaned. "Silence her Kelda."

"She has teeth breaking through."

"Well, do something about it!" Grimalkin snapped.

Kelda found the comfort cloth on the floor and stuffed it into the babe's maw, she took to it immediately suckling upon it and her cries stopped.

Grimalkin looked down at the fallen King and Queen, Sebastian was a quivering shell that somehow clung to life, but could no longer do anything to impede The Dark Lord. Queen Marie Ann lay over her husband, she had no fight left within and from her sockets dripped tears and blood.

"Ironic how you have fallen to the very sword that was wielded by your kin and used to protect your kingdom for these past few centuries." Grimalkin said as he inspected the blade. "But as there will be no more Hartwaker Kings, then there is no more need for a sword." The Orb of Quirinus pulsated and glowed as he lifted Reignmaker aloft, dark energy ran through his arm into the sword and the steel sang high and long before the evil Warlock brought it down with force and watched as the blade broke into several shards of useless steel. The Dark Lord examined the beautifully crafted phoenix hilt and let it fall to the floor.

"Now only one thing remains..." Grimalkin smiled, "my crown!"

Vai-Ra had continued to hold onto it through the whole ordeal, in fact she had barely been apart from it since her farda had left all this weeks ago, she also still held her new toy tightly, she did not want to part with either.

"Shall we kill the babe?" Kelda asked.

"I am not sure," Grimalkin pondered, sliding Hex back into its scabbard, "I have not decided yet."

"But I shall take the crown nonetheless." He smiled at Vai-Ra and held out his hand towards her, "I will take that little one." Magic seeped from his fingertips and circulated in the air, an invisible force tugging at the golden crown that remained in the clutches of the Princess. There was resistance as the child refused to let go of it and stared at the one eyed Demon that scowled at her.

"She is a strong one, no?" Asked Kelda astonished by the babe's will power, Grimalkin said nothing but The Orb of Quirinus glowed even brighter and more magic was sent to retrieve the crown. Finally the crown came loose and hovered away from her reaching hand toward a new Master. Grimalkin clutched the crown and sighed with relief, finally he had his most sort after prize. Vai-Ra was not too concerned and focused on her wooden toy.

"It is mine!" Said Grimalkin, the gold twinkled in the reflection of his magenta eye.

"My Lord, you have it!" Came a gravelled voice.
He turned to the door to see General Feng and a troop of Goblin soldiers including Sluug, Brood, Kraag and the sorry looking sight of Pooka concealed by a huge helmet.

"Indeed I do General." He smiled.

General Feng made eye contact with the dying King and grinned sadistically.

"You have found the Man King I see, my Lord."

"Yes." Grimalkin smiled. "But you look disappointed General."

"I had wanted to be the one to bring you his head."

"There is still breath in his lungs, General, you may still have that honour if fate allows."

"You pay me a great honour." Feng bowed thankfully.

"What news have you of the conquest?" Grimalkin asked his General.

"It is done." Feng said proudly, pushing out his wide chest to display his fresh marks that he had etched into his chest plate. "The Kingdom is yours."

"Excellent." Grimalkin hissed.

"Shall we start to rebuild, if there is to be a coronation?" Feng asked.

"No, General, we shall not be staying here."

"But is this not your birthright, my Lord?"

"It is nothing but rubble and its stench of Man revolts me. We return to Mount Quirinus and to the darkness of the East."

"As you command, my Lord." Feng bowed.

"As for a coronation, I have waited so long for this moment that I shall crown myself here and now."

The walls seemed to close in around them as The Black Imps all gathered around to witness such a prestigious occasion, the Goblins followed the lead of their General and bent knees to their Dark Lord. Pooka hung at the rear reluctantly, his guilt for what he had done had started to eat away at him and when his eyes met the fallen King and Queen who were both barely alive. The King's breaths were extremely slow and blood seeped from the huge wound in his chest and dribbling from the corner of his mouth as his eyes remained frozen in a sad stare. The Queen weeped of a broken heart, her body weak from the mystical torture that Grimalkin had imposed on her and the hollow socket that once homed a beautiful blue eye behind long fluttering lashes now barren and void of anything but pain and suffering. Pooka lowered his head, the massive helmet that had been placed upon it almost fell off as he wallowed in his own self pity, only to raise his head again and for his gaze to meet the poor child locked in the grasp of Kelda the Witch.

"What have I done?" He whispered to himself, his dark eyes filling with moisture.

Grimalkin looked at the tiny half breed and scowled at him.

"Join your brothers and sisters Pooka!" He hissed.

"He's no brother of mine!" Whispered Kaarg who scowled at the runt as he shuffled forward and joined the troop.

"This crown is as much yours as it is mine." Grimalkin smiled. "You should be honoured! If not for your discovery in the Scrolls of History, then none of this would have been possible."

Pooka's dark, round eyes unleashed the tears they were holding back and they ran freely down his leathery cheeks and disappeared into the thick hair that surrounded his face.

Luckily for him the ill-fitting helmet concealed his emotions from his Master.

Grimalkin gazed upon the crown again the way a marda would a newborn babe, he took a deep breath and he exhaled long and loud, whistling through his craggy teeth like the wind that carried through the Kayalian Mountains.

The Dark Lord was almost overcome with emotion, but would obviously spill no tears, especially not in front of his disciples.

"Let it be so." He said and with that he lifted the golden band that was intricately engraved with flames and several Phoenix, the crown that had sat on the heads of almost every Hartwaker monarch of the past. Now it was being lowered on the head of a dark Elf, a Warlock, a Demon. The crown touched his hairless skull gently, it was cool on his skin, producing a wave of gooseflesh that blistered down his spine.

"Hail the..." Kelda began but was interrupted by a snap of Grimalkin's jaws.

"No!" He smiled, "I am of Elfish birth and of God's blood. I have magic sweeping through my veins, no crown of Man will sit upon my head. I shall wear a crown that is fitting of my stature."

The Orb of Quirinus started to glow and the enchanted black armour rippled again like ink, Grimalkin took the Orb in his hand where it shrank to the size of a small hanging fruit, and he placed the Orb in the centre of the crown and amazingly it seemed to absorb the Orb. It glowed vigorously and then a black substance that mimicked that of his armour seeped out and consumed the golden crown, turning it as black as shadow.

Even the Phoenix design was replaced by Dragons that resembled Demios and sharp black shards rose from the band in stuttering sizes. A crown of jagged black now sat upon his head, The Orb of Quirinus glowing subtly with pinks, purples and white.

"Wonderful!" Kelda cried and clutched the babe tightly, much to the child's discomfort, on hearing her cry out. Queen Marie Anne reached up towards them but she was halted by Grimalkin's staring gaze.

"Halt!" He hissed and pointed his finger towards her, the Orb began to glow and caused a surge of power through the Warlock, so much so that he began to mirror the shimmering of the Orb.

"My first decree as King of Maglore will be that all Hartwaker Queen bitches will be destroyed!" Grimalkin unleashed the power within and energy surged towards the fallen Queen engulfing her in magenta flame. She screamed as the flame bit at her hair and flesh until it abruptly stopped with the flick of Grimalkin's fingers, leaving her skin burned to a crisp, but amazingly still alive, she collapsed next to her King, but she did not even have any moisture left of draw a tear.

"All hail the King! Whisperer of Dragons, Spawn of Sloore, The Dark Lord, Grimalkin!" Kelda sang with a shrill cackle and the Goblins followed suit chanting loudly.

Pooka dropped his head and wept, silent tears fell to the ash coated carpet and he noticed a comfort cloth that belonged to the little Princess, he scooped it up in his long hairy fingers and lifted it to his nose underneath the massive helm. He inhaled the wonderful scents that had been absorbed by it, the smell of soap and roses and cherry blossoms danced around his nostrils and then he lowered the cloth to see the bleeding King and the burnt Queen on what would become their final resting places.

Demios announced his arrival with a high-pitched shriek that echoed around the shadowy walls of the tower, it sunk its claws into what remained of the balcony, disturbing more stones to fall around him. He spread his wings out wide and screamed again, before what resembled an attempt of a bow with its long neck.

"Demios!" Gleamed Grimalkin, "I am so glad that you could join me on this special occasion."

Demios screamed back and shook his head from side to side as Grimalkin approached the gigantic beast and stroked him under his chin, this comforted the Dragon and it closed its eyes as if it were as delicate as a kitten.

"Your presence indicates to me that the West burns?"

There were of course no words spoken from the Dragon, but Grimalkin had that mystic way of communicating with the creature and he smiled, obviously delighted with the information that Demios had brought him.

Vai-Ra began to holler at the top of her lungs and the sound just made Grimalkin grimace.

"Shut that child's mouth!" He growled. "It is time that the child paid for the sins of her parents."

Pooka's eyes doubled and without thinking he scuttled forward.

"Please my Lord, all the babe needs is her comfort cloth." Pooka cried.

487

Grimalkin sneered at the half breed with disgust and then smiled.

"Are you volunteering to watch over the babe, Pooka?"

"Aye!" He spat in angst, he knew that it was the only way to save the child, "I will my Lord, I will."

Pooka ran to Kelda and snatched the babe from her clutches, she hissed at him trying to swipe him with her claw, but he was too quick on his feet and was able to allude the Witch's attack. He cradled the child in his arms, she was half his size and he struggled to hold her as she flayed in discomfort, but Pooka handed her the cloth and she immediately placed it into her mouth and began chewing on it, so comfortable was she that she began to fall asleep.

"We have finally found a use for the Runt!" Brood laughed. "A nursemaid!" He added and was joined by a roomful of mocking laughter, even The Black Imps chattered their teeth in a manner to jeer him. He cared not and made for Grimalkin on the balcony to show his dark Master that he was capable of caring for the child if he would will it.

"Firstly take off that ridiculous helm." Grimalkin spat and Pooka removed the helmet and let to fall to the broken balcony, his eyes were wide and pleading, if he could do one thing to avenge his guilt it would be to rear the child.

"I would like to give you the following gifts Pooka."

"Gifts?" Pooka queried cautiously. "Master has never given me gifts before."

"That is your first gift, I am relieving you of your position as... as whatever it is that you are and do." Grimalkin waved away nonchalantly everything that Pooka had ever done for him in once sentence.

"Yes, you will no longer have the burden of serving me as we move forward into The Dark Reign."

The Goblins mocked and japed about it being about time and that he did not belong with them anyway.

"Oh!" Pooka gasped in surprise and tried not to seem too excited about the prospect. "Thank you my Lord."

"I ask for only one more thing and you shall be free to leave."

"Anything!" Pooka bowed holding the babe tightly as she slept, "I shall do anything you ask my Lord."

"Kill the child!" Grimalkin hissed, his working eye burning with depravity as he stared at a dumbstruck half breed.

"Kill the child?" Pooka gasped, immediately feeling sick at the thought of such a heinous act.

Sebastian grunted and yet more blood spewed from his mouth and the Queen who was blistered from the flame squealed and began to cry again, but she had no way of stopping what was about to take place.

"Yes," Grimalkin spoke casually as he stepped away from him and towards his troop of followers who all wore matching smiles, "dispose of the brat over the falls and then you may leave."

"I...I cannot..." Pooka stuttered.

"Then that is your choice." Grimalkin sighed. "If you do not kill it then I have many others that would gladly step

Grimalkin said and Feng nodded, unsheathing Flesh-Stripper and hoisting it above his head.

Pooka had already witnessed enough horrors to last him a lifetime and he hollered his words, "I am ready!" interrupting the beheading of an already dead King.

"What?" Cried the Goblins in unison, they were dumfounded that Pooka could be capable of doing something like this.

"The half breed shows a spine after all." Grimalkin smiled.

"I am ready to do what needs to be done if it means my freedom?" Pooka asked.

"It does." Grimalkin replied, "I have no need of your services."

"Very well." Pooka said and with that released the swaddled rock into the falls.

Everyone looked surprised but Grimalkin actually looked proud, that he was able to take Pooka who was weak, feeble and considerate for all forms of life and turn him into a murderer.

"Excellent!" Grimalkin hissed. "You may leave us Pooka!"

Pooka would not wait around for the Warlock to change his mind, he scooped up the helmet and checked on the babe who was still fast asleep, curled up in the deep confines of the helmet and made for the door, moving as fast as he could down the spiralling stairs.

"I promise I will not let any harm come to you child. I have failed the realm, but I will not fail you."

492

As Pooka made his escape, Grimalkin's words echoed through the stairwell.

"Now the reign of Hartwaker is truly over and with no one left to oppose my rule let The Dark Reign begin!"

There was a hideous cheer and then a sudden ringing of steel as sword met stone and King Sebastian was relieved of his head.

CHÃPTÉR 41

TÉÃRS ÖF GÛÏLT

ven after all these years Pooka remained troubled by this period in his life and retelling the story brought back many unwanted memories. As he looked around his class, glazed eyes that mirrored his own stared back at him sadly. All but Jasson who appeared to hide his emotion with an angry brow.

"How could you!" Jasson growled, his face was blemished with outrage, as tears rolled around his lids threatening to spill forth.

Pooka's head dropped with embarrassment, his long ears fell in front of his face, he hoped they would conceal his shame.

"Jasson!" Gasped a teary Xen. "How dare you speak to Pooka in that manner."

"Well..." Jasson whimpered, "...he...he deserves it!"

"Jasson I..." Xen snapped, but she was interrupted by the dejected sigh of her teacher.

"No, Xen, your brother is right."

Pooka lifted his head and looked out at the children he had been teaching the histories of Maglore to for several years and felt embarrassment. Now that they knew the truth of his past they looked at him differently and he was consumed by shame.

"I look around you all now and I see some confusion, some sorrow and some anger." His eyes met Jasson's and he looked away.

"You are all so young and have had little experience of life outside the safety of the kingdom's walls. The decisions you face daily are, forgive me for saying, but insignificant in the grand scheme of things."

Jasson looked at him in disgust for those words.

"How would you ever now what we go through? You could never know!" Jasson barked.

"Oh but I do." Pooka replied. "My words are not meant to anger you, but to make you understand that time has changed. You have everything you could ever desire, you are fed well and live in luxury. You are all from Houses of great wealth and you shall want for nothing."

"We cannot help being born into rich families, Pooka." Xen said.

"That is my point exactly, Xen." Pooka smiled. "You cannot judge me for my past demeanours for you have not lived the same life. Growing up as a half breed species, to my knowledge the only one of my kind." He shrugged. "Imagine growing up and being rejected by your own kind, having no place with your own race, you cannot even fathom how that feels can you?"

The class looked at him and shook their heads in unison, even Jasson's brow seemed to soften as understanding was slowly seeping in to his pigheaded mindset.

"I never chose that life, it was all chosen for me." Pooka continued on. "All I wanted was for someone to take notice of me, to care for me, to love me and I never had that."

Tears seeped down his face and several of the children followed suit.

"I do not say any of this for you to feel sorry for me, I have done that enough myself to last a life time. I tell you so you may understand the hardships I faced and that the decisions I made were not my own. Decisions made out of necessity, ones that kept me alive."

"B-but..." Jasson stuttered choking on his emotion. "It was your fault, all of it!"

"I think it is unfair to lay all the blame upon Pooka." Xen snapped. "He did what he had to survive, can you not understand that?"

Jasson said nothing, but looked away from them all, shielding his emotions from the others.

"Blame me, I understand. I blamed myself for many years. Guilt is an extremely difficult thing to live with. I know that my actions helped Grimalkin execute his plans to take the realm and I can never be sorry enough for that, but I was just a pawn in The Dark Lord's game, if I had not have done what was asked of me I would have been tortured until I relented or worse I would have been executed."

"You see!" Xen stood defiantly. "Pooka had no choice."

"There's always a choice!" Snapped Jasson.

"There is." Pooka smiled. "And life is also about making the wrong choices so that we may learn from them."

They looked at Pooka and many nodded and smiled understanding exactly what he meant, Jasson could still not bring himself to look at him and remained in an emotional slump in his chair.

Pooka left the safety of his own seat and moved slowly down the steps and headed out into the sea of desks. The children in their seats towered over his small stature, glazed eyes of sadness, frustration and pity met his gaze, but he only had eyes for Jasson. He stopped for a moment at Xen's seat, placed a hairy hand on her desk and smiled at her. She smiled back, eyelids batting back tears and placed her young hand on his, whispering to him, "I understand."

The words of sentiment warmed his heart and he smiled, patting her hand in gratitude for her kindness and understanding.

Pooka made his way to Jasson's desk all the while his thoughts were with Xen and what a fine woman she will make, her compassion for others would put her in good stead for the career that she longed for in politics.

As he approached Jasson he began to speak again, his croaking voice breaking the silence.

"I took Vai-Ra to make amends for those past transgressions, if I could keep her safe from Grimalkin's clutches then I thought that would bring me redemption."

497

Jasson wiped his eyes and looked at Pooka, he saw the sadness for the mistakes he had made in his past life and warmed slightly.

"What happened next?" Jasson sniffed.

"Well, there is still much to tell." Pooka smiled.

Jasson gazed into Pooka's eyes but said nothing.

Pooka could still sense the resistance from Jasson and knew that it would indeed take a long time for him to forgive him.

"Maybe you will forgive me in the end, but as I say the whole story has still yet to be told."

CHÃPTÉR 42
Ã WÏZÃRD'S ÉXÏLÉ

agmai arrived at Windmast Castle in a sudden burst of thick smoke and shards of lightning.

He was too late.

It had taken almost everything he had to use a travelling spell to make the jump from The Isle of Zodiic to the land of Calgaras and for several moments he lent on his crooked wooden staff, gasping for breath. He had left Lennoc back on the secret island, to look after the Giant child, Kendal. Lennoc did so want to accompany the Wizard and help fight against his brother Demios and rid the realm of this darkness, but the argument was one sided and the Wizard would not hear of it, someone had to be stay for the wellbeing of the last Giant in existence.

He finally composed himself and looked around the broken remains of the once mighty Windmast Castle.

"Impregnable!" He murmured to himself, this was the word that had always been associated with the castle.

"Nothing it would seem is impregnable." He sighed.

The Sun of Seylm gazed down on him from high above, the West still locked in its routine of night and day and not effected by Grimalkin's dark hold that he had over the East. The rays shimmered from it like hot tears, weeping for the loss of so many innocent lives.

"More death, more grief," Pagmai murmured, "and for what? Power and coin." He shook his head, they were two luxuries he had never sort. Knowledge and discovery had always been his vice and that is why he was here now standing in the rubble of the demolished great hall of Windmast Castle.

"If the walls could talk." He murmured to himself and he looked around the remains of the once majestic castle, watching on as plumes of smoke rose from the fallen stone and splintered wood. Piles of dead bodies lay festering in the hot rays of the Fervor sun, the atrocious scent besieged the Wizard's nostrils and he was forced to turn away from such a sight.

"The walls will talk!" He said defiantly.

He needed to know what had happened and so he closed his eyes, calling again on his dwindling inner powers and he faded into a trance where he saw everything. The whole sordid saga played out before his weary eyes in rapid succession, yet his mind was able to take every tiny detail in and remember it. Dragons burning and crushing those that opposed them, Black Imps creeping out from the shadows and ambushing the unknowing soldiers, devouring their faces with their jagged, chattering teeth. Goblins in their droves sliced through the unprepared guards of House Hartwaker. By the time they were fully aware of what was transpiring it was too late, the only solace that Pagmai took from the ordeal was that some escaped to freedom, hopefully to fight again another day. He saw the great Head Knight, Sir Winstone Vespa fall and many other names that he had seen written in the scrolls for their valiancy cut down by Goblin and Cyclops. Maids and stable boys devoured by Feral and Bat-Fiend, it was too much for his old eyes to take and they began to weep until he found himself in the royal chamber in the highest tower of the castle and watched as the events played out before him. He fell to his knees and wept at the sight of Queen Marie Ann being devoured by the magenta flames and as the child was cast over the falls with reckless abandon.

"The King is dead, long live the King." He murmured as the King's head left his body and was hoisted into the air by Grimalkin who laughed and laughed as if what had played out before him was nothing but a farce.

He returned to the moment and found himself in the chambers, knelt on the scorn carpet as ash floated around him. The King's headless corpse lay before him, the sword of the Hartwaker's left broken and The Queen burnt black, her skin still blistering.

"What travesty!" He wept, "if only..." he began and then realised his words meant nothing and the guilt would be his to carry with him for the rest of his days. He rose and then something pricked at the corners of his mind and his brow contorted with confusion.

"What did I see?" He asked himself. "There was something in those visions, something not of truth..."

501

He closed his eyes and ran the visions through his mind again at ridiculous speeds until he came to the small half Troll, half Goblin holding onto the swaddled child in his arms, then he smiled and his eyes were opened wide.

"The Princess still lives!" He gasped. "Clever little half breed, very brave, yes, very brave."

He gazed around pondering his next move, he was almost depleted of his power, but the realisation that the child was still alive gave him hope and sent a rush of energy throughout his veins. He spied the broken blade of Kings past and scooped up the hilt and trailed his ancient finger over the intricately etched Phoenix design. He took the shards of steel too and then shuffled over to a flag that somehow still hung on the wall defiantly, although it was singed by fire and covered in its ash, but the Hartwaker crest still stood out prominently in its golden thread. He wrapped the hilt and the broken blade in the flag and cradled it to his chest.

"I must leave a piece of me..." He closed his eyes and thought long and hard, "...a piece of me to relay this message of what I have witnessed."

Energy flowed through him again and amazingly a second version of himself stepped away from his body. This other version of him was transparent and flickered wildly as it looked at the Wizard, it was if Pagmai's soul had stepped out from the confines of his physical form.

"Excellent!" Pagmai smiled, but his head swayed and he almost lost his balance, but managed to be kept upright by the helping hand of his duplicate.

"You shall remain until she comes, how ever long that might be." He said, his breaths under some duress. "You will relay the message to the true heir to the throne."

The transparent version of himself nodded to indicate that it understood and it glided like some ghost over to a chair in the corner where it sat silently. Pagmai held the remains of the sword closely and closed his eyes again, within the blink of an eye he reappeared in a cloud of smoke and flickers of lightning at the mouth of a cave, a mass of sand under his feet. He opened his eyes and again he stumbled, swaying from side to side and using his staff to hold himself upright, but this time it had all been too much and he fell to his knees in the sand, dropping the staff and the wrapped sword. He breathed heavily, knowing that he must now conserve his strength and power. His skin hung off him and he looked ancient, time was rapidly falling away from him, he gazed around at the beach on which he knelt, his vision was returning now and he could take in the beautiful Isle of Zodiic before him, The Mirror Sea reflecting the sunlight idyllically and with such beauty before his eyes he wondered how there could be so much evil in the realm.

"You were not away for too long Wizard?" Came the booming voice of Lennoc.

Pagmai turned to see the gigantic red scaled Dragon emerge from the mouth of the cave.

"Are you okay?" Lennoc asked.

Pagmai nodded, retrieving his staff and strenuously pulling himself up to his feet.

503

"Are you sure?" Lennoc questioned. "If I may say you look like what awaits you in Kendal's clouts."

"Very amusing!" Pagmai scoffed, "I am happy to see that you still have your sense of humour."

"Was it as severe as we had thought?"

"Worse!" Pagmai sighed heavily.

"Then all is lost." Lennoc growled, he was the largest of all Dragon's and quite possibly the most powerful creature in the realm, but even he would not be able to take on Grimalkin's army, not alone and he knew that Pagmai's life was hanging on by a fine thread, he was no longer powerful or well enough to go fighting wars against a Warlock and his Shrouded Realm.

"Not quite." Pagmai grinned, it was a gesture that Lennoc had not seen in centuries, it was the mischievous grin of his youth. "The Princess still lives."

"What good is a babe against such a mass of darkness?"

"She will not remain a babe." Pagmai smiled. "She will grow, with royal blood running through her veins, the blood of a..."

"Hartwaker!" Lennoc interrupted.

"Indeed!" Pagmai nodded, "I have left a message for her at the ruins of Windmast for her to one day find."

"How long will that be?"

"I do not know." He shook his head sadly. "Memory is no longer my friend I fear."

"But you are sure she will come?"

"I believe that in my heart, yes." Pagmai smiled. "She will be the best weapon to use against Grimalkin, for he does

504

not know that she still lives, that will need to be kept a secret for as long as possible. The element of surprise is everything."

From the cave came a loud gurgling cry, like the rumblings of a hungry bear.

"Kendal calls for you." Lennoc snapped, "I am not made for nursing."

Pagmai slowly made his way through the sand, gripping the staff tightly.

"So what should we do next?" Lennoc asked.

"You must return to Vollox, where you stay until you are called upon."

"When will that be?" Lennoc growled, "I want to fight now!"

"Now is not the time my old friend, only when a new army rises will it be your time again."

Lennoc reluctantly agreed and asked. "What of you?"

"I shall remain here in exile and hopefully become forgotten. My time grows short and I have no magic left within, but I shall linger on until that day that she comes."

"She will come here?"

"Yes."

"Why would she come here?"

"To retrieve her birthright." Pagmai said and he unwrapped the broken fragments of Reignmaker.

CHÃPTÉR 43
BÉTWÉÉN FÍRÉ ÃND DÃRKNÉSS

nder the shroud of night, Pooka scuttled along the banks of a river that leaked from Adeve's Vein. He wore a hooded cloak to conceal his appearance in case Grimalkin had a change of heart and sent a horde for his head.

He held Vai-Ra tightly to him, she had slept for most of their journey and had been easily soothed back to sleep by Pooka with the child's comfort cloth and the wooden toy that her farda had given her. He emerged on the outskirts of Emsme in Tendor, it was deathly quiet, and only a few candles burned in the small wooden structures that made up the village. Pooka crept through the broken cobbles of the road that ran through the village and noticed that windows and doors had been barricaded heavily. Word must have reached the village and they had taken the best precautions of an invasion as they possibly could. Pooka knew that the small towns and villages of Maglore were never on Grimalkin's list, he had even said that he wanted to keep most of the population of Man alive to continue their ways.

"What is it to be a King if you have no slaves to do your bidding?" Pooka whispered, recalling the words of his old master.

Several lights flickered in the windows of a large tavern at the head of the trail, Pooka repositioned the babe in his arms and moved forward towards it. At the door he could hear the voices of many, discussing what was taking place all around them, the darkness in the East, the fire in the West and they were trapped between the unknowing ways of evil, trapped and terrified. Pooka looked down at Vai-Ra and noticed that she was awake, rubbing her gums on her new wooden toy.

"Oh, you are awake." He smiled and she giggled at him.

"It is time for me to leave, little Princess." Pooka whispered. "Your time will come and when it does I shall return to aid you in anyway I can." Tears started to swell up in his round dark eyes and the child looked at him in confusion as he placed her on the doorstep of The Withering Tree.

"I will make amends for my failures I promise. I will be here watching over you and when it is time we shall be reunited."

The babe began to cry and Pooka, placed the comfort cloth in her mouth, but she rejected and reached for him, dropping the binturong to the doorstep, she wanted Pooka. He wept openly, he had never been wanted before and it made his heart swell. He let the babe grasp his long hairy finger in her tiny digits, the touch seemed to soothe her.

"I shall return, little Princess." He said retrieving his finger and picked up the wooden toy and placed it in her lap,

507

but she began to cry as he backed away from her, "I promise you."

He knocked the door and then quickly merged in with the shadows of the silent village. The door creaked open slowly and the round face of Ernest Copperpot peeked his head around the door and his eyes grew wide when they caught sight of the snivelling babe lying on the doorstep.

"Blooming heck!" He cried. "It's a blooming baby it is!" He bent down to the child and she looked up at him with a queer look on her face. His face must have looked very odd to her from upside down and she began to giggle, grasping her wooden toy and waving it at him.

"Hey!" He gasped. "That's my..."

"What's going on out here!" Cried his farda from back in the tavern. "You have been told about opening this door, Ern. We need to keep it locked until we know what is going on." His voice was stern and commanding as he stood looking down at Ernest who was dumbstruck, holding the wooden binturong that he had carved for King Sebastian several moons ago.

"Well?" Arthur asked his son, hands grasping his hips, his rotund stomach jutting out proudly.

"It's a..." Ern stuttered and pointed to the child that his farda seemed to have missed.

"Bloody hells bells!" He gasped. "Agatha!" He yelled.

"What is it? What's the lad done now?" She sighed and then she saw the child and gasped, grasping her hands together tightly and holding them close to her ample bosom. "A little babe!".

"But where did it come from?" Arthur asked, looking out onto the street, his eyes squinting into the darkness.

"Well, we can't leave the poor babe there now can we!" Agatha swooned, barging past Arthur almost knocking him over in the process to get to the child, she scooped her up in her arms and made ridiculous sounds to the child. Vai-Ra laughed loudly at such silliness.

"We are not keeping this child." Arthur said defiantly. Agatha carried the Princess into the tavern and Ernest followed close behind, still clutching the wooden toy and wearing a bemused expression.

"Agatha?" Arthur cried, but he was ignored as she sat down next to the fireplace, sitting the child on her thick thigh, she bounce her up and down and Vai-Ra laughed excitedly.

"Oh what a little sweetheart!" She cooed.

"We cannot keep this child!" Arthur fumed.
She ignored him.

"I forbid you to fall in love with that child!" Arthur growled sternly, and then his eyes met those sparkling green emeralds, they captivated him and a smile broke under his mass of moustache.

"What a little sweetheart." He whispered as she reached out towards him and he hoisted her up and smiled at her mimicking the same noises that Agatha was making toward the babe. Vai-Ra reached out and tugged on Arthur's moustache, he winced with discomfort and handed her back to Agatha who chuckled at him.

"Well, I guess she can stay until whoever left her here returns."

As Agatha removed some of the swaddle that was wrapped around the child a small scroll of parchment fell out onto the floor. Arthur picked it up and unravelled it and read it aloud, "My name is Vai... That's all it says."

"Well at least she has a name." Ernest said.

"Little Vai." Agatha swooned again.

Vai-Ra reached out to Ernest's wooden toy and became increasingly restless.

"But this is my binturong that I made for..." Ernest spoke, but was interrupted by Agatha.

"And you want to give it to Vai as a gift, oh how sweet of you Ernest." Agatha rubbed his hair and he allowed Vai-Ra to take the wooden toy and she suckled on its head, changing the colour of the smooth wood with her heavy saliva.

"Lock the door, there's a good lad." Arthur said to his son with a pat on the back and as Agatha and Arthur gathered around the child Ernest walked toward the open door asking himself how she came to have the toy in her possession, as he closed the door on the night.

Pooka had watched on and certain that he had made the right decision he disappeared back into the shadows of the silent town of Emsme.

CHÃPTÉR 44
FÃLLÉN HÖÜSÉS

nd so in one bleak night the realm of Maglore had been desecrated, innocent blood was spilt, flesh was burnt and walls fell. Several of the Higher Houses of Maglore were eradicated, families that had distinguished histories, some of them spanning over centuries, now meant nothing within this new regime, this Dark Reign.

Not one Man could say that Lord Grimalkin's plan was not faultless, if they did then their tongues would have been knotted with lies, his battle strategy was flawless. Grimalkin utilised his evil army of mercenaries and miscreants to their full potentials, all of them attacking in numbers and striking at the Higher Houses all at the same time. There was no time for the armies of these Houses to react and in doing so it also eliminated the possibility of cavalries intervening to defend their allies. Some may argue that it was the Dragons that tipped the scales in his favour and maybe that is true, without their wrath then it may have been a different tale, but the fact still remains that his plan was executed perfectly and immaterial of the Dragons presence Man was still blind to the attacks.

Each Higher House and family fell quickly, leaving no noble legacy behind other than ash and bone to be remembered by. The House of Sitruc had had a long illustrious history hidden in the seclusion of Valtora and their Kingdom under the Flowers, their refusal to join those that dwelled above in times of need did not save them when 'The Yellow Hornet' Laasp reaped their land in mere minutes. The Fairy race was eradicated in the blistering heat of Laasp's flames and their beautiful kingdom withered like the flowers around it. Only one of their kind remained, a lonely, drunk Prince staggered into Valtora, only to be greeted by the burning corpses of his people, some he had called friends, some he had called foe, some family, it had mattered not to Laasp's ruthless flame for it knew no prejudice. Prince Ekim collapsed to his knees as he cradled in his arms the blistered remains of his marda, Queen Oleander, it was the most sobering experience of his life and as the colour drained from his drooping wings so did the last flame that scorched the Kingdom under the Flowers.

The mightiest race in history, the Giants of Kanka taken by surprise and hacked to death by a horde of bloodthirsty Cyclops in their cots as they slept. Any Giants that resisted were consumed by Demios' magenta flame, even the most powerful species on two legs could not withstand the attack and the mighty House Brockonbak collapsed leaving only one remaining child left to be reared by an ancient, powerless Wizard.

512

The impenetrable fortress of Hammillda, home to the fearsome warrior Dwarves under the rule of House Hammillaxe were massacred in the darkness as The Children of the Shrouded Realm run amuck, seeping out from the shadows and devouring their innards without so much as a fallen wall. The cantankerous Dagyan 'The Defiant' died on his jagged throne of black stone consumed by a dozen or more Black Imps, without even given the chance to wield Lungblower. Only Miglay 'The Mindful' was able to escape the horrors of Hammillda, but even he fell to his injuries, becoming the last of his race to fall.

Many prestigious names from the Scrolls of History were mutilated as they made their stands against Grimalkin's dark horde. The House of Tudor fell to the vigorous lashes from Maddox's spiked tail and then overrun by the creeping and crawling of The Black Imps. The Tudor Hall of Elken was not equipped to defend such an assault. Bravely Lord Grayhorn Tudor stood defiant in his courtyard with Preserver gripped in his hands and with fight in his heart he stepped forward to protect his own, but when the mighty Maddox slogged into the courtyard. The brave Lord had met his match as a rage of flame melted him where he stood, his liquid flesh and blood left to seep into the crevices of the cobbled stones. That was all it took for the people of Elken to abandon their domain.

The Hall of Kalfahr had stood majestic for over a century, linked together with the crown as the royal cavalry, but even they stood no chance as General Feng led the onslaught with the entire Goblin army as well as Demios' wrath against House Lacey. The gigantic weeping willow tree that had become synonymous with the House became ignited in the flame of Demios, its delicate leaves engulfed in the sharp pink flames, which acted as the beacon to the rest of the army to move forward and take Windmast. But Demios was not yet done with the Hall of Kalfahr. Head Knight, Sir Sebastian Smythe locked the doors to keep the Lacey family safe and gripped his battle axe known as Cutter, swiping it through dozens of oncoming Goblins, even his vicious words that he spat at them was to no avail as Demios circled the walls of the hall and loomed above the brave Knight. Even when eye contact was made with Dragon and Knight, Smythe growled obscenities at the beast before the black serpent unleashed a streak of flame that saw him destroyed, his flesh blackened to ash before he collapsed in a pile of broken bones. Lord Trent was an old Man but was not one to flee his issues. He lambasted his Head Knight for locking him inside the keep with his family, he thumped the door relentlessly to get out and face whatever horrors awaited them as his family stood huddled in a circle whimpering. It was his wife Kirstelle who noticed that her husband had become mad with the lusts of war and his actions would see them all dead. She was a Lacey through marriage and a Hartwaker through blood, related to The King himself as an auntie and daughter of Harold Hartwaker II, a Princess herself, if times had have been different, then she may very well have been Queen.

She left her husband to save her daughter Danelle, her son Triant and her grandson Magam, leading them out through a secret passage way, but their escape was all too late, when the keep's doors gave way and a pack of ruthless Ferals destroyed the doors, which fell on Lord Trent crushing his old bones beneath their bulk. The Ferals snouts and teeth were thick with viscera, they had tasted Man blood and liked it and now they found themselves in frenzy. They immediately picked up the scents of the fleeing Lacey's and hurtled towards them, some of them getting in each others way and stopping to fight with each other. Danelle held onto her marda's arm as she tried to pull her into the tunnel, but was left holding just her arm when the Ferals ripped her limb from limb, it was too much for Danelle who screamed, the sound reverberated around the tunnel and agonised the young lad Magam's ears before he witnessed his auntie Danelle dragged from the tunnel. Magam's farda was not a brave Man but swallowing hard he knew that he must do something, that his son's safety was the most important thing and he unsheathed the family sword from his scabbard, which had been named Weeping Willow after their beautiful tree that shaded them in times of need. He handed Magam the sword and told him to stay within the tunnel, Magam cried with pleas for his farda to stay, but Lord Triant needed to avenge the deaths of his farda, marda and sister and he left the tunnel, sliding the wooden panel back in place behind him. Magam heard the shrieks of his farda as he was torn apart by the unrelenting Ferals. There was nothing but silence and Magam held the sword tightly as he sat on the cold stone of the damp tunnel and wept, but his plight was far from over when he heard the sudden thumping against the wooden panel, constant

515

was it that it sounded like the drums of war. A huge Feral burst through the flimsy panel and skulked into the tunnel, filling it with its immense size. The Feral's face heavily scarred from past scrapes with Man's steel, its spotted fur was matted heavily with fresh blood, which dripped from its fangs as it picked up on Magam's scent. Magam could not run, he was frozen within his own fear and stayed seated on the floor, weeping loudly. The Feral stalked him, almost smiling, pink fangs glistening in the glare of a distance torch further down the tunnel. Magam pointed Weeping Willow towards its snout, the narrow blade quivered as the Feral sniffed at it and then barring its teeth and gums growled. Magam closed his eyes tightly, hoping it was all dream and when he opened them again the beast would be gone. It was no such dream, but Magam could not understand why he had not yet been slaughtered where he sat and slowly opened his eyes to see the Feral still there, staring at him with inquisitive eyes, eyes that mirrored his, moist with tears. The beast sniffed at the lad's mop of hazel hair and then gazed at him again before backing out of the tunnel slowly and leaving him be. Magam breathed a sigh of relief and finally made his way through the tunnel and out of the kingdom of Lacey, never to return.

A small band of able Men from Trinpola were ripped through and picked off, one by one by the devious Grey Shadow, Tazak, on seeing this the rest of Trinpola returned to their homes and barricaded themselves in, too terrified to move forward and help their allies at Windmast Castle.

516

The House of Blood in Winaldo, which had been home to House Bloodgaard for many years and had strong ties with the royal family stemming back to the Age of Man. Founding Farda of the House of Bloodgaard, Torant was a huge help to Grayfall Hartwaker when he took the power away from the Elves, even cementing their alliance by King Grayfall wedding Torant's sister Elizabett. But there was no way of them coming to the aid of their allies when Demios attacked and unleashed flame upon the forges, they erupted and all hands were needed to try to put out the raging inferno before it took hold of the residence. They failed and the greatest forgers of weapons and steel dwindled to nothingness.

Sir Brand Bloodgaard, Knight and Lord of the house was furious and broken, but managed to lead a small group of Knights to Windmast, but it was too late and the war was already over. Bloodgaard and his Knights disappeared as short time afterwards.

House Smythe was a small House that dwelled in a manor in Foxall, they had no real army to speak of so would have been no help to Windmast Castle as it fell. The family were known for their reputation as fabulous boot makers, wizards with leather some had said and when Grimalkin's Goblin Army forced entry to Smythe Manor they were unprepared for such savagery. The family sword, Tenderheart had seen little battle throughout its life and now hung above the mantle of a huge fire, its fine blade layered with dust and not blood.

517

Lord Killian Smythe and his wife the Lady Rachell were caught unawares in their bed, enjoying each others bodies as they had done for many years, but still had yet to be gifted with a child. Lord Killian was unable to fight off the Goblin horde of Sluug, Kaarg and Brood slithered around the bed and dragged Rachell out from the confines of her sheets as naked as the day she was born. Brood held his blade to her throat and whipped his tongue over her breasts as she whimpered, this drove Killian into a frenzy but was quickly subdued by a hefty blow from Sluug. Lady Rachell was groped deep in-between her legs by Brood and Killian was forced to watch Brood molest his wife as she cried. Brood threw her to the ground and she rose on all fours, her arms and legs trembling Brood licked his lips at the sight before removing his loincloth and slid his blade gently down her spine teasing her of what would come if she were not cooperative. Sluug and Kaarg laughed as the small inferior figure of Pooka watched on with the huge helmet covering his entire head and cried. Rachell knew it would probably mean her death, but she had to try and she reached underneath the bed and retrieved a used chamber pot, quickly unleashing the contents of it over Brood's face, covering him in urine. Sluug and Kaarg laughed at Brood's predicament and then the chamberpot was broken over his head and all laughter ceased as they dropped the half conscious Lord to the floor and cornered Lady Rachell as she tried to flea. Brood grabbed her by the hair and drove the knife into her spinal cord, she collapsed onto the bed and her legs quivered from the severed nerves. Sluug drove his meaty fist into Lord Killian's face again

518

and again relentlessly, breaking several of his teeth and turning his face into a bloody pulp. Kaarg then squatted over him, rubbing herself up against his naked body and then laughed about the Lord enjoying it. Poor Rachell could do nothing as Brood entered her and she watched on as Kaarg removed her love's Manhood and then ate it. When finally the House's Head Knight arrived it was all too late, the Goblins had gone and he was met with the dead bodies of his Lord and Lady.

Sir Reginald Plume had been known as 'The Knight of Wine' and perhaps if he had not have been down in the wine cellar indulging in his Master's stock then the tale may have been different. He fell to his knees and wept with guilt, the circumstance was very sobering to the Knight and after several battles with himself about taking his own life he finally left to join with Sir Brand Bloodgaard and his band of Secret Knights.

Tendor's Hive House was spared fire and brimstone because the Vespa family made the finest tasting hornet honey known in all the land and it was rumoured that Lord Grimalkin was very taken with its sweet taste that he had forbid the destruction of the House so that it could carry on making delicious honey. But there were of course some casualties, Lord Nathaniel Vespa was gagged and tied and made to watch as Goblins savaged his family, leaving them heavily scarred and mauled, but alive. Some of them wished that they were dead when they glanced at their reflections later on that day.

Even the East of Maglore felt Grimalkin's wrath, in Zalenta at Freedom Place which was home to the producers of the finest textiles and silks in the realm, House Forrestor came under scrutiny. Lord Ganteth who ran the House was sadly made an example of when he was decapitated as the family sat around their banquet table. Sir Cale Daley the House's Head Knight was knocked unconscious by a club wielding Goblin and left unable to halt the evil hordes proceedings. Lady Florence sat defiant at the table as her two children Eemma and Olivier clutched an arm each and shook with fear as Goblins invaded their dinner, crawling over the table and eating the succulent pieces of meat that had been prepared for the Forrestor family. Lady Florence was the sister of King Sebastian and how the Goblins howled with laughter when she threatened them with her brother's wrath. Silent tears fell when they informed her of his death and her children clutched her tighter still, until a cleaver met her pretty slender neck and her head joined that of boar and poultry on the family table. When Sir Daley woke he found the children still holding on to the headless corpse of their marda, their eyes wide and trembling, their rosy cheeks splattered with her blood.

Other Higher Houses that were left spared were House Bythe for their breeding of colts and House Seaclau whose family fortune had been built on the fishing of the finest carp found in the Salted Sea. Several other Lesser Houses were left alone again due to what they could do for the realm. House Craven for their dairy that specialised in milk and cheese. House Crone for the brewing of ale and rum. House Dunhurst for their poultry farm. Houses Neidhart and Lunggate were unarmed and continued to forge weapons and coltshoes. Mantel for their furs and skins and House Plume for their fine berry wines.

The Great City of Shantanga was not so fortunate, its future had been left in the hands of the savage Beast-Men known as Zwulf. Led by their leader Purge, they ripped the city to shreds taking it for their own. Lord Edmund Swanclaw who was warden of the city was seen fleeing the massacre on his luxury ship, White Swan. He gave up his seat and kingdom freely and did not look to help the people of the city or indeed even look back at its burning buildings as he sailed away across The Salted Sea.

The ancient architecture of the city was defaced and wrecked by the uncultured Zwulf, no building or monument was off limits to their vandalism, even the magnificent Temple of Adeve, with its white stone structure and exquisite carvings of Adeve within its massive pillars. The temple was overrun and almost demolished, statues of Adeve decapitated and the domed roof of stained-glass shattered. Remarkably none of the Adevian Monks were hurt due to the quick thinking of the elder Brother of the order, Brother Bernard, who led the monks to safety through several tunnels and far below the surface into secret caverns, where they remained as Purge ruled the fallen city above.

Pooka wandered around the room as he put the finishing touches to his story.

"And so Lord Grimalkin took his place as King of the realm choosing to rest upon a throne of skulls and bones." He said.

"Skulls!" Gasped several children disbelieving of his words.

"Aye, my children." Pooka nodded. "The skulls of every Lord and Lady that had fallen during the Dark Reign were brought to Mount Quirinus and in the old hall where The Mystic Circle would meet for council now sat an almighty throne of death. A place for Grimalkin to rest while he meticulously mulled over his next dastardly intention."

"What were his intentions?" Xen asked. "Surely he had everything he desired?"

"That is always the problem with people of power my dear," Pooka smiled. "They always want more. Whatever they have its still not enough."

"And what did he crave?" Asked Danell in a tender, anxious voice.

"Total darkness." Pooka announced in a loud voice that made the children jump. He chuckled to himself and returned to his seat at the head of the class.

"The eradication of light! Only with the realm in total darkness could he be all powerful."

"But that would mean slaying 'The Light Bearer', Ulla." Xen added.

"Indeed!" Pooka replied.

CHÃPTÉR 45
THRÖNÉ ÖF BÖNÉS

he dark castle of Mount Quirinus was now the residence of Lord Grimalkin, The Dark King of Maglore. The hall that for centuries played host to Mystic Circle meetings, now lay barren of such communal discussions, for there was only one rule now, that of The Dark Lord himself.

The elegant carpets, wall hangings and tapestries had been removed, erasing any memory of The Mystic Circle's existence. All of it stripped bare to reveal nothing but black stone. Grimalkin had chosen to keep the vast gape that was blasted through the castle wall, he enjoyed the bitter breeze that swept through from the Kayalian Mountains' coldest peaks and to better keep his evil eye on his realm. The dark walls were now decorated with flags that displayed his own royal sigil that he had created for his Dark Reign. He believed that he should have a crest to show his stature and importance and so a contorted dragon in silver thread was embroidered on a base of lavender cloth, and hung from every room within the gloomy castle walls of Mount Quirinus.

The most outrageous change that The Dark Lord had made to the hall was that of his distasteful throne that he had constructed, a massive arrangement of bones and skulls, the broken remains of fallen Man. The skulls of the Lords and Ladies of the Higher Houses had been collected and brought to the new ruler where they had been arranged to act as his seat. King Sebastian's skull took a place of honour on its armrest and left loose so that Grimalkin could handle it whenever the urge took him, some say that he even spoke to it as if to ask the old King's guidance in affairs of the crown, or maybe it was to never let the King rest by plaguing him even in his death.

On this day he sat upon his Throne of Bones, the black shards of his crown rising upwards as if to pierce the haze that hung in the sky, keeping The Orb of Quirinus secure in its clutches. His single eye of magenta was half hidden under a scowling brow, his other eye now long gone, leaving behind a dark barren socket, that was heavily scarred with raised pink tissue that ran from the top of his head to his gaunt pale cheek. The scar an unwanted memento from Queen Marie Ann, one that he was never likely to forget. His enchanted armour that he wore the night that the Hartwaker King fell was now displayed in a prominent position in the hall, with the black blade, Hex sheathed and reclined against it casually. Both armour and sword called to him with its hypnotic shimmer, but Grimalkin no longer had any need for garments of war, there was no longer anyone to oppose his reign. He sat clad in black robes of the best silks and cottons known in the land, beautifully embroidered with silver and lavender thread that mimicked the Dragon motif of his sigil.

Kelda the Witch was at his righthand as always, as close as a shadow, almost close enough to copulate. Her glazed eyes glistened with admiration for her Dark Lord as her snake-like tongue whispered in his pointed ear.

To his left stood G'nora, the hooded stargazer, who still kept his distance and was terrified to be so close to The Dark Lord. He remained tight lipped on many discussions and only gave his opinion on matters concerning what was written within the stars, his words would have no doubt fallen on deaf ears if he would have spoken his mind anyhow.

But these were not the only members of Grimalkin's congregation, six Knights that formed his royal guard stood in various corners of the hall, clad in the blackest armour and menacing helms that were crowned with steel sharpened wings and visors shaped like the face of a Dragon with rows of teeth smiling sadistically. Luscious velvet capes of black flickered in the cold breeze unveiling a lavender lining, each of them wore a sword at their side and gripped spears tightly. They remained unmoving, some had even said un-breathing, it was unknown who or what dwelled in these suits of armour but they were deadly and loyal to The Dark Lord's reign. They had gained a reputation for being ruthless and aggressive, known to all now as The Silent Six.

Grimalkin sat on his throne seeming indifferent with the world he had recreated in his dark image, long black fingernails tapped out a rhythm on the skull that belonged to Sebastian

Hartwaker while he waited for Kelda to finish delivering information.

"General Feng is here with the mercenaries you called for my Lord"

"Excellent!" He hissed, his brow rising and his eye shimmering with anticipation. "Bid them entry."

"As you wish my Lord." She whispered and disappeared into a dark mist that glided through the air and slid silently underneath the doors to the corridor the other side of the throne room.

The doors opened with authority and the black mist glided back around the room and back to her rightful place at her Dark Master's side, returning to her physical form once again.

General Feng marched into the hall, his armour rattling aggressively as he entered, green hand gripping the hilt of Flesh-Stripper that was nestled safely in its sheath at his hip. A Goblin quickly followed holding aloft the new Goblin sigil on a pole. The sigil was of course a tradition of Man, but as Grimalkin himself had now taken a flag and whisperings from The Great City of Shantanga that a Zwulf sigil was now displayed from black flags at its towers, then the Goblins had to follow suit. The cloth was black and torn to symbolise the hardships the race have gone through over the centuries, but the design was that of a Man skull splattered with the real blood of fallen Man. Feng now ruled the Goblin race at Hammillda that was once the home of the Dwarves. He always wore his armour to show his history in battle, to show all who gazed upon his chest plate how many had fallen at his feet.

"Ah, The Man-Slayer returns! General Feng, welcome, welcome!" Grimalkin announced and greeted his General with a smile.

"My Lord!" Feng said dropping to a knee and bowing before his Dark Master.

"Yes, yes rise my friend, rise." Grimalkin said impatiently, gesturing with his clawed hand for the Goblin General to stand, which he did.

"I have gathered the mercenaries my Lord."

"Show them in, show them in!" Cried Grimalkin as he clapped his hands together with excitement.

"Come!" Shouted Feng and he moved aside allowing Grimalkin to gaze upon the most vile hunters known to the realm and beyond. Ten mercenaries marched forward and stood in a line, all of them bowing their heads in respect of their Dark Lord.

"My, my what a malevolent mix of miscreants!" Grimalkin grinned relaxing on his throne, as well as one could when it was made up of skull and bone.

"So tell me General, who do we have here?"
Feng stood proudly his chest expanded as though it would burst from the chest plate that confines it, he spoke in a loud and coarse tone as if his throat was gargling rocks. As he announced each mercenary, they stepped forward and bowed in tribute to The Dark Lord.

"Kramlin, 'The Barbarian' of Raw Cliff!"
A large Man stepped forward and bowed, his hair was as bright as the skin of a zestful orange, and wore black and red war

527

paint across dark eyes of hate. He wore leather straps and fur in attire fitting for one that dwelled in the mountains. He clasped a large hammer of war within his coarse fingers with another sheathed at his back. Curiously he wore several different variations of hammers around his waist on a thick belt.

"Impressive!" Grimalkin sneered, "I hear that the people of Raw Cliff do not follow the ways of past Kings."

"We spit on Man and the false laws that were put in place to suit themselves." Kramlin growled and with that spat a wad of saliva onto the dark stone slabs.

"Then we share the same sentiments 'Barbarian'!" Grimalkin smiled.

"Qui-Claw, 'The Raider of Tangotta Island'!" Feng called and Qui-Claw stepped forward to join Kramlin. He was a wide bald Man, with the darkest skin that was consumed with raised scars all over his body. He wore tan cured Feral leathers and a sash and belt that held many sharp daggers.

"Your scars interest me 'Raider'," Grimalkin asked, tapping his fingernails on Sebastian's skull, "are they of ceremonial value..."

"From battle my Lord!" Qui-Claw grinned to unveil a mouthful teeth that had been filled into points.

"Good, good!" Grimalkin nodded.

"The Jackal Brothers, my Lord!" Feng snorted, his eyes immediately turning to slits as if the two flea bitten twins that stepped forward could not be trusted.

"Worm Jackal." The taller twin spoke.

"Skab Jackal." Said the smaller twin, then both them grinned a smile that was filled with rotting teeth. "At your service!"

They bowed low, displaying mischievous twinkles in their eyes. The Jackal Brothers' bodies were patched with hair and had horrendous looking faces that not even a marda could love, they were half breeds, an awful formation of Man and Troll. They both held clubs in their hands, Worm's was tipped with spikes.

"Oh yes, your reputations spread far and wide." Grimalkin cackled, "I shall be sure to have an audit undertaken on the silverware when you leave."

The Jackal Brothers cackled along with The Dark Lord.

"Bru'can Shore," Feng growled. "The Pirate Soldier!"

A young Man strode forward, each step displayed his arrogance. He wore a suit of armour once worn by the soldiers of Shantanga, but it was heavily scraped and looked as though had been attacked by the salts of the four seas, removing all shine from its steel. He hardly bowed his head that was hidden under a visor-less helmet and span a spear around in his hands nonchalantly.

"I can never quite trust a Man that turned his back on his own." Grimalkin pondered aloud. "From a soldier of Man to a pirate…"

"I will do what needs to be done!" Bru'can snapped.

"Address The Dark Lord correctly pirate! He is your King!" Feng snarled, he still had no love for Man, any Man.

"My apologies!" Bru'can sighed arrogantly, his eyes never leaving Feng's and he bowed. "Your Majesty."

Grimalkin's eye quivered for a moment, it was one of distaste for the soldier turned pirate.

"I give you Raasp, 'The Sheddder' from the Isle of Dikaku."

A beautiful female Repteel stepped forward a whip at her hip and sword sheathed at her back. Her bluish hair was long and tied in a tight braid that fell down to her hip and her whole body was covered in scales like a Serpent, tinted with tones of green and blue, but her face was exquisite as an ivory statue.

"Your Majesty," she hissed as she bowed, "it shall be an honour to serve you."

"The pleasure is all mine, Raasp." Grimalkin smiled, Kelda sneered at the Repteel out of jealously, she wished no other female to share her master's affections.

"It has been an age since I have cast my eyes upon... forgive me a slip of the forked tongue..." he laughed, "I seem to have done it again!"

Flirtatiously they both laughed back and forth at his little puns.

"I meant to say, it has been an age since I cast my 'eye' upon a Repteel. I thought that your race had become extinct."

"No, Your Majesty, we chose to dwell in the solitude of Dikaku." She paused as if she had more to say and then plucked up the courage to do so. "Well, the others do, but I long for blood on my blade and coin in my purse."

"Good! Very good!" Grimalkin smiled.

"My Goblin horde!" Feng cried proudly. "You know of Brood, Sluug and Kaarg."

"Indeed I do."

"They have volunteered for the quest."

"Most excellent!" Grimalkin smiled as the three Goblins stepped forward and bowed before him.

"We only live to serve you, Dark Lord." Brood smiled.

"Sno-Klop! 'The Mammophant of the Mountains'!" Feng cried and his voice was lost in the heavy footfalls of a Cyclops, draped in the fur of an auburn mammophant and gripping a large axe made of ivory in his massive grip.

"Majesty!" He boomed and bowed low, his one huge eye closing in respect as his long greasy hair hung down his scared face.

"My, my what a specimen!" Grimalkin swooned, "I would not wish to meet you on a dark cold night my friend."

"Or even a warm one." G'nora scoffed and then his eyes grew wide having realised what had slipped from his mouth.

"Very good G'nora, very good!" Laughed Grimalkin clapping his hands together, G'nora smiled and then breathed a sigh of relief, luckily for him his Master was in good spirits this day.

"Well, what a motley crew you all are, absolutely delicious!" Grimalkin growled as he rose from his throne.

"I have taken Maglore. Its future lies within the palm of my hands, but I am not yet satisfied." He sighed as he slowly stepped down the steps of bone.

"The East is caressed with the dark haze and I grow stronger with each passing season, but it is still not enough."

He reached the dark stone slabs and slowly he walked the line of mercenaries that listen eagerly to his words.

"I want Maglore plunged into total darkness!" He seethed. "That is where a group of misfits with your special skillsets come in."

The mercenaries glanced at each other, some of them know each other and there is pure hate there, for in their line of work, none of them have ever been associates, to share wealth with another mercenary is not something they agree with.

"Ulla, The Lighter Bearer, alludes me."

Bru'can scoffs under his breath, and it did not go unnoticed by Grimalkin, who carried on with his speech.

"For darkness to fully shroud this realm and for my power to be absolute I need you to find that bitch that walks the West. There will of course be riches beyond your wildest dreams for the person or group that brings me the creature alive."

"Alive?" Brood said with some sadness in his voice, "I had hoped to slit her throat myself"

"I appreciate your dedication to the cause Brood, but I must be the one to have the satisfaction of draining that bitch of her life force."

"Of course my Lord." Brood bowed.

Bru'can stepped forward, he was originally from The Great City of Shantanga and had at one time been a pirate as part of the Crimson Clan, so his travels had taken him away from the realm and he knew little of Grimalkin's reputation so had nothing to fear.

"I thought there would be more of a challenge than to slay a unicorn!" He laughed, "I do not have time to waste chasing silly creatures around the realm!"

The other mercenaries stood dumbfounded at his defiance and those nearest to him shuffled away, not wanting to be associated with what was surely now the walking dead.

He attempted to take his leave and Feng stood in his way.

"How dare you disrespect The Dark Lord!" Feng growled and gripped the hilt of Flesh-Stripper ever so tightly as if he would unveil its biting blade and slice it across Bru'can's throat.

"Do it Feng!" Bru'can replied matching the sentiment with a twirl of his spear, "I would be glad to be the one to put the mighty Man slaying Goblin out of his misery."

"Leave him Feng!" Grimalkin announced walking back towards his skeletal dais. "He may leave us…"

Bru'can barged past Feng and walk towards the door.

"…leave us in death!" Snarled Grimalkin angrily.

Bru'can stopped and turned around to answer the statement with defiance in his eyes.

"Who will do this? Any of you worms move and I'll have your tongues!" Bru'can sneered.

Grimalkin swivelled on the spot and with The Orb of Quirinus glowing wildly he pointed a clawed finger at the disobedient mercenary and unleashed a wicked strike of lightning that shredded the Pirate Soldier's flesh from his bones. His charred remains collapsed into a heap on the floor.

"Feng!" Grimalkin called. "My trophy." And with that Feng retrieved Bru'can's smoking skull and threw it through the air, it was caught easily in Grimalkin's hand and he sniffed at the skull, taking in its fresh vapours.

"I adore the scent of freshly burnt flesh, it does please me so."

He smiled sadistically and disposed of the skull onto the pile that made up his massive dais and throne.

"You have your orders, now leave me!" Grimalkin growled as he started his ascent once more.

The mercenaries bowed and quickly took their leave.

"Are there anymore orders my Lord?" Feng asked as Grimalkin collapsed back onto his throne grasping Sebastian Hartwaker's skull.

"Bring me The Light Bearer General and there shall never be any orders to ask of you again."

His pale clawed hand squeezed the skull with such force that it caused several cracks to slither across its cranium.

CHÃPTÉR 46
Ã CHÃPTÉR'S ÉND

o no one opposed him?" Jasson barked with annoyance. "Why did it take so long for someone to make a stand against him?"

"Fear." Pooka said sitting back down in his seat.

"Spineless cowards!" Jasson scowled thumping his desk.

"What of the band of rebellious Knights?" Xen called out.

"As shrewd as ever Xen, you have been reading your history scrolls." Pooka laughed. "There was a band of Knights that led an uprising not long after Grimalkin had taken the crown, they were known as The Secret Knights."

"The Secret Knights!" Jasson whispered.

"Oh, do tell us about them, Pooka, please!" Xen pleaded.

"Oh I will," Pooka said, interlocking his longer hairy fingers together on his lap. "But that is a tale for another time."

HÏGHÉR HÖÛSÉS

HÖÛSÉ HÀRTWÃKÉR

House Hartwaker is the Royal House of Maglore founded by King Grayfall I after 'The Rage of Man' war which saw Man overthrow Elf rule.

Windmast Castle is home to House Hartwaker and resides to the west of Maglore in Calgaras. After Man took rule the caste was renamed Windmast as way of a tribute to Grayfall Hartwaker I's farda whose name was Grayfall Windmast.

The castle rests proudly upon a great waterfall, which makes it almost impossible for attackers to invade its impregnable walls.

The House sigil is a flaming Phoenix in golden flame on a blanket of red.

The House arm is a broad blade greatsword known as Reignmaker that has been wielded by each Hartwaker monarch during their reign.

House words: "Hartwaker's always rise"

HÖÜSÉ VÉSPÄ

House Vespa is one of the oldest Houses within Maglore and has had strong connections with House Hartwaker since its inception.

The House's first Lord was Sinclair Vespa, who served alongside Grayfall Hartwaker I in the war that saw Man take control of the realm away from the Elves.

There have been several marriages within House Vespa and House Hartwaker that has further strengthened their alliance, but House Vespa has never been a drain on the Royal House, House Vespa made its fortune making the finest hornet honey in the land.

The House resides in a luxurious manor known to all as Hive House in the flatlands of Tendor. Hive House is blessed with several acres of land that is swarming with hundreds of apiaries.

The House's sigil is a fluttering hornet of gold and black on a blanket of amber.
The House arm is a slender bladed sword known as Stinger.

House words: "We are all but workers in the hornet's hive"

HÖÛSÉ TÛDÖR

The House was formed by Lord Mason Tudor, who was known as Mason 'The Mind' and served as consort to Grayfall Hartwaker I for the majority of his reign before passing on from stomach illness in 37AE.

The family's reputation has been built on their hunting ability, each generation of Tudor's have bred some of the best trackers and hunters in the realm. The House has always seen the Great Elk that roams the Elken Wood and Hartfelt Woods as sacred. The creature's numbers had started to decrease through poaching and the Tudor's have taken it upon themselves to protect this creature.

The House resides at Tudor Hall, surrounded by several wooded areas known to all as the land of Elken.

The House's sigil is a springing Elk of gold on a blanket of forest green.

The House arm is a longsword known as Preserver.

House words: "Serve and preserve"

HÖÜSÉ SMŸTHÉ

House Smythe is a relatively small House that has built up a reputation for being fabulous boot makers. Known as being wizards with leather and for using juug and heifer as the main material in their work.

The House has little army to speak of but does have an important connection with the Royal House with Lady Phylomena Smythe being joined with King Cecil Hartwaker in matrimony and supporting him as Queen consort until his death in 213AE. Phylomena was marda to five Hartwaker siblings, three of which reigned as King of Maglore. Smythe Manor resides in Foxall near the West-coast of Maglore, it had been strategically situated there for its numerous plots of land that has vast amounts of grazing juugs.

The House's sigil is a seated fox of gold on a blanket of burnt orange.

The House arm is a relatively unused longsword known as Tenderheart.

House words: "Tender fingers and tender hearts"

HÖÜSÉ SÉÃCLÃÜ

The Seaclau family is a wealthy House that has built its vast fortune through fishing of the finest carp found off the East-coast of Shantanga in the Salted Sea. The House was formed by a former sailor, Lord Arguile Seaclau, known to all as 'Captain', or 'Carp-Catcher'. On an expedition to Tangotta Island he realised that the Salted Sea was overflowing with all manner of carp. Arguile saw this as a huge opportunity and built his first ship, 'The Silver Carp' and when he returned from his first trip, his net swollen with carp, he knew that this was his future.

The home of the Seaclau family is Golden Carp Place which sits majestically on a hill not far from the Great City of Shantanga with a beautiful view of the Salted Sea from each of its windows.

The House also had a Royal connection when Lord Arguile's daughter, Lady Katherine Sealcau was wedded to King Willem Hartwaker. As the Queen consort she gave birth to four Hartwaker children, three of them reigning as King.

The House's sigil is a golden carp on a subtle blanket of marine. The House arm is a curved blade known as Snapper.

House words: "Little fish are sweet"

541

HÖÜSÉ BLÖÖGÄÄRD

House Bloodgaard has the oldest and strongest relationship with the Royal House, its founder Torant Bloodgaard was the best friend of Grayfall Hartwaker and helped him take the realm for Man's rule.

Torant unfortunately died in battle and never lived to see his friend take the throne, but he was a huge reason why Man succeeded. Torant was Grayfall's Head Knight and Royal blacksmith, he was even responsible for forging the famous royal blade, Reignmaker. Torant's sister, Elizabett went on to wed Grayfall Hartwaker which strengthened the bond between the two Houses as they moved forward together. Many years later Annette Bloodgaard wed King Roxon, but sadly passed away during childbirth.

The Fortress of Blood was built on their forging of steel and resides in Winaldo and homes several huge forges as they continue to make the finest armour in Maglore. The House's sigil is a golden boar on a blanket of burgundy.

The arm of House Bloodgaard is a heavy broadsword known as Hog Tooth.

House words: "Forged by blood and steel"

HÖÜSÉ FÖRRÉSTÖR

Jest Forrestor was known as 'Lord Fancy' for his flamboyance and daring choice of clothing. He singlehandedly built House Forrestor's fortune from his expertise with a needle and thread, but with a modern vision using the finest silks when creating his garments.

Meena Forrestor had been betrothed to King Brode II, but it was a match that never came to fruition when 'The Boy King' was assassinated during his coronation. Instead Meena was matched with Brode II's uncle and next King, Grayfall II. In later years Princess Florence Hartwaker was matched with Lord Lucas Forrestor which strengthened their bond with the birth two children, Eemma and Tomas.

The House's home is known as Freedom Place and is situated in Zalenta surrounded by the exquisite Lakes of Freedom.

The House's sigil is a flaunting black crane on the finest silk of lilac tone.

The House arm is an elegant and slender blade known as the Sleeping Crane.

House words: "The needle is mightier than the sword"

HOUSE BYTHE

The House was founded by Laur Bythe, he had a strange ability to communicate with and train wild colts. Laur built the House of Bythe on the reputation that they produced the finest colts in the realm.

House Bythe have supplied the Royal House with their steeds for generations, but although their connection was firmly built of business the bond was strengthened when Lady Saara Bythe wed King Harold III and reigned alongside him as Queen consort for many a year, becoming marda to Princess Kirstelle.

True Colt Manor was once a feeble stable where founder Laur Bythe slept with the colts, now it is a beautiful home with acres of land in Lupiin.

The House's sigil is a majestic rearing colt of gold on the purest white cloth.

The House arm is a short sword, it's pommel fitted with a tail of colt hair that belonged to Laur's personal steed called Proper Charlie, the blade is known as Soothsayer.

House words: "War is won on the backs of colts"

HOUSE LACEY

House Lacey was founded by Marn Lacey, a great warrior who became known as 'The Ram' an alias that he acquired for constantly using his head as a weapon during battles.

Marn was a childhood friend to Grayfall Hartwaker I and helped Man take control of Maglore. House Lacey have acted as the Royal cavalry for generations of Hartwaker rule, the Horns of Lacey becoming a synonymous sound during battles of Man.

The bond between House Lacey and House Hartwaker has been reinforced over the past generations with marriages of two Hartwaker Princesses. Daughter of King Brode Hartwaker I, Princess Tessandra wed Lord Paoul and went on to marda four children. Princess Kirstelle joined Lord Trent Lacey in matrimony, bringing Danelle, Triant and Magam into the world. The family live at a fine castle called The Hall of Kalfahr under the shade of a gigantic weeping willow.

The House arm is a short sword with a curved blade, known as Weeping Willow.

House words: "Mouth to horn, hands to hilt"

HÖÜSÉ SWÄNCLÄW

House Swanclaw have been entrusted with wardening the largest city within the realm of Maglore, The Great City of Shantanga.

The arduous task of running the city has been bestowed upon several members of House Swanclaw for generations and each Lord has done so with loyalty and respect for the crown.

One of the advantages of being the Lord of the Great City is an elaborated palace of bronze that overlooks the city, a throne seated at a wide window to gaze upon its town square. The most recent Lord, Edmund Swanclaw has taken advantage of his role and abused his power, the words of the house seemingly lost on him and looks only for the dollin he can generate to line his own pockets.

The House of Swanclaw are also responsible for the Royal sleet in the East, Lord Edmund has even taken it upon himself to have his own ship constructed, a gigantic ship with majestic white sails, its wooden structure trimmed in gold and bronze, that he calls 'The White Swan'.

The House arm is a slender sword known as Cygnet.

House words: "Loyalty and respect for the crown"

HÖÜSÉ CÃLGÃRÃS

The Elf race became the first species to rule the realm of Maglore, originally ruled collectively by three Elves. Queen Eva Quirinus ruled in the East from the dark castle upon Mount Quirinus in the Kayalian Mountains. King Egron Lunarc ruled the heart of the realm from his Egron Tower in the deserts of Lunarc and finally in the West King Argo Calgaras from his castle atop of a great waterfall.

Argo Calgaras was a poisonous King always craving more, he manipulated the other two rulers into believing that they were at war with each other and made each believe he was firmly with them. He betrayed them both to take rule of the entire realm.

Many called him 'Argo the Eternal' believing that he was immortal and would never relinquish his grip on the throne, but he had taken Man for granted and Grayfall Hartwaker led an onslaught against the Elves showing them that they were not immortal as they so believed. 363BM saw the end of the Elf race and Man took throne and rule for their own.

The House arm is a longsword known as Madrigal.

House words: "The Rightful claim be with Elves"

547

HÖÜSÉ HÄMMILLÄXÉ

The Higher House of the Dwarf race, a race that was built on hard work and stubbornness. The first known Dwarf was the legendary Uggol Breakspeare who was an exceptional architect who was responsible for the creation of several castles including Windmast, Quirinus and Hammillaxe. Since then building and forging have become synonymous with Dwarves.

The Dwarves stubborn and grumpy nature worsened as generations passed, envious of Elf and Man they waited patiently for their time to rule. Their rule finally came when Haggart Hammillaxe ambushed Maglore's then King Brode Hartwaker I using a secret passageway through the King's Falls, beheading him in his own throne room and drinking his blood from the royal chalice. His reign lasted eleven years before the crown was taken back by Grayfall Hartwaker II. The race would go on to remain disgruntled and hateful of Man, even though King Sebastian Hartwaker gave them their own independence, there was never any love lost between the two races.

The House arm is a war-hammer, one side forged with an axe, infamously known as Lungblower.

House words: "Strength in defiance"

HÖÛSÉ SÏTRÛC

The Royal House of Fairies was one of the first Houses created in the realm of Maglore, founded by the self-proclaimed 'Fairy King' Algamoth Sitruc.

The Fairies used their magic to create a beautiful 'Kingdom Under the Flowers' in the tranquil fields of flowers, in Valtora. Their magic protected them for generations from those that walked above caring not for the battles of Man, Elf and Dwarf they kept to themselves and away from such needless politics, something that has never changed.

On Algamoth's death, the crown was passed to his daughter Oleander making her Queen of the Fairies, her rule was as eventful as her farda's had been for life never changed in the Fairy kingdom. The family name would live on through her two sons, Prince's Ekim and Valian, their farda's identity unknown.

Fairies abilities have never really been fully explored and probably never will, but many historians believe that even Fairies did not understand how powerful they truly were.

The House arm is a thin, narrow blade known as Lullaby.

House words: "Peace for those under the flowers"

HÖÛSÉ BRÖCKÖNBÄK

Surely the Giants are the most powerful race that ever graced the realm, although some would argue that honour should be bestowed upon Dragons, but Giants have both might and numbers.

The Giants were similar to the Fairy race were they liked to live a quiet life away from the battles of other races that seemed consumed with the need for power and riches. But unlike the Fairies, Giants would fight if they needed to and on many occasions have joined forces with Man in their battles against Dwarves, for they knew that Man's rule would benefit them more than Dwarves.

The Giants settled in Kanka in the Hills of Brockonbak where they dug huge holes within the hills and lived quite comfortably away from the prying eyes of other races. It is said that there are vast tunnels that connect all the Giant's homes together within the hills.

The House arm is a broadsword as big as a Man, known as Grave-Digger.

House words: "We stand alone, we stand tall"

550

THE MYSTIC CIRCLE

The Mystic Circle was formed by 'The Grand One' Pagmai, a powerful Wizard who longed to bring those with gifts together to keep them safe and nurture their abilities to help the realm.

Pagmai travelled the realm with the great Dragon, Lennoc 'The Red' to find those with gifts to join his circle. It was during this adventure that he met his true love Holleet Seaclau, a beautiful Witch that captivated him and immediately joined him in his cause. Together they discovered the empty castle atop Mount Quirinus and took it for themselves to form The Mystic Circle.

It created a home for those who were made to feel like monsters for having such amazing gifts and those that could read the messages that were written in the stars above. The Circle grew quickly and welcomed all who had been bestowed with these gifts, with no prejudice.

The Mystic Circle's arm is an enchanted black longsword known as Hex, only ever used once by Pagmai at the battle known as 'The Rage of Man'.

House words: "We are decided"

LÖRD GRÏMÄLKÏN

Lord Grimalkin used devious means to manipulate his way out from the shadows to become ruler of Maglore.

The realm became absorbed by Grimalkin's Dark Reign and for many years Man lived in fear from the creatures that emerged from The Shrouded Realm to wreak havoc.

Many creatures that were once loyal to the Shrouded Realm left Sloore and sided with Grimalkin who now held all the power in the realm. Sloore was furious at Grimalkin's defiance, but due to his fear of Dragons ze would not leave hirs dark dwell to seek revenge.

But even with all the power of rule, Lord Grimalkin still wanted more, he could not enjoy his rule until he had total darkness. Mostly he sat restlessly upon his Throne of Bones waiting impatiently for The Light Bearer, Ulla to be seized and brought to him to be executed, somehow the Unicorn still manages to elude her pursuers.

The arm of Grimalkin's House was of course the enchanted black longsword known as Hex, that once belonged to The Mystic Circle.

House words: "I am the prophecy"

552

THE GOBLINS

The Goblins were heavily rewarded by Lord Grimalkin for their assistance during the birth of the Dark Reign. General Feng was so instrumental in making Grimalkin's dark vision a reality that he was showered with riches and power. No longer would Goblins hide and cower in the dark corners of Sloore's Dwell, Feng now ruled his Goblins from the dark fortress of Hammillaxe in Hammillda, the former dwelling of the now seemingly extinct race of Dwarves.

The Goblins now run riot raping and pillaging the towns within the realm, leaving Man to live in constant fear of their heinous attacks.

General Feng has plans to take the great City of Shantanga from the grip of Purge and his Zwulf Beast-Men, this is something that Grimalkin has backed, but only when the Light Bearer has been slain will The Dark Lord allow it.

The House arms are the serrated blade known as Flesh-Stripper and the spiked mace, Man-Eater.

House words: "Freed from shadow"

THE ZWÜLF

Now calling himself 'The King of the Beast-Men' Purge did nothing to help Lord Grimalkin with other matters of his Dark Reign and instead remained in the relative safety of the Great City of Shantanga.

Purge and his Beast-Men ravaged the city leaving it in ruin, all but the high walls that surround the city. The gates were locked and the walls manned by guards night and day letting no one leave or enter. Those people that remained within its walls were beaten and raped, those that were executed were eaten by the savage horde leaving everyone in fear for their lives.

Several underground resistances have been assembled, but all their attempts to take back the city have failed, each leader that has been seized have paid for it with their heads, heads that now sit upon spikes in the town square as a warning to any other would be rebels.

The arm of Swanclaw, a golden blade that was known as Cygnet was left behind by former warden of the city. Purge has taken it as his own renaming it 'Spit'.

House words: "To the beasts go the spoils"

THÉ RÚLÉ ÖF MÃGLÖRÉ

BM: BEFORE MAN   AE: AFTER ELVES   DR: DARK REIGN   *: DID NOT RULE

ÃRGÖ CÃLGÃRÃS

Argo reigned from 0BM to 363BM and was known as 'The Elf King' and 'Argo the Eternal'. He was the first official monarch of the realm, dismissing the claims of fellow Elves Queen Evaa Quirinus and King Egron Lunarc.

His arrogance became his undoing, truly believing that he was immortal, but during 'The Rage of Man' uprising he felt the wrath of Grayfall's Reignmaker and on seeing his own innards spill out from his gut was enough to make him realise that he was indeed mortal after all.

GRÃYFÃLL HÃRTWÃKÉR I

Grayfall reigned from 0AE to 58AE and was known as 'The Man King' and 'Grayfall the Just'. He had grown tired of the Elves selfish rule, taking whatever they wanted from Man and giving the realm nothing in return. It was Grayfall that was the first to stand up against their rule and show Man that there was another way, why should they be ruled over by these arrogant Elves? Many followed his cause and Grayfall and his army of Man were victorious taking throne and crown in the name of House Hartwaker. His reign saw several hardships including the three years of The Black Plague that took many lives. Many tongues wagged that this dreadful disease was Argo's revenge and their were whispers that maybe the Gods were angry at Man and did not believe that they should rule. Grayfall died peacefully in his sleep at a ripe age of 91.

*TÖRÃŊT HÃRTWÃKÉR

In 2AE, the first son of Grayfall was birthed stillborn and therefore did not rule.

RÖBÏŊ HÃRTWÃKÉR I

Robin I's reign was short at only one year, ruling from 58AE to 59AE, he was known to all as 'Robin the Unready'. Robin was never the right sibling to take the crown, but the laws of heirship were clear and he was the next in line for the burden of rule. His early demise came when an unexpected eclipse shrouded the Moon of Tenaj and 'The Goblin King' Grotte and his Goblin army used the advantage of darkness to lay siege to Windmast Castle. King Robin was unready for such a siege and was slaughtered for his ignorance.

WÏLLÉM HÄRTWÄKÉR

Robin's brother, Willem avenged his death and drove the majority of the Goblin army back to Lake Salivia, where Salinka 'The Water Dragon' gorged herself on Goblin flesh. Willem Hartwaker was then crowned King becoming known throughout the realm simply as 'The General' for his expertise as a strategist of war. During his reign which lasted from 59AE to 112AE, a war of beliefs broke out between the Cult of Crypor and the Adevian Monks both of them believing that their belief was truth. There were needless losses of life on both sides before King Willem intervened and explained that one had the right to believe whatever they wanted to believe. The Cult of Crypor refused to agree with The King's words but it was enough to end the war between them. The Cult took solitude in the Kayalian Mountains where they festered in their hatred and bitterness. Willem died aged 86 at the banquet table in the Great Hall, choking on a tough piece of wild boar.

HÄRÖLD HÄRTWÄKÉR I

Harold was the first born to King Willem and had a very short tenure as King with nothing of merit to write about. He reigned for only a few seasons during 112AE and 113AE when he fell from his colt in the courtyard of Windmast Castle and suffered a broken neck and for this would always be known to the people as 'Harold the Ungraceful'.

BRÖDÉ HÄRTWÄKÉR I

Brother of Harold, Brode took to the role as King with much vigour and enthusiasm, earning him the moniker of 'Brode the Eager'. His reign ran from 113AE to 136AE, the time was filled with exciting tales which King Brode revelled in, he yearned for adventure and longed to leave his name written in the Scrolls of History for evermore, he did exactly that. Some started to call him 'Brode the Brave' as he shied away from no battle or incident and always met it head on with Reignmaker in hand and he did it all with pride in his heart and a smile on his face. But 130AE his moniker was changed once more when he did what no King, or Man for that matter had ever achieved or even thought possible, The King slayed a Dragon in combat! This historic event came known in lore as 'The Ballad of the King and the Dragon', story has it that Grosa 'The Bronze' had been attacking several settlements and towns and gorging himself on Man flesh, burning crops and eating livestock. King Brode I rode to meet the beast and in an epic battle managed to slay the Dragon, injuring his leg and hip in the process, injuries that would forever effect his mobility. From then on out he became known as 'Dragon Slayer' and even had special armour forged from the thick bronze coloured scales of the fallen Grosa. But during 'The War of Two Kings' Brode Hartwaker I's adventure came to an abrupt halt when 'The Dwarf King' Haggart Hammillaxe gained entry to Windmast Castle taking Brode by surprise and beheading him in the great hall of House Hartwaker.

BRÖDÉ HÄRTWÄKÉR II

It was 136AE and King Brode Hartwaker I was dead. A Dwarf
now sitting upon the throne in Windmast Castle, Brode's
brother Grayfall looked to increase morale in Man by
crowning his nephew, the son of Brode as the new King. A
coronation was staged to crown the young Prince, the
ceremony was held at Hive House in Tendor with House
Vespa playing host. King Brode II was crowned, a reign that
lasted minutes. Before the crown could even settle, an arrow
met his head and he fell dead on the steps of his dais.
Assassinated by an unknown archer, which sadly earned him
the moniker in the Scrolls of History as 'The King for a Day'.

HÄGGÄRT HÄMMÏLLÄXÉ

Haggart 'The Arrogant' sat on the throne within the great hall
of Windmast Castle, a throne that had now seated Kings of
Elf, Man and Dwarf. The Dwarf Regime had begun, a cruel
reign for those that lived with Maglore that lasted from 136AE
to 147AE. He ruled arrogantly and cared not for any race but
Dwarves. But he grew paranoid of the world outside the castle
walls and when he heard news that Grayfall Hartwaker had
amassed an army of Man and Giants to march against
Windmast he fled back to what he believed the safety of
Hammillda only to have been outsmarted by Grayfall who was
waiting their for him. Grayfall slaughtered Haggart on the

cobbles of his own courtyard ending the Dwarf King's reign after eleven years.

GRÃYFÃLL HÃRTWÃKÉR II

Grayfall Hartwaker II became affectionately known as 'The Conqueror' and 'Dwarf Slayer' his tactics had helped win back the crown putting an end to 'The Dwarf Regime' birthing the Second Age of Man. Grayfall II was gracious in victory and gave Haggart's sons Dagyan and Miglay back their castle if they knelt to him which they did. The Man King went on to make a speech that a son should never be punished for the sins of the farda.

Grayfall ruled in relative peace only minor battles were ever fought during his reign, the battle of most notoriety was known as 'The Colossal Collision' in 149AE where a band of gigantic Cyclops advanced on the Giants of Kanka kidnapping their children to eat. The Giants fought back but were outnumbered by this evil horde of Cyclops. King Grayfall II and his army of Man were enough to tip the scales in favour of The Giants.

At the age of 67, in the year of 166AE Grayfall II passed away from a weakness of heart.

HÃRÖLD HÃRTWÃKÉR II

The firstborn son of Grayfall II was Harold II, named in tribute of his ungraceful brother who he had loved dearly.

560

Harold II reigned from 166AE to 185AE in peace with no anguish of note. He became known as 'Harold the Kind' and went out of his way to help the people of the realm, it was a happy time for Maglore. At 45 years he died from a stomach illness.

RÖBÏN HÄRTWÄKÉR II

Brother to Harold II and second born son of Grayfall II, Robin II was young and many said too immature to sit on the throne at all. His reign lasted less than a year during the span of 185AE to 186AE, but it was not due to battle or plague that his life was taken so early. Robin II had known very little of war, he grew up in the peaceful times that his brother Harold II had nurtured and had spent his time with other meaningful pursuits, namely the chasing of girls. It was this pastime that earned him the moniker "Robin the Romantic" and in some instances "Robin the Risky". His downfall came when he fallen in love with his marda's handmaiden, to prove his feelings to her he scaled a large tree in the gardens to retrieve a rare owlex egg. The romanic gesture to his betrothed was laughed at by all onlookers as the young King was up to his tricks again, but the merriment was soon halted when he slipped and fell to his death.

CÉCÏL HÅRTWÅKÉR

If anyone was born to be King it was Cecil Hartwaker, the last born son of Grayfall II, many said that he was the sibling that was most like his farda. Cecil longed for adventure and for battle and he did not have to wait long until he got his wish. During the Deerheart Games, The Goblin King, Grotte led a surprise attack on the unknowing nobles. Goblins tore through the crowd and even some of the unsuspecting jousting Knights. It is written in the Scrolls of History that Cecil left his royal seat and cut his way through dozens of Goblins as he made his way to the centre of the jousting field where he was joined by several other Knights to take on the oncoming Goblin horde. Cecil's white tunic was covered in blood which was the reason he was given the monikers 'Red Cecil' and 'The Bloody King'. In his triumph he wounded the mighty Grotte who retreated back to Sloore's Dwell only too be rejected by his master and cast-out of The Shrouded Realm for his constant failure, where his own kind were said to have turned on him and ripped him limb from limb. But after all his bloody adventures, ironically the King died peacefully at sleep in 213AE.

* HÅRÖLD HÅRTWÅKÉR III

Cecil's firstborn son was born with disabilities of the spine and legs, his skull was swollen. He spoke no words, the only thing to ever spill from his lips was the constant string of saliva that would have to be wiped by his marda several times an hour. Due to his ailments he had been seen unfit to rule and it was decided that his brother would indeed take the crown instead. In 208AE at the tender age of 15 years 'The Twisted Prince' was dead, many tongues have wagged indicating that his marda, Queen Phylomena suffocated her poor Prince when she could stand his suffering no more.

RÖXÖN HÄRTWÄKÉR

Roxon was crowned King at age 11, earning the moniker of 'The Boy King' and 'Roxon the Young' but they were monikers that would soon change. One event to recall was known as 'The Raid on Raw Cliff'. The savages of Raw Cliff had been leaving their mountain home to raid towns and villages in God's March, Kalfahr, Winaldo and Shanoli. King Roxon took some of his best Knights in a raid of their own, an arduous journey that took them several weeks, for climbing mountains was no easy feat, finally they made it to Raw Cliff but in their exhausted state they were ambushed and captured. Roxon managed to escape his confines and slay the ringleaders of the raids and seeing all the other dwellers of the mountains take a knee before him on snow and ice, he did all this before even freeing the Knights. But it wasn't his adventures as King that are remembered by the Scrolls of History, the names 'Roxon the Haunted' and 'Roxon the Unfortunate' are the names that are best remembered. Roxon was wed to Annette Bloodgaard, she was young and beautiful and the king was besotted by her bestowing on her titles of affection like 'My Petal' and 'The Delicate Flower' after a few turns of the moon she fell pregnant and the pair were delighted. In 236AE Prince Arn was born during the hottest night in the Season of Fervor, he was born very small and there was nothing that marda's milk nor physician's medicines could do to help. It was even said that, 'The Grand Wizard' Pagmai visited the child and marda but told them that there was nothing that magic could do to help them. Tiny Prince Arnie passed away after just seven days of life, quickly followed by his marda Annette of a broken heart. Roxon was consumed with grief and after several weeks he took his own life by stepping from the balcony of the Royal Tower into the raging waters of the King's Falls.

*ARN HARTWAKER

Did not reign. See Roxon Hartwaker.

VIKTOR HARTWAKER

Viktor I was more than ready to rule after his brother's death, but not for want of adventure or to protect the realm but for the power that came with the crown. Viktor was despised by his kingdom and earned such monikers as 'Viktor the Pig' and 'The Drunken King' for good reason he had no interest in affairs of the kingdom and politics, even the thrill of spilling blood on the battlefield (a trait that he was exceptional at) had lost all its thrill. Viktor spent his days in his bedchambers enjoying wine, ale and women. Viktor had no wife but he did have a child, a bastard son from a night of debauchery with local whore. His son Ohen despised him and although he was allowed to live in the castle and was bestowed with the Hartwaker name the boy had no want for the crown.

Times spent on the battlefield had waned and his brother Sebastian Hartwaker, who was Viktor's Head Knight and Consort was sent to clean up The King's messes that he caused with his mouth. Viktor had been dismissive of The Cult of Crypor and their beliefs, which they had not taken kindly too and started to sabotage local towns crops, and intercepting The King's deliveries of much needed wine. Viktor was angry but refused to help his people personally, instead he left Sebastian to clean up after him. Sebastian tracked down The Cult and put an end to their ways by executing the ringleaders. By 238AE, just two years into his reign the kingdom had seen enough and he was poisoned by an unknown assailant. Many tongues wagged of this mysterious assassin although the assassination was thought by many to be political to remove him from the throne, there were others that thought the whore who was marda to his bastard child that was responsible. Even his bastard, Ohen was fingered by some as the boy fled the kingdom soon after his farda's murder and was never heard from again. Some tongues even wagged that it was his brother Sebastian that poisoned his wine, so that he could take the crown for himself, but there was never any evidence to this claim.

* ÖHÉN HÁRTWÁKÉR

The son of King Viktor did not reign as King, it may have been that he would never have ruled due to him being a bastard, but he was of Hartwaker blood and therefore some would say that he was the rightful heir to the throne. But after Viktor's demise he was nowhere to be found, the people called him 'The Lost King' for a time before he became forgotten altogether. Ohen's whereabouts to this day remain a mystery.

SÉBÁSTÏÁN HÁRTWÁKÉR

Some say that Sebastian Hartwaker is the greatest King to rule the realm of Maglore, earning such monikers as 'Sebastian the Worthy' and 'Sebastian the Obliging' but in close circles he was called 'The Reluctant King', never wanting to wear the crown or sit upon the throne. His days as a Head Knight for his brother's would have suited him, filled with adventure and battle, but with Viktor's rule came the burden of politics that was left strewn at Sebastian's feet. When it was time for Sebastian to take the throne he wanted to make changes to the realm that some thought folly at first. His first decree that was all races would rule themselves, he had said many times that a King cannot rule over those that he does not understand and with that he called a great meeting at Windmast Castle calling for all the rulers of each race to

566

parlay in the great hall where he gave them their independence. The other races were indeed thankful but after several years they cared not for Man and only for their own, leaving them unwilling to join with any battle that they would be needed for. He also decreed that no longer would a monarch's rule fall with the male heir and Queens will also be able to rule the realm. Sebastian's story has been told of dark visions and a foolish quest to bring the realm together and we all know what happened to a reluctant King that only wanted to do good.

LÖRD GRÏMÃLKÏN

Lord Grimalkin took the crown and throne for his own in 257AE (or in modern Scrolls of History, 0DR) and has reigned unopposed for 15 years. He sits atop his Throne of Bones in the dark haze of the East and continues his search for The Light Bearer.

OTHER WORK AVAILABLE

NOVELS

Secret Hunters Horde: Monster Home

Secret Hunters Horde: Finding Condor

Vatican: Angel of Justice

Vatican: Retribution

Vatican: Unholy Alliance

Blood Stained Canvas

Maple Falls Massacre

Dinner Party

Fear Trigger

Welcome to Crimson

COMING SOON

Magpa: Sorrow

Follow author Daniel J.Barnes on social media
@DJBWriter on Facebook, LinkedIn, Instagram & Twitter.

Proud to be part of the Eighty3 Design family.
For all your website and graphic design needs.

www.eighty3.co.uk

Printed in Great Britain
by Amazon